E.R. PUNSHON
COMES A STRANGER

Ernest Robertson Punshon was born in London in 1872.

At the age of fourteen he started life in an office. His employers soon informed him that he would never make a really satisfactory clerk, and he, agreeing, spent the next few years wandering about Canada and the United States, endeavouring without great success to earn a living in any occupation that offered. Returning home by way of working a passage on a cattle boat, he began to write. He contributed to many magazines and periodicals, wrote plays, and published nearly fifty novels, among which his detective stories proved the most popular and enduring.

He died in 1956.

Also by E.R. Punshon

Information Received
Death among the Sunbathers
Crossword Mystery
Mystery Villa
Death of a Beauty Queen
Death Comes to Cambers
The Bath Mysteries
Mystery of Mr. Jessop
The Dusky Hour
Dictator's Way
Suspects—Nine
Murder Abroad
Four Strange Women
Ten Star Clues

E.R. PUNSHON

COMES A STRANGER

With an introduction
by Curtis Evans

DEAN STREET PRESS

"Death has no advantage, but when it comes a stranger"

(FRANCIS QUARLES)

INTRODUCTION

With *Comes a Stranger*, E. R. Punshon's eleventh Bobby Owen detective novel, the author found inspiration for his plot in remarkable contemporary real life events, to which he circumspectly alluded in an author's note at the beginning of the book. In this introduction I discuss the novel without reference to the actual events that inspired its composition. *The latter subject I address in an afterword, which readers should peruse only after they have finished the novel, on account of major plot spoilers contained therein.*

During the course of his murder investigation in *Dictator's Way*, the Bobby Owen detective novel that immediately preceded *Comes a Stranger*, Detective Sergeant Owen, like other handsome, well-born fictional crime solvers of his day, such as Dorothy L. Sayers's Lord Peter Wimsey and Ngaio Marsh's Inspector Roderick Alleyn, falls in love with one of the suspects in the case: Olive Farrar, lovely owner of a chic London hat shop. In *Comes a Stranger*, Bobby and Olive, who happily proved not to be the actual guilty party in the earlier novel, are engaged to be married. The couple are chastely spending some time in the country, Bobby staying in Wynton Village at the Wynton Arms, and Olive at nearby Wynton Lodge, country home of eccentric Miss Kayne, an old friend of her family, and the locale of the world-renowned Kayne library.

The Kayne Library, which was brought into existence by Miss Kayne's late father and now "perhaps the finest collection of books in private hands," is the object of considerable contention as the novel opens. Over the library imperiously presides the intimidating noted bibliographical scholar Mr. Broast, timorously assisted by his wallflower secretary, Miss Perkins. However, the library is under the sole control, during her lifetime, of Miss Kayne, pending any compelling evidence brought forth by the trustees--Miss Kayne's cousin, Nathaniel Kayne, and her near neighbor, bibliophile Sir William Winders--of maladministration on her part. Both of the trustees are desirous of finding just such evidence, Winders because he wants to replace Mr. Broast as librarian either with himself or someone loyal to him, Nathaniel Kayne because he hopes to close the library and sell off the books to the University of Wales, pocketing a big profit. (Under the terms of the will he is Miss Kayne's heir.) For his part, Bobby has the impression that Miss Kayne, who has devoted her life to nurturing her father's brainchild, "felt towards that wonderful collection of books a little as Frankenstein felt towards the monster of his creation."

At the end of chapter five a report comes to Sergeant Owen of, most classically, a body in the library, yet when he arrives upon the scene he is unable to locate said body. However, a bullet-riddled corpse, this one definitely verified, soon turns up in the sunken lane through Wynton Wood, and Bobby's assistance thereupon is secured by local law enforcement to help them solve this most perplexing problem, one that will see more deaths before it is untangled. A slashed portrait, a tale of an old lover's long-hidden poems, an American with the remarkable, Elmer Gantry-ish name of Bertram A. Virtue and a box of forget-me-nots all play parts in one of E.R. Punshon's most beguiling tales of mystery.

Along the way the reader is treated to some superb examples of the author's engaging wit and wisdom. The county constable, Major Harley, is much enamored with Freud and theorizes throughout the novel that sexual repression may be a factor in the case:

> "Repressed sex instinct. Knew she wasn't attractive to men and wanted to make other people think she was. I've known instances. It's all in Freud. He knows."

Later:

> "Repressed sex instinct again," explained the Major. "She was in love with him. Didn't you notice the way she talked about his good looks?...I've known cases—these sex-starved, unattractive women. Pathetic, you know."
>
> "Yes, sir," said Bobby.
>
> "These sex-starved women…" [The Major] left the sentence unfinished except for shaking his head doubtfully. "Freud, you know," he said abruptly.
>
> Bobby didn't know, so he made no reply, and the Major shook his head again.
>
> "Anyhow, first glimpse of a motive we've had," [the Major] pronounced. "Very good looking young fellow....The girl is obsessed by him. She knows she has no chance. It grows on her. She can't have him in life. She will in death. Sex starved. That's it, perhaps. Worth considering."
>
> "Yes, sir," said Bobby, though what he meant was "No, sir"....

Later Bobby discusses the case with Olive, mentioning Major Harley's pet theory about the manic compulsions of sex-starved women ("Freud, you know"), which the spirited Olive ripostes with keen feminist insight:

> "It's very horrid of him," said Olive. "Why is it always women who are supposed to be sex starved? Why not men for a change?
>
> "Well, I suppose men needn't be if they don't want."
>
> "Women needn't either, need they? Not now, not to-day. My gracious, walk along Piccadilly, if you're a girl, I mean, and see how many men are willing to relieve any symptoms of sex starvation. Piccadilly may not be flowing with milk and honey, but it certainly is with the most obliging men. Sex starvation fiddlesticks....Sex starvation is just a phrase invented by gentlemen who don't want to run any risk of suffering from it themselves, blast them. It's all a dodge to make women easy."

Olive herself is a London career woman, owner of "Olive, Hats," and contemplates marriage to Bobby with some level of trepidation: "All very well to talk about sex equality, but the eternities remained, and what a woman gave, she gave, and could never have again. But what a man took, he took and could go on taking, so where was your equality?" Somewhat undercutting this observation Punshon adds that, nevertheless, after Olive sees Bobby looking at her, "no thought was left in her any more, only a great wish that she had more to give and ever more." Readers unimpressed with this last sentiment should compare it with Margery Allingham's observations on marriage and feminine sacrifice in her detective novel *The Fashion in Shrouds*, also published in 1938; I think they will find Punshon the more modern of the two authors in this regard.

Comes a Stranger inaugurated the period of, arguably, Punshon's finest crime fiction, and it was highly favorably received by English reviewers. (Mystifyingly, it and the next six Bobby Owen detective novels were not published in the United States.) Reviewing *Stranger* in the *Spectator*, Punshon's Detection Club colleague Nicholas Blake (the leftist poet Cecil Day Lewis) conceded that while the novel "reverts to that venerable crime chestnut, the Body in the Library" (this four years before the publication of Agatha Christie's celebrated Miss Marple detective novel of that title), "Mr. Punshon garnishes his crime with a wealth of bibliography which adds to its fascination." *Comes a Stranger* was, he declared, "a first-rate story" with a "terrific climax." On this score, Mr. Blake will get no argument from me. It is a great pleasure to welcome *Comes a Stranger*, a mystery set in a library of precious rare books that is itself the rarest of E.R. Punshon's detective novels, back in print after nearly eighty years. Classic crime fiction fans are in for a rare treat.

Curtis Evans

AUTHOR'S NOTE

Because this story was suggested by, and is indeed founded upon, certain recent occurrences, on which, however, for good reason, little emphasis was laid in the public press, it is all the more necessary to insist that neither personages, incidents nor localities have any resemblance even in the slightest degree, to actual places, persons, or events.

There is, there never has been, any library, public or private, in any way resembling the Kayne library. The owner, the trustees, the librarian, are all equally creatures of the imagination, and have no relation to any person, living or dead.

Certain liberties, too, for the purposes of the tale, have been taken with the facts of bibliography. There is, for example, no reason to suppose that Caxton did in fact print an edition of the *Travels of Sir John Mandeville*, even though it is a little surprising that so popular a work—a 'best seller' for centuries—did not pass through his press. But it is hoped that such liberties as have been taken are of comparatively minor importance, and that if, by any remote chance, this work falls into the hands of the expert bibliographer, he will not find in it too much to arouse indignation.

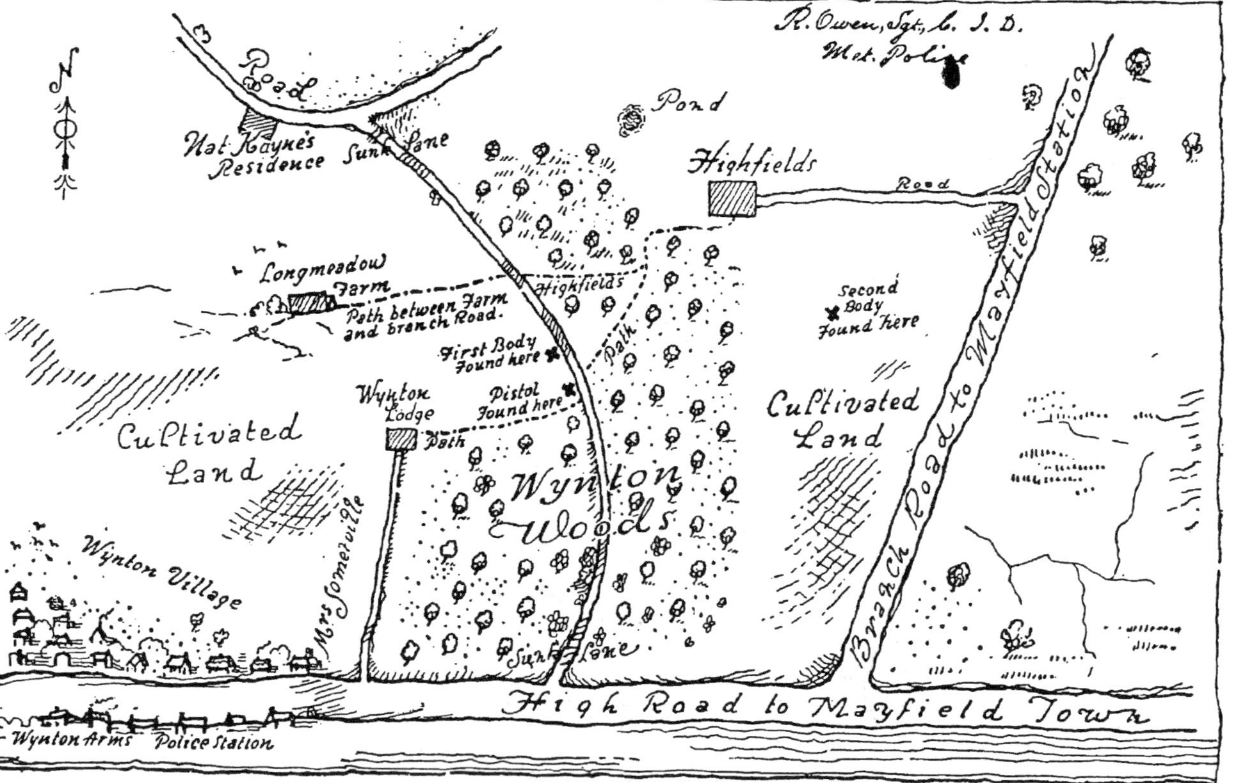

SKETCH MAP OF WYNTON LODGE AND DISTRICT, NOT DRAWN TO SCALE

CHAPTER I
THE PERFECT MURDER

"You see," explained Miss Kayne, wheezing a little, her tiny voice issuing as it were with difficulty from the mountainous flesh encasing it and her, "I was so interested when I saw that paragraph about dear Olive engaged to a detective. So exciting."

"Oh, yes," answered Detective-Sergeant Bobby Owen, polite but bored, wondering vaguely why everyone thought a detective's life exciting when in reality it consisted chiefly of routine work any city clerk would think deadly dull.

"Because, you see," Miss Kayne went on, "I committed a murder once myself."

"Oh, yes," said Bobby brightly, getting ready to laugh as soon as he saw exactly where the joke was supposed to lie.

"The perfect murder," mused Miss Kayne in her small and distant voice. "I think—the perfect murder."

"Indeed," said Bobby, still brightly, still wondering what, exactly, was the joke, and when he would have to laugh.

"You would call it that, wouldn't you?" Miss Kayne went on, looking at him earnestly, "when there's never even any suspicion—when the murdered person just vanishes and is never even missed, and no questions are ever asked?"

"Well, I suppose so," agreed Bobby. "Only it doesn't happen like that, you know."

"Are you sure?" she asked.

"Why, er—" Bobby said, a little taken aback by the direct question, by something forceful, too, he seemed to feel in it.

"Do have another cup of tea," she urged. "Or a whisky and soda? You would prefer that? If you'll ring the bell, Briggs will get it."

"Oh, no, thanks, I never touch spirits in the day time," Bobby explained. "Sometimes at night just before going to bed. But that's all."

The conversation languished. Bobby supposed the subject of the perfect murder, of the victim who vanished and was never even missed, had now been exhausted. Certainly this enormous old woman, sunk in fat, her swollen feet in great, shapeless slippers, so ponderous that, as he knew, for Olive had told him, it was all she could do to rise from her chair without assistance, in no way suggested a murderess.

Bobby was paying this visit at Olive's request, and because it is part of the duty of the newly-engaged to present themselves for the inspection and approval of the friends and relatives of the other party. Miss Kayne was, he knew, a very old friend of Olive's, though one from whom she had not heard for a number of years till there had appeared paragraphs in the papers announcing their engagement. The papers noticed it, because it came as a sequel to a sensational case of murder that on account of its political aspects had attracted general attention, and so there had been various headlines about Romantic Sequel to Sensational Political Killings.

As a result there had arrived a letter from this old friend of Olive's, asking her and Bobby to spend a week at Wynton Lodge, Miss Kayne's residence in the village of Wynton, near Mayfield, a town of some size. Wynton Lodge was, too, the home of the famous Kayne library Miss Kayne's father had built up through many ardent years, till now it had a world-wide reputation. Olive had accepted the invitation, glad to renew an old friendship, but Bobby's duties at Scotland Yard had only permitted him to run down this afternoon on his new motor cycle for which he had just finished paying, and now was wondering for much he could sell it again, since, in view of his engagement, pots and pans, curtains and carpets, were all becoming of more importance than motor cycles.

So far it had proved rather a boring visit. Of course, Miss Kayne was an important person, as the owner of the celebrated library that held all sorts of bookish treasures. But then Bobby did not know much about books, nor was he overwhelmingly interested in them. He was wondering now what to say next. He wished Miss Kayne would make some remark, and with something of a start he realized how closely she was watching him from small, malignant eyes, deep hidden like knives in ambush behind huge rolls of fat. It was almost as though she expected him to take her remark seriously. It was almost as though she challenged and defied either him or the impersonal authority of the law that sometimes he represented. Then he supposed that perhaps she was annoyed because he had not yet seen the point of her joke about the 'perfect murder', and had made no suitable response. Or perhaps she didn't like detectives, or perhaps she just simply didn't like him, or, more probably and naturally, merely thought it was a pity a girl like Olive should be throwing herself away on a detective-sergeant of police.

He wished Olive would come back. She had gone to see if they might visit the famous library. He let his gaze wander out of the window to rest on the tall, blank wall of the annexe built out from the main body of the house, like a thrusting arm, wherein the great Kayne collection of books was contained. There were no windows, it was just a great blank wall, like that of a gaol or a fortress to guard some secret prisoner.

Silly, of course. What secret prisoner could a famous library hold? But why should a library be built like a gaol?

Suddenly he became aware that Miss Kayne was shaking with a hidden, silent mirth. Her laughter seemed to run all over her huge body, and yet it found no outlet in sound.

Even her chair, an enormous construction in solid oak, shook with it, and her cushions that were about her like a sea. There she sat and rumbled with an inner merriment, but a merriment in which her small, bright, deep sunken eyes had no share, for in them as they peeped out at Bobby he thought he recognized a secret, hidden hate. She said:—

"That's the library building you're looking at, the Kayne library."

Was it the library she hated, he wondered? Or something that the library stood for? Or was he himself, for some reason, the object of her anger?

"I was wondering," he said slowly, "why there are no windows."

"South wall," she explained. "When my father built it he wanted no windows on that wall because he thought direct sunlight might be bad for the books, their bindings especially."

"I see," said Bobby.

"There are windows on the other wall, the north wall and at the west end," she told him. "They all have steel shutters, though."

"Steel?"

"Protection against burglars," she explained. "Some of the books are very valuable. Against burglars—and fire."

Her mirth had ceased now, but she pronounced this last word with a strange and puzzling accent, lingering on it as though she loved its sound and yet dreaded it as well. A strange old woman, Bobby thought, and with a certain disquiet his mind returned to that declaration of hers about the perfect murder she said she had once committed. Nonsense, of course, and yet those small, malignant eyes of hers were still watching him, he saw, like enemies in ambush.

"We must take every possible precaution against fire," she said again, and again her small, clear voice lingered on the final word.

"Oh yes, of course," agreed Bobby, who knew, for it was common knowledge, that there were many valuable treasures in the Kayne library.

There was the *Glastonbury Second Psalter*, for instance, snatched from under the very nose of the British Museum authorities hesitant on an authenticity now triumphantly established, so that the thousand pounds for which it had been purchased had increased tenfold. Or those so precious fragmentary pages of the *Travels of Sir John Mandeville*, printed by Caxton. Till their discovery by Mr. Broast, the Kayne Library custodian, in the South of France, it had not been known that Caxton had ever printed the Mandeville *Travels*, even though the guess had often been hazarded that so popular a work was almost certain to have passed through his press. The discovery of these fragmentary pages—a score of them, twelve consecutive—the sole relics of an edition that otherwise had vanished utterly, provided therefore a first class sensation, and the eight odd pages had been sold for enormous sums, mostly in America. The other pages, the consecutive ones, remained in the library, all offers, no matter how extravagant, being sternly refused. No wonder, then, that precautions like steel shutters were employed against theft and fire. Only it was odd how strangely that thin, remote voice of Miss Kayne's lingered upon this last word, as though it held for her some dreadful and unnamed attraction.

"A penny for your thoughts," she said unexpectedly, as though she had guessed something of what was passing through his mind. He had the idea indeed that there was little those small, bright eyes of hers did not see, and little, too, of what they saw that when they saw they did not hate. In quite a different tone she said: "Well, when are you and Olive going to get married?"

"We haven't settled anything yet," he answered.

"Money, I suppose," she said. "It's all money in this world. Money. Are detectives well paid?"

"Not detective-sergeants in the Metropolitan police," Bobby answered ruefully.

"Olive has a business of her own?"

"Her hat shop, you mean? I don't think it does much more than pay the rent. Bad debts, for one thing."

"Collect 'em," said Miss Kayne.

"Can't, sometimes, when there's no money. And Olive says it's often worse when there is money. Apparently when you've a five figure income ordinary bills are beneath your notice, and if you're asked to settle, then you take offence, and there may be a bill paid, but a customer lost."

The old woman nodded, nodded at least as far as the folds of fat around her neck permitted her to move her head.

"Olive told me about that," she said in her tiny, distant voice, that sounded almost as if she were speaking over a telephone. "She said you ought to be promoted soon, and then it would be all right."

Bobby shook his head doubtfully.

"Goodness knows when that will be," he said. "Things aren't too comfortable in the London police just now."

Bobby hesitated. He knew very well that Olive had accepted Miss Kayne's invitation not only for old friendship's sake but also because she thought Miss Kayne, as a rich and influential woman, acquainted with many important people, might be able to help Bobby to that official recognition Olive felt it was so unfair he had not yet been granted. More likely to do harm than good, Bobby thought privately.

But Miss Kayne might as well know how things were. He went on.

"It's this business Lord Trenchard started of bringing in an officer class. Every policeman used to feel he had as good a chance as anyone else in the force. Now he feels that the first thing he'll be asked when he goes before a promotion board is what his father did. Just like a new boy at school. 'What's your father do?' Then the kid's classed, for good. Like that with us, too, now. 'What was your father?' is the first thing the Promotion Board wants to know. If you say your father was a doctor or a parson, well, they purr and you get through. If you say he was a navvy or a farm labourer, they look down their noses and the odds are you don't."

"That doesn't affect you, does it?" Miss Kayne asked. "You're the officer class, too."

"Oh, I fall between two stools," Bobby explained. "I'm not one of the Hendon lot and I don't much want to be, so I'm out there. At the same time the old style policeman classes me with them, so I'm out there, too. Lord Trenchard thought the police only existed to protect society, and he only saw society as a society of the rich, so he thought he had to bring in chaps from the rich classes to keep the police loyal. They were loyal, but loyal to the community, not to a class. The Trenchard result is that for the first time the police are split with class feeling—some of them feel they are only there as servants of rich people, and the rest don't like it, and none of them know quite where they are."

The door opened then and Bobby forgot everything else as Olive came in. She gave him a quick, smiling, hesitating glance, a little as though she were wondering still who it was to whom she had now trusted herself, and her future, and why she had done so, and whether it had been quite wise, and what would he do with her? For indeed a half of her gloried in the surrender she had made and a half of her was afraid. All very well to talk about sex equality, but the eternities remained, and what a woman gave, she gave, and could never have again. But what a man took, he took and could go on taking, so where was your equality? And then she was Bobby looking at her and at that no thought was left in her any more only a great wish that she had more to give and ever more. Neither of them noticed how the small hidden gaze of the old, fat woman, immobile in her huge arm-chair, went darkly from one of them to the other, and then back, nor, if they had, would it have been easy for them, or anyone, to guess what meaning lay hidden in those remote and secret eyes.

"Does Mr. Broast say it'll be all right?" she asked suddenly.

"Oh yes, he was quite nice about it," Olive answered. "Miss Perkins says he's in a good temper today, in spite of its being Inspection."

"You saw him yourself?" Miss Kayne insisted, a little uneasily, as though she were afraid of any misunderstanding—though, after all, Bobby reflected, the library was hers, and Mr. Broast only a salaried employee.

"Oh yes," Olive answered. "Miss Perkins said he was in the cellar, and I had better go and ask him, and so I did."

Was it then necessary, Bobby wondered, for Miss Kayne to ask her librarian's permission before she sent her guests to view her treasures?

"The cellars? What was he doing in the cellars? Was he alone?" Miss Kayne asked, her voice suddenly a note higher.

"Oh no, Sir William and Mr. Nat were there, too. They were looking at an old printing press. Mr. Broast was explaining something."

Miss Kayne made no further comment. She seemed, as it were, to withdraw herself into the lethargy of her gross, enormous body. Olive touched Bobby on the arm and they went out together, Miss Kayne apparently hardly conscious of their withdrawal.

CHAPTER II
THE CUT CANVAS

Outside, Bobby said to Olive:

"Well, you did tell me Mr. Broast ran the whole show pretty well on his own, but I didn't know you meant it was like that."

"It might belong to him," Olive agreed; "Miss Kayne never interferes." She added: "You would almost think she hates the library and everything connected with it."

Indeed this was the impression Bobby himself had been conscious of, as if Miss Kayne felt towards that wonderful collection of books a little as Frankenstein felt towards the monster of his creation. Perhaps she felt that her life, her father's life, had been made too much a mere accessory to the creation of the library. Under her father's careful and somewhat complicated will, she was the owner for life, but only for life, and old Mr. Kayne, very much afraid his daughter might marry someone who would prefer its very considerable value in money, had taken great pains to make sure that the library should be kept together in perpetuity.

The will, however, gave her very wide powers of administration, though these were, in fact, exercised almost at his own discretion by Mr. Broast. Within the four walls of his domain his word alone had authority. It was he to whom application had to be made for permission to examine or consult any of the treasures in his charge; he who decided such purchases and sales as seemed desirable or necessary.

For the library had been built up by old Mr. Kayne, a comparatively poor man, through a system of extraordinarily successful dealing in books. When he had started to collect, rarities were easier to find, both in Great Britain and on the continent, than is the case today, and he had been one of the first to realize that there was a fresh and eager—and wealthy—market in the United States. His discovery of a printed form of Indulgence issued to some local magnate who had contributed towards the expenses of the war against the Turk, and that had almost certainly, from the similarity of type and paper and for other technical reasons, been drawn off as a kind of trial, or test, previous to the printing of the great Gutenberg or 42-line Bible, had been a first-class sensation. It had also been extremely profitable, for the name written in on the printed form happened to be that of an extremely wealthy American business man who had in consequence been prepared to pay a fancy price for a document he claimed, on the strength of this resemblance of names, had been issued to an ancestor. There was too, the discovery of those few famous leaves proving that Caxton had, in fact, printed an edition of the *Travels of John Mandeville*.

In this way, buying precious things cheap, securing for them a judicious publicity, and then selling them at a greatly increased figure to purchase others more precious still, old Mr. Kayne had not only succeeded in building up what was perhaps the finest collection of books in private hands, but in making, as it were, the library pay for itself and for a cost of maintenance that was naturally considerable. It was a method still followed by the present custodian, Mr. Broast, who since the death of his employer, under whom he had worked for many years, had not only been retained in charge by Miss Kayne, but was allowed by her to exercise almost entirely his own discretion in all matters of business and administration.

By the terms of his will, however, Mr. Kayne, always haunted by that vision of a possible spendthrift husband for his daughter, or of one more interested in the cash value of books than in the books themselves, had given a right of inspection to the ultimate heir, his brother, Nathaniel Kayne, and to Sir William Winders, a rival collector, part dearest friend and colleague, part deadliest enemy and hated and dreaded rival. These two had power, acting jointly, if they were not satisfied with the upkeep of the library or the general results of the sales and purchases effected, to ask the Courts to order a formal inquiry, though with the provision that they were to be personally responsible for the costs if the investigation proved without reasonable grounds.

The general effect was that the library remained the sole property of Miss Kane for life except on clear proof of serious mal-administration and that all her rights and powers were in fact exercised in her name by Mr. Broast.

After her death, if she died unmarried or without male issue, the library was to pass to Nathaniel Kayne, the testator's brother, to him and his heirs direct in the male line, always under the same strict precautions to provide for proper maintenance. On any failure in administration, or any failure in the male Kayne line, the library passed to the University of Wales, that being selected as a young foundation comparatively badly off and by no means likely to let slip any chance of securing such a treasure as the Kayne library.

In drawing up his will, old Mr. Kayne had evidently had two main ideas: one that for as long as possible the Kayne family, and the other that it should never suffer the usual fate of private libraries and be dispersed by public auction. The testator's brother, the Nathaniel Kayne mentioned in the will, had been dead a good many years, but his rights and duties under the will had passed to his son and heir, the Nathaniel Kayne mentioned by Miss Perkins to Olive, and of whom it was generally believed, since he was known to be in need of money, that the moment he came into possession he would sell his rights, as the will permitted to be done, to the Welsh University.

In spite of a general belief that Mr. Broast held his position by right under the will, that somewhat lengthy and verbose document made no mention of him, except once or twice in reference to the advice that might be given by the librarian. He remained, as he had been under old Mr. Kayne, an employee subject to the usual notice of dismissal, but in practice he acted as the owner, merely asking Miss Kayne for her signature to documents when it was necessary in law, but otherwise acting entirely on his own responsibility. He even resented the monthly inspections Sir William Winders and Mr. Nathaniel Kayne had power to carry out, and that they seldom omitted, for Sir William lived in hopes of finding out something which would enable him to get Mr. Broast dismissed, and himself, or a nominee of his own, placed in charge, and Nathaniel would have been equally glad of a chance to negotiate on a cash basis with the university authorities. Inspection days, therefore, tended to be days of open battle, and on them, as Mr. Broast's secretary and assistant, Miss Perkins, had remarked, Mr. Broast's temper was apt to be distinctly uncertain.

So far, however, the hopes of Sir William, the expectations of Nathaniel, had remained unsatisfied. Impossible to find any fault with a management at once scholarly, efficient and financially successful. Mr Broast seemed, indeed, to have inherited old Mr. Kayne's flair for sensational discoveries in the book world, and only two or three years previously had purchased for a low figure and sold for a sum large enough to cover all library costs for some years, the prayer book used by Bishop Juxon at the execution of Charles the First together with the Bishop's own copy of that one time best seller; the *Eikon Basiliké*, of which some sixty editions and translations appeared within a year of the king's death, a record to arouse the envy of even a twentieth century best selling novelist. The copy had, too, a feature of extraordinary interest in that on the fly leaf, beneath the Bishop's signature, had been written the word 'Remember' by apparently the Bishop's own hand. It was a word, since it presumably referred to the one mysterious injunction given by the king to the bishop on the scaffold itself, that according to report had added a couple of thousand pounds to the value of the book. True, the authenticity of the prayer book had been disputed, but the pedigree of the *Eikon Basiliké* seemed satisfactory, though it was only Mr. Broast who had appreciated the unique interest of that 'Remember', or had identified the crabbed, difficult signature as that of the Bishop.

Another clause in the will provided that the library had to be open to the public once a month, so that the ordinary citizen, too, might have a chance to wonder at and admire so many bookish treasures. It was not a privilege, however, that the ordinary citizen ever showed any great eagerness to exercise. On some of these monthly open days only one or two visitors put in an appearance, though occasionally there would be an influx when char-a-bancs would arrive with bands of tourists or sometimes with chattering companies of schoolgirls.

These days, too, were a sad trial to poor Mr. Broast, interfering with his work, breaking in on the solitude and peace he loved, keeping him in a flutter of anxiety lest some precious book or manuscript might disappear or some act of vandalism be perpetrated. He mobilized the whole household on these occasions to act as watchdogs. Even poor Miss Kayne herself, grumbling and reluctant, was uprooted from her favourite chair to sit at the entrance and see that all visitors duly signed the great visitor's book, while Mr. Broast, his little secretary, Miss Perkins, Briggs, the butler, kept constant watch and ward. Even the cook and the maids were called on at times, though Mr. Broast never felt that they were a remedy likely to be much better than the disease. As for Miss Perkins, she generally ended the day under notice of dismissal, though that was never mentioned again, since it would have been impossible to find anyone else so willing, so industrious, so prepared to be entirely at Mr. Broast's beck and call—and above all, so cheap.

"A fool, a giggling little fool," Mr. Broast would snort indignantly; "totally uneducated—doesn't know a word of Greek or Hebrew, didn't even know what a colophon was or a signature when she came. But no worse than most other giggling fools of girls."

He never added that she was content with a salary of twenty-five shillings a week, was prepared to work all hours and every day, and seemed willing to endure the worst edge of his sharp tongue and general bad temper.

In fairness, though, it must be agreed that Mr. Broast's monthly fits of nervous anxiety had some justification. There was the awful occasion when a young woman visitor had been found lighting a cigarette in one of the book recesses!! One prefers not to dwell upon the subsequent scene. Mr. Broast's pet nightmare was fire. He even refused to have artificial lighting in his beloved library. Work after dark had to be done by the light of portable electric torches, of which a supply was always kept on hand—though in the house, not the library. Warmth in winter, recognized as necessary, not for the human element but to preserve the books from the effects of damp, was provided by hot water pipes, Mr. Broast feeling that hot water was little likely to cause fire. One can imagine, therefore, his emotion when he was someone actually holding a lighted match to a glowing cigarette, the match no doubt to be thrown, still burning, on the floor, the cigarette end destined most likely for some waste paper basket.

There had been further complications, too, when the girl's father brought an action for assault and battery. Altogether a most unfortunate episode. Again, only three or four months ago, the glass of the show case enclosing the *Second Glastonbury Psalter* had been mysteriously broken, nor had the culprit ever been discovered. The sound of the smash had brought Mr. Broast and Miss Perkins and one or two visitors, those near enough to hear, running at full speed, in time certainly to frustrate any attempt at theft if that had been contemplated, though the Psalter itself did not seem to have been touched, but not quickly enough to catch the culprit. Presumably the guilty person had instantly fled elsewhere, perhaps down to the cellar where an old fifteenth century printing press was always an attraction. Anyhow, he had never been identified, but the incident had been disquieting. It had to be admitted, therefore, that Mr. Broast had some excuse for his displays of nerves on open days, though, as little Miss Perkins remarked between two giggles, that was no reason for being rude to visitors or for refusing permission to use the library to readers and scholars whose credentials did not happen to quite satisfy him.

Bobby, only mildly interested in even the rarest and most precious of books, would have preferred a quiet stroll with Olive to the library inspection, for which Mr. Broast had just given what was apparently so rare and gracious a permission. But for one thing rain was threatening, and after all the Kayne library was famous the world over and worth a visit. Besides, certain reminiscences of libraries he had known in his Oxford days suggested that this one, too, might provide quiet and unobserved nooks and corners, where it would be possible to persuade Olive to turn her attention from bibliographic to more personal subjects. As they made their way down the long corridor that led from the room where Miss Kayne usually spent her days to the door—fireproof—admitting to the library annexe, he said to Olive:

"Miss Kayne seems a queer old bird. She informed me she had committed a murder once."

"What?" exclaimed Olive, startled.

"I suppose it was some kind of joke," observed Bobby doubtfully. "I couldn't see the point."

"I don't think murder's anything to joke about," declared Olive, shivering slightly at memories still vivid.

"She said that was why she was interested in your being engaged to a detective," observed Bobby. He added complainingly: "Everyone in the blessed place seems to know all about me. There was an old boy at lunch at the Wynton Arms wanted to know if it was true I belonged to the C.I.D."

"A little man with grey hair and a big nose and horn spectacles?" Olive asked. "That would be Mr. Adams. He came here specially to see something in the library, and Mr. Broast wouldn't let him. There was an awful scene."

"Why did Broast object, do you know?"

"Oh, it was something rather specially precious, and Mr. Broast says he doesn't know Mr. Adams, and Mr. Adams has no credentials, and he's not going to let every Tom, Dick, and Harry paw over things they don't understand and can't appreciate, and Mr. Adams—well, Miss Perkins says she thought murder was going to be done, only finally Mr. Adams went away, and now he is waiting for credentials to show he really is a serious student. He had to send to America for them, and he's awfully furious. There was another scene with Miss Kayne, but she wouldn't interfere, she never does."

"I suppose that's what he meant," Bobby remarked. "I gathered he thought I ought to go and arrest somebody, but I couldn't make out who or why. Then another fellow started to pump me. I had to shut him up. A long-legged fellow, rather good looking, fair. An American, too, I should say."

"He sounds like a boy I saw in the village last night, after Sir William Winders called to give inspection notice. He has to do that you know, or probably Mr. Broast wouldn't let him in. It's a sort of general armed neutrality among them all, at least when it's nothing worse."

"Well, this chap seemed to want to know a lot. Told me America was just crazy about Scotland Yard, and I told him that was just too nice, but if he wanted to know anything he must make written application. We weren't allowed to talk. That choked him off, it always does if you talk about written application."

"I wonder what he's here for," Olive said. She went on: "I'm not sure, but I think I saw someone like him prowling about outside the library the other night."

"Did you though? Can he be up to anything?"

"Mr Broast is awfully nervous about burglars," Olive remarked. "Not so much about fire, though. You don't think this man's a burglar, do you?"

"Oh, I expect he's all right," agreed Bobby. "I didn't recognize him, and he didn't look like a crook, but then crooks never do. It's only that he seemed to want to know such a lot. It's all a bit queer—and then Miss Kayne making silly jokes about murderers. You've known her a good time, haven't you?"

"Ever since I was quite a kiddy. Poor Peter's father was doing my portrait—it's at the Tate now, but they don't show it because it's supposed to be so old-fashioned. He was doing old Mr. Kayne at the same time, and Miss Kayne used to come to the studio with her father. She used to give me chocolates and pet me, and afterwards she had me here sometimes for holidays, after mother went to live abroad. But after I joined mother I didn't hear of her again for a long time—not till she read about our engagement in one of the papers. When I saw her again I hardly knew her," Olive added. "She used to be ever so pretty."

"Who? Miss Kayne?" Bobby asked incredulously.

"Well, come and look," Olive said.

They had been talking in the corridor, and now she led him back a few steps and into the dining-room. A portrait hung there, above the fireplace. It showed a lively, pleasant-faced, good-looking girl with small, regular features and a rather charming air of friendly eagerness, as of one hurrying to say 'Yes' to life and all that it might bring Bobby, staring at it wonderingly, could vaguely trace a sort of dim resemblance to the swollen features and enormous bulk of the old woman he had seen, ponderous and silent in her great oak chair. He said:

"That's not Miss Kayne, is it?"

Olive nodded.

"Peter's father did that, too," she said slowly.

"But—well, how old... I mean..."

He did not say what he meant, but Olive understood.

"It's rather dreadful, isn't it?" she said. "That was done about twenty-five years ago. She would be twenty-six or seven then. She can't be much over fifty now."

Bobby continued staring at the portrait. What strange circumstances could have changed the bright and vivid girl of the picture into that sombre, swollen mass of flesh he had just left? Life can be strange, life can be hard and bitter, but between this picture and that reality there seemed to be an abyss altogether unaccountable.

"Oh well," he said, telling himself it was no business of his. He said to Olive: "You aren't staying any longer, are you?"

"I am sorry for her," Olive said.

Bobby scowled. He interpreted this remark quite rightly as an intimation that Olive meant to stay as long as Miss Kayne wished, or as long as Olive could spare the time. Then he went nearer to the picture. Something had caught his eye. He said:

"There's a tear in the canvas. Do you see? There."

"No. Where?" Olive asked.

"Across the throat," Bobby said. "The canvas has been slit right across there where the throat is."

Olive looked. It was plain enough when pointed out. The painted throat had been cut across, and though the slit had been repaired it was still visible when looked for. Olive turned away with a slight shudder.

"Let's go into the library," she said. "I told Miss Perkins we wouldn't be long."

CHAPTER III
THE LIBRARY

They went through the great fireproof door that admitted from the house to the library annexe. Beyond was a small, square lobby, containing a chair, a writing table on which lay a huge visitors' book, on one wall a portrait of an elderly gentleman in a frock coat, and opposite it an enormous 'No Smoking' placard.

"Mr. Broast has a 'no smoking' complex," Olive said, seeing Bobby looking at this.

"Well, it's big enough all right," observed Bobby. "Who is the old gentleman?"

"Miss Kayne's father," Olive explained. "Afterwards Mr Albert always said it was the worst thing he ever did."

"It's not so bad," decided Bobby, examining it critically. "A bit photographic, perhaps."

"That's just what Mr. Albert always said himself," observed Olive with a touch of surprise in her voice. "He said a camera would have done as good a job. He told me once it was about the only time he hadn't been able to get hold of his subject at all, as if there were something Mr. Kayne was keeping back, something secret in him, something of himself he wasn't going to let anyone else know about if he could help it."

The thought came into Bobby's mind that Miss Kayne, too, had given him the same impression, a feeling of something held back and hidden, something that only constant watchfulness and effort prevented from thrusting itself into the open. Olive said teasingly:

"You ought to have been an art critic."

"No such luck," sighed Bobby. "What do they keep it here for?" he added, thinking of the other portrait, that of Miss Kayne, to which this seemed the natural companion.

"It does seem funny, doesn't it?" agreed Olive, and then there opened the door, again heavy and fireproof, that admitted from this entrance lobby to the main library hall.

Through it there fluttered nervously, rather like a startled canary hopping from perch to perch in its cage, a small, slight, youngish, frightened looking woman, wearing a brown overall, with mouse-coloured hair, dull, slightly inflamed eyes behind heavy horn spectacles, small, indeterminate features, conveying altogether a general air of timid and apologetic insignificance. When she saw Olive and Bobby she giggled and said breathlessly:

"Oh, I'm so sorry." It was how she began almost all her sentences. "Oh, I do hope I haven't kept you waiting."

"Oh no, we've only been here a minute," Olive answered reassuringly. "Miss Perkins is Mr. Broast's secretary, Bobby. I know you've heard about Mr. Owen, Miss Perkins."

To her great annoyance Olive found she was blushing as she said this. Miss Perkins giggled again. She generally did. She clasped her hands and gasped:

"Oh, I'm so sorry; oh, it's so romantic, isn't it?" She giggled once again. Bobby and Olive exchanged glances, two minds with but a single thought, and that regrettably tending towards assault and battery. Miss Perkins, noticing nothing, managed yet another giggle, and panted out: "Oh, it must be so Wonderful to be a detective, and find out everything. You do, don't you, Mr. Owen, Everything?"

"I don't know about everything," said Bobby.

Believe it or not, Miss Perkins produced another giggle. Bobby looked despairingly at Olive. Olive scowled at him to tell him he must be patient and then said:

"Must we sign the visitor's book, Miss Perkins?"

"Oh, yes, please; oh, I'm so sorry," said Miss Perkins, fluttering over to the table. "Oh, I do think it ought to be 'Distinguished Visitors', don't you, Miss Farrar? Because Mr. Owen's quite famous, isn't he? And you, too, I'm sure, so it oughtn't to be just 'Visitors', ought it?

"I'm not famous," Bobby declared, with a touch of temper in his voice so that Olive gave him another warning frown.

"Oh, a detective," protested Miss Perkins as she might have said the Prime Minister, or the Director of the B.B.C., or a film star, or any other of the truly great and mighty. Once more she giggled, and then from a drawer produced a book smaller than the giant volume on the table and more elaborately bound. She pushed it across to Bobby, murmuring reverently as she did so: "A detective's so wonderful, finding out things all the time, isn't he?"

Bobby, rather than endure another giggle, duly signed, though with a strong mental reservation about the "distinguished". Olive signed, too, and Miss Perkins thanked them and said she was so sorry, and presented them each with a small printed card containing once more the prohibition against smoking within the library precincts. It was, she explained, with her accustomed mixture of apology and giggle, a strict rule that every visitor's attention must be drawn to this regulation.

"Even if the King himself came—" said Miss Perkins, and then relapsed into awed silence, overcome entirely by the mere thought of such a happening, "Only I do think he would be Interested, don't you?" she added, recovering slightly.

They both agreed that His Majesty would certainly be Interested, and Miss Perkins said she was so sorry, though for what did not quite appear, and then ushered them through the second fire-proof door into the great hall of the library itself.

The first impression was that if an all-pervading gloom, a kind of sea of shadows, through which one dimly perceived row upon row of books, shelf upon shelf, stretching away into invisibility and the unknown, and again the thought of secrecy, of reserve, of something kept away and hidden stole into Bobby's mind, as though this vast place of shadows were a place of secrets, too, as though each one of these thousands of books held its own message it would reveal but with reluctance.

The library rose to a considerable height, its roof barely seen in the darkness that seemed to cluster beneath it. Till they were nearly lost in this gathered darkness, the shelves of books rose up in ever-ascending sequence. Along the walls there ran two iron galleries, by which access to the books could be obtained. The galleries themselves were reached by spiral iron stairways placed at intervals. At the west end of the hall these galleries were three in number, the topmost one dominating, as it were, the floor of the library. Olive whispered to Bobby that on open days, when the public were admitted Mr. Broast sometimes took his stand there, so as to watch from this place of vantage and make sure no one was misbehaving. On the floor, at intervals of two or three yards, bookcases were arranged at right angles to the walls, making, as it were, a succession of small bays. The book-cases, however, did not reach quite to the sides, so that on the walls the shelves were continuous and a clear passage by them allowed. From each side these bookcases extended about a third of the way across the width of the hall, so that in the centre was left a wide passage way in which, as well as in some of the heavily shadowed bays, stood a few show cases. Miss Perkins, who had followed Olive and Bobby, said with her inevitable giggle:

"Oh, please, I'm so sorry, but Mr. Broast said I was to show you some of our wonderful, wonderful treasures. I always say 'ours'," she explained apologetically, "I'm so Proud of them. Mr. Broast said he was so sorry, but would you please excuse him till he's finished talking to Sir William and Mr. Nat."

"Oh, yes," said Bobby, supposing he must have been mistaken in thinking he had seen a figure detach itself from where the shadows lay thickest in one of the bays and slip silently away behind those book-cases, row upon row of them, that stretched out from the walls like so many clutching fingers.

He supposed it was because he wasn't much of a bookish person that this place made so odd, so unpleasant an impression on him, a place of secrecy and reserve, it seemed to him, of hidden activities, of ancient knowledge and of unknown powers concealed between the covers of all these books but ready to spring into activity again at the call of those who might have power to release them. He remembered how often libraries had been burnt in past ages, and he thought he understood something of the mind of those who had put them to the flame.

"I wouldn't mind so much," he thought, "if only there were more light," and he looked with disfavour at the south wall, where the rows of books were unbroken by any window. On the north wall there were windows certainly, but even they were provided with great steel shutters, and now that it was growing late on this day of cloud and drizzle, the northern light, dim at the best, had almost gone. The architect had intended the high west window to provide most light, but it had been given heavy curtains, and then, too, the book cases arranged at right angles to the walls threw heavy shadows across the floor. No wonder, thought Bobby, that little Miss Perkins's eyes were so red and inflamed if she had to work all day in a gloom like this.

She was mingling now giggles, ecstacies and apologies over one of the showcases, and behind her back Bobby flew signals of distress, even of incipient rebellion. He really felt he could not stand much more of Miss Perkins and Olive took pity on him and said:

"I think Mr. Owen would like to see the printing press in the cellar if I might take him down there."

"Oh, I'm so sorry," said Miss Perkins, fluttering nervously towards a door near by and then back again. "Oh, Mr. Broast might want me. He does sometimes," she assured them nervously, "especially when it's Inspection— so unnecessary, I always think, don't you?"

"Don't bother to come with us," Olive said. "I know the way. Then if Mr. Broast does happen to want you, he won't have to wait."

"Oh, thank you so much," Miss Perkins said earnestly. "You're always so thoughtful, Miss Farrar."

Olive acknowledged this compliment by giving the fluttering little woman one of her warmest smiles, said thank you so much and not to trouble, manouevered Bobby and herself through the door leading to the cellar and got the door firmly closed before Miss Perkins could succeed in following them, as in her vague, undetermined way she seemed inclined to do. At the bottom of the stairs, once he was sure they were safe, Bobby said solemnly:

"Olive, if anything could make me love you more than I do, it's your rescuing us from that awful woman."

"You must be nice to the poor little thing," Olive told him severely, "I feel so awfully sorry for her."

"Not me," said Bobby, "I feel most awfully sorry for anyone obliged to have anything to do with her. Is she always like that?"

"Well, she was a bit worse than usual," Olive conceded. "I think she was nervous. I think she imagines detectives are liable to put you in handcuffs and march you off to prison at any moment."

"Little fool," growled Bobby.

"Now, Bobby," Olive rebuked him, "you are not to talk like that. She's had a dreadfully hard life. It would have made most people hard and revengeful, and it's better to giggle, isn't it?"

Bobby, not greatly interested in Miss Perkins, now Miss Perkins was no longer there, thought the occasion appropriate for an interlude. Olive reminded him that they were there to look at a very interesting fifteenth century printing press, still in working order, and in fact used by Mr. Broast at times when he happened to want any printing done. Indeed it was understood that he intended himself to print on this press the new catalogue now in course of preparation. It was a task he was quite capable of carrying out, for he was an expert printer, and always protested that everyone interested in bibliography, whether as an expert, as a collector, or commercially, ought to be fully equipped in practical knowledge of all the details of book production.

Until the introduction of the linotype machine and other recent developments of the same order, there was little difference between the early printing presses and those in current use. This one, standing in the cellar of the Kayne library, had been kept in good order, and visitors regarded it with awe when told that it might well have been used by Caxton himself, or more probably, from certain indications, by that Thomas Rood, of Oxford, for whom as a printer, at one time, priority even over Caxton had been claimed. All round the press against the cellar walls was piled high that miscellany of lumber that so soon accumulates. Behind it, hardly an inch of wall was visible. The only light here came from two windows, half sunken and heavily barred, and the whole place was heavy with the damp and sullen odour of mould and of decay.

"Why on earth don't they clear all this rubbish out?" Bobby asked. "The place only wants a little ventilation. Is this the only cellar? There ought to be another so you could get a current of air through," he added, remembering that Miss Kayne had spoken of cellars in the plural.

Olive said, however, that there was no other, and tried to interest him in the printing press. But Bobby didn't care two hoots for ancient printing presses when Olive was there and they were alone. He agreed the press was in wonderfully good order, cleaned and oiled and ready for use, and awfully interesting, of course, and with that the press was forgotten and the interlude resumed till a familiar giggle sounded from above to recall them to more mundane things.

"Oh, I'm so sorry," said Miss Perkins, fluttering in her vague, helpless way at the head of the stairs, "but it's Mr. Broast. He's asking where you are."

"Tell him I'm showing Mr. Owen the old press," Olive called back, hastily smoothing hair that somehow had got ruffled during the showing process. "We'll be up in a minute."

She sternly repressed Bobby, who tried to put that minute to a use inconsistent with Olive's felt need of reconditioning her hair. They heard Miss Perkins's giggle die away in the distance, and Bobby, cross at the waste of that minute he could have put to such good use, said:

"Well, I'm glad I haven't got to put up with that eternal giggle."

"It's not eternal," said Olive severely. "It's only that the poor thing's nervous, and you're not to talk about her like that."

"All right," said Bobby meekly. "I won't, I suppose there are worse things in life than a giggle, though it doesn't seem so at the moment. Does she get on all right with Mr. Broast?"

"Well, she's cheap," Olive explained. "I don't know how she manages on what she gets. She never seems to want a holiday. She's good at shorthand and typing, too, and she did it all by herself."

"Did what?"

"Shorthand and typing, she taught herself both, and I think it was awfully clever of her."

"So do I," said Bobby without conviction.

"Nobody's a bit fair to her," Olive said, "just because she's nervous and shortsighted and giggles. When she was a little kiddy, her mother ran away from her husband with some man. There was a divorce and the husband allowed her to be given charge of the child. Then he shot himself, the blackguard his wife had run away with and married after the divorce, deserted her when he had spent all her money, and her own family, and her former husband's family, refused to have anything more to do with her or with the child. Finally she died or something. She had left the poor little kiddy in some cheap lodging-house and at first sent money to pay for her keep. Then one day she sent her boxes and a message to say she was coming herself and that was the last heard of her. When the money stopped coming, first the landlady sold the contents of the boxes—at least, everything that was worth selling, Miss Perkins has a few things still. Afterwards the landlady kept the child out of charity, she said, but really because she saw a chance of getting a maid-of-all-work on the cheap. Charity pays in the kitchen. Miss Perkins didn't mean to stop there, though. She taught herself shorthand and typing, and it takes something to do that by yourself at night in your bedroom after you've been cleaning and scrubbing and cooking and washing up all day, sixteen hours on end attending to lodgers. She learnt typing on the keyboard of a broken machine she got from a rag and bone man. It was all to get money to try to find her mother again, but he never did. I think it was rather wonderful of her, even if she is nervous and does keep giggling. I expect I should have been washing dishes still in that woman's scullery."

Olive had grown quite flushed with the warmth of her defence, and Bobby was not so much interested in it as in thinking how becoming that flush was to her thin and pale cheeks, though indeed just recently that thinness and that pallor had seemed to grow less pronounced. He kissed her suddenly.

"You're wonderful," he said, "and if you say so, Miss Perkins shall giggle as much as she likes—I can't say handsomer than that."

CHAPTER IV
THE LIBRARIAN

Entering the main library hall from the cellar, Bobby and
Olive saw standing there a little group of three men. One,
who seemed to dominate the other two by some innate force
of personality, so that it was on him the eye rested first, was
a tall, thin man, whom Bobby guessed at once to be so Basil
Reardon Broast, the custodian of the Kayne library. His
hair, plentiful still, and worn a trifle long, was snowy white,
though his easy and upright carriage, the bright intensity of
his clear, blue greyish eyes, the swift certainty of his
movements, showed plainly that as yet age had laid no
withering touch upon his powers. Nor was there anything
here of the scholar's stoop that Bobby had remarked in Mr.
Adams, his acquaintance of the Wynton Arms, nothing of
the scholar's dim and peering gaze. In his hand he held
gold-rimmed spectacles, it is true, but he only wore them
for really close work. At a distance his sight was still good.
He wore a small moustache and a small, pointed beard,
both now perfectly white, and his curved, arrogant nose
stood out like the beak of a bird of prey. A distinguished-
looking figure, Bobby thought, though one that suggested
more the man of action, the leading politician or the
controller of some great business, than the timid, unworldly
and retiring scholar of tradition. In his youth he must have
been strikingly handsome, and with his flashing glance, his
upright figure, his finely carved, ascetic features, he still had
the air of one fashioned to dominate and to command.

His two companions were both big, heavily-built men,
one much older than the other. This elder man had a large,
flat face, but well-formed features and a good forehead,
though with a small chin jutting out obstinately beneath a
little pursed-up mouth. A face of many contradictions,
Bobby thought, and one that in youth must have been
handsome too, though never with that air of arrogant,
compelling beauty of which the librarian still showed traces.

The skin, too, was blotched and unhealthy looking, and the eyes showed beneath them a puffiness that suggested a tendency to self indulgence. The third member of the little group was a tall, exceedingly handsome youngster with hair that was a mass of yellow curls, features of classic perfection, that 'schoolgirl complexion' the advertisements talk of, a head beautifully modelled, though perhaps a little small, and set on square, athletic shoulders of a singularly graceful body. At the moment, however, these remarkable good looks of his were somewhat spoiled by a black and scowling expression and the nervous twitching of his rosebud mouth. Bobby indeed had the impression that he had just been shaking his fist at one or other or both of his companions. At the opening of the cellar door, when Olive and Bobby came in, he swung round, gave them an even blacker scowl, and then marched away. They heard Miss. Perkins's nervous giggle, they heard the library door banged with considerable force, and in a whisper Bobby said to Olive:

"Who is the film star in the naughty temper?"

"Nat Kayne, Miss Kayne's cousin," Olive answered. "He is the heir and he is always wanting to get the library sold to the Welsh University because then he would get a half share at once. The other man is Sir William Winders, the senior trustee."

Mr. Broast had watched Nat Kayne's stormy exit with a kind of amused and yet regretful tenderness. He made an expressive gesture with those fine, white hands of his as if to say that to the young much must be excused and then came forward and very pleasantly introduced himself and Sir William.

"We were all quite excited," he said smilingly, "to know Miss Olive was bringing a real live Scotland Yard detective to visit us. Evidently only a spotless conscience would allow its owner to get engaged to a detective."

"Police," growled Sir William, who seemed less inclined to be amiable, "used to be a very decent set of men—getting a bit above themselves now. Fussy. Cars and all that," he concluded vaguely, from which Bobby instantly deduced that there had been some trouble about speeding or leaving a car unattended or something of the sort.

"Can't fuss too much with the deaths on the road what they are," declared Mr. Broast with another smile at Bobby. "Sometimes I wish they would fuss a bit more. But I don't suppose Mr. Owen has much to do with the traffic problem?"

"No, nothing at all," agreed Bobby, and began to be aware that for all the smiling ease Mr. Broast showed, those clear, bright eyes of his were regarding his visitors with an almost fierce intensity.

Natural enough, no doubt, that Olive's friends should be keenly interested in the policeman on whom they probably—and reasonably—considered that she was most foolishly throwing herself away.

"And then," Mr. Broast continued, "I had a special reason for feeling so interested when I knew you were a detective officer. A very special, personal reason."

"Oh, yes," said Bobby, suddenly afraid that Mr. Broast, like Miss Kayne, was about to declare that he also had in the past committed the perfect murder. Bobby was quite relieved when Mr. Broast merely continued:

"Because, you see, I'm a detective, too."

"Indeed," murmured Bobby.

"Much of my work," explained Mr. Broast, "lies in tracking down rare editions, association books, and in identifying them by all manner of small details. I could tell you a story of how I traced the Caxton Mandeville leaves half across Europe. You start after your murderers from a dropped button or a burnt-out match, and the end is the gallows. I start—once I did so literally—from the burnt match, and I end with the discovery of a book perhaps unique."

"Prefer your sort of hunt," growled Sir William. "Hate to think of hanging people," and he shuddered slightly, with a kind of uneasy sensibility his somewhat heavy and slow appearance did not quite suggest.

"The excitement of the hunt must be much the same in both cases," said Mr. Broast. "I daresay when Mr. Owen lay his hand upon the murderer's shoulder, he feels much the same sort of triumph that we do when we run to earth say a complete set of *Pickwick Papers* in original paper covers, or, as I did last year, a copy of the quarto edition of *Titus Andronicus* that till then no one had even believed existed. A triumph, that, a triumph to equal any of Mr. Owen's," declared Mr. Broast with a kindling eye, a flushed cheek, at the memory of that ecstatic moment.

"I don't think we feel much triumph," Bobby said slowly. "What one does feel is duty done and the knowledge that peaceful folk can sleep safely in their beds again."

"Does that follow?" Mr. Broast asked. "Surely a murder is never committed without a cause, and surely a cause for murder seldom repeats itself?"

Bobby shook his head.

"Murder breeds murder," he said. "There's the sense of power for one thing. A murderer may begin to feel himself a kind of god with power in his hands of life and death over lesser mortals. Or again he continues to kill for security, to make himself safe. You remember *Macbeth*? The start is just one murder—that of Duncan. But that one leads to many more—inevitably."

"Surely that hardly applies under modern conditions," Mr. Broast argued. "My point is that it may be necessary once, but that necessity would hardly arise again. In *Macbeth*, the environment and circumstances were quite exceptional."

"They always are, unique rather," Bobby said.

A faint giggle from behind heralded the fluttering approach of Miss Perkins.

"Oh, I'm so sorry," she said. "Briggs says Miss Kayne is asking for Mr. Nathaniel."

"Tell her he's gone," Broast said abruptly, and Miss Perkins fled, evidently so scared by his sharp tone that she even forgot her customary giggle.

"I'll be off, too," Sir William said. His large, flat face was a little pale, his hands shook slightly. "Don't like this sort of talk," he muttered. "Murder, hanging. Ugh." One unsteady hand went to his throat and pulled at a collar he seemed to be finding too tight. "Sets you dreaming," he complained. "I shall dream to-night. I shan't sleep."

Muttering adieus, he hurried away, and Miss Perkins had by now sufficiently recovered from her recent fright to contribute once more her accustomed giggle as she let him out.

"Well, if our friend doesn't sleep, he won't dream," Broast remarked, looking after Sir William's retreating form with a smile that was more than half malicious, Bobby thought. "He's a very nervous type, very nervous," the librarian continued. "Ought to have taken up something less exciting than book collecting."

"I suppose it is awfully interesting," observed Bobby, though without much conviction in his tone.

"It leads you on, leads you on, just like you say murder does," declared Mr. Broast and chuckled over a joke that he evidently thought excellent, but that Bobby considered in poor taste. Perhaps the librarian felt something of Bobby's unexpressed disapproval, for he added: "But Winders was right—murder's not a pleasant subject. Unnecessary to talk about it. We'll forget it, shall we?" He paused to smile again, as though he found a secret amusement in this suggestion, and went on: "You must look at some of our treasures, Mr. Owen. All that section behind you for instance is devoted to my Incunabula—in the general sense of books printed before 1500. Really of course the word means books produced before printing was properly organized in any country so that America and Australia have their own Incunabula. After all, the word only means swaddling clothes. But these of mine are all pre-1500."

"I suppose they are awfully valuable," Bobby remarked.

"Well—er—to be perfectly frank, their value's a good deal exaggerated in popular idea. Of course, there are exceptions—the great 42-line Bible, for instance, or the 36-line Bible for that matter, and others of real interest. But most of them are just school books—Delectuses, Latin grammars, Donatuses. Catlo's Delectus had a big circulation in the fifteenth century. I was offered another copy the other day. The owner wanted a thousand pounds for it. He thought I was trying to swindle him when I suggested—well, a good deal less. But after he had tried the Museum, and Christie's, and one or two other places he was glad to come back and take what I gave him. All the same, Mr. Owen, they form the foundation on which the library has been built up. But for them"—Mr. Broast's voice took on a slow solemnity of tone—"the Kayne collection would never have come into existence."

"Oh," said Bobby, quite puzzled. "You mean you began with them?"

"Not quite that. I use them as counters—trading counters. I am always ready to buy any—at a fair market price. Then I put them on the shelves. I've got three *Hours of the Virgin* there at present—two of the Sarum use and one York. It was the laymen's prayer book at that time, you know. Some rich man hears of the library and comes to look round. He has money—he wants culture. The possession of a few rare books or paintings give him that, he thinks, gives him an aroma of that taste and scholarship he does not even begin to understand. As a favour, therefore, I let him buy one or two Incunabula. I can tell you, Mr. Owen, that word alone has been worth hundreds of pounds to the library. Lots of people find it most impressive; it seems to have the same effect on them that Mesopotamia had on the old lady in the story. I can often sell for twenty, fifty, even a hundred times what I gave."

He chuckled delightedly, and Bobby gave a polite smile, though wondering inwardly whether all this was quite honest. But collectors always had, he supposed, their own standards, and then, too, the purchasers Mr. Broast described were all probably rich enough to gratify their vanity and their wish to be looked upon as patrons of art and learning. Probably they got full value by being able to say to their friends that they had secured the treasure they were showing from the famous Kayne library ('didn't half like parting, either'). Probably, too, the higher the price they could quote, the greater the interest and admiration displayed by their friends.

As honest as a good many other business deals, Bobby decided. Was it not written long ago that between buying and selling sin sticketh close as the mortar between bricks?

"Now, this other section I don't sell from," continued Mr. Broast, who, with his strange, uncanny sensibility, seemed to know what doubts were passing through Bobby's mind. "Complete," he said proudly, "complete and unique. Every book without exception published by the Aldine Press—eight hundred and twenty and three, and every one represented here."

"How interesting," said Bobby, who had heard of the Aldine Press, and to show his general knowledge and interest he added: —"I suppose you've the Elzivirs, too?"

Mr. Broast gave him a baleful glare.

"I wouldn't have an Elzivir on my shelves except to sell again," he snarled. "Second rate in every way, printing, scholarship, everything. The only thing about them was that they were small so they would go in your pocket. That's how they got to be so fashionable, people dancing attendance on kings or great nobles could read them while they were waiting for admittance—at least they could if they had good eyesight. Now the Aldine books—serious scholarship and clear and lovely printing. They were the first to think of making printing fine. And there they all are, on my shelves. Not a gap."

"I suppose they'll be worth a lot of money," Bobby said.

Mr. Broast bestowed on him another and still more baleful glare.

"We don't use the money measure of value here," he snapped. "I've no idea what they would fetch at auction, if that's what you mean." He paused to give those serried ranks of ancient books just such a look as a mother bestows upon her new-born child. "The whole history of early European printing, of the birth of European thought is there," he said slowly. "Those shelves, Mr. Owen, tell the growth of the human mind during those years—and I can give you no idea of their monetary value."

"I'm sure it's awfully interesting," said Bobby meekly, feeling a bit suppressed.

"Money value is a kind of measure of general value, don't you think, Mr. Broast?" asked Olive, rallying to Bobby's rescue.

"I daresay you're right, my dear young lady," agreed Mr. Broast, benevolent again.

With those swift, sure movements of his, light on his feet for all his white hairs as any youthful athlete, he passed on a few yards and paused before other shelves, beckoning Bobby and Olive as he did so to follow him.

"There," he said, pointing to one of the higher shelves. "You see those Miltons? Now they have a money value, more accidental than real in a sense. I expect you know there were eight issues of the first edition of the *Paradise Lost*."

Bobby tried to look as if this fact had been familiar to him since childhood. Olive however said:

"I thought a first edition meant it all came out at once?"

"All printed at once," Mr. Broast corrected her. "There was no demand at first. Perhaps you do know," he added, with a sidelong, slightly malicious look at Bobby, "the story that Milton sold the poem for £5. He was probably still suspect as an adherent of the Puritan party and no one wanted to have too much to do with him or his writings. So when *Paradise Lost* was printed, only a few copies were issued for sale. When they had all been bought then a few more were bound up and put on the market. There were eight of these issues altogether, each with a different title page, during the two years from 1667 to 1669 till the whole printing was disposed of. Well, copies of each issue are on that shelf. That has what I call genuine value—genuine bibliographical value. But they have, too, a very much increased money value because each single copy has association value from having belonged to some celebrated man. The signature of Lord Shaftesbury is in one volume, the bookplate of Samuel Pepys is in another, though I had to take off one or two of no interest that had been put over it. There's the bookplate of his friend, William Hewer, in another, and the last of the series has Dryden's signature. If it is ever necessary to sell—I hope it won't, but maintenance costs are heavy and of course we're private and independent so we don't get any help. But if sale is ever necessary, and I would rather part with association books than others if I have to, I expect the set would fetch a big price. I've been offered £5,000, but I was able to say 'No, thank you' at the time. If I have to sell, it will be at auction, and we shall see what we shall see. Probably some rich fool," he added, looking vicious, "will buy them just for showing off and boasting and publicity."

"Isn't it rather wonderful to have found them all belonging to famous people?" Olive asked.

"It is indeed," said Mr. Broast and chuckled as if he found his luck amusing. "Now I'll show you something of real interest, the Mandeville leaves—money value and real interest in them," he said and slipped away.

"They're his chief treasure," Olive whispered to Bobby. "They're only shown to special people—you must have made a good impression, darling."

"I didn't think I had," confessed Bobby. "You never know where to have him. One minute he talks of nothing but how much the things are worth and the next he snaps your head off if you mention money."

"I think he has two standards," Olive said, "two standards and two moods. Sometimes he's the perfect bookman and sometimes the complete book dealer. But the book lover is fundamental. He's awfully proud of having the complete set of the eight Milton issues, but if he had to he is quite willing to cash in on their accidental value because they all once belonged to famous people."

"I used to be awfully fond of Dryden," Bobby said. "I got him for a prize once—the other chaps in my Form had influenza so I came in on top. I remember I spouted that thing about none but the brave deserve the fair one speech day." He put up a long arm to the shelf above that Mr. Broast had pointed to, and took down the last of the eight volumes. He opened it and in a puzzled tone he said: —"The fly leaf's blank, there's no name at all."

With his swift eager step, as of one who knew there was little time so every passing minute must be used, Mr. Broast came quickly back to them, and when he saw what Bobby had in his hand, he gave him a look so fierce, so deadly in what seemed an intensity of rage, that Bobby fairly jumped.

"Oh, I'm sorry," he stammered, "I just wanted to look at Dryden's signature."

"It isn't there, is it?" Mr. Broast said softly, yet the anger in his eyes unabated. "No, I've just remembered. I took it to show a friend and put another copy in its place."

CHAPTER V
MURDER REPORT

Though nothing more was said, though Mr. Broast plunged at once into a description of the Mandeville leaves, as he called them, yet there still persisted a faint atmosphere of restraint, of unease. More than once Bobby thought he perceived the librarian's swift, piercing glance flashed at him for an instant and then away again. It was as though something of suspicion, of doubt, even of fear conveyed itself in those quick, flashing looks.

"Hang it all," Bobby said to himself irritably, "what's the matter with the fellow?"

Mr. Broast went on talking. It appeared that no record existed to suggest that Caxton had ever printed an edition of Sir John Mandeville's *Travels* and yet it had always seemed likely that a work of such popularity must have passed through his press. Something, some quite obscure reference in which Mr. Broast had seen a significance no one else had noticed, had put him on the track. He had followed it, he explained, from one faint indication to another.

"Just like a detective following up the clues in a murder," declared Mr. Broast with another of those quick, searching glances that Bobby had come to expect.

These clues had taken him to the south of France, to an old château there, to the farm to which most of the château furnishings had been removed at the time of the French revolution, on to another château where these furnishings had gone on the Bourbon restoration, finally to an old house in Le Puy where the last survivor of the family lived with many of the old family relics.

There in an attic, in an old chest, Mr. Broast told how he had discovered, used as packing for the broken binding of an ancient housekeeping book containing old recipes, these precious leaves. He had paid the price, a quite exorbitant price, demanded for the housekeeping book—it was old and interesting and worth in itself a pound or two, and Mr. Broast had paid, after suitable bargaining to avert suspicion, the £20 demanded for it, thereby confirming the expressed opinion of the owner that the Paris dealer who, when consulted, laughed at such a figure, was of an 'indélicatesse extrême.'

Bobby gathered, however, that great care during these negotiations had been taken to avoid any hint escaping concerning the precious packing that was in fact the sole object of Mr. Broast's desire, and whereof the value ran into four figures. Again Bobby wondered whether that sort of thing was quite honest. Most collectors, he supposed, would argue that their superior knowledge deserved reward, but was not that a little like the argument of the robber baron that his superior strength deserved reward? No such scruples, however, troubled, it was plain, Mr. Broast, who chuckled cheerfully over his own cleverness in buying for so little something of such rare value without the seller ever suspecting for one moment what he was parting with. Indeed, it was true that but for the acumen and perseverance shown by Mr. Broast these precious pages would probably have remained for ever lost and unknown, their value unsuspected.

"What the whole book itself, intact, would have been worth," he said, "I hardly dare think. Probably it got worn out in time, came to pieces, and no one was going to bother much about an old book in a foreign language that probably by that time no one could read. Finally most of it would disappear and these few leaves got used for packing. Twelve are consecutive, part of the epilogue, including, by a miracle of good luck, the colophon. Eight were odd leaves. We had to sell those," added Mr. Broast regretfully, "though I must say we got a whacking price. But the consecutive pages, including the colophon, are here."

Bobby and Olive duly admired the almost sacred relics, and Mr. Broast explained that the chief value of the colophon was that it gave the date; it showed that this book was the first ever printed anywhere in English.

"It antedates both the *Dictes and Sayings of the Philosophers*—we have a superb copy of that, by the way—and the *History of Troy* printed in Bruges, and supposed to have been actually the first book printed in English as it was also the first book printed in French. Now the Mandeville *Travels* comes first, in English and in England, and incidentally proves that Caxton was at work in England before he set up the 'Red Pale' press. There is the *Dictes*," he added, pointing to a locked case. "I believe I'm right in saying it's the finest copy known—mint condition. The book next to it is a copy of the 1557 edition by Tottel of poems by the Earl of Surrey and Sir Thomas Wyatt. The Bodleian has the only other known copy, but it's not in such good condition."

He went on to show others of his treasures, including an indulgence granted to a knight of Surrey, whose name and that of his wife had been written in in now faded ink.

"A trial sheet for the *Dictes*, as I've proved conclusively," Mr. Broast told them, and pointed out various small technical details on which he relied for proof of the *Dictes* connection. "No doubt drawn off preliminary to beginning the actual printing of the *Dictes*. A precaution to make sure everything was right. Name and date left blank, you see, to be filled in later on. In fact, a printed official form issued in blank to be filled up as required."

With extreme awe Bobby regarded this progenitor of all those official forms that since have filled the world with their monstrous brood.

There were other treasures to be shown, though none that quite so keenly interested Bobby, whose whole life indeed was cribbed, cabined and confined, by endless printed forms, stretching out as it were to the crack of doom, or at any rate till long after he ought by rights to have been able to sign off.

None the less, though all this was very interesting, Bobby was not sorry when the tour of inspection drew to an end. There were so many things he wanted to say to Olive, and so far he had hardly a chance to be alone with her for more than a few minutes at a time. He had managed to wangle permission to leave duty early and had got down here in good time, before lunch indeed and with a strong hope that he might get an invitation to have that meal at Wynton Lodge. But when he rang up from the village inn, the Wynton Arms, to announce his arrival, instead of the invitation to lunch he had so optimistically hoped for, he merely received the information that Miss Kayne and Miss Farrar were lunching out.

So he had been obliged to get his meal at the Wynton Arms in the little, low-beamed dining-room, in the company of Mr. Adams, the stooping, dim-eyed scholar in horn rimmed spectacles who had, it appeared, quarrelled so violently with Mr. Broast, and of the tall young American who, like Mr. Adams, had discovered from local gossip that Bobby was connected with Scotland Yard and had tried, not very successfully, to engage him on the subject of police work.

Now therefore that this duty tour of the Kayne library seemed to be drawing to a close, Bobby began to indulge in hopes that he might soon get a chance to have Olive to himself for a little. He was due back in town that night, but there was no need to make too early a start, so there was still time they could spend together if opportunity were permitted, and then they heard once more Miss Perkins's apologetic giggle.

"Oh, I'm so sorry," she said as she fluttered towards them through the shadows that lay so thickly and so heavily in this home of learning and of gloom, "Briggs has just brought a memo from Miss Kayne It's a message from Sir William Winders, Miss Kayne took down when he rang up. He says he is going to run over in the car after dinner, and he wants to be sure of finding you disengaged."

"Oh, very well," Mr. Broast answered, though Bobby thought he looked for the moment a little annoyed or disturbed, as if this proposed visit were not too welcome. "I'll ring him later perhaps. There are several letters I ought to write to-night," he added in a vexed tone.

"Yes, Mr. Broast," said Miss Perkins, and fluttered away again into the shadows from which she had emerged.

They were indeed so heavy now that Mr. Broast had to produce his pocket torch to light Bobby and Olive to the door, and Bobby thanked him very much and said how interesting it had all been, and when they were safely outside, with the heavy fireproof door closed behind them, Olive said with some surprise in her voice:

"I've hardly ever known Mr. Broast be so nice and take such trouble."

"Didn't look so awfully amiable," observed Bobby, "when he saw me with that Milton. Did he think I was going to pinch the thing?"

"I expect so, darling," Olive answered cheerfully. "He did look furious, didn't he? He's always in a panic about fire or burglary or visitors—especially visitors. He suspects them all, like cats in a dairy. He's got a revolver somewhere for protection against burglars, and I'm sure he would use it."

"Has he though?" said Bobby. "Hope he's got a licence. I thought he was never going to stop showing us things— awfully interesting of course, but I came along to see you, not a lot of old junk."

"Bobby," protested Olive, horrified at this description of treasures and rarities famous all the world over. She added: "Ever since he heard about you, he has been calling himself a detective. I expect that's why he was so nice."

Bobby felt a little doubtful whether 'nice' was quite the word.

"Got a temper of his own," he remarked. "Looked as if there had been been a good old row with those other two."

"There's always some sort of upset when it's Inspection," Olive told him. "He hates it so, and then it takes him away from his work and he has to answer all sorts of questions. They would be only too glad to catch him tripping. They are always as rude to each other as they can be, especially Mr. Broast to Mr. Nat, because Mr. Nat doesn't know anything about it, and so Mr. Broast gets chances to score off him. I expect that's what's happened to-day, and why Mr. Nat went off in such a paddy. All Mr. Nat wants is to sell, so he can get his share of the money."

"Would Miss Kayne consent? Has she the power?"

"I think Mr. Nat says they could apply to the Courts for permission, I don't know exactly. He's tried to talk her over and Mr. Broast was simply furious. Of course, if anything happened to her, it would be different. He would have a much stronger position then."

"Funny sort of business," observed Bobby. "I suppose there's never been any talk of Miss Kayne marrying, has there?"

Olive stopped and stared at him.

"Bobby," she asked in a small, slightly-awed voice, "you do ask such funny questions."

"Why, what's there funny about that?" he asked, puzzled, puzzled, too by something indefinable in Olive's tone.

"It's just—" she said and paused. "It's because—" she said again and paused once more. "Somehow," she said slowly, "you always ask just the questions that count."

"Does that count?" he asked. "If it does, I didn't know."

Olive was still looking at him a little strangely.

"I suppose it's being a detective," she said. "I suppose things must come together in your mind and then you ask just the one question that matters."

"My dear girl," Bobby protested, "I don't in the least know what you are talking about."

"Yes, that's just it," Olive explained. "You don't know, you couldn't know, and all the same... Bobby, Miss Kayne told me something. It's a sort of secret, she doesn't want anyone else to know."

"Olive," said Bobby gravely, "you must remember I am a man under authority. Anything told me—"

But Olive laughed and interrupted, giving his arm an affectionate squeeze.

"You old silly," she said, "it's nothing to do with that sort of secret. Only it's so funny you should ask that just when I was thinking about it. Because Miss Kayne began to talk about our being engaged and she wanted to know if I was awfully happy, and of course I said I was—Bobby, be quiet, of course I had to say that, even if I was breaking my heart in secret, when I am most likely—Bobby, when you've quite finished, and if you don't, I shan't say another word. She said she had been engaged, too, once, and, well, it's rather sad and I did feel so sorry for her. She said the man she was engaged to was awfully clever and wrote wonderful letters and lovely poetry in them, But her father didn't approve, and then he died—I mean the man she was in love with. And she fretted so much her father always wanted to burn the letters, and so to keep them safe she buried them."

"Buried them?"

"Yes, that's the secret, in a tin box, in a waterproof wrapping. Now she thinks she would like to dig the up and have them published in a book. She thinks they were such lovely letters and some of the poetry so beautiful, they oughtn't to be lost. So she told me whereabouts she buried them, that's the special secret I'm not to tell anyone, even you, until she makes up her mind. Only she said if anything happened to her or anything special happened, then I was to tell you and ask you to help me get them and you and I are to decide."

"Morbid sort of idea," Bobby said. "Reminds one of Rossetti burying his poems with his wife and then digging them up again."

"Oh, it's not like that," Olive exclaimed. "This isn't a grave."

"Good thing, too," said Bobby, "only what does she mean—we're to decide. Decide what?"

"Publication, that's what she said. About publication," Olive answered.

"Well, it's about the rummiest idea I ever heard of," Bobby grumbled. "I don't see why she picks on you for the job either. Why can't she do it now herself, or put it in her will or something?"

Olive had no explanation to offer, and Bobby, a little tired of the Kayne library and everything connected with it, was glad to direct the conversation to more personal matters.

They managed to secure an hour or two to themselves, and then came dinner. It proved but a dull meal. Miss Kayne hardly spoke, and Mr. Broast, talkative as he had been in the library, was not equally taciturn, though Bobby caught now and again sharp glances thrown at him with that curious intensity of expression of or expectation he had seemed to detect before.

Presently, however, a reason came out. Mr. Broast believed he had caught sight of someone prowling about in the grounds near the library where no stranger had any right to be, and he was very worried. He had called out, but whoever it was had vanished without making any reply. A burglar in his opinion. Perhaps that Mr. Adams staying at the village inn. Mr. Broast had had his doubts of Mr. Adams from the first, and now he felt them more than justified.

"Told me he was connected with the University of Nebraska," said Mr. Broast darkly. "No credentials to show, though. In my opinion, he had never been near any University in his life. He wanted to see the Mandeville leaves, wanted to photograph them. Delighted, of course, to give every facility to anyone from any university of standing, but then, is he? Or is he wanting to see what he can pick up? What do you think, Mr. Owen?"

Bobby suggested warning the local police constable, though privately of opinion that the stooping, blinking Mr. Adams looked little like any burglar he had ever met.

After dinner it was nearly time for Bobby to depart. He lingered as long as he dared and then started off. Olive wanted to come with him as far as the Wynton Arms, where he had left his motor cycle, but the night was dark, the road unlighted and the weather uninviting, with a faint splutter of rain beginning.

So Bobby set off alone. On his way he had to pass the building that was both the local police station and the home of the resident village constable. The door was open, and in the little room that served as an office two people were talking loudly. Bobby, wondering what was happening, stood still for a moment before going on and then the policeman, a man named Mills, who had never had to deal with anything much more serious than a theft of poultry or an unlighted bicycle lamp, came running after him.

"Beg pardon," he said. "I saw you passing. It's Mr. Owen, isn't it? It's the talk here, belonging to Scotland Yard, up at London."

"Yes, why?" asked Bobby, guessing that for some reason he was wanted back in town at once.

Constable Mills paused to wipe his forehead. In the light of the gas lamp above the door he looked pale and excited.

"There's a gentleman come in," he said, "American gentleman, staying at the Wynton Arms. He says there's been murder done up at the Lodge in the library, he says he looked in and saw a dead man lying there all over blood."

CHAPTER VI
SECOND REPORT

Behind Mills, framed in the lighted doorway of the little police station, stood the tall, still form of the young American who at lunch that day, at the Wynton Arms, had tried to get into conversation with Bobby about his work. To Bobby, now, it seemed there was something intent and wrought-up in his attitude as he stood there, leaning a little forward, like the gambler who, having placed his stake, watches and waits for the fall of the roulette ball. Bobby looked at his watch. He saw that it was nineteen minutes past ten. He said to the American:

"What is your name?"

"Virtue," the other answered. "Bertram A. Virtue."

The gas light above his head shone with a yellow radiance on his features, made indeed a kind of aureole about his head. Natural perhaps that a man who had hastened there with such a tale of violence, of death, of murder apparently, should have that tense, excited air. He was tall, well made, athletic in bearing, distinctly good looking, with his fair hair, blue eyes, fresh complexion, well-formed, regular features, though the nose, with its wide nostrils, inclined perhaps a trifle too much towards that variety known as the 'snub'. Bobby noticed, too, that his ears were smaller than usual, with pointed tops, and were set closely to the head so that the lobes seemed almost to sink into the cheek. It is always well to pay special attention to the ears, for they are distinctive, difficult to disguise, always useful for purposes of identification. In spite of the tense restraint in which he held himself, his long, pliant fingers were restless, twisting themselves with and round each other. All this Bobby took in, as he had been trained to do, with one quick, intent look, and then he said:

"You state you saw a dead man in the Kayne library?"

"That's so," Virtue answered.

"We had better get along there immediately," Bobby said. "Please come, too." He turned to Mills. "You've got a bike? Good. Anyone else here? Only your wife? Ask her to ring up your inspector at once and tell him what's happened. Don't stop her to do it yourself, let her. Get your bike out and get along to the Lodge as quick as you can. Mr. Virtue and I will follow—we'll foot it, quicker than waiting to get hold of a car. Can you run, Mr. Virtue?" Virtue nodded. "Come along then, sooner we're there, the better."

They started to run. Hampered both by the darkness and by their own lack of familiarity with the road, they could not, however, use their best speed. Side by side they ran, their feet loud in the darkness of the night. Bobby had a fleeting thought that the sound of their running would alarm the whole village. He noticed, too, that Virtue ran easily and lightly, like a man in good condition. Half-way to the Lodge, Mills passed them, riding furiously. Three-quarters of the way to the Lodge, they found him crawling out of the ditch into which he and his cycle had gone together in the dark, head first.

"The bike's smashed up," he said as they arrived. "I've hurt my ankle or something," he said, trying to limp along.

"Never mind the bike," Bobby said. "Come on as quick as you can—crawl if you can't walk. Come on, Mr. Virtue."

They raced on together. Before them showed the lights of the Lodge, hitherto screened by the trees that lined the road. Questions were forming themselves in Bobby's mind as they ran together, side by side. He wished he could stop and ask some of them. He wished he could watch his companion's face. But the darkness hid it, and one cannot run and race through the night and ask questions at the same time.

He remembered that Mr. Broast had complained of having seen someone prowling about in the Hall grounds near the library after dark had fallen. Virtue's breathing was quiet and regular, as though this physical exertion had in some way relieved his excitement. His story sounded curious, fantastic even, and yet why should Virtue tell it, if it were not true? The truth may be fantastic at times, and life can take on the quality of a nightmare, but what possible motive could any apparently sane man have for inventing such a tale? Then surely it must be true, and yet there was a clear memory in Bobby's mind, both of those steel shutters to the library windows he had understood were invariably closed at nightfall and of that other fact that in the library there was no artificial light at all.

Through his mind raced these facts as his feet raced along the road, and now they were in the short drive that led up to the Lodge. The library annexe was on the other side of the building and to reach it they would have to go right round the house. Bobby's plan had been either to go himself or send Mills round to the library to watch outside, while the other of them entered through the house. But Mills was not there, and Bobby did not wish to let Virtue out of his sight. They were at the front door now. Bobby tried it. It was unlocked, and he opened it and entered without stopping to knock or ring. This was no time, he felt, for ceremony, and he supposed the noise they made in entering would at once bring someone on the scene. He had noticed the position of the service door, and he went towards it, meaning to call for someone to come. As he approached it, it opened, and Briggs appeared, looking very startled. He stood still when he saw Bobby. Bobby said quickly:

"I'm here as a police officer. A man has been seen in the library annexe. Is it open? have you a key? I it one of those?"

He pointed as he spoke to a cabinet with a glass door he had noticed hanging on the wall, containing various keys.

"The two bottom at the right are for the library doors," Briggs answered. "I can ask Mr. Broast for his—he's in his room."

But Bobby was in no mind to wait. Every moment might be of importance. The man Virtue had seen might not be dead for that matter, but only injured, and the difference of a minute might mean the difference between a saved life and a lost. Bobby caught hold of the handle of the cabinet and gave it a violent pull. It had been locked but both it and the lock were of poor construction. With a splintering of wood the door gave way. Bobby took the keys. He said to Briggs:

"Tell Mr. Broast at once. Where are the ladies? don't disturb them yet if you can help it."

He hurried on, Virtue close at his heels, Briggs, watching them over his shoulder in a very doubtful and bewildered manner, was hesitatingly ascending the stairs. He said as if he had just thought of it:

"The ladies have retired for the night, sir."

Bobby and Virtue went on down the passage along which Olive had conducted Bobby that afternoon. They came to the big, fireproof door that shut off the library annexe from the house. Bobby opened it and they went through into the lobby. The second fireproof door, giving admission to the library hall, Bobby opened, too, and they went in.

The darkness was intense. No gleam of light showed, no breath of air stirred, the silence was broken only by the sound of their own hurried and uneven breathing. Bobby flashed around the beam of his pocket torch, a thin ray of light that left the darkness deeper on each side. To and fro he sent it, searching. It showed only row upon row of books, silent and waiting as it were. He had the idea that they were all watching him, a little scornfully, a little scornful of all transitory things, of all happenings in time and space, remembering in their eternal calm, in the wisdom and the knowledge of the past that they enshrined, how little all the fret and fuss of the passing hour mattered compared with their perpetuity. Impatiently Bobby shrugged his shoulders, as if to throw off these ideas the sombre heavy silence of the library seemed to impose upon him, and, moving a yard or two to one side, he directed the light of his torch along the open passage way that ran the length of the hall below the windows on the north side. There was nothing to be seen, no prostrate body, no sign of any struggle. He threw the light next on each window in turn. Apparently, of each one, the shutters were securely fastened. Bobby said:

"All the shutters are closed. Which window was it?"

"The middle one. I noticed that."

"If you could see in through it, the shutters must have been closed since. Anybody there must have been moved, too."

He walked on towards the indicated window. Virtue followed. He said:

"The body was lying there."

He pointed to a spot exactly in front of the window and midway between the two transverse book-cases that here made one of the successive open bays into which on each side the floor of the library was divided. There was nothing unusual to be seen, no sign of any struggle or of any other happening.

Bobby said:

"I think you told Mills the body you saw was covered with blood?"

"Yes, not covered exactly. There was a good deal on the—" He paused and went on: "—from a wound in the chest."

"Did you see any weapon? what sort of wound? big, small, from a stab, an open cut? a gash?"

"I'm not sure," Virtue answered. "I was too upset to look very closely. I think it was a small wound, a stab most likely, or it might have been a bullet wound. I don't know. There seemed to be a good deal of blood. It was all over the front part of the body."

Bobby was stooping down. He looked very carefully at the floor. He even lifted the coco-nut matting which here served for a floor covering. He said:

"I can't see the least trace of any blood."

Virtue said nothing He stood still and upright. He was apparently deep in thought, but he did not seem troubled by the incredulity in Bobby's tone. Bobby went on:

"Did you notice what time it was when you saw all this?"

"Yes. I remember looking at my watch. I didn't know what to do. I'm a stranger here. I didn't know what a Britisher would do. I thought I had better go find police."

"You didn't think of giving an immediate alarm, of rousing the house?"

"I suppose I thought some of them inside must know already," he answered. "I daresay I was a bit scared of what might happen if I knocked up the folk indoors. It's a bit disturbing when you're a foreigner and never been in the country before to run across what looks like a murder. I just stood and stared and felt mighty scared and then I left quick as I knew how to find police."

"Was the window wide open or did you see through the glass? Did the shutters show at all? were they partly closed, I mean?"

"The window was shut. I could see through the glass. It was the bright light shining through it outside I noticed first. I didn't notice shutters or curtain or anything like that. I knew at night the library was always shut up tight as could be. That's what made me wonder when I saw the light, why I came across to look."

"Where did the light come from?"

"I didn't notice. The rest of the place was all dark. It was light all round this part, light was shining out through the window, too, but every other place was dark."

"Curious," observed Bobby dryly, "for I understand the library has no artificial lighting system of any kind."

"No—no lighting?" Virtue repeated. For the first time he seemed startled, taken aback. "But there must be—stands to sense. I mean—" He paused and then said doggedly:—"Well, I don't know about that. Maybe there was a torch fixed somewhere. I saw what I told you, and there must have been light someway for me to see by."

Bobby made no reply. He was feeling more and more puzzled. The library door opened. They both turned. Briggs was standing there. He said:

"I can't find Mr. Broast. He's not in his room. Is anyone here?"

"We haven't found anyone, but we haven't looked everywhere, and this gentleman is quite sure he saw— something," Bobby answered. "He attends to them himself. It's always as soon as it's dark."

Bobby examined the shutters again. They were all carefully locked, securely fastened on the inside. He asked Briggs to get two of the electric torches, the most powerful there were, from the stock kept in hand for use in the library when work had to be done after dark. Telling Briggs to remain by the doorway, Bobby, Virtue accompanying him, made a hurried search of the library and the cellar below. It did not take long. There were few hiding places. They found nothing. All seemed in perfect order.

"If there was a dead body there, it has been moved."

"That's so," Virtue agreed. "There was a body here and it has been moved. I'll stake my life on that. Now it's up to you."

"Yes," agreed Bobby.

"Up to you," Virtue repeated slowly, and Bobby thought he was putting emphasis on the words, "up to you to take that for a start and find out what it means."

"If it means anything," Bobby said.

"I get you," Virtue said in the same slow and heavy tones. "I know what you mean. You think maybe I'm crazy or lying. I suggest the most thorough and careful search of the whole building and I claim the right to be present. I realize I am responsible. You can prosecute for what you call 'public mischief'. Very likely, too, I am liable for damages—libel, or malicious scandal or something of the sort. Well, I've a right to defend myself. I claim there has been a dead body here, and I say it has been moved. I claim that a thorough and complete search must be made, and I claim the right to be present."

"You are claiming a good many rights," Bobby said, "and I don't know myself that you have any rights to claim any one of them. Your statement so far seems entirely unconfirmed."

"You're a swell detective, aren't you?" Virtue said. "I've heard quite a lot about you in the village. They've all been talking. You can get at the truth of anything according to them. Give him a brick, they've been saying, and he'll build a row of houses. Well, I've shown you a brick, build your house from it, get at the truth from it."

"That sounds like a challenge," Bobby said.

They were both silent then. Bobby was very puzzled. He did not in the least know what to make either of the man himself or of his story. It sounded preposterous, utterly incredible indeed, and yet there was an accent of sincerity, of an almost passionate conviction in his low, intense tones. Bobby continued:

"Anyhow, it's not up to me. You're wrong there. I'm only in this by accident. I happened to be here and the village constable felt a bit out of his depth and asked me to help. Just a coincidence." He paused when he had said this, for it was as though something stirred deep down, down in his consciousness and told him it was no coincidence at all. "Oh well," he said, "it's nothing to do with me. I'm Metropolitan police. This is the local people's show. They'll carry on.

They'll decide what to do. I shan't have anything more to do with it after they take over."

"But you're from Scotland Yard, aren't you?" Virtue asked. His voice sounded curiously disappointed. He said: "I thought Scotland Yard was the boss show over here, did it all?"

"The local police have sole authority in their own districts," Bobby answered. "Scotland Yard is only the headquarters of its own local police in their own district, which happens to be the London area," and he was more convinced than ever that this bit of information was a heavy disappointment, both surprise and shock to Virtue.

They were interrupted by the belated and limping arrival of Mills, looking a good deal the worse for wear after his adventure, with torn clothing, a scratched face, a dragging leg. He was helping himself along with a stick he had got out of a hedge near his accident. Bobby asked him how soon they might expect help and he said that he didn't suppose the inspector would be long. The chief constable, Major Harley, might come, too, he thought. The major did not live far away, and quite probably the inspector would have rung him up to report such a sensational story.

"If it's that way, the Major might get here first," Mills said. "He won't have turned in yet."

"I hope someone will be along soon," Bobby said. "I oughtn't to be in this at all by rights."

"Well, sir, you're Scotland Yard, you see," Mills said mildly, "and if it's murder—well I never heard tell of such a thing, not down our way, and there was me all alone and this gentleman coming in and saying what he had seen and all."

"The body seems to have disappeared," Bobby said. "I can find no trace of it, no trace of blood either or of any disturbance."

"I saw it," Virtue interposed doggedly. "It was a man about thirty. A thin, long face,, high cheekbones, very strongly marked eyebrows, a bit of a snub nose, a bit like mine, only bigger. Moustache with waxed ends, the lobe of the left ear not sticking out like most people's, but attached to the head—quite distinctive."

A sort of strangled gasp came from Mills. Bobby looked at him. He was staring at Virtue as if he had seen a ghost, and when he tried to speak no words came at first. Then he stammered out:

"But that—well, that—if that don't beat all."

They were interrupted by Briggs who had disappeared from his post at the door but now came back.

"It's the 'phone, sir, I heard it ringing and I went to see," he said to Bobby. "It's Mrs. Mills, and she wants to speak to Mills or to you, sir. She sounds excited, she says it's important."

"I'll answer it. I'll go," Bobby said.

"Miss Farrar just come downstairs, sir," Briggs added. "She heard voices."

Bobby went through into the hall where the 'phone was situated. Olive was standing at the foot of the stairs. She said:

"What's happening? Briggs said you had come back. Is it a burglar? Briggs said Mr. Broast was out?"

"It isn't a burglar," Bobby said. "I don't know what it is except that it's crazy. I must answer the 'phone."

It was ringing again. Bobby took the receiver and spoke. He heard Mrs. Mills's excited, stammering voice that said:

"Oh, please, it's from Longmeadow Farm, Mr. Chapman's, and he says Mr. Nat is there, Mr. Nat Kayne, shot dead where he found him in the sunk lane through the wood, isn't it awful? whatever shall I do?"

CHAPTER VII
LEN HILL'S STORY

For one bewildered moment, in the first instant of his astonishment, Bobby thought this must be the body of the dead man the young American claimed that he had seen through the library window, in some mysterious manner carried away to a lane in a wood where it had now been found. But then he remembered Nat Kayne as he had seen him for a moment earlier in the day. No resemblance to the description Virtue had given, a description, too, that Mills had appeared to recognize, but that had certainly not suggested Nat Kayne to him or he would undoubtedly have said so.

It was something else then that had happened, but was it coincidence, or was there connection?

No time to think that out now, Bobby told himself.

He began to speak quickly over the 'phone. He told Mrs. Mills that he himself and her husband would go on at once to Longmeadow Farm, that he would attend to what was necessary in the way of summoning help, and that all he could do was to be careful to answer any further 'phone calls and make a note of any message received. Then he spent a few hurried minutes ringing up the chief constable and learning that that gentleman was already on his way to Wynton Lodge, and in getting in touch with the nearest county police headquarters to inform them of this new development, and to ask them to send a doctor and further help. He added, giving his name and rank in the Metropolitan police, that he was accompanying Mills forthwith to Longmeadow farm, Mills having managed to lame himself in a cycle accident, and being therefore to some extent incapacitated.

In the middle of all this phoning, getting wrong numbers, waiting for a reply,—it all took time—he heard Olive say something. He turned round. She was standing a short distance away, looking towards the stairs. Half way down them stood Miss Kayne in a loose Chinese dressing gown, all sprawling, scaly dragon, that seem somehow to emphasize the grossness of her enormous bulk. She was standing motionless, her small, sunken eyes staring out, intent and angry, from the pits of flesh in which they were sunk. She had an ebony stick with a crook handle she used to support herself with, but this she was now holding up in an odd attitude as of mingled menace and triumph. She stood there like a brooding, malign Fate, and slowly she lifted her ebony stick to point with it towards the passage leading to the library door. It was a gesture that seemed to wave on invisible agents of her hate, and then in that small voice of hers which gave the impression of having to struggle for utterance and yet possessed penetration and a clarity of its own, she said:

"It's come then... has it come?... what's happening in here?"

Bobby had no time to wonder what she meant, though he thought her gesture conveyed less surprise than a kind of hopeful or even triumphant rage. He found himself remembering the odd tale Olive had told him of how this old fat woman had once had a lover and of how she had buried his letter and his poems in a secret place. There flashed into his mind a conviction that there must be some connection and then he told himself there could not be, and that anyhow there was not time now to think about that. The 'phone claimed his attention. He turned to it and he heard Olive say:—

"I don't know... something... I don't think it's burglars."

"Burglars!" Miss Kayne pronounced the word with scorn, dismissed it with a gesture. She pointed her ebony stick at Bobby. "What's he to do with it? what's he come back for?" Then she added: "What's he found out?"

Bobby hung up the receiver.

"There's been an accident, apparently," he said. "I don't know what. At a place called Longmeadow. I expect Mills will know it. May we borrow your car, Miss Kayne? We ought to get over there as soon as possible to see what's actually happened."

"Nat Kayne?" she asked. "Has something happened to Nat Kayne?"

"Why do you think of him?" Bobby asked, startled.

Again she made that dark, slow gesture towards the library.

"Something's happened there," she said. "In the Kayne library. What happens in the Kayne library—" She left the sentence unfinished. "Suppose I say I will not let you have the car?" she said.

"Then I shall have to take it without your permission," Bobby answered.

She emitted an odd kind of half-choked chuckle.

"Take it, then," she said, "and drive fast. Then you may all break your necks and that might be best for some of us." He turned and began to climb the stairs again, slopping heavily upwards in her great shapeless slippers. Over her shoulder she said, as she laboured upon the ascent: "Let me know as soon as you can if young Nat is dead."

Bobby made no answer nor did his expression change. Of that he was sure, he had trained himself to keep full control of his features. But she seemed to read the truth, for she paused and turning, supporting herself by the banister rail, she said:

"Why, then, if he's dead, there's only one Kayne left— me." She said to Olive: "Where is Mr. Broast?"

"I think he is out," Olive said. "I don't know."

Miss Kayne greeted this with her half-choked chuckle and then started to resume her ascent. Looking back at Bobby she said to him:

"Well, get to work, Mr. Detective."

It had been a nightmare scene, with that old fat woman brooding in hatred from half way up the stairs. But Bobby had no time to spare just then for trying to think out its implications. He asked Olive to be ready to explain to the chief constable on his arrival what had happened. He told Briggs to lock the library door, to remain there on guard, and to see that no one entered. If anyone, his employer or any one else, Mr. Broast, for instance if he returned, insisted on entering and Briggs could not prevent it, then he was to warn them that the police would regard it as highly suspicious. He also asked Virtue to wait with Briggs for the present. He supposed Virtue might take the opportunity to disappear, but that risk had to be accepted. If he did vanish, that would be a kind of confession, and probably there would be little difficulty in picking him up again. Then he told Mills to wait for him at the front door while he ran round to the garage and got out Miss Kayne's car. He had heard that Miss Kayne kept no chauffeur. The car was generally driven by Mr. Broast or by Briggs. It was only rarely that Miss Kayne made any use of it. With all possible speed Bobby brought the car round to the front of the house, picked up Mills, and started.

Mills knew Longmeadow farm and the Mr. Chapman who occupied it. Mr. Chapman was a churchwarden, a leading Conservative, was believed to be more prosperous and successful than most farmers, and was understood to entertain hopes of being made a magistrate some day, if the 'Reds' were kept out. By 'Reds' Mr. Chapman, who read one of the national papers and believed it all, meant everyone who didn't vote for the Conservative party. Bobby guessed that Mills did not much like him. Apparently Mr. Chapman was a somewhat authoritative gentleman, a little fond of laying down the law according to his own interpretation, and then expecting Mills to execute it.

"Reported me once for not arresting some lads that had been blackberrying," Mills said resentfully. "The inspector came over special and said as how I was right, but it ain't so nice to be reported—and if you're reported they're always ready to think it's along of you being wanting in tack or something."

Bobby nodded comprehendingly. 'Tack' is indeed the first essential in a policeman's equipment, and Bobby was glad of the warning that Mr. Chapman was one of those people in dealing with whom 'tack' is always necessary. Mills, dropping the subject of Mr. Chapman, and having directed Bobby, who was driving, which route to take, went on:

"It's a rum start altogether about that body the young gentleman says he saw."

"You recognized the description?" Bobby asked. "Someone you know?"

"Well, sir, it's this way," Mill explained. "There's a young lady what does for Mr. Broast, writing his letters and such like."

"Miss Perkins?" Bobby asked, wondering what on earth that giggling ineffectual little person with her eternal refrain: 'Oh, I'm so sorry,' had to do with this complicated affair.

"That's her," said Mills. "Very quiet, respectable young person, though there's some laughs at her and calls her a softy, but what's it to do with them if she is, if so be she gives satisfaction?"

"Nothing at all," agreed Bobby. "Do you mean the description was like some friend of hers?"

"In a manner of speaking," answered Mills. "When she come first there was a bit of talk about how she told everyone as how she wouldn't be here long, on account of going to be married, and she got to showing round a picture of her young man. I seen it myself, like most everyone else. A fair joke it got to be, and everyone laughing about it behind her back, and some of the women saying she was just putting it on like and she wasn't no more engaged to no one than the babe unborn. Just swank like, if you see what I mean."

"Yes," said Bobby. "Well?"

"Well, sir," said Mills earnestly, "struck me all of heap like, it might have been that there photo the American gentleman was telling of, particular when he said that about the end of the left ear being stuck to the cheek like. I remember noticing that particular."

"Smart of you to notice it," Bobby said approvingly. "Your inspector ought to owe you a pat on the back. Only— what does it mean?"

"Ah," said Mills profoundly, "that's what's worrying me, though I hadn't the education to put it in them words."

"Worrying me, too," said Bobby. "Where does Miss Perkins hang out? at the lodge?"

"No, she lodges with Mrs. Somerville. Walks to the Lodge every morning and stops all hours. Dinner and tea there, and Mrs. Somerville gets her breakfast and supper, and keeps it hot for her when she's late. Mrs. Somerville's is along this road, the last house on the right."

"I suppose she'll be in bed," Bobby said. "Anyhow no time to stop now. But it might be a good idea to get hold of that photo."

"That's the house," Mills said. "There's a light in her room—getting ready for bed. That's her at the window," he added.

Miss Perkins's profile was in fact plainly visible. She was sitting at the open window, smoking a cigarette, presumably before retiring.

"Damp night to be sitting there," Bobby remarked, though in fact the splutter of rain had ceased and the air was close and heavy enough to make an open window desirable in spite of the pervading dampness.

They had left behind now the village, and Miss Perkins enjoying her cigarette, and by a dark, deserted road with so many twists and turns in it Bobby had to drive slowly and with caution, they came presently to a large farm-house. There were lights in the window and a general pervading air of bustle and excitement. When the car stopped before the front entrance a short, thick-set man came out to greet them.

"Too late, Mills," he said. "Dr. Blythe is here—got here just in time to see the poor fellow die. This gentleman a doctor?" he asked, looking at Bobby.

"No, I'm a police officer, London," Bobby explained. "Mr. Mills asked me to come with him to see if I could help. Mills has had an accident and hurt his leg unfortunately, so he is a bit handicapped."

Mr. Chapman looked as if he thought that was just what one would expect from Mills, and then led the way into the house and up the stairs into a small spare room where in all the stillness and majesty of death lay that young man whose physical vigour and beauty had so impressed Bobby in the brief glimpse he had had of him only a few short hours before. An elderly man who was in the room turned to them as they came in.

"Never recovered consciousness," he said. "Died almost as I got here. Not that I could have done anything. Three bullet wounds in the chest. Bad internal bleeding."

"No possibility of suicide then?" Bobby asked.

"None. Three wounds, each one probably fatal. It's a wonder he lived so long. Fired from a distance. No sign of burning on the clothing. No marks on the hand."

"Was any weapon found?" Bobby asked Mr. Chapman.

"No, the men had a look round, but they didn't see anything. It was Len Hill found him—we heard him running and shouting just as we were turning in. We're early folk here, soon after ten it must have been. Said there was a chap shot in the lane through the wood and he reckoned it was Mr. Nat Kayne. So I got some of my men together and we found him and brought him in. My wife rang up Dr. Blythe as soon as we knew, and Mills, too. Murder, that's what it is. Murder."

They went downstairs, and Bobby asked Mr. Chapman a few more questions. Mr. Chapman was quite willing to talk, and so was Len Hill, the man who had made the discovery. Hill was an under-gamekeeper on a neighbouring estate, and hearing shots had concluded poachers were at work, though even at first he thought that queer since poachers are usually careful to work silently, and also it had struck him that the reports had had a quality of sound different from any he was used to.

"Sharp like," he told Bobby.

It had been exactly ten o'clock when he heard the shots and went to investigate them. He had found the dying man lying in a sunk lane, providing a short cut for foot passengers to and from the village, who thus avoided the rather long detour by road that would otherwise have been necessary. On his giving the alarm Mr. Chapman and several of his men had gone with him, bringing back the wounded man on a stretcher improvised on the spot from branches cut or broken from neighbouring trees.

Bobby reflected that this probably meant that every likely clue on the spot had been thoroughly trampled out of existence. Half a dozen heavy booted men moving excitedly to and fro in the vicinity would leave little trace of what had happened before their arrival. No good saying so, however. The mischief was done for one thing, and for another the first necessity had been that the injured man should receive attention. Then, too, the thought of murder had probably occurred to no one. Accident or suicide at first it would be put down as, and only later would the grim thought, certainty, of murder begin to be entertained.

Both unfair and useless, then, to complain, but all the same bad luck that there probably remained no chance of gleaning any information from even the most careful inspection of the scene of the crime.

In reply to a question Hill had no doubt about finding the exact spot, even now, in the darkness. But he did not see what the good would be.

"You won't see nought," he said, "not till daylight."

"It's the weapon," Bobby said. "We ought to get hold of the weapon if we can possibly."

Another car arrived. It was Major Harley. He had driven on from Wynton Lodge. He was a brisk, quick-spoken, apparently capable man, and he agreed at once, as soon as he understood the position, to Bobby's suggestion that a search should be begun immediately for the weapon used.

"Most important to find it," he agreed.

"He undertook, too, to 'phone the Scotland Yard authorities, explain the circumstances, and secure permission for Bobby to remain on the spot for the time.

"I shall tell them I consider it most fortunate to have an experienced officer here from the very start," he said.

Two or three of the farm labourers agreed to accompany Bobby and Len Hill to make a renewed search for the weapon, and Mr. Chapman allowed them to provide themselves with stable lanterns. They started off accordingly and as they went Len Hill said:

"I don't wonder the Major thinks it rare luck there should be a Scotland Yard man here. Never been a murder in these parts before that ever I heard tell of, and when one happens, there's a London man right on the spot."

Bobby said nothing, but again there came a little nagging thought in his mind that perhaps there was no coincidence at all, that perhaps his arrival in the village, his known occupation, had merely been the spark serving to bring about an explosion that time and circumstance had long since prepared.

CHAPTER VIII
POINTS OF INTEREST—A TO K

The search failed, nor was it long before Bobby found that he was meeting with failure, too, in his efforts to keep up the interest and the enthusiasm of his voluntary helpers. His idea of a search was to cover the whole ground, inch by inch, each searcher assigned a definite area as his own responsibility. These farm labourers' idea of a search was to plunge about here and there in what looked likely spots and then give up. But the police never give up. Their job is simply to make sure, success or failure being merely incidental. Then again, as was pointed out to Bobby with much force by more than one of his helpers, they had their work to do next day. Mr. Chapman would expect them all to be at their jobs as usual in the morning and anyhow what was the good of messing about in the dark any longer?

One by one therefore his volunteers, the first flush of excitement and interest over, slipped away. Bobby had indeed been deserted by almost all of them when presently a message came from Major Harley, summoning him back to the farm. Glad to abandon a task that was plainly beyond one man's capacity, Bobby returned accordingly, and found the Major waiting by his car.

"They've been giving you the slip, haven't they?" he said as Bobby came up. "Not much good trying to do anything more to-night, anyway. We must wait till morning. Lot to do then. I've been fixing things up. You had better come back with me and we can have a talk. Mills has been telling me a queer sort of yarn about some young American—can't make head or tail of it myself."

Bobby obediently took his seat in the car and they started. When they reached his home, the Major left the car standing outside the front door with the remark that now the rain had cleared off and it looked like remaining fine, he wouldn't bother about opening the garage.

"Want the car again soon enough," he said as he led Bobby into the house and across the hall to a small room he used as his office when at home. There was a tray with sandwiches, whisky and soda, and coffee in a vacuum flask, waiting for them, and they were both glad of the refreshment. Seating himself comfortably and waving Bobby to another chair, he said:

"Now, then, what's all this about a dead body seen in the Kayne library?"

Bobby repeated the story in careful detail, and the chief constable listened with close attention.

"What do you make of it?" he asked when Bobby ceased.

"It seems incredible in itself, and equally incredible that anyone should invent such a story," Bobby answered slowly. "I haven't got beyond that as yet, sir. Immovable object and irresistible force problem. Mr. Virtue seemed very strong on wanting to search the whole library. I thought that seemed quite genuine. I suppose Mr. Broast would consent?"

"He's very touchy about that blessed library of his," observed the Major, a little doubtfully. "There's no confirmation of Virtue's story, and there seems evidence it can't be true in the fact that there's no artificial lighting. And if Broast says he closed the shutters as usual—well, how could anyone see anything, dead body or living man or anything else?"

"Yes sir, quite so, sir," agreed Bobby. "I should be inclined in a way myself to wipe it out. Of course, Virtue can be questioned again. We hadn't much time to ask him anything. Only there is one thing. Mills says the description Virtue gave of the dead body he claims he saw is just like a photograph in Miss Perkins's possession."

"I know," said the Major. "Mills told me. Very odd. I don't see how it can be a mere coincidence."

"No, sir, I think coincidence can be ruled out. The left ear peculiarity is decisive."

"How about this for an idea?" the chief constable asked. "Virtue killed Nat Kayne and then reported this yarn to Mills to prove an alibi. How about time and distance?"

"The murder was at ten o'clock, according to Len Hill, at least, that's when he says he heard shots," Bobby answered. "It must be about two miles from where it was committed to the village. Mills says Virtue turned up at about a quarter past ten. Virtue is a good runner, I saw that. It would be possible. He wasn't out of breath at all when I saw him, but it's down hill and he could cover the two miles in ten minutes or so and have a minute or two to get his breath again. It's possible but only just. He might have had a bicycle."

"Check that up," said the Major. "Someone may have seen him—heard him if he ran the whole way."

"Yes, sir," agreed Bobby. "But there's this again. It's doubtful if he had ever even seen Nat Kayne. There seems no motive at present. He has only been in England three months I think he said. And I don't think Nat Kayne had ever been in America. That applies to Miss Perkins also, I imagine. I should suggest as a starting point investigating the apparent connection between Miss Perkins's photograph and the description given by Mr. Virtue."

The chief constable nodded and made a note.

"Looks as if they might be confederates. Very valuable stuff in the Kayne library. May have been after it. Broast is always nervous about burglary attempts. Anyhow, there's Starting Point A."

"Yes, sir," agreed Bobby. "I thought of that, too, only it does seem going a long way round, if it was all a put up job to get a chance to do a spot of burglary. Complicated."

"If it's Virtue and Miss Perkins working together," the Major pointed out, "they're amateurs, and amateurs are like that—complicated. Try to be clever. You say Virtue pressed for an immediate search. He may have reckoned that would give him his chance. Broast was out, wasn't he? Chance for Virtue to slip something in his pocket while you and Mills were searching—something like these Mandeville pages, that are worth money."

"Yes, sir," agreed Bobby, "only if it's that way, why did he draw attention to Miss Perkins, if they were working together, by describing a photograph of the man she's engaged to? Mills says she started showing it round as soon as she got her job at the library. He says some of the women didn't believe her—she's never worn an engagement ring. They seem to think she invented it to show off."

"Might be that," agreed the Major, who liked to keep up-to-date with all the newest theories. "Repressed sex instinct. Knew she wasn't attractive to men and wanted to make other people think she was. I've known instances. It's all in Freud. He knows. Well, call that Starting Point B.—why did she show the photo round the village?"

He made another note and Bobby went on.

"There's another thing I don't understand. I mean Miss Kayne's attitude. The Kayne library is famous all over the world pretty well. It's extremely valuable—fame and fortune in one for its owner. And yet she gives me the impression— well, it's almost as if she hated the place. I've seen her look at it just as you imagine an old Hebrew prophet might have looked at an image of Baal."

"I expect it's a little like that," the Major said, "the false god to whom her father sacrificed. He spent all his money on it. Her life, too; that was sacrificed as well. She never had any youth No social life. No friends. The library and nothing else."

"Wasn't she engaged or nearly engaged at one time?" Bobby asked.

"Goodness, no, never any man in her life," the Major answered. "I doubt if she ever saw anyone in trousers except old professors and bookworms—and the villagers of course. It was all her father and his books."

"But if she hated—"

"Oh, that was only afterwards, after his death. That left a big gap in her life, and I suppose she began to feel then how much she had given up, and all for nothing, now she had lost interest in the library when her father had gone."

"I see, sir," said Bobby and hesitated, remembering what Olive had told him. But there seemed no object in repeating a story that could have nothing to do with recent happenings and that, although it had not been told under any pledge of secrecy, was still a matter of purely private interest. Probably neither Miss Kayne nor Olive would wish it repeated unless for good reason. He said: "I understand all the money old Mr. Kayne spent on the library he made out of it, that his discoveries and dealings made it self-supporting?"

"Oh, he used his private means as well, every penny almost," the Major answered.

"Did Miss Kayne ever object or grumble?"

"Not while he was alive," the Major answered. "In fact, I never heard of her grumbling about the financial side. I don't see how she could. There's a fortune there, and the Courts would certainly give permission for a sale if she pressed for it. She just seemed to lose interest, that's all. Natural enough."

"Yes, sir," agreed Bobby. "Though I should like to call that Point C.—why Miss Kayne's attitude to the library changed."

"Oh, all right," said the Major and made a note though without much conviction—Bobby suspected he put a note of interrogation against it.

"There is one point I think I ought to mention," Bobby went on. "Miss Kayne told me this afternoon she was interested in my being a C.I.D. man because once she had committed a murder."

"Eh?" said the Major, startled. "What's that?"

"The perfect murder, she called it," Bobby added.

"Nonsense," said the Major.

"Yes, sir," agreed Bobby. "I thought it was a kind of joke at the time. I didn't pay it any attention. Some people like to joke about my job. Only now—well, now this has happened it seems a coincidence. I don't like coincidences." He hesitated, remembering once more what Olive had told him of the love passage in Miss Kayne's life and her tale of the buried love letters and poems which had reminded him so much of the strange Rossetti affair. Perhaps it was reading about that had suggested the notion to Miss Kayne. Another queer thing was the damage done to the portrait of Miss Kayne hanging in the dining-room. But it was always wiser to avoid cluttering up the consideration of a case by bringing into it the non-essential. He would bear the two things in mind, he decided. If the course of events in the future seemed to make it desirable to do so, he would mention them. "All the same, sir, I think we ought to call it Point D.," he added. "I mean, Miss Kayne's saying that."

The Major was looking grave. He seemed to attach as much importance to this point as to anything Bobby had said so far. He made a note accordingly.

"You think," he said, "it suggests some sort of uneasiness—anticipation? It might. Don't like it. She's not a woman to make jokes as a rule. Only there's no possible motive why she should want Nat Kayne out of the way. He made no difference to her about the library, one way or the other, and there's never been any ill-feeling between them."

"No, sir," agreed Bobby. "I'm told there was disagreement between Mr. Broast and Nat Kayne. When I was being shown over the library this afternoon I couldn't help seeing what looked very much like a quarrel between him and Sir William Winders and Mr. Broast. Kayne went off in what looked like a very bad temper."

The major nodded and looked grave again.

"Call that Point E.," he said. "Very important. Everyone knew there was bad feeling. Perhaps that's what Miss Kayne was hinting at. Nat Kayne wanted the library sold and that meant Broast out of a job—out of control of the library anyhow, a little like trying to get the baby away from its mother."

"I understand Mr. Broast was out at the time of the murder," Bobby said.

"I believe he always took a stroll late at night," the Major remarked. "As it happens I've met him once or twice when I've been prowling around on some job or another. He had an idea a walk before bed made him sleep better. He told me once a good brisk walk, wet or fine, was his cure for sleeping badly. After dinner he went to his own room—he lived at the Lodge, you know—attended to his letters. He used to speak them into a Dictaphone for the Perkins girl to type next day. When he had finished he went for a walk, so it was quite usual for him to be out at that time."

"I had forgotten one thing," Bobby said. "I remember now Miss Perkins came in with a message for him that Sir William was driving over to see him that evening—I rather thought at the time perhaps it was about the quarrel there had been with Mr. Nat Kayne."

"Hum," said the Major. "Sir William, eh? Does he come into it, too? Perhaps they can alibi each other. Anyhow, that's Point F., eh?

"Yes, sir. Point G., I think," suggested Bobby, "might be finding out what caused the quarrel I saw. Kayne looked murderous enough as he went off, and if he felt like that, perhaps the others did as well—either Mr. Broast or Sir William."

"Sir William, Sir William," muttered the Major uneasily. "I can't think—very influential, very leading family and all that. Of course he must be asked. Point G. then—yes, Point G., undoubtedly."

"Point H.," continued Bobby, "might be where was Sir William at the time of the murder, and whether he heard the shots."

"Point H.," agreed the Major gloomily. "His family have been settled here since—oh, since the Conquest pretty well. Oh, yes, point H., undoubtedly. Of course, Sir William is one of the library trustees, but he didn't want to sell. He's almost as cracked on books as Broast—used to be a great friend of old Mr. Kayne's when they weren't trying to do the dirty on each other over some dog-eared old volume you would have expected to get for twopence. But they were great friends when they weren't at each other's throats."

"Queer business, this book collecting," Bobby said thoughtfully.

"It is," agreed the Major with conviction. "Do you want that put down as Point I.?"

"Well, sir, I thought myself Point I. might be checking up on Mr. Adams. But we can call that Point K."

"Who is Mr. Adams?" demanded the chief constable. "Haven't heard of him before. Where does he come in?"

"He is stopping at the pub here," Bobby explained. "He says he is interested in bibliography and wanted to examine the Mandeville pages. Mr. Broast wouldn't let him see them, and there was a row. Then this evening, early, Mr. Broast told me he had seen someone hanging about the library, in the Lodge grounds, just before it got dark. He thought it was Adams. Adams claims to be a professor at the University of Nebraska. Broast says he doesn't believe it, he seems to suspect Adams of wanting to steal the Mandeville pages. I suppose they are valuable?"

"Broast calls them priceless," the Major agreed. "Difficult to dispose of, though. What started the trouble with the Nebraska gentleman?"

"Just that Mr. Broast wasn't satisfied with his credentials. I must say Mr. Adams doesn't look like a burglar to me."

"Point K. all right all the same," declared the Major; "that is, of course, if it does turn out he's not what he says and the Nebraska people don't know him. We'll cable them and see what they have to say. Of course, if they're prepared to vouch for him—" The Major paused and looked worried. "Where's all this link up with the murder of poor young Kayne?" he demanded. "Does Broast think Adams was employed by Kayne to burgle the Mandeville leaves and they quarrelled or anything like that? Or what has he got in his mind?"

"I don't know, sir," Bobby answered. "I haven't seen Mr. Broast since quite early this evening." He paused and added in tones he made as colourless as he could: "I think I mentioned before that Mr. Broast was apparently out at the time of the murder."

"Oh yes, yes, so you did," agreed the Major and looked thoughtful.

Bobby said:

"Am I right, sir, in thinking Mr. Broast has a revolver? I suppose, if that's so, the number and make will be in the firearms register?"

"And all that, I suppose," sighed the Major, "will be point L. I'll look up particulars about Broast's revolver in the morning." He got to his feet. "Look at the time," he said, "and we must make an early start. Breakfast at seven. I rang them up from Chapman's to tell them, and to have a bed ready for you. You had better turn in now and get what sleep you can. Even a couple of hours is better than none."

CHAPTER IX
POINT M, TOO

Scanty sleep and hurried breakfast brought Major Harley and Bobby to Mrs. Somerville's house so early next morning that Miss Perkins was not yet visible.

Mrs. Somerville, however, was bustling about in a very excited state, divided between the necessary morning tasks and sudden darts to the door in the hope that someone would appear who really knew what had actually happened the night before. Early as it was, rumours were already abroad, the only point on which they agreed being that a dead body had been found in the sunk lane through the wood. Mrs. Somerville's interest was the greater in that she herself had been out the night before and had actually passed by the spot where the lane entered the wood.

"So it might have been me as like as not," she pointed out, a trifle tremulously, "and never shall I get over it, never."

"What time was this?" Bobby asked, wondering if she, too, had heard the shots.

But it appeared that she had reached home almost exactly at ten. She was quite sure of the hour, because Miss Perkins had been sitting up waiting for her, busy sewing and listening to the wireless. Miss Perkins, a little peeved perhaps at being kept up beyond her usual bed time, had switched off the wireless the moment she heard Mrs. Somerville returning, made some remark about the late hour—she was generally in bed by ten or soon after apparently—and had gone straight up to her room where Bobby remembered he and Mills had seen her sitting at the window, smoking a final cigarette presumably, when they passed by in their car on the way to Longmeadow farm. As ten was the hour at which Len Hill heard the shots, it was evident Mrs. Somerville had been indoors at the time of the murder. Seeing Bobby glance first at the clock and then at his wrist watch, she remarked that her clock was always right because they set it each day by the wireless signal, though indeed it was the wireless programme itself by which they went in that house almost as much as by the clock. They knew what was on, what coming on, when it began, when it ended, indeed it appeared as if she personally regulated her whole life by wireless. And she remained convinced that last night she had had the narrowest possible escape.

She seemed to think, too, that the errand of her two visitors was to assure themselves of her safety, expressed her appreciation of their concern for her well being, and looked quite surprised when they explained that they wished to see Miss Perkins. Knowing that it would be better to give some reason, if the wildest tales were not soon to be in circulation, the Major added that Mr. Broast reported having seen a stranger hiding near the library in the Lodge grounds and that it was necessary to know if Miss Perkins had also seen him.

Mrs. Somerville accordingly went upstairs and knocked at Miss Perkins's door, returning with the information that she would be down in a minute.

"She doesn't make an early start, she hasn't to be at the Lodge till ten," Mrs. Somerville explained, "and I don't blame her for wanting her rest, her not being strong, and needing it, working all hours, too, like a driven slave, and the only chance she ever has for a breath of fresh air when she's coming and going to work."

"Too bad," said Bobby, while the Major, scowling and impatient, for he had some domestic experience of what "down in a minute" might mean, was looking alternately at his watch and the door, "does she never take a little walk in the evenings before bed?"

"Oh, no, fair wore out she is when she gets home and glad enough to rest with a bit of sewing and the wireless. She always says she's quite got out of walking in a manner of speaking with sitting all day with those musty old books."

"She ought to try cycling," Bobby suggested; "she could still be sitting and yet have exercise and fresh air all the same."

"Well, now, it's funny you should say that," Mrs. Somerville remarked, "for it's what I'm always telling her, me being a great one for cycling. But some way she can't learn. Nervous. That's what it is. Goes all of a wobble and flop over and then she won't try again. She says the first time she ever tried to go alone, before she came here, she ran right into a baker's cart and might have been killed, and now it's just as if she couldn't manage her arms and legs and in a manner of speaking no sooner she's on than she's off. Nervous."

As if to confirm this verdict there became audible, floating to them down the narrow cottage stairs, the sound of Miss Perkins's nervous little giggle.

"Oh, I'm so sorry," she said, fluttering down the stairs. "Isn't it Awful? It doesn't seem as if it could be, not here, not Murder. Oh, do they know who it is was killed?"

Major Harley hesitated. He was an official and thoroughly imbued with the official view that none of the public should ever be told anything that could possibly be kept from them. None of their business, anyhow. But Mr. Nat Kayne's name would certainly soon be known, indeed was probably already known throughout the greater part of the neighbourhood.

"It's Mr. Nat Kayne," he said.

Mrs. Somerville gave a faint scream and said it couldn't be, not Mr. Nat; why, she had seen him herself only the day before as well as ever he was in his life. Miss Perkins stood still and frozen. Her face grew ghastly, a kind of wild bewilderment showed in her expression. The two men watched her curiously. Mrs. Somerville's babblings died into silence, as though abruptly extinguished. In a low, uncertain voice, Miss Perkins said:

"No... no... no... not him."

Neither the Major nor Bobby answered her. Mrs. Somerville began to look frightened. About the girl there seemed such an agony of dread and doubt as though even the balance of her reason shook. She lifted a slow hand and crooked a finger at them, at Bobby and the Major. She said in the same low, uncertain voice:

"It isn't—true. It isn't—true. No."

"I'm afraid there's no doubt," Major Harley said.

"It can't be," she repeated. Then when they did not answer she seemed to draw herself together, by an effort of every force of will and nerve that she possessed, recovering a self-control that had nearly left her altogether. She put her hands together and held them before her. She said,

"Nat Kayne... it is Nat Kayne? Nat... not Nat?... not someone else?"

"No, it is Mr. Kayne," the Major repeated, a little offended by her use of the dead man's Christian name.

"Ah, yes," she said. "I see." She stood upright and still. Then she said: "How did it happen? It was in the sunken lane through the wood?"

"Only think of it," interposed Mrs. Somerville, "and all the many times I've been that way myself, and him such a good-looking young gentleman, almost like some of them that's in the pictures."

"Yes, it was in the lane, about ten last night," the Major said.

"In the lane at ten last night," Miss Perkins repeated, and still her looks, her voice, her manner, were a little wild. "Last night at ten while we were sitting here, listening to the wireless."

"You were, but not me," said Mrs. Somerville, "I had only just got in, and him such a nice gentleman, with a pleasant word for all."

"Yes, he had, hadn't he?" agreed Miss Perkins. She seemed more natural now, her self control more assured. She said: "He was handsome as a dream—a Greek god. Mr. Broast said so himself. He was shot—did you say he was shot? Do they know who did it? Why? why should… anyone? Him? Why should it be him?"

The major explained that every possible step was being taken to discover the murderer. At present they hadn't much to go on, even the weapon used by the murderer had not yet been found, though a careful search was being made.

"We couldn't do much last night," he told them, "but I arranged for some of my men to be there as soon as it was light. We'll find it, if we have to go over the whole place with a comb."

"When you do find it," Miss Perkins said, "most likely that will show who it was."

The Major remarked that at any rate it would be a very useful and significant indication, and then went on to explain that the object of their visit was to know if Miss Perkins could confirm in any way Mr. Broast's statement that a stranger had been seen lurking near the library, and, if so, if she could give any description of him. But Miss Perkins, it appeared, had seen nothing herself. Mr. Broast had mentioned the incident to her, and had seemed disturbed. But that was all she knew. Mr. Broast was always nervous about burglars, she added.

The Major thanked her, said they would like a statement from her in writing, and so managed to get her alone with himself and Bobby into the little front sitting-room, while Mrs. Somerville, called away to take in her morning's supply of milk, exchanged news and confidences with the milk-man, and acquired much prestige from the fact that she had recently been conversing with the chief constable himself, who was even then actually in the house, along with another detective gentleman.

In the little parlour Major Harley was saying:

"There's something else we wanted to mention, Miss Perkins. It's a rather odd story we've been told about something seen in the library last night."

On a nod from the chief constable Bobby repeated as exactly as he could Virtue's tale of the body he declared he had seen through one of the library windows. She listened gravely and in silence, without that perpetual giggle of hers, without once interrupting to say she was so sorry, without even any of those exclamations of surprise and incredulity Bobby felt would have been natural. It seemed indeed as though she were hardly attending, or, rather, that she was finding it almost impossible to keep her attention on what she was listening to when her mind was full of the tragedy of which she had just heard. When Bobby ceased she seemed to draw herself together. She said:

"It sounds very funny, doesn't it? I should think he made it up. It's the young American gentleman you mean, the one that's staying in the village?"

"Yes," said Bobby. "You've seen him, I suppose."

"Only once," she answered. She gave her little giggle again, and seemed now to be more like her usual self. "He's very nice looking," she said. "Not like Mr. Nat, though." She paused and her face seemed as it were to crumple up, though only momentarily. Recovering herself, she went on: "You don't think it was him, do you? Why should he? I mean, why should he want to shoot Mr. Nat? They didn't know each other. He called at the library Wednesday, I think—Mr. Virtue, I mean. He wanted Mr. Broast to let him go over it. Mr. Broast wouldn't. He said he hadn't time, he said he wasn't going to act as guide to every fool of a tourist that came along. He said he didn't like Americans anyhow, except when they buy his books he wants to sell and then he always asks more from them than he would from anyone else. They keep asking questions, trying to find out things, poking about everywhere. Mr. Broast hates that. Mr. Virtue wrote once or twice, too, but it didn't make any difference."

"Did Mr. Virtue give any special reason for wanting to see over the library?"

"I don't know, I don't think so; of course it's awfully famous," answered Miss Perkins. "I'm so sorry." Then she added: "How could he see anything at all—Mr. Virtue, I mean? There's no lights in the library and shutters, too."

Bobby questioned her on this point, but she was quite clear that the shutters had been closed as usual at dusk. She had helped in the task herself and she was sure all of them had been carefully fastened. Of course, they might have been opened again. That was possible, evidently, but, if so, she knew nothing about it, and did not understand who could have done such a thing without the knowledge of Mr. Broast or of herself or the inmates of the house.

"The dead man Virtue saw, if he's telling the truth," observed Major Harley, "might have opened them himself to escape by."

Miss Perkins screamed faintly, said not Two dead men, oh, not Two, and then apologised and said she was so sorry.

"Difficult to understand," agreed Bobby. "Now, Miss Perkins, there's something else we have to ask you about. Please be very careful in answering." He repeated slowly, emphasizing each detail, the description given by Virtue of the features of the body he said he had seen. When Bobby had finished, he said: "Does that description suggest anything, bring anything to your mind? Please think carefully?"

Miss Perkins was gaping at him. She had every appearance of utter astonishment. She said slowly:

"It sounds just like a friend of mine. I've a photograph. Only it can't be. How can it?"

"Do you mind letting us see it?"

"The photograph?"

"Yes, please."

"But it's silly," she protested. "It's just silly."

"It does seem extraordinary," Bobby agreed. "That's why we have to ask about it."

"I don't understand," she repeated. She was plainly uneasy and alarmed, on the defensive. Not that there was now in her expression that extremity of horror and of wild amaze she had shown before. It was more a kind of incredulous astonishment she displayed, mingled with a sort of alert doubtfulness. Suddenly she gave her familiar giggle. "Oh, I'm so sorry," she said. "I'll go and get it."

She left the room and they heard her run upstairs Major Harley said:

"She's upset. I can guess why. Eh?"

"I'm afraid I can't, sir," Bobby said, for indeed at the moment he saw no reasonable explanation.

"She'll bring someone else's photo," the Major went on. "You see if she doesn't. It'll be a pointer."

Bobby wondered why, and in what direction. Miss Perkins came back. She was normal again now, once more her usual fluttering nervous self, full of giggles and apologies.

"Oh, I'm so sorry," she said. "Oh, I expect it's this one, isn't it?"

The one she showed answered in fact very closely to the description Virtue had given. The abnormality of the left ear was plainly visible. On the back Bobby found the name and address of a New York photographer.

"Would you mind telling us who this is and where he is now?" Bobby asked.

"I'm so sorry," Miss Perkins said helplessly. "I'm afraid... what I mean is... you see..."

"Our information," interposed the Major, "is that it's the young man you're engaged to?"

"That's right," she admitted. "I am," she said defiantly. "It's quite true. Only he's abroad." She hesitated, looked pitiful. "He's been abroad a long time," she almost whispered. "Sometimes I think he won't come back."

"I see," said the Major, a little awkwardly. "I'm sorry to have to press you. I'm afraid it's necessary. Of course, it's all quite confidential. We shouldn't bother you about your private affairs unless we had to. It's necessary to investigate this story Mr Virtue tells, especially in view of what happened last night. In a case of murder everything must be cleared up."

"Murder?" she repeated. "Murder—couldn't it have been—an accident? a mistake?"

The Major shook his head. One shot might be an accident, he agreed, not three. Three meant deliberation, determination, He took up the questioning now. Bit by bit he got her simple story from her. She had been born in Fromavon the great west-country port. She had never known her father or any relatives. There was some quarrel and her mother had left them. When her mother died, they refused to have anything to do with her or help in any way. She had been brought up by the woman in whose charge her mother had left her, together with a small sum of money to pay for her keep. When that became exhausted the woman had continued to give her shelter, but had turned her into a useful, unpaid little maid-of-all-work. She had managed to teach herself shorthand and typing, and had obtained work in London and then her present position with Mr. Broast. It was when she was in London she had met Mr. Cadman, the original of the photograph. They had become engaged, but he had been obliged to return to America on business. She admitted she had not heard from him since his departure, and it was quite plain she had little hope that any message would ever arrive. Apparently she had nothing more to tell, and after a few more questions they thanked her, asked permission to keep the photograph for a time, and so departed."

"Pathetic little thing, pathetic little story," said the Major, as they settled themselves in their car. "Repressed sex. Most likely she was never engaged to this Mr. Cadman at all. Probably they met, he may have taken her out once or twice perhaps, somehow she got hold of his photograph, and she imagined all the rest of it. Pure romance. Did you notice how really distressed she was about poor Nat Kayne's death?"

"Yes, sir," agreed Bobby slowly. "I didn't quite understand—I thought of calling that Point M. I mean, whether there is some connection or explanation we don't know about. I thought she was going to collapse utterly."

"Repressed sex again," explained the Major. "She was in love with him. Didn't you notice the way she talked about his good looks? I'll bet a good deal she's got hold of a photograph she shows of her fiancé. I've known cases— these sex starved, unattractive women. Pathetic, you know."

"Yes, sir," said Bobby.

"Anyhow, it seems clearly established there can be no connection between her and Virtue," decided the Major. "We had better see him next and hear what he has to say for himself."

CHAPTER X
THE PHOTOGRAPH AND MR. VIRTUE

On their way through the village to the Wynton Arms, the Major stopped at the little police station and spent there a few energetic moments at the 'phone and reading reports that had come in. Having thus assured himself that the various orders he had issued were being carried out, he joined Bobby, who had waited in the car outside. He said to him:

"Nothing about the pistol yet. If it doesn't turn up, I'll offer a reward. Of course, the murderer may have it in his pocket still. Anyhow, I can't have all my men tied up in that wood, wasting their time raking it over. Plenty for them to do. We aren't like you people in London with a force twenty thousand strong to call on."

Bobby fairly gasped. Twenty thousand men to call on, perhaps, but twenty thousand jobs for them to attend to, and press and public all ready to raise a howl if a constable wasn't always there just when and as required.

"Well sir," he began in a voice trembling with indignation, but the Major wasn't listening. He said as he started the car:

"I wonder if they would give the kids a holiday from school. If I could get them turned loose on the job and the pistol is anywhere about they might find it. Sharp eyes, kiddies have. Might try it, only then I should have to warn them not to touch it, and of course they would and probably shoot themselves. Then the fat would be in the fire. Better not try it, perhaps. Oh, there's a temporary authority through from London about you, and it'll go in at once for confirmation—detailed for provincial assistance. Here we are," he added as they drew up before the ancient inn, one half of which looked as if it might tumble down at any moment while the other half was brand new in red brick and sham half timber. "What's happening, though?"

An ancient-looking car was standing before the inn. An elderly man walked briskly from it towards the car. Mr. Drew, the landlord, stood at the inn threshold, looking on. Robins, porter, garage attendant, and general factotum, was in the act of placing a suit-case in the car. Bobby said:

"That's Mr. Adams, the man Mr. Broast said he saw—hanging round the library last night."

"Doing a bunk, eh?" said the Major darkly. "Looks bad. Can't have it, anyhow."

He jumped out. Mr. Adams saw him and with a startled air jumped in and shouted to his driver to hurry. The Major shouted to him to stop, and the driver was evidently not quite sure which to obey. The Major said:

"Police."

Magic word. The driver doubted no more where obedience lay. Mr. Adams put his head out of the window.

"What's the matter?" he asked. "I can't wait. I've a train to catch."

"Sorry," said the Major. "I'm afraid you'll have to miss it. I am making inquiries into a murder that took place last night."

"I know nothing about any murder," Mr. Adams asserted angrily. "Why should I? Nothing to do with me. Most inconvenient."

"Murders often are," said the Major dryly and opened the car door.

Obeying the hint this gesture conveyed. Mr. Adams alighted, though with evident reluctance. He was small, thin, elderly, with hair already grey, a pale, thin face, a big nose, and short-sighted, peering eyes behind large, horn-framed glasses. He did not look very prosperous—he did look eminently respectable. A timid, rabbit sort of little man, Bobby thought, though he knew well enough that timid, rabbit little men can do desperate things at times. Certainly, he looked exceedingly nervous now, with his shaking hands and frightened eyes, and his voice that seemed not fully under his control. He said:

"I consider this an outrage. I have a train to catch. I shall consult my solicitors."

"You are, of course, fully entitled to legal advice," agreed the Major. "Will you let them know at once—there's a 'phone here or you can wire? Until you have a reply, perhaps you will be good enough to wait at the police station."

Mr. Adams fairly jumped. Evidently he did not like the suggestion at all. He began to perspire slightly, and he tried to bluster. A feeble effort. He protested again that he knew nothing about a murder, this murder, any murder. If, as he understood from what was being said, the victim was a Mr. Nat Kayne, then he had never even seen Mr. Nat Kayne in all his life. Oh, yes, he supposed he did know Mr. Nat Kayne's as one of the library trustees, but what had that to do with it? But here's the Major cut short his protests by asking Bobby to go round with him to the police station, there to await the arrival of the solicitors not yet sent for.

"No time to waste," the Major told him. "You are only making a lot of unnecessary trouble by forcing me to detain you for inquiries. Much more sensible if you would answer a few questions. For you to decide, of course."

"Oh, very well," said Mr. Adams petulantly. "Most inconvenient. Most annoying. A train to catch. It's nothing to do with me. I'm not concerned with their quarrels. If there was anything wrong at the library, nothing to do with us."

"Have you any reason to suppose there was anything wrong at the library?" the Major asked.

Mr. Adams looked first startled, next alarmed, then cunning.

"If there's been a murder, it looks like it, doesn't it?" he said, and bustled away to dismiss the still waiting car and have his suit-case taken back to his room.

It was an opportunity the Major took to ask the landlord when this urgency to depart had first become apparent. He learned, as he had expected, that nothing had been seen of it till the gossip about the death of the unfortunate Nat Kayne had reached the inn.

"Thought as much," said the Major grimly, and Bobby said to him:

"Did you notice, sir, Adams said it has nothing to do with 'us'? Why did he say 'us'?"

"I'll ask him that," said the Major, and then Mr. Adams came back and repeated his readiness to answer any reasonable questions without waiting for his solicitor's presence.

"I warn you, however," he said very severely, but a little like a rabbit issuing a severe warning to the man with the gun, "I shall seek advice on my return to town."

"Very good," said the Major. "Very wise, too, if I may say so. But I must ask you to wait a few moments. My business here is really with someone else." He turned to the landlord, who had been listening to all this with great interest, not sure whether to be worried at the idea of having had a murderer staying in the house, a thing little likely to add to its popularity, since who wants to run the risk of sleeping in the next room to a murderer? and his certain knowledge that for days to come his bar would overflow with customers eager to know all about it and to discuss it over innumerable pots of beer. "Mr. Drew," the Major went on, breaking in upon his doubtful thoughts, "you have another American gentleman staying there, I think?"

"Yes, sir, Mr. Virtue that'll be, he's at breakfast. He's the only American gentleman here."

"Oh, yes," said the Major, glancing at Mr. Adams, who indeed neither looked nor spoke like an American. "Well, we can go into that afterwards. Mr. Virtue first."

There was a movement within the doorway and Virtue himself stepped forward. How long he had been standing there, hidden behind the landlord and the half-open door, it was impossible to say, though plainly he had overheard a part at least of what had been said.

"About last night, I suppose," he said quietly. "I don't know anything about this murder they're talking of. I don't think there's anything I can tell you about that. I can't even begin to guess whether there's any connection between it and what I saw. Of course, any questions you want answered—"

He left the sentence unfinished. The landlord showed them into a dreary, stuffy, unaired little sitting-room he called the lounge, and kept for the use of his guests, though to judge from its appearance none ever used it, as indeed was no wonder, when the bar and the garden were so much more attractive. However, its sombre, heavy appearance gave it a certain air of suitability for such an investigation as was now in progress. The landlord undertook to see they were not disturbed, as he undertook also, in answer to whispered instructions from the Major, to keep an unobtrusive eye on Mr. Adams, and give warning if that gentleman showed any renewed signs of attempting to take his departure.

"Not as he can have done the murder," Mr. Drew assured them, "him being here in his room last night. Went up early. Said he had letters to write and wanted to be quiet. Must have been nine or thereabouts when he went upstairs."

"There is no cause for suspicion whatever as yet," said the Major sternly, for he wanted no gossip, and Mr. Drew protested that he quite understood, and only his respect for a chief constable prevented him from winking, indeed wink he did at Bobby, who promptly winked back, since a wink is both a friendly thing and quite non-committal, and yet goes far to establish mutual understanding.

"Now, Mr. Virtue," the Major began when they were alone, while Bobby got out his notebook, "I want to hear from yourself your account of what you saw last night. Then I shall want you to put it in a written statement and I want you, please, to be very careful to be as accurate as you can in every detail. You understand that in view of what has happened since, your story has to be regarded much more seriously."

"I don't see how it joins up," Virtue said slowly. "I do not." He was looking pale and nervous, and Bobby guessed that he had not slept much. He went on: "If there's a join up, it's mighty strange. If there isn't, and it's only coincidence, well, that's stranger still. What I want to suggest is a mighty close search of that library. I suggest going over it with a small tooth comb. Maybe you might find an explanation. And I want to claim that I ought to be present."

"It won't be very easy to get permission to do that unless your story is confirmed in some way," the Major said. "Mr. Broast may very reasonably object. Mr. Virtue, I should like to warn you that we take a serious view in this country of any attempt to mislead the police."

"So we do in my country," answered Virtue steadily. "Mighty serious." He added: "I don't want to mislead any one. I don't understand what's happened. All I want is to get at the truth."

"Then I trust we may expect your full and frank co-operation," said the Major, but not much as though he were building on it. "You understand we have already made some inquiries. It has been pointed out to us that there is no artificial lighting in the library."

"I know," Virtue answered. He added: "I saw what I saw."

"We are also informed that the shutters to the windows are always closed and fastened as soon as it's dark, and that that was done as usual yesterday."

"I saw what I saw," repeated Virtue. "I say again, there ought to be a search made, and I ought to be there when it's done. I stand by what I say, and if I'm proved wrong—well, I suppose it's up to you then. Your call." He added abruptly: "It's this killing has me rattled. I don't get it."

He did indeed look troubled and disturbed. Bobby reflected that when he spoke of what he claimed he had seen in the library he appeared calm, composed and certain. Whether the story were true or whether he had invented it for some inexplicable reason, he evidently intended to stick to it. But any reference to the murder showed him disturbed and hesitant.

The Major said:

"I should like your full name, address here and in America, and occupation, please."

"Virtue, Bertram Arnold Virtue. I stay at the Bloomsbury Hotel, London. Some of my baggage is parked there now. Home address, Grand Rapids, Michigan. I'm in business there. At present, on a holiday trip in Europe."

"Any special reason for visiting Wynton?"

"The Kayne library," Virtue answered. "The Blue Guide says you ought to see it. I tried, but got turned down. Tourists not welcome apparently."

"What time did you go out last night? had you any special reason? what took you near the library building? It's on private property."

"I went out about nine, I suppose, or thereabouts. I'm not sure to a minute. I thought I would like a stroll before bed. I just happened round by the library. Then I saw a light shining through the window. I thought it queer. I knew it was shut up tight after dark. I went across to see what was on. I saw what I saw. That's all."

Bobby, taking notes diligently, noticed this phrase. He could not help remarking:

"That's the whole question, Mr. Virtue. What you did in fact see."

"Yes, that's so," agreed Virtue.

The Major frowned. He was puzzled. Also he felt this was in a way a waste of time. The pressing investigation was not the incomprehensible story Virtue told, but the tragedy in the sunken lane. And yet it might be they were interlinked, though it was difficult to see how. He went across to Bobby, looked at his notes, then whispered an order. He made as if his questioning were over and went towards the door. Bobby stood up. Virtue looked relieved and said abruptly:

"I'll stop on a day or two in case you want me."

Bobby said:

"Thank you. Oh, one thing more. You gave a very clear and vivid description of the appearance of the dead man you say you saw in the library. A recognizable description."

"Yes," said Virtue. "Hadn't you better make it public? Some one might know it."

Bobby found himself wondering if that was a genuine suggestion or just a piece of bluff. He said:

"Miss Perkins, the typist at the Kayne library—you know her?"

"The girl who looks like a wet fish and giggles every time she opens her mouth?"

"She has a photograph of her fiancé she showed us," Bobby said. "It answers very closely to the description you gave us."

Virtue stared, gasped, looked very astonished. Then he said sharply:

"Nonsense. That's absurd. See here, are you trying to pull some police trick on me?"

"I am making a simple statement of fact," Bobby answered quietly.

"Mean to tell me," demanded Virtue, "that this Perkins girl has a photograph of someone she says she's engaged to and it's like—I don't believe it."

"It's the fact all the same," Bobby told him.

The quietness of his tone seemed to convince the other. Virtue sat down abruptly. He looked utterly bewildered, even a little afraid.

"I don't understand," he muttered. "Well, it's just not possible. Have you got it? Can I see it?" he asked.

Bobby looked at the Major who nodded. Bobby produced it. Virtue said slowly:

"That's it all right. That's a photograph of the dead man I told you I saw lying on the library floor. Where did this woman get it from?"

CHAPTER XI
INFORMATION RECEIVED

Neither Bobby nor Major Harley made any reply, nor did Virtue seem to expect one. He had an air of being utterly at a loss, of being a little frightened. He got up and went across to the window, as if he experienced a need for fresh air. He turned round and said:

"It's not possible. Well, I mean it can't be like that." He came back to his chair and sat down again, leaning forward, knocking gently his clenched hands together. His surprise and bewilderment seemed perfectly genuine. "In God's name, what's it—mean?" he demanded suddenly. "This Perkins girl—has she ever been in America?"

At a nod from the Major Bobby referred to his notebook. He said:

"She states she was brought up in Fromavon, got work in London, came here two years ago. She gives names and dates that can be verified."

"Well, now then," Virtue muttered. "She claims she was engaged to—him?" he asked, nodding at the photograph.

"That is her story," Bobby agreed. "She says she met him in London and they became engaged. He returned to America just before she got her post here. She has not heard from him since. She gave the impression that she doesn't much expect she ever will."

"He returned home two years ago?" Virtue repeated thoughtfully. "She's never been there herself? She doesn't much expect she'll ever hear from him? I don't get it."

"Mr Virtue," interposed the Major, "have you ever been in England before?"

"No. It's my first trip."

"Had you any special reason for taking a stroll last night?"

"I just thought I would have a walk round."

"Do I understand you to say that it was ten o'clock precisely when you were outside the Kayne library, looking through the window?"

Virtue did not answer for a moment or two. He looked steadily at the Major, steadily and thoughtfully. He said presently:

"I get that anyway. You mean you think I faked the yarn to give myself an alibi for the murder? It was ten when the shooting happened, wasn't it? Anyway that's what they were saying here."

"Shots were heard at ten exactly according to our information," the Major answered with professional caution.

The young American took out his handkerchief. He was paler even than before, his mouth twitched nervously. He wiped his forehead on which a slight perspiration had gathered. He said slowly:

"Looks like I've gotten myself into a bad jam. Didn't expect my first European trip to finish in a British hanging party. Only why should I want to shoot up a man I've never even seen, never heard of till a few days ago?"

"We're concerned with facts, not with motives," the Major answered. "Mr. Virtue. You tell us an extraordinary story. It presents features we find it difficult to accept. If we find we can accept it, no doubt it gives you a satisfactory alibi. If we are finally unable to do so, we shall have to ask ourselves what purpose you may have had in putting it forward. If there is anything else you care to say—anything to explain your visit here, your interest in the library, this photograph, we shall be happy to listen."

"I can't explain the photograph," Virtue said. "There's something behind that. I don't know what; I can't even guess. I suggest Miss Perkins should be asked some more questions. About my trip over here. I told you I was in business in Grand Rapids, Michigan. It's a furniture factory. Virtue furniture is pretty well known. 'Virtue in name, Virtue in nature,' is our slogan. You'll see it plenty places over home; magazines, newspapers, so on. It mayn't mean much, but it pulls. We have a standing paragraph, too, we bring out every so often. About virtue coming from the Latin, and meaning strength, and strength was what the old Romans stood for, and so does our furniture stand for it to-day, and about how the old Roman Empire lasted a thousand years and our furniture lasts longer than that. I tell you, honest, our publicity has taught the American people more Roman history than all the college professors put together in a row. It's been a grand line of talk to hand out."

"Is it your own business?" asked the Major.

"Gosh, no, I'm just one of the executives. The family hold all the units between them, though. We're incorporated on a unit basis. I hold fifty myself. There are five thousand units in all. We value them at about a hundred dollars each. I suppose in time I'm likely to inherit some more."

"Who had the direction of the business?"

"Well, of course, there's a board of executives, but there's the trustees on top. They're the real bosses, if it comes to a show down. Things are a bit difficult because a cousin of mine disappeared on a trip to Europe more than ten years ago. He held most units but he never interfered much or took much interest. Books were his line, crazy on them, spent all his money collecting."

"Books? He collected books?"

"He did so. Give him some worm-eaten old book and he'd pass up woman, wine, and song without turning a hair. And he liked them all right too, but different someway, not like books. He did a lot with old Mr. Kayne. Mr. Kayne got James A. Junior—that's my cousin, the one who disappeared—a complete set of first editions of John Smith's works."

"John Smith?" asked the Major, who had not known there was an author of that popular and familiar name.

"Yes, Captain John Smith—you know, one of the founders of Virginia, president at one time. Princess Pocahontas saved his life. You remember the story? Spoils it a bit that she married someone called Rolfe instead. We claim to be descended from her through the Randolph family; and if we can't prove it true, no one can prove it isn't, so it gets by. Result is we're very keen on the John Smith legend, and James A. was mighty pleased when old Mr. Kayne got him first editions of all John Smith's books— and what's more, each blessed one of them with the autograph of a famous person to show it had belonged to him at one time. Your Lord Falkland, the Duke of Buckingham—the one Felton outed—Lord Shaftesbury of the letters, and the prize one of the lot, Nell Gwynne. Made a unique set and worth a lot—and I tell you, James A. paid top figures, too."

"Very interesting," said the Major, slightly puzzled, "but I don't quite see..."

"Very interesting," agreed Bobby, and his mind went back to that series of the various issues of the first edition of Milton's *Paradise Lost*, each of them containing the autograph of a famous man, even though that of Dryden had been missing from the copy he had picked up.

It seemed the Kayne library had indeed many treasures; and Bobby felt his mind, as it were, searching, probing, wondering, as if vaguely knowing that in these series of ancient autographed volumes was somehow concealed a clue to the murder of the night before in the sunken lane through the Wynton wood.

"Spent his money like that," Virtue went on; "he had a pile came to him from an aunt, so he was independent. He hadn't a big share in the business then. It was understood he had the aunt's money, so his elder brother was to have the business. Well, James A. started off on one of his European trips, and while he was away his father—my uncle Art—and his brother, Art, Junior, were both killed in an auto smash. That meant their business interests passed to James A. under an old will. Since then, we've never heard a thing of James A., whether he's alive or whether he's dead. We traced him here, to this village. He had had a talk or two with Mr. Broast, showed him a rare book he was very proud of, printed by Caxton, swell copy, the *Dictes* it was."

"*Dictes*?" repeated Bobby, remembering that was the title of a rare and fine specimen of Caxton's work Mr. Broast had seemed proud the library possessed.

"Yes, Apple of James A.'s eye, it was. Well, from here we traced him to Dublin. He had a girl with him. He often had. Seems they created a disturbance and were asked to leave. That wasn't a bit like James A. We didn't believe it was him at first, but the hotel people still had his photo; the girl with him had amused herself by sticking up in the dining-room and throwing knives at— Had too much to drink, probably. It was him all right, the photo, I mean. He had a trick of giving his photo to girls he picked up, his technique, so to say, to persuade them he really loved them alone, that sort of thing."

"This was ten years ago?" Bobby interrupted quickly.

"More," Virtue answered. "I get you. Sounds like it was him gave this Perkins girl the photo she showed you? But that was only two years back, she says, and ten years back, she must have been only a kiddy. Don't seem to fit, does it? Because, if it was James A. Miss Perkins means, well, where has he been all this time, and how's he been living? Doesn't seem possible to me it was him."

"It certainly seems difficult," Bobby agreed.

"After the Dublin affair there was no trace of him," Virtue continued, "till his baggage turned up in a Paris hotel. It had been registered through from London and never claimed. And that's all we ever knew. Awkward for business, because he and his mother between them hold a majority of the units, and no one knows whether he is alive or dead—not that there's much chance of his being alive after all this time."

"Can't you get his death presumed?" asked the Major. "That could be done here. The courts would do that on application. After less than ten years. That would be the normal procedure."

"Yes," agreed Virtue, "but aunt—his mother, I mean—won't stand for it. She won't have it he's dead—expects him to walk in any day. It's about all that keeps her alive, poor soul. And she's got it into her head that presuming his death is just taking away his last chance. If we could get actual proof, she would be more satisfied. But she's not going to have it presumed, and the trustees back her up good and hard. You see, if death was presumed, the trust could be wound up and that means they would lose their fees—five thousand dollars a year. Well, they don't see why that should happen any sooner than it's got to. It's a lump of overhead for us to carry, only it's not so easy to dig folks out of a nice fat job like that. They tend to hang on. Also they're an obstructive element. They don't want to develop. Why should they? If we went big, if we sent our sales up ten times over, if we covered ten times the territory we do, their fees would stay the same. Not a cent more. So they want to stand pat, play for safety, refuse consent to any development scheme, and the result is we are getting more and more tied up all the time. It's getting to mean a lot to the family to find out for sure what happened to James A."

"That is your errand over here?"

"That's so."

"Have you had any success yet?"

"Well, you know, I haven't been on the job so long," Virtue answered.

The Major was looking worried and perplexed. He did not see clearly where all this tended. Very specially, he did not see what connection there could be between the disappearance of a young American ten years ago and the mysterious murder of poor young Nat Kayne it was his pressing duty to investigate.

"It's because of your cousin's connection with the Kayne library as a buyer of books from it that you are here?" Bobby said suddenly

"That's so," Virtue agreed.

The Major go to his feet.

"Mr. Virtue," he said, "I don't profess to understand your story. I don't think you have been entirely frank with us. We shall make further inquiries, and we shall have to ask you for a formal written statement. For the moment things can be left as they are. There is a good deal to attend to. In the meantime, I will ask you to think over your position very carefully and consider whether there is not something more you can tell us to make the position plainer. Also I must ask you to undertake not to leave here for the present."

"That's all right," Virtue answered. "I realize I'm in a jam. But I've nothing to do with any shooting. Why should I?"

The Major made no answer. He opened the door and went out. Bobby, in the act of following him, said to Virtue:

"Much better tell us all about it, you know."

"Well," Virtue answered slowly, "there is such a thing as jumping out of the frying pan into the fire. I've got to consider my position pretty carefully. I'm a foreigner here and I've got to think twice before saying anything."

Bobby nodded, wondered what Virtue meant by talking about out of the frying pan into the fire, since surely suspicion of murder was itself rather a very hot fire than a comparatively cool frying pan, and caught up with the Major who was standing by his car outside, looking at some papers a messenger had just brought him. He glanced up, as Bobby came near and said:

"Well, what do you make of all that?"

"Sounded to me, sir," Bobby answered, "as if Virtue believes some clue to what happened to his missing cousin is somewhere in the library—some book perhaps he bought or wanted, or something like that. Mr. Broast refused to let Virtue see over it, so he invented this story as a way of getting a search made. You remember how he kept insisting on what he called his right to be present?"

"Preposterous," growled the Major. "Absurd. Does he think there's a dead body hidden behind the books on the shelves somewhere?"

Bobby said nothing. The Major flung down the papers he was holding. Very red and angry looking, he said:

"I suppose you haven't got it into your head this has anything to do with Miss Kayne's telling you she had committed the perfect murder?"

Bobby continued to say nothing. The Major got more and more red, more and more angry-looking. He picked up again the papers he had just thrown into the car.

"I can't spend any more time running round," he said. "Everyone's waiting for orders. Half of them can't blow their own noses till they've had official instructions. It's incredible, anyhow, Miss Kayne! You might as well suspect a bishop. Preposterous. Incredible."

"Yes, sir," agreed Bobby, "only things so often are, aren't they? Incredible world altogether, sir, if I may say so."

"Hang it all, man alive," protested the Major. "Why should she? how could she? When could she? This fellow is said to have been missing ten years—ten years—and he had nothing to do with anyone here, except that he bought books. Good customer, too, apparently, paid a high price. Well, you don't murder a man because he's buying the books you want to sell, do you?"

"Well, sir, of course it does seem a poor way to encourage trade," agreed Bobby. "When I was in the library yesterday Mr. Broast showed us a set of Milton, each copy with a famous autograph in it except one I looked at. Mr. Broast was very annoyed. It was Dryden's autograph I wanted to see. Mr. Broast said it was in another copy. He seemed very upset. I don't know why. I noticed he sold the missing Mr. Virtue a set of someone's books that all had autographs of famous people in them, too."

"Well, why not?" asked the Major. "I believe Broast is famous for that kind of bibliographical discovery. What about it?"

"I don't know, sir," Bobby answered. "I just noticed it. Point N. sir, so to say."

The Major grunted.

"We've got to remember it's a murder last night we've on our hands," he said, "not an American missing ten years ago. I would like to know what's behind that girl's story, though. Have to talk to her again as soon as there's time."

He got into the car. Bobby followed, and they were just about to start when Mr. Adams came out of the inn. He had been watching them through a window and now he came hurrying out. But the Major greeted him with a scowl.

"No time now," he said. "Everything's hung up—even if there's been a murder there's all the usual work to attend to. Owen, you hear what Mr. Adams has to say and then report to me."

"Very good, sir," said Bobby.

The Major made another grab at his letters as Bobby prepared to alight, and he looked very worried.

"I've got to see about these," he said. "Can't have everything else at a standstill. There's Broast, too, got to see what he has to say. Sir William, as well. We've got to know what that quarrel was about you spoke of."

"Yes, sir," agreed Bobby. "I believe Sir William motored across to see Mr. Broast last night. I was there when the 'phone message came. He would have to pass where the sunk lane enters the wood. He may have seen something."

"Well, look into it," said the Major. "Get rid of Adams first and then see Sir William and hear what he has to say and report back to me. I shall be busy till lunch or later. If Sir William has anything to say bring him over with you. We can lunch here."

"Very good, sir," said Bobby again.

He alighted. The Major started the car and drove off. Bobby said to Mr. Adams, who was looking half inclined to retreat again:

"There is something you wish to say?"

Mr. Adams hesitated, looked very uncomfortable, coughed, and said nothing.

"I suppose," Bobby went on, "you have your passport with you? Could I see it?"

"That's just it," sighed Mr. Adams. "I haven't got one—at least, I mean, not an American one. I suppose you will be making inquiries about everyone here in view of this most unfortunate occurrence so I feel it advisable to explain. I have no connection with the University of Nebraska or with any University. I am a British subject and I live in this country."

Bobby looked at him doubtfully.

"Your correct name and address, please?" he said.

"I deeply regret," said Mr. Adams primly, "that in the circumstances I feel unable to answer your question. I trust you will believe me when I say how really unfortunate I feel it that I am obliged to decline to give you any information whatsoever."

CHAPTER XII
LIBRARY SCENE

"Oh," said Bobby, somewhat taken aback. "Dear me," he said, "someone else, I suppose, who prefers the frying pan to the fire?"

"I fear," said Mr. Adams, "I do not altogether succeed in grasping your meaning."

He stood there, mild and respectable, his hands folded together, peering short-sightedly from behind his glasses, looking exactly like a meditative sheep. And Bobby reflected that while a pig may be the symbol of obstinacy, as a matter of fact a sheep is often ten times harder to move. The pig may want to go its own way, the sheep merely remains immobile. Bobby turned to Robins, the inn factotum, who was hovering near, and asked him to bring his motor-cycle from the shed where it was stored. Then he said to Mr. Adams:

"Well, of course, if you won't answer my questions I shall have to ask you to come along to the police station."

"I regret," explained Mr. Adams mildly, "to seem disobliging, but I fear I must decline. It would be an entirely useless waste of time."

"Mr. Adams," said Bobby, "do you know a murder was committed last night near here?"

"So I am informed by current report," replied Mr. Adams. "I trust you do not need my assurance that I am entirely ignorant of the circumstances surrounding such a lamentable occurrence."

"Your assurance seems pretty badly needed," retorted Bobby. "You admit you are here under a false name and description. Also we have information that you were seen near the library building, in private grounds so you were trespassing anyhow. That was last night."

"I imagined I had been seen," agreed Mr. Adams. "I heard someone shouting. It is why I departed. Mr. Broast, I presume?"

"What were you doing there?"

"I regret that as I have already informed you certain circumstances make it impossible for me to offer the explanations I would otherwise gladly impart to you."

"Now you just understand this, Mr. Adams," said Bobby crossly. "No circumstances excuse withholding information from the police—above all in a murder case. Do you know what is meant by being an accessory after the fact?"

"I am not," confessed Mr. Adams, "well acquainted with legal phraseology. I should be inclined to presume that it indicates—er—some degree of complicity. That I beg you to believe would be an entirely erroneous impression. I think I may go so far as to inform erroneous impression. I think I may go so far as to inform you that I was in my room, engaged with my correspondence, from about nine o'clock, or very soon after, till the hour appropriate for retirement. That, if I am correctly informed," he concluded, "is what is known as an alibi."

"You didn't go out at all?" Bobby asked.

"I remained the whole evening from nine onwards within the privacy of my apartment. The correspondence with which I was engaged was of primary importance."

"What was it about?"

"I have already explained," replied Mr. Adams gently, "that until the matter has received further and careful consideration I am unwilling, indeed unable, to submit to interrogation."

"That exposes you to grave suspicion," Bobby pointed out, not quite sure yet whether to be angry, bewildered, or merely amused by the other's calm and gentle obstinacy, a little like that of a feather pillow you can pommel as much as you like with remarkably little effect.

"It is an attitude on your part I must confess appears to me distinctly unreasonable," declared Mr. Adams in mild protest. "I was within my room at the moment when this unfortunate young man met his death. I was in no way concerned with him, I had no dealings with him whatever.

To the best of my knowledge I have never even seen him. I was aware, naturally, that he was a trustee of the Kayne library, but I gathered he was concerned solely with the financial aspects. I doubt, I seriously doubt," said Mr. Adams with a touch of heat coming into his calm and level tones, "if he would have known the difference between a signature and a colophon—incredible as that may seem to most of us."

Bobby, who had no idea himself of the technical meaning of the word 'signature' in bibliography, passed this over.

"I believe," he said, "you had applied for permission to visit the library and had been refused?"

"I perceive you have taken steps to obtain certain information," observed Mr. Adams. "I presume in the course of your official inquiries. It is, however, not entirely accurate. It was permission to examine closely the Mandeville leaves that was so remarkably refused me. Mr. Broast chose to behave in a manner I can only describe as—unprecedented. Yes, unprecedented," repeated Mr. Adams firmly. "He literally—I choose the word with deliberation— he literally snatched the camera from my hands. It is one of considerable value, nor is it my personal property. For a moment he appeared to contemplate inflicting serious and deliberate injury on it. He contented himself with removing the roll of film and destroying it by exposure."

"Had you taken any snaps?" Bobby asked.

"I had secured two of the *Jason*, to my mind the most remarkable exhibit in the library."

"I thought the Mandeville pages were that?" observed Bobby, who had not before heard of the *Jason*.

"In my considered opinion," said Mr. Adams with such a slow solemnity of utterance as the head of a state might use when speaking of issues of peace and war, "the Fust and Schoeffer *Romance of Jason* is the most important production known to bibliographists. Although I am aware the statement may be disputed, I consider it proved that this, the only copy known, is the first book ever printed, anterior to the *Psalter* issued in Mayennce in 1457, anterior to the 32-line Bible, anterior to the great 42-line Bible, commonly known as the Gutenberg Bible. No one," said Mr. Adams, warming to his theme, "can deny that the Gutenberg Bible necessitated the usage of an enormous fount of letters—about 2,700 to the page. It follows, therefore, of necessity, that that fount of letters must have been in existence, and it may be concluded had been previously made use of. So great an undertaking as the 42-line Bible could not possibly have been launched without previous trials. Of these undoubtedly the *Jason* was the first actually completed. For certain technical reasons which I could not fully explain to you without the use of diagrams, I consider that the letters used in the *Jason* of which it is merely perverse to doubt the genuineness, were some of those subsequently made use of in the printing of the Gutenberg, or 42-line Bible."

"Yes, very interesting," interposed Bobby, fearing that this lecture would continue indefinitely. "You took a photograph of it and Mr. Broast objected?"

"He returned, contrary to my expectations," explained Mr. Adams, "as I was in the act of securing photographs of the Mandeville leaves. As I have already mentioned, he chose to behave with the most extraordinary violence. Further he used language of a regrettable, even curious nature. I use the word 'curious' in its technical sense of improper or obscene. He described me as the son of—er—of a female of the canine species. It is an appellation," he added, in his voice a touch of nostalgia Bobby did not at the moment understand, "I have not heard employed for a considerable period."

"What happened then?"

"I obtained re-possession of my camera which Mr. Broast had—er—impelled somewhat abruptly in my direction. I considered it undesirable to engage in further controversy, more particularly undesirable on the lines of physical encounter apparently contemplated by Mr. Broast, if I may judge from the gestures he was making with a ruler he had taken from his writing table. I therefore withdrew, ignoring both the language of Mr. Broast, and the books and other loose objects he directed towards me. One, a particularly heavy tome of, I am inclined to think, the late eighteenth century—probably a volume of sermons and of small or indeed of no interest—came into violent contact with the central portions of my back. A discoloration of the skin is, I am informed by one of the male attendants at this inn, plainly visible. Indeed, at the moment I lost my balance, and Mr. Broast so far forgot himself as to indulge in a cachinnation of unseemly merriment."

Bobby both looked and felt very puzzled. This tale of a violent scene between Broast and Adams was curious, but he could not see any connection between it and the murder of young Nat Kayne.

Mr. Adams continued:

"I admit that at the moment I was aware of a sensation not highly dissimilar from those one experienced during the late war before going over the top. Cold feet, we used to call it, I remember. Mr. Broast had called my attention to the fact that he possessed a revolver and that he considered he would be fully justified in its employment. It recalled vividly to my mind the extreme distaste I have always entertained for firearms, a distaste much heightened as a result of my very unpleasant term of service in the army."

"Did you see any fighting?" Bobby could not help asking.

"I was wounded three times," Mr. Adams told him. "I was presented with a D.C.M. I am glad to say I have since mislaid it. I find it most unpleasant to be reminded of the occasion. Yet I was not to blame. A German soldier advancing with considerable precipitation, projected himself on the point of my bayonet. A repulsive experience."

"Was that what you got the D.C.M. for?"

"That and because, not having been notified of the receipt of orders to retire, I therefore continued to make use of a machine gun that chanced to be in my proximity. Under appropriate conditions a machine gun, the trigger being subjected to adequate pressure, continues to eject bullets to a considerable number. The credit for this seems to me to belong to the machine gun itself and to its manufacturers. On this occasion, however, that credit was assigned to me, as I was subsequently informed in hospital. I was glad of it at the time, as the language of sergeants was often considerably modified when directed towards those in the ranks to whom that decoration had been awarded. In my case this was especially desirable, as sergeants often expressed a measure of dissatisfaction with the state of my equipment and with the difficulty I often found in keeping step and such other matters as seem of importance to the somewhat infantile military mind—of which," Mr. Adams added musingly, "the police mind frequently reminds me."

Bobby gave it up.

"Well, look here, Mr. Adams," he said, "I am afraid unless you choose to tell us a little more about your identity, the chief constable is almost certain to want to detain you for inquiries. I shall let him know at once what you've told me. I should like your promise to remain here for the present. I am afraid if you make any attempt to leave it will probably be thought necessary to arrest you."

"On what charge?" snapped Mr. Adams with an unexpected force and decision that seemed reminiscent of his military days.

"Accessory after the fact," retorted Bobby. "But that will be for Major Harley to decide. May I have your promise to stay here for the time?"

"I have already consented to do so," replied Mr. Adams. "It is perhaps as well to await here a reply to my letters. If I change my mind I will let you know. I repeat I have no knowledge of, and am in no way concerned with, the death of this unfortunate young man."

With that he made Bobby a stiff little bow and went back into the inn, leaving Bobby entirely puzzled.

There had been this violent scene with Broast that might have an explanation other than that put forward by Adams, for indeed there seemed no reason why an attempt to photograph the Mandeville pages should cause such an outburst of anger and the use of such threats. Mr. Adams acknowledged, too, having known of the existence of a revolver, and his army record seemed to suggest that in spite of his usual placidity there was a formidable side to his character. It was certain, too, that he possessed information of some relevance and importance, or why should he refuse to answer questions?

Robins came up now with the motor cycle Bobby had asked him to fetch. Bobby said to him:

"Did you see Mr. Adams last night at all?"

Robins considered, trying to remember.

"Only when he went out to post his letters somewhere about half past nine," he answered finally.

"Oh, yes," said Bobby, remembering that Mr. Adams had denied leaving his room. "Did you see him come back?"

Robins shook his head. He had been going past the front entrance to the inn on some trifling errand when he noticed Mr. Adams slipping out with letters in his hand. He had never given it another thought. Why should he? The door was always open till eleven or after, and anyone could slip in or out without any great risk of attracting attention. That Adams had been seen going out was pure accident occurring could be greatly lessened by the careful choice of a suitable moment. Inquiries would have to be made, but probably with small chance of success. For the moment, Bobby supposed, all he could do was to make a report to Major Harley and then go on to Highfields, the residence of Sir Williams Winders.

It was a fairly large house, standing in three or four acres of private grounds, the home of a man very comfortably off, if not of great riches. All its inmates were evidently in a state of considerable excitement, much intensified by the sight of

Bobby, whose names and profession, even before the murder, had been passed from mouth to mouth.

"Never anything so awful known in these parts in mortal memory," the butler informed him, "the only thing like it was when a tearing, rushing motor cycle ran into young Mrs. Lewis's perambulator she was wheeling full of potatoes, and everyone thought at first the baby was there, too, along with the potatoes, only it wasn't by the mercy of Providence, as Vicar said himself when he heard of it. Sir William is terribly upset."

"Can I see Sir William?" Bobby asked.

"Terrible upset he is," the butler confirmed. "Couldn't believe it—when I took his tea in this morning and told him, I thought he would faint, he came over so pale and trembling. So you can tell what a shock it was."

"Yes, indeed," said Bobby.

"In a fair state, he was, and when he got up, that restless it seemed he couldn't settle, felt like he must find out what was being done. He was going to 'phone Major Harley first, and then he thought he would go and inquire himself. Wouldn't even wait for breakfast, but started off to walk through the wood."

"Didn't he take his car?" Bobby asked.

"No, said he would walk, it's not so far by the short way into the sunk lane through the wood."

"That would take him past the spot where Mr. Kayne was shot, wouldn't it?" Bobby asked.

The butler shook his head.

"No, the path comes out into the lane lower down than that, nearer the Lodge; at least, the lower path does, there's another as well," answered the butler. "Anyhow, Sir William changed his mind and just walked round by the pond and home again. Seemed quieter like then, and said it wasn't fair to bother the police, and we must wait, and he would have his breakfast first, though it wasn't much he took, except coffee. And upset we all are, knowing Mr. Nat as we did here."

"Sir William and he were friends, weren't they?" observed Bobby.

"Sir William knew him when he was that high," declared the butler indicating some eight inches from the ground, "and they were both of them library trustees, too, so it brought them together, not that Mr. Nat knew much about books, not like Sir William, a real expert he is. Makes him feel it, and then, too, he was over to the Hall to see Mr. Broast last night. I reckon he must have come back along the sunk lane not more than twenty minutes or half an hour after the murder. It's a mercy," said the butler fervently "it wasn't him too."

"What made him walk? Doesn't he generally take the car?" Bobby asked.

It appeared that Sir William was fond of walking. It helped him, or so he thought, to keep down a certain tendency to increase of bulk. He had always been a great walker. Sometimes, of course, he took the car, but it was almost as quick to go by the footpath and the sunk lane as to motor round by the road. It was quite common for him to pay a visit to Mr. Broast after dinner, and they often sat up late, arguing, quarrelling, disputing, over the various problems of bibliography. On these occasions, when Sir William was late home, he let himself in by the side door, left on the latch. So here was yet another, Bobby reflected, who had no alibi, who must indeed have been quite near the scene of the murder at the time it happened.

CHAPTER XIII
MISS KAYNE ACCUSES

Sir William Winders was a tall, bigly made, elderly man, a little inclined probably to put on flesh, but still vigorous and upright. That he was in a highly nervous and excited state was both evident and not unnatural, since the violent and sudden death of a friend and neighbour must have touched him deeply. But Bobby thought, too, there was fear in the deepset, uneasy eyes overhung by bushy brows, in the continued restlessness of movement, in the constant licking by the tongue of lips dry and parched.

He received Bobby in the breakfast-room, a pleasant, book-lined apartment overlooking the garden, in the distance the dark mass of Wynton wood, and, to one side, a glint of reflected sunshine suggesting the presence of that pond whereof the butler had spoken.

Sir William began to talk at once, without waiting for any question to be put him. Sometimes seated, sometimes shifting from one chair to another, or moving about or standing, he talked at length of the shock the news had been to him, of the impossibility of understanding how such a thing could have happened to disturb the serenity of their quiet countryside, of his absolute certainty that no one in the neighbourhood could have been guilty of such a crime.

"Don't you think it must have been an accident or suicide?" he asked abruptly.

Bobby shook his head. Suicides do not shoot themselves three times over. The same consideration applied to the accident theory. Bobby had been content to listen for a time. Listening in silence to those anxious to talk is useful from many points of view. It gives opportunity to form an impression of the speaker. Besides, in a flow of unchecked talk often more is said than would be elicited by questioning.

"An unbelievable thing to happen, I can't tell you what a shock it was," declared Sir William for about the tenth time; "I can't understand it, I can hardly believe it," and Bobby, watching him attentively, grew more and more certain that either he knew or he suspected something.

But Bobby continued to say nothing, and he had the impression, too, that his silent watchfulness was having, as silent watchfulness always has, its effect upon the other's nerves and self-control.

"Well, I suppose there's something you want to know," Sir William snapped suddenly. "Not that there's anything I can tell you. I don't know anything. I can't make it out. The very last thing I should have expected to happen, the very last. A quiet little place like this. I nearly walked across to the village to see what was being done, and then I thought you people would probably have your hands full, and I thought, too, perhaps you might be coming up here, as I knew young Kayne. Co-trustee, you know. So I made up my mind to stay in case I missed you. Always the way. Turn your back for two minutes and that's the moment someone calls. So I thought I wouldn't. I thought I would stop indoors just in case."

"You have not been out at all this morning then?" Bobby asked.

"Not a soul in the house been anywhere, none of us know anything except gossip—the postman and the milkman and the rest of them."

There seemed a discrepancy here, reflected Bobby. The butler had said that Sir William started out before breakfast, went as far as the wood, and then changed his mind and returned. But the difference was one susceptible of easy explanation. Sir William might only mean that he had not gone as far as the village, and he might easily consider that his uncompleted work was too un-important to mention. He might even have quite genuinely forgotten it for the moment. Nevertheless, a little disturbing that Mr. Adams, too, had denied having been out when he had in fact been at least as far as the wall post box, a few yards from the inn. No doubt, he, too, might have thought so brief an excursion not worth mentioning. This coincidence in forgetfulness seemed, however, to be worth remembering. Bobby went on to ask a few more routine questions and then said:

"I daresay you will remember seeing me in the Kayne library yesterday afternoon, just as Mr. Kayne left after he had been talking to you and Mr. Broast—a little heatedly, I thought."

Sir William, seated now fairly jumped in his seat. The man's nerves were on edge, Bobby thought. He seemed quite literally jumpy. Bobby reminded himself that he must not draw hasty conclusions. Murder of a friend, a neighbour, a co-trustee might well make any one nervous. Sir William stammered:

"Oh, was that you?... I saw some one... I didn't realize... you mean you noticed...?"

"Well, no one could help, could they?" Bobby said. "It was pretty evident there was some sort of quarrel, and that Mr. Kayne was very excited. I remember remarking that he looked quite murderous. Only it is he who has been murdered. Major Harley thought it would be as well to ask if you mind informing us what the dispute was about and why Mr. Kayne appeared so angry. It may be of help in our investigation. I am sure you understand that. My instructions are to ask you to make a statement in writing."

Sir William looked more and more uncomfortable. He fidgeted in his chair, he huddled down into it as if for all his size he hoped somehow that in it he might escape notice. At last he mumbled:

"Oh, it was nothing, nothing of any consequence."

"Of consequence enough," murmured Bobby gently, "to upset Mr. Nat Kayne. He appeared very disturbed."

"What I mean is," Sir William said reluctantly, "it was just the same old thing we have been over hundreds of times. Nat always lost his temper about it. Regular thing. He wanted the library sold. He didn't care or know anything about books, and he wanted his slice of the purchase money as soon as he could get it. Broast and I objected. Nor was it Miss Kayne's wish. Her desire and ours was to keep the library intact."

"With Miss Kayne, you, and Mr. Broast objecting, he had no chance of getting his way, I suppose?"

"Certainly not, not unless he could prove neglect—or—or anything unsatisfactory. The terms of the trust are quite clear. But he always lost his temper. Tried to bully. Naturally Broast resented it. So did I, for that matter."

"I suppose it would have meant a lot to Mr. Broast if there had been a decision to sell," observed Bobby. "He would have lost his post."

"Oh, well, as far as that goes, he would soon have had his choice of another," Sir William answered. "He is about the leading expert in his line in the world, I should think. Besides, in the event of a sale he is entitled to five years' salary as compensation. He gets £200 I think, though he doesn't always draw it."

"How is that?"

"Well, he lives at Wynton Lodge, he never takes a holiday, he buys a suit of clothes about once in five years, if he wants a little pocket-money he draws a few pounds on account of salary. I expect the library owes him a thousand or two. That, and the thousand he is entitled to as compensation, would enable him to start a business of his own. His reputation would soon make it go. Knows more about books and printing than any man alive, and I know enough about them to know that."

"You are an expert, too?" Bobby asked.

"Not like Broast," Sir William said. He seemed less nervous now. He even smiled. "Most of what I know, Broast has taught me. He has a nose for a rare book, smells 'em out, sort of sixth sense almost. Show him a pile of a hundred volumes and he'll pick out instinctively just the one that's really interesting. It's entirely thanks to him that my collection of first editions of the Caroline poets is complete—unique, I believe. I've the quarto illustrated Quarles no one else had ever heard of till Broast and I found it in a pile of uninteresting old stuff at Sotheby's—bought it for fifty shillings. No one knew it was Quarles. My Americana, too. I've the *Psalter* that was the first book ever printed in America, and the American *Sartor Resartus* that came out over there when no English publisher would look at it. My Edgar Allen Poe's, too. I've the 1827 *Tamerlane*, and a complete set of the *Southern Literary Messenger* which published much of his early work, as you remember."

Bobby could not truthfully say he remembered what he had never known. So he said nothing, and Sir William continued:

"That reminds me. Perhaps I ought to tell you poor Nat Kayne seemed worried about a letter he had received from some American visiting this country, from an hotel in London."

"Oh, yes," said Bobby, who thought this might be interesting.

But Sir William, though Bobby questioned him closely, knew nothing more about it. Nat Kayne had talked in a vague, excited way about having received such a letter, had seemed to think it might be important, but without explaining why, and had also said something about a coming personal interview with the writer. Neither Mr. Broast nor Sir William himself had paid much attention to him. Nat Kayne had tried vague bullying threats before in his attempts to force a sale. He had even got a firm of solicitors to write a stiff letter.

"Ridiculous, of course," said Sir William, "bluff, very weak bluff, too. Broast wrote back and told them not to make fools of themselves—said they might succeed in bluffing a poor widow or an ignorant working man, but he was neither, and they needn't try their dirty tricks with him. Hot correspondence. He told them finally that if they tried to carry out the inspection they talked about—of course, they had no right to do any such thing—he would turn the garden hose on them. Oh, I can tell you, when Broast gets his blood up—well, things happen."

And Bobby found himself wondering if murder was one of the things that happened when the fiery tempered librarian got his blood up. And he wondered, too, if this sidelight on Mr. Broast's character had been given intentionally. A quiet, shy, scholarly man to all appearance but in defence of his beloved library, what might he not be capable of? Bobby decided it was time to inquire into another point.

"I think you paid Mr. Broast a visit last night?" he said.

Again Sir William, whose manner had been growing more confident and assured, became alarmed. His nervousness returned, his eyes grew wary once again. He hesitated, and Bobby felt certain that his first impulse was to return a flat denial, but that then second thoughts told him denial would be useless.

"Yes," he said. "I walked over after dinner. I suppose that means I must have passed quite close to where the murder took place—not very pleasant."

"You walked—you didn't go by car?"

"No, I walked, I generally do when I'm going to the Lodge. It's as quick going through the wood as having to drive all round by the road, even without the trouble of getting out the car. I've no chauffeur, you know. Can't afford one."

"I was only wondering what made you change your mind?"

"Why? I didn't, I almost always walk, unless I'm going on somewhere else."

"I happened to be there when you rang up," Bobby explained. "I was talking to Mr. Broast when your message was given him. I am sure the word 'drive' was used, not walk."

Sir William looked faintly puzzled and shook his head.

"I am sure I said 'walk', not 'drive'," he repeated. "I rang up myself, and I am certain I said I would walk over. I had no intention of getting out the car."

"I see," said Bobby. "There is a path through the wood, I believe?"

"Two as a matter of fact. They both run into the sunk lane, one higher up than the other. It runs right on to Chapman's place—Longmeadow Farm. The other curves round a lot, joins a footpath to the high road and then ends up in the sunk lane."

"Which one did you take last night?"

"The lower one. There's not much in it. One is as short as the other. Sometimes I take one, sometimes the other. Last night I took the lower one. Why? Does it matter?"

"Impossible to say at present," answered Bobby. "The murderer can't have been far away. You saw nothing? heard nothing?"

"Nothing at all."

Sir William was quite clear about that. He insisted he had seen nothing, heard nothing. He hinted it would be a long time before he would care to come back alone through the wood at night. He hoped he was neither a coward nor superstitious. All the same, there would be no more taking those paths at night. As regards time he was not clear. He had not noticed. He believed he had started out about nine, but after rather than before. He did not walk fast. It would probably be about half-past nine when he emerged on the open space at the back of the Lodge where he had expected to meet Mr. Broast. On this occasion he had not seen the librarian, and after waiting a little he had decided they must have missed each other and he had returned home.

"Broast and I often met like that for a chat before turning in," Sir William explained. "That's why I am so sure I said I would walk. If I had said drive he would either have waited in for me or met me along the high road. Broast invariably goes out for a stroll before bed, says it's the only way he can be sure of sleeping. He has rather converted me to the same idea. I often do the same thing—take a stroll before bed, I mean. And if I have anything to talk over with Broast, any bibliographic point to consult him about or anything like that, I often meet him then, and we have our talk without any risk of being overheard. Once—it was before the time of the present secretary, Miss Perkins, you've seen her—we lost a superb example of the Aldine *Hypnerotomachia* through something the girl who was Broast's typist at the time let out. And another time it was a copy of the rare Tom Jones in boards I lost because Miss Kayne got talking—the Tom Jones edition in boards is worth perhaps a couple of hundred, you know, while a copy in leather any bookseller would be glad to sell you for a fiver. So now if we hear of anything we want, we prefer to talk it over when there's no chance of being overheard."

"You take an active interest in new acquisitions for the library?" Bobby remarked.

"We help each other, we work together," Sir William explained. "Collectors often do—make up the gaps on each other's shelves."

"I see," said Bobby. He wished he knew more about bibliography. It was all very interesting, but a little confusing, too, and hard to remember. Odd, for instance, that an edition bound in boards should be worth so much more than one bound in leather. He said:

"Was there anything special you wished to discuss with Mr. Broast last night?"

"No, nothing, only the little upset with Nat Kayne," answered Sir William, not too willingly Bobby thought.

"How long did you wait before giving Mr. Broast up?"

"Oh, about half an hour, I suppose. I remember hearing it strike ten. Then I came home."

"Through the wood, I understand?"

"It's the only way unless you go right round by the road."

"You didn't hear any shots?"

"No, I heard nothing. I don't suppose the sound would travel far in the wood, and I should be somewhere near the gate that leads into the Lodge grounds. I suppose I got in about half past ten or a quarter to eleven, and then I sat up reading before I went to bed. I came in by the side door. I didn't disturb anyone, no reason to. They are generally all in bed early, we're not late folk in the country."

Bobby calculated that, assuming this story to be true, Sir William had returned though the wood by the sunk lane and the path, during the interval between the discovery of the dying man by the gamekeeper, Len Hill, and Hill's return with the help from Longmeadow Farm he had gone to summon. By turning off at the lower path, as he said he had done, Sir William would miss by a few yards the actual scene of the murder, and presumably he would be indoors, or at any rate well away, before the Longmeadow party arrived. Only—was he speaking the truth?

Then, too, there was that odd discrepancy between his statement that he had not gone out this morning and the butler's account of his early stroll by the wood and the pond. If he had really intended to go to the village, surely he would have had some breakfast first? and why had he, after going out and changing his mind, not come straight back home, but instead gone round by the pond, two or three hundred yards out of his way? Had he expected or hoped to meet someone there? If so, whom? It was difficult, Bobby told himself, to find a threat connecting these things.

It would be necessary, too, to investigate this tale of a letter the dead man had received from an American visitor to London, and that had apparently so much excited him. Possibly Virtue might know something. Inquiries could be made in London, too.

When he had secured Sir William's somewhat reluctantly given signature to the note he had taken of this conversation, Bobby departed. On his motor-bicycle he covered the distance to the village at a rate of speed stimulated by the thought of luncheon, for it was growing late now and he was decidedly hungry. Slackening his speed he came into the village street and there, before the little police station, he saw Miss Kayne's not very modern car drawn up, with Olive sitting at the wheel. She opened the car door as she saw him approaching and he jumped down and went up to her. She said:

"Oh, Bobby, I am glad you've come. There's been a frightful scene between Miss Kayne and Mr. Broast, and she's talking so wildly and seems so strange. She says the library's been robbed, and it's Miss Perkins, and I'm sure it isn't, how could it be?"

"Miss Perkins?" Bobby repeated, and at that moment Miss Kayne came heavily out of the police station and stood on the threshold, filling the doorway completely with her enormous bulk, as she lifted her long ebony cane and pointed it directly at Bobby.

CHAPTER XIV
MUCH DISCUSSION

For a moment or two they all three remained like this, immobile, and Bobby heard Olive draw her breath sharply between her teeth. He knew she was experiencing a feeling of tension, of drama, and he shared it, and yet he did not know why, for what was there tense or dramatic in the sight of a fat old woman standing in a doorway, pointing with an ebony cane? He supposed, vaguely, it must come from some underlying excitement, some as it were subconscious knowledge of dark, strange currents lying just below the surface.

Miss Kayne lowered her cane and came quickly towards the car. Bobby noticed that for all the heaviness of her swollen body, the clumsiness of those enormous slippers in which her feet were still encased, she yet moved with an unexpected speed. It surprised him a little, for he remembered that in the house she had seemed to find it difficult to rise from her chair without help, to ascend the stairs to her room without labour and effort. In her thin, far off voice that seemed as though it only escaped from her with such difficulty, she said:

"Detective, what have you found out, detective?"

"Very little so far," Bobby acknowledged.

"Detectives never do," she told him. "No one ever finds out anything. Things find themselves out."

"I think that is true," Bobby agreed.

"Things find themselves out," she repeated, "and there's nothing that can stop them." She climbed into the car. "Not even detectives," she said, "not even if you bury them, not even if you forget them or try to but you can't. Major Harley will do his best to stop them coming out, of course, in spite of what I've told him. Forget-me-not is the flower detectives ought to wear. Remember that, young man. I'm tired. Olive, take me home."

"You won't mind if Olive comes back afterwards so we can have lunch here?" Bobby asked. "I'm staying on to see if I can be of any help, so I'm on duty, and I don't know when I shall have another chance to see anything of her."

"You mean you want to ask her about me?" Miss Kayne said. "No harm in that, though there's nothing she can tell you. You've heard about what was buried years ago? Olive's told you? You know? Or do you? Don't you? Shall you want to dig it up again?"

"I might perhaps," agreed Bobby calmly, "if I knew where to look."

"Find out, if you can," she retorted. "It's a detective's job. Olive knows, but then she has promised not to tell."

"She told me so," agreed Bobby.

"Take me home, it's tired me telling things to Major Harley," the old woman said again to Olive. To Bobby, she added:—"Perhaps some day I'll tell you myself, but I don't think I will."

"There are thing perhaps you might tell me about the library," Bobby remarked. "You know Mr. Virtue says he saw a dead man there last night."

"That was a lie," she said, "that was the truth. Do you understand, Mr. Clever Detective?"

"I think perhaps that I might make a guess," he answered gravely. "Now you've told me so much, won't you tell me some more? Will you tell me why you hate as you do anything so famous and so valuable as your library? Surely a collection of old books is harmless enough?"

She sat forward in her place and stared at him in silence. Then she said:

"I think the man is really clever. At any rate he knows what questions to ask, even if only a fool would think books were harmless. Why, they're deadly, that's why they are often censored and burnt." She leaned further forward. She almost whispered. She said: "Yes, I hate the place, and some day perhaps I'll burn it down. Olive, I'm tired, tired with talking to this young man of yours, tired with all I told Major Harley. Take me home. Then you can come back. She won't be long, young man."

She made a gesture of farewell. Olive started the car. Bobby watched them go. He had an idea that what she had said was extremely important and enlightening, and yet also he felt that he did not understand it. While the conversation was fresh in his mind he wrote it down, as nearly word for word as he could remember, in his note-book, and he thought that perhaps if he tried long enough and hard enough he might discover the meaning he felt sure lay hidden in it. What in especial had she meant by saying in the same breath that Virtue had told the truth, had told a lie, and then asking him if he knew what that meant? A challenge, he felt, to discover her true meaning, and he shook his head doubtfully as he told himself the challenge was one it was going to be difficult to meet successfully.

He reflected, too, that she had never said anything about Miss Perkins and the accusation of theft launched against her of which Olive had told him. Perhaps that had been mentioned to Major Harley and he was dealing with it. An improbable accusation, Bobby thought. If anything had been stolen from the library, how could Miss Kayne know it when she hardly ever entered the place? Mr. Broast would know if a single book were out of place, but apparently the accusation came from her and not from him. Then again, Miss Kayne hardly ever came in contact with Miss Perkins, so utterly distinct was the life of the library from that of the Lodge. Miss Perkins had lunch and tea there, it was true, but she had them alone, in the little anteroom where she did her typing.

He put his notebook back in his pocket and entered the building just as Major Harley came hurrying out, carrying in one hand a packet of sandwiches and with a bottle of beer sticking out of his pocket. He said to Bobby:

"Oh, it's you. Did you see that Kayne woman? She's mad. Insisted on seeing me. Then she never said a word. Sat there. Simply sat there and never opened her mouth."

"Oh," exclaimed Bobby, astonished, "why, she said she had told you—"

"Sat there," interposed the Major resentfully, "and never opened her mouth. Sat there like a Chinese Buddha. Never spoke a word sat there like a fat old hippopotamus and never got a word out. I asked her what she had come for, and then she got up and waddled off. Mad, quite mad."

"Yes, sir," said Bobby mechanically, his mind busy seeking some reasonable explanation, since he did not for one moment believe that Miss Kayne was mad. He went on: "Miss Farrar told me there had been some sort of quarrel or scene between Miss Kayne and Mr. Broast, and that Miss Kayne afterwards talked about Miss Perkins, and said she was dishonest—accused her of stealing books from the library, as far as I could make out."

"Miss Perkins? that's the typist woman, isn't it? Well, if she thinks so why doesn't she lay a complaint? Or does she mean she thinks Miss Perkins murdered Nat Kayne?"

"She didn't say so, sir," Bobby answered cautiously.

"It's worth considering," said the Major. "These sex-starved women…" He left the sentence unfinished except for shaking his head doubtfully. "Freud, you know," he said abruptly.

Bobby didn't know, so he made no reply, and the Major shook his head again.

"Anyhow, first glimpse of a motive we've had," he pronounced. "Very good looking young fellow, Nat Kayne. The girl is obsessed by him. She knows she has no chance. It grows on her. She can't have him in life. She will in death. Sex starved. That's it perhaps. Worth considering."

"Yes, sir," said Bobby, though what he meant was 'No, sir', for the suggestion did not seem to him much worth serious consideration.

"Oh, well," said the Major. "You saw Winders? Had he anything to say?"

"He agrees he was not far away at the time of the murder," Bobby answered. "He denies hearing any shots. He agrees there was constant difficulty with Nat Kayne, who was trying to force a sale of the library, but apparently with no chance of succeeding. Still, it was a constant source of quarrels between him and both Sir William and Mr. Broast. The most curious thing about that is that Miss Kayne seems to dislike the library intensely, and never enters it if she can help, and yet she supports the other two against Nat Kayne in refusing to consider selling. Inconsistent apparently. Another small inconsistency is that Sir William says he rang up to say he would walk over to meet Mr. Broast last night and the message as delivered was that he would drive over. That apparently is how he and Broast missed each other. Sir William also says that Mr. Nat Kayne seemed worried about a letter he had received from an American visiting London."

"Virtue," snapped the Major. "Follow that up. Anything else?"

"I don't think so, sir. I think I've mentioned all the points in Sir William's statement that seemed to me important. I have it here as he signed it. I expect it might be as well to ask him if he would care to amplify it later on."

"Very likely he will," agreed the Major. "Wonderful how people's memories improve at times. We'll see about that later. Get your lunch now. I've got to go to Mayfield—other things to attend to. Have to get my lunch in the car on the way. I'll read Winders's statement, too. I'll be back as soon as I can. Then we'll go and see Broast and hear what he has to say."

He nodded and departed. Bobby added his report of the morning's proceedings to the already formidable and always growing pile of documents dealing with the case, and then went on to the Wynton Arms, where Olive soon joined him.

"I don't know what to make of Miss Kayne," she told him, looking very worried, "or what she means about poor little Miss Perkins. I'm sure she wouldn't steal anything. I asked Mr. Broast, and he only laughed. I don't believe anyone could take a pen nib out of the library without his knowing."

"Well, let's feed," Bobby said, and during the meal he chatted resolutely of other things, though indeed they both found it difficult to keep out of their talk the one subject occupying their minds. Their meal finished and themselves established with cigarettes and coffee, Olive said:

"Bobby, tell me, why is all this happening as soon as you get here?"

"That," Bobby answered grimly, "is what I'm wondering—wondering quite a lot. It may be merely coincidence. Coincidences do happen, and very odd ones, too. Only it's so easy to say 'coincidence' and leave it at that. And if it isn't coincidence then there's a reason, and it's the reason we've got to dig up. Once we've got that, we shall know where we are—or have some idea. At present I've none. I suppose everyone in the place knew about my job?"

"I expect so," said Olive, looking a little self-conscious. "Everyone always seems interested. I don't say you're a C.I.D. man now when people ask me. I say you're a policeman, and then they look down their noses and think of me bringing you sandwiches and coffee in a thermos flask while you're directing traffic."

"If you did, you would get it in the neck," observed Bobby. "Policemen aren't supposed to need mundane things like sandwiches and coffee."

"Well, if it isn't coincidence, it's rather horrid," Olive said, frowning anxiously.

"There's one thing I wanted to ask you about perhaps you can help in," Bobby went on. "You know that yarn Virtue told us? You heard Miss Kayne say first it was a lie and then it was true, and I was to guess what that meant—Major Harley's guess, by the way, is that she's mad."

"She's not mad," Olive said slowly. "She's something—I don't know what."

"That's how I feel," agreed Bobby. "The funny thing about Virtue's story is that the rather full description he gave of the body in the library he says he saw, exactly resembles a photograph in Miss Perkins's possession she says is of her fiancé, though apparently he has gone back to America and she doesn't seem too confident of ever hearing of him again. Now, what does that mean, and what possible connection can there be between whatever it does mean and the murder of Nat Kayne? Virtue has never been in England before, Miss Perkins has never been in America, and Nat Kayne had nothing much to do with Miss Perkins, and apparently they had never seen Virtue."

"What do they say themselves?" Olive asked.

"Virtue seemed genuinely astonished, says he can't understand it or explain it. Miss Perkins will have to be questioned again. By the way, while I am thinking of it—there's a pond near Sir William Winders's place, isn't there?"

"Yes. Why? There used to be fish in it and I used to try to catch them when I was here years ago. I never did."

"Is it deep?"

"I don't think so. Not very. Why?"

"I was just wondering," Bobby answered. "To return to Miss Perkins. Major Harley is always talking about her being sex starved."

"It's very horrid of him," said Olive. "Why is it always women who are supposed to be sex starved? Why not men for a change?"

"Well, I suppose men needn't be if they don't want."

"Women needn't either, need they? Not now, not to-day. My gracious, walk along Piccadilly, if you're a girl, I mean, and see how many men are willing to relieve any symptoms of sex starvation. Piccadilly may not be flowing with milk and honey, but it certainly is with the most obliging men. Sex starvation, fiddlesticks."

"I suppose Major Harley doesn't quite mean that," observed Bobby.

"No, he's just muddled between the old kind of licence and the new. You can't starve in a world overflowing with fodder if you want it. Sex starvation is just a phrase invented by gentlemen who don't want to run any risk of suffering from it themselves, blast them. It's all a dodge to make women easy." Olive paused and snorted. "Silly," she said, "when we all are already. Only poor little Miss Perkins isn't like that. You can always tell."

"I suppose," agreed Bobby tolerantly, "she is rather a dull little thing."

"She needn't be if she didn't want," retorted Olive. "She's got quite good features and have you never noticed her teeth? They're lovely, perfect. If she had taken half the trouble about herself she must have gone to to learn shorthand and typing, she would be all right. If she permed her hair, and looked after her skin and dropped in a smile sometimes to show off her teeth, and attended to herself generally, and thought about her dress, and didn't wear those spectacles all the time—she only needs them for close work and pince-nez would do and make all the difference— she would look just as smart as anyone else. As it is—well," asked Olive in a voice of awe, "did you notice her hat? It was awfully rude of me, but I just couldn't help saying something."

"What did she say?"

"Oh, she just giggled in that silly way she puts on. I don't think she was a bit interested. She's the only girl I ever met who isn't—in hats I mean. As for men, you would think she didn't know they existed."

"Well, then," said Bobby, "how does that fit with her showing a photograph all round the village and telling everyone it's her fiancé?"

"It doesn't."

"Doesn't what?"

"Doesn't fit?"

"No, only it does, because it's what she did, so there you are. Only nothing seems to fit. Lots of odd things but none of them have any possible connection with Nat Kayne's death. They are all just on the fringe so to speak. I don't get it. There's another thing. At the Lodge when I was there Miss Kayne seemed hardly able to get out of her chair without help. When she was leaving the police station just now, she seemed quite nimble."

"Oh, she can get about quickly enough when she wants to," Olive answered, smiling a little. "She suspected one of the maids of having a key to her bureau and taking money and stamps from it. She let the girl see her in the garden and then nipped back into the house as quickly as anything and caught her in the act. It is difficult for her to get out of a chair or go upstairs, but on the level ground she gets about easily enough—when she wants to."

"I thought it was like that," observed Bobby. "She gives the idea of having a kind of reserve of energy—a sort of hidden heat she can turn into action if she wants to. Do you remember what time she went up to bed last night?"

"We said good night as soon as you had gone. I went into the dining-room for a book, and when I came back she had gone upstairs. I didn't notice the time exactly."

"You couldn't say for certain that she did actually go upstairs then?"

"No. I suppose she did. Why shouldn't she? She said she was. Why? Oh, Bobby, you don't mean you think it might be—her. Oh, that's horrible."

"I don't think it," Bobby hastened to re-assure her. "It's only that we've got to consider everything. If Miss Kayne can get about as quickly as it seems she can, it would have been possible for her to get from the Lodge to the sunk lane and back again in the time. There's not the least indication that she did. And I suppose she has a motive. It's her library and Kayne was trying to force a sale."

"It's too terrible to think of," Olive said.

"Don't think of it," Bobby told her. "Besides, she seems to hate the very thought of the library. Perhaps she really wants it sold and was backing up Nat Kayne on the quiet."

"Why should she?" Olive said. She added: "She's been so strange all day—ever since we heard. She keeps saying one thing leads to another. Why does she say that? What does it mean?"

"It's true enough anyway," Bobby said. "One thing does lead to another. Broast will have to be questioned next."

"I would much rather think it was him," Olive muttered. "I don't like him."

"Well, I think he is a more likely choice myself," agreed Bobby, "but there's not enough to go on yet. He has a motive of sorts, too, —not that Nat Kayne had much chance of forcing a sale apparently, but he may have got on Broast's nerves, always talking about it. One never knows. Fixed idea of sale on Nat Kayne's part, fixed idea of stopping him in Broast's mind. It might be. That would make Broast the most likely person. Of course, there's Virtue, too. Or Mr. Adams. Miss Perkins seems to be Major Harley's choice."

Olive smiled faintly.

"Poor Major Harley," she said, "he's terribly worried, and I don't think he is very clever. Anyhow, you can tell him Miss Perkins is no more sex starved than she is food starved."

CHAPTER XV
THE STOLEN REVOLVER

When Bobby returned to the little village police station that had become, for the time being at least, the centre of the investigation, he found Major Harley returned from

Mayfield and very deeply immersed in the report of Superintendent Killick, the officer in charge of this district, to whom had been delegated the duty of visiting Nat Kayne's home and endeavouring to secure there any information that might throw light on the circumstances or the motive of the murder.

"Not much in it," decided the Major at last. "Nothing to help that I can see. No trace of correspondence with Virtue. Lived with his mother and a sister. Did a bit of farming—dairy, chiefly. Director of a company, 'Gay Doings, Ltd.,' owning two or three roadhouses. Said to dabble a bit in stock and share dealing, and generally believed to be pressed for money. Explains why he wanted the library sold, so that he could get his share in cash, but not much guidance otherwise. Not known to have any love affairs. Good reputation generally, but not much liked. Bit quarrelsome, apparently, argumentative sort of person, but nothing known of any serious trouble. Had an important engagement that night after dinner with the chairman of 'Gay Doings', who had promised to call when motoring past on his way somewhere else. There was some talk of extending 'Gay Doings" operations apparently. Kayne was keen on it, and was very disappointed when the chairman rang up to say he couldn't call that night as he had been delayed in starting and it would make him too late to stop at Kayne's place, Kayne told his sister it was only a put off to avoid making a decision. He seemed angry and restless, and after a time said he would walk over to Wynton as he believed Broast and Winders were up to something and he would try to catch them out. Nothing there to help us, I'm afraid. We knew before there was bad feeling between Kayne and the others, and we knew he was shot on the way to the Lodge. Leaves us just where we were."

"Yes, sir," said Bobby. "May I see the report, sir?" he asked, for it seemed to him that it established at least one fact that might be of extreme significance, both in itself and because it carried with it implications of still greater importance.

The Major handed it to him. A constable came in to say Major Harley was wanted on the 'phone, from the Coroner's office at Mayfield. As there was no extension, the chief constable had to go to the instrument to answer the call. When he came back he said to Bobby, still busy with the report:

"Well? Noticed anything?"

"Sorry, sir," Bobby answered. "I'm trying to think it out. I'm afraid I'm a bit slow," he added apologetically. "I always have to mull things over before I can get them clear in my mind."

"Being quick is everything in police work," said the Major severely. "In my opinion speed is the essence of detection." He was rather pleased with this aphorism, and decided to remember it for future use, perhaps at the next meeting of chief constables; and Bobby said 'Yes, sir' in a very respectful voice, and continued to let the details of Superintendent Killick's report turn over and over in his mind in that kind of half unconscious manner which sometimes, but only sometimes, ends in bringing the truth uppermost.

"The inquest date is settled, anyhow," the Major went on. "Day after to-morrow, but it'll be purely formal to allow of the burial taking place. There'll be an adjournment to allow us to continue inquiries. The next thing, I think, will be to push along and see if Broast can tell us anything useful. We shall have to find out, too, where he was around about ten o'clock last night. Perhaps we ought to have seen him first. He'll have had time to think out a story if he wants to."

"He would have had time to do that anyhow," Bobby pointed out. "And if any one starts telling lies, it's always a useful pointer."

"Yes, if we can find out they are lies," agreed the Major in a very gloomy and doubtful voice, and Bobby refrained from remarking that distinguishing between lies and truth was precisely their business.

When they arrived at Wynton Lodge, Briggs, the butler, informed them that Miss Kayne had retired to her room, Miss Farrar was somewhere in the grounds, and Mr. Broast was in the library as usual. He conducted them there, and in the small anteroom left them in the charge of Miss Perkins, who looked up from her typing to greet them with her customary nervous giggle.

"Oh, I'm so sorry," she said. "Is it about the photograph? have you brought it back? what does Mr. Virtue say?"

"He identifies it as resembling the man he states he saw here last night, dead or seriously injured," answered the Major. "He has no explanation to offer."

"Oh, I'm so sorry," said Miss Perkins, "but I haven't either."

"Such a coincidence," the Major told her sternly, "requires an explanation. I am afraid we shall find it necessary to question you further."

Miss Perkins merely produced again that exasperating giggle. The Major glared and then asked if Mr. Broast was disengaged. Miss Perkins said, "Oh, yes, certainly," and as they passed through from the anteroom into the library proper, she added to Bobby:

"It's Mr. Virtue you ought to ask questions."

"Oh, we shall," Bobby promised her, and then she giggled again, and said it was that way, please, and they would find Mr. Broast at his desk.

"You know," the Major said to Bobby as they proceeded in the direction indicated, "it's a bit awkward. Nothing much we can do if a man invents a silly yarn about a corpse where there certainly isn't one, or if a girl likes to pretend a photograph she's got hold of is the sweetheart she hasn't got but wishes to goodness she had."

"No, sir," agreed Bobby, "only I would like to know how Virtue came to describe the original of the photograph and who that original is."

"Must try to find out if he ever had a chance to see it," the Major remarked. "The girl seems to have shown it about pretty freely. Perhaps he heard it described."

They had paused to exchange these whispered remarks, but now they came to the open alcove at the end of the library where Mr. Broast worked. He was busy with a 'block' book, technical points of which he was noting down to use as evidence in support of his belief that printing from movable type was in clear line of development from these early 'block' books printed from whole blocks in which letters had been carved. He received his two visitors without surprise, waved them to chairs, returned to his place behind the writing table so heaped with piled up papers and pamphlets like columns, book after book one on top of another, as to remind one of many-towered Ilium, and said:

"It's about this tragic affair, I suppose. I'm afraid there's nothing I can tell you. But I understand there's some wild tale about a dead man having been seen here—does that mean Nat Kayne? How could that be possible? and there's something about a photograph... isn't there?"

Major Harley produced it.

"Do you recognize this at all?" he asked.

Mr. Broast took it. He put it on the table before him. Resting his chin on his hands he stared at it long and thoughtfully, nor could Bobby, watching him intently, detect any sign of emotion, yet none the less felt sure that to the librarian it conveyed some meaning. His eyes still fixed upon the picture, he said:

"Will you leave it here? I should like you to leave it here."

"I'm afraid we can't do that," the Major said, and then he added: "Why?"

"I thought I might remember," Mr. Broast said. He got to his feet. His eyes were still upon the photograph. He said: "If I ever knew any one like that, I've forgotten." He made a slow gesture of a deep contempt. "I have other things to think of more important," he said, "but if you left it here I would keep it on my table and perhaps I might remember." He shrugged his shoulders. "The past is past," he said; "and if it returns what does it matter? Take it away."

As he spoke he picked up the photograph and with a gesture of something like defiance handed it back to the Major.

"That's all as far as I'm concerned," he said. "Where did it come from?"

The Major did not answer. He said instead:

"We understand there was some kind of quarrel or dispute between Mr. Kayne and yourself and Sir William Winders. Could you give us particulars?"

"He wanted us to sell. Both Sir William and Miss Kayne objected. That's all. Sir William was a little impatient, naturally, at the way in which Mr. Kayne would insist on bringing up something that had been decided over and over again. Sir William got quite cross yesterday. He told Kayne he was behaving like a fool. Kayne made some sort of insolent retort. They both lost their tempers. Of course Kayne was entirely in the wrong. He had no business to keep on worrying like that. Quite ridiculous."

"What was your own attitude?" asked the Major.

"In my opinion selling would be an almost criminal act of folly," answered Mr. Broast at once. "Not that my opinion matters. I'm a paid servant of the library. Miss Kayne is the owner. Winders and Nat Kayne are the joint trustees—were I suppose I should say now. Miss Kayne has complete control, and the trustees have merely powers of inspection."

"Who takes Mr. Nat Kayne's place? Do you know?"

"I rather think I do," the librarian answered, though with some reluctance. "I really am not sure. Perhaps only for the time. I should have to refer to the will to be sure."

The Major went on to ask a few more questions. Mr. Broast's replies only confirmed what they knew already. Regarding his own movements, he explained that he had gone to his room almost immediately after dinner on the previous night, in order to attend to his correspondence. It was his habit to speak his letters into a Dictaphone, Miss Perkins typing them afterwards from the records. He finished fairly early, about half past nine or a quarter to ten, he supposed, and then he had waited for a time, expecting Sir William, who had rung up to say he was driving over for a chat. That was not unusual. They had many interests in common, apart from Sir William's position as library trustee. After a time he assumed that Sir William must have changed his mind, or that something or another had prevented him from carrying out his intention. It was, Mr. Broast explained, his own invariable custom to take a brisk walk before bed as a means of inducing sleep, and he had gone out as usual, soon after ten, probably, as soon as he felt it was useless waiting any longer. So far as he knew no one saw him go. He remembered looking into the drawing-room, but it was empty, and he took it that the two ladies had gone to bed. Briggs and the maids were presumably in their own quarters. He had not seen them, and he supposed they had not seen him. He had been out his usual thirty or forty minutes, and on his return had entered by the front door, which was unlocked as usual. He locked and bolted it on his return, also as usual. So far as he knew no one had heard or seen him. No reason why anyone should. His habits were well known and well established. His evening walk before bed was his sole outdoor exercise, and it was quite regular. So far as he knew no one could confirm his statements, but was confirmation really necessary? Mr. Nat Kayne was an extraordinarily ignorant and uncultivated young man but one to whom Mr. Broast had no ill will. He would pick up a rare first edition and handle it as though it were a shilling magazine just bought from a railway book-stall. He was inclined to be bumptious, and aggressive, too, but he had little to do with the library except on inspection days, and even then seldom had much to say to Mr. Broast.

"He really thought," explained Mr. Broast, "that a librarian was just a clerk with a certain knowledge of books, exactly as a man in a bank is a clerk with a certain knowledge of figures. His ignorance was too gross even to be offensive. I really believe his chief interest in life was football pools. I understand he spent four or five shillings every week, and a very great deal of time, over them, and was highly elated when on one occasion he won one of the prizes offered."

"He won something once?" exclaimed the Major, much impressed, for indeed he had never before heard of such a thing.

"I gather all his forecasts were correct on that occasion, so he won what they call the pool. Very remarkable. His share came to seven and ninepence, as a great many others were correct that week, too. He was very excited by his success, he thought it highly encouraging."

Bobby, frowning over his notebook, wondered if the librarian had really been as indifferent to Nat Kayne's activities as he now pretended. Suppose, for example, there had been hints of Miss Kayne being inclined to yield to her cousin's importunities? True, there had been no sign of that as far as seemed to be known. But Broast might have been aware of under-currents unknown to others. Again, had Broast really been as little touched by Nat Kayne's ill-bred behaviour as he now claimed? He had used the word 'offensive'. And had he really remained entirely aloof from the quarrels between the two trustees? It was to be remarked, too, that the alibi he put forward had no independent evidence to support it, and he admitted having finished his letters in time for him to have reached the scene of the murder by ten. Apparently it would have been easy for him to slip both out and in again unperceived.

On one point Mr. Broast was emphatic. He repudiated with scorn the mere possibility of there being even a modicum of truth in Virtue's story.

"Barefaced lie, pure invention," he declared. "The shutters were closed, and how could he see through them? Even if the shutters had been opened again, which they weren't, for there was no one to do it, he could have seen nothing in the dark."

"He suggested," remarked Bobby, "that the light might have come from a strong electric torch."

"Nonsense," snapped Mr. Broast. "Just a pack of lies. There's a lot of rare valuable stuff here. That's what he was after. Hired by some rascally collector perhaps—some of them would stop at nothing. Or perhaps he's a collector himself. The tale he told was his first move. He was trying to get in here when I wasn't present. Then, while your men were searching for a dead body that didn't exist, would be his opportunity to pocket something."

The Major looked impressed. Put like that, it sounded plausible. He remembered, too, that Virtue had admitted that one of his relatives was 'crazy' about books and first editions and so on. Perhaps that relative was himself. There had been, too, his insistence on his right, as he had called it, to be present at the search he demanded. All very suggestive. Major Harley glanced at Bobby, who, as a matter of fact, was thinking on much the same lines. He said:

"We are of course considering every possibility. A cable has been sent, asking for information about Mr. Virtue's identity and standing, though at present there does not seem much reason to think he is concerned in the murder. There is one more little matter and then I think we shan't have to worry you any more at present, though I'm afraid I can't promise we won't return. It's possible there may still be information you can help us with. We have not been able to find the pistol used, so as a matter of routine we are checking all we know of. Apparently Kayne was shot with a three-two, and I think I'm right in saying you have a permit for a Colt revolver, a three-two?"

"Yes, it's here," answered Mr. Broast, pointing to one of the drawers of his writing table. "Very necessary. We have to admit the public once a month. Anyone could easily lay hands on items worth thousands of pounds."

"I suppose you've missed nothing lately?" the Major asked.

"Certainly not," snapped Mr. Broast. "I take my precautions. That is what I have a revolver for—in case of emergencies. I know how to use it, too. I took lessons."

The Major glanced at Bobby. This seemed finally to dispose of the vague accusations Miss Kayne had seemed to want to make against the little typist. Mr. Broast closed with a bang the drawer he had been looking in and opened another. He said:

"It ought to be there. Of course, any thief would have to know what to take and what to leave." He pointed to a shelf near. "One of those books," he said, "is the Caxton *Dictes*, almost perfect copy—mint condition. It would fetch a nice little sum at auction if anyone got the chance and knew enough to pick it out."

"Most interesting," murmured the Major, looking at the indicated shelf and wondering which was the volume referred to, since to him they all seemed much alike. He added: "You won't mind our taking your pistol away for examination?"

"No. I can't see it," Mr. Broast said. He opened yet another drawer. He closed it and looked at them. "It's gone," he said uneasily. "It's been taken. Someone's stolen it."

CHAPTER XVI
THE PHOTOGRAPH AGAIN

In spite of the sharp questioning to which he was subjected, Mr. Broast either could or would tell them no more. The revolver had been there and now it had vanished, and that was all knew. He was not even certain when he had seen it last. Not for some days he thought. He scowled and frowned a good deal, too, at the questioning to which he was subjected—he was certainly not blessed with the most equable of tempers—and often returned testy answers. Finally he refused flatly to say anything more, and tried to order the Major and Bobby out of the library, whereupon he had to be reminded sharply that a case of murder was under investigation.

"If you take that attitude, Mr. Broast," Major Harley said, "I shall certainly 'clear out' as you express it, but you will accompany me. I shall detain you for inquiries. Before you force me into action of that kind, I suggest you had better think well."

"You have no right to do any such thing," almost shouted Mr. Broast. "You've no warrant."

"I don't need a warrant," retorted the Major, "to detain a person under grave suspicion of complicity in murder who refuses to answer questions."

Mr. Broast had been standing up and hammering on the table with his clenched fists, had indeed looked almost as if preparing to launch a physical attack on them in spite of his age and the fact that they were two and he only one. But at this he sat down abruptly. His face, flushed with anger, turned very pale. Trembling a little, his voice stammering and low and different indeed from the tone he had been using, he said:

"Good God, you don't mean you think I shot young Kayne?"

"You are under the gravest suspicion, much intensified by your present attitude," retorted the Major.

"Why on earth do you suppose I should want to do anything like that?" demanded the librarian. "I had hardly anything to do with him."

"It's not a question of 'why' at present," answered the Major. "It's still a question of 'who.' The murder was committed with a three-two revolver. You are known to have had one in your possession and you are unable to produce it. You are unable to offer any independent confirmation of your statement that you were in your room at the moment of the murder. Mr. Kayne was a trustee of the library and on his death you take his place."

Broast was fidgeting nervously with the various articles on his desk. He said after a pause:

"It's simply absurd to suppose I had anything to do with it. Why should I? The trustee business is merely formal— merely a precaution against Miss Kayne marrying some-one unsuitable. I'm sorry if I lost my temper. I apologize. I'm afraid I didn't understand. I never, never in my wildest dreams," he declared with emphasis, "expected to be under suspicion for murder." He paused again, glaring at them challengingly. He gave a harsh laugh. "I suppose next," he said, "I shall be accused of murdering the original of that photograph you've got there. It wouldn't surprise me. Is that the next item?" he asked with a dark irony.

"All we require at present is that you should answer the questions put you," the Major retorted. "You may refuse to do so. You may require the presence of a lawyer if you wish. You understand that our questions are connected with our inquiry into the murder of Mr. Nat Kayne. Are you willing to answer them or do you refuse?"

"Certainly, certainly I am perfectly willing," Mr. Broast answered now. "I must apologize again. I am afraid I didn't quite understand at first. If you really think I murdered young Kayne or the man whose photograph you've got there and that I've hidden the body—well, you are perfectly welcome to look on all the shelves to see if I've got it tucked away somewhere behind the books. To me, this young American's story sounds obvious invention. If you think differently, if you take seriously this tale of something seen through thick shutters in the dark—" He shrugged his shoulders with an evident sneer. "After all," he said, "it should be easy to find a hidden body here. I haven't had much time to hide it, have I?"

The Major paid no attention to this. He asked a good many more questions, repeating some of them over again, but he always got the same answers, and he got no further information. Probably, Mr. Broast agreed, everyone knew he possessed a pistol. Probably most of them knew where he kept it. Most of them could have taken it, if they wished, and waited their opportunity. Young Kayne himself, for that matter, or his co-trustee, Sir William.

"The ladies as well," went on Mr. Broast. "Miss Kayne, Miss Farrar," this last name he accompanied by a malicious glance at Bobby, "my typist, Miss Perkins, the rest of the servants, including the charwomen who come in to clean, that sham American professor, Mr. Adams—I suppose it would not occur to you he might be worth questioning?"

"He has been interrogated," the Major answered. "Anyone else?"

Mr. Broast added the names of one or two other visitors.

"Including," he finished with emphasis, "the young man whose preposterous story seems to interest you so much, who says he saw a dead body here at the moment when there was actually a dead body not far away. To my mind, highly suggestive."

Major Harley observed that the point had not been overlooked, and after one or two more questions he and Bobby retired. Mr. Broast made no attempt to accompany them to the door, and when he and the Major reached it, Bobby looked back and saw Mr. Broast standing there in the shadows at the further end of the library, watching their departure. It was growing late now, and in that dark and airless place of gloom, cut up by the transverse book-cases into little bays where all day long the light was dim, already the coming night lay heavily. This library seemed to Bobby no place of peace and calm and learning, but of lurking evil, a place of darkness and old death, a place of hidden whispers and secret device, and the aged, white-haired librarian, standing there in the distance, watching them with a malign intentness, gave him the impression of an ancient spider for ever spinning webs in which his victims were to be entangled.

Major Harley, unimaginative army man as he was, seemed to experience something of the same feeling.

"Wants some air here, some light, too," he muttered. "I don't like the place. I don't like the man. Inhuman. He would commit a murder as easily as you or I would eat our dinners."

"Only," said Bobby thoughtfully, "not without cause."

He turned abruptly and walked back towards Broast. He had seen him lift his hand. He had seen something gleam in it. As he approached the librarian raised his hand again, and again there was something bright and hard in it. Bobby walked on. Broast slipped away behind some book cases. Bobby paused. Broast appeared again from behind. He had slipped round somehow. His smile was dark and thin. He was holding in his hand a small electric torch. Bobby wondered if it was that he had seen or if it had been something else. Broast said:

"You have forgotten something?"

"Not at all," Bobby answered, looking at him steadily.

If it had been a pistol in his hand, the weapon had probably now been well hidden. Bobby went back to the Major.

"I thought I saw a small pistol in his hand," he explained. "When I got up to him, he was holding an electric torch. If it was a pistol I saw, he hid it again."

"Oh, well," the Major said thoughtfully.

They opened the heavy, fireproof door and went into the ante-room where Miss Perkins was sitting before her typewriter, though she was making no attempt to use it. She looked up when they entered, and then got to her feet with her accustomed giggle.

"Oh, I'm so sorry," she said, "but I couldn't help hearing a little—I mean, when Mr. Broast was talking. He has such a penetrating voice, hasn't he? especially when he's at all upset."

"I shouldn't have thought anything could have been heard through that door when it was shut," observed the Major, looking at it.

"Oh, no, only it wasn't shut, it was open," explained Miss Perkins, giggling again. "I'm so sorry, but it was."

"How was that?" demanded the Major.

Miss Perkins did not explain. Instead she said:

"So I couldn't Help hearing, could I? It's so dreadful about Mr. Broast's pistol being lost, isn't it? Only I'm sure you can't think he would murder Anyone—not even Mr. Kayne, even if he did Dislike him so much."

"Why do you think he did?" demanded the Major sharply.

"Mr. Broast always said so himself," answered Miss Perkins, "only of course he didn't Mean it—I mean to say, not like that. Because if people murdered everyone they disliked, it would be so Dreadful, wouldn't it?" She stopped to giggle again, and then went on: "Oh, I'm so sorry, only I do think now, though it's most Unpleasant, perhaps I ought to confess."

"Confess?" snapped the Major, startled. "Miss Perkins, please remember this is a serious matter."

"Oh, yes, indeed it is, isn't it? that's just what I've been thinking," said Miss Perkins, looking more like a frightened canary than ever, too frightened even to produce her accustomed giggle. "Only of course it isn't Really important, only it isn't Quite True what I told you about the photograph, I mean to say, about its being his, because I haven't got one, not of him, and I daresay now he never really meant it, and when I told people they didn't very often look as if they believed it, so when I found the photograph, and Mrs. Somerville didn't know who it was, and hadn't ever seen it, and no one else here had ever seen it either, I thought it might have been him if I had ever had one, and so I mean to say I said it was him, and he really was an American gentleman, and when I saw this one had New York on the back, I thought perhaps it was Meant, so I didn't think it was Really Wrong, at least not very. I mean to say, with me expecting a letter every day, and always looking in the paper to see when the post was in from America."

"Good God," said the Major feebly, looking at Bobby as though asking for help to stand up against this torrent of words to which Bobby himself had been listening with close attention.

"May I put a few questions, sir?" he asked, and when the Major nodded a relieved assent Bobby proceeded to try to disentangle the facts that Miss Perkins's involved observations seemed to contain somewhere.

Ultimately it emerged that Miss Perkins had no special reason to think Mr. Broast disliked the dead man, other than the fact that a good deal of quarrelling went on between them all, the two trustees and the librarian, jointly, variously, and severally. Nat Kayne was quarrelsome argumentative, and resentful. Sir William was authoritative and bullying. Mr. Broast was prickly, hated interference, contemptuous of all opinions that did not coincide with his own. Fertile breeding ground for displays of bad temper, but hardly for murder, Bobby thought. As regards her own corrected story she now told, Miss Perkins insisted that she had, in fact, been very friendly with a young American during her term of employment in London. He had taken her out a few times to dinners and theatres. What grounds had really existed for her belief that he was actuated by anything more than a good-natured sympathy for a pathetically lonely and helpless woman, did not appear. A few kisses seemed to have passed, nothing more. But Bobby, watching her more attentively now, remembered what Olive had said about Miss Perkins's potential good looks being quite up to the average if she would only try to make the best of herself. He noticed specially the perfection of form and regularity of her small white teeth Olive had mentioned. After all, there are few girls who do not possess at any rate a share of attractiveness, real ugliness is as rare as great beauty, even though Miss Perkins did seem as much inclined to emphasize her bad points as are most of her sex to bring out their good ones. She admitted quite frankly though that there had been nothing of the nature of a formal engagement.

"We understood each other," she said, and seemed to think that was all that was required.

Then the young man returned to America, promising to write, and assuring her he would be back soon. Even at the time when she came to take up her new post in the Kayne library, she was growing uneasy at his prolonged absence and silence. She had already declared herself engaged, Mr. Broast having complained, at their first interview, of her predecessor's interest in young men that had interfered with attention to work. So Miss Perkins had told him he need not be afraid of that in her case as she was already engaged. She told Mrs. Somerville the same thing when engaging her room, but Mrs. Somerville, more curious than Mr. Broast, had asked questions. When, therefore, Miss Perkins found, pushed away behind a drawer in a wardrobe in the room given her, a photograph of an attractive young man, taken in America, she had apparently regarded it as a kind of omen or promise. While she was still looking at it, she said, Mrs. Somerville came into the room, and at once jumped to the conclusion that it was the 'young gentleman' Miss Perkins had spoken of. Certain doubts Mrs. Somerville had not entirely concealed being thus laid to rest, Miss Perkins had allowed her assumption to go uncorrected, and had afterwards shown the photograph to others in the village to make sure she was safe in adopting it as that of her missing fiancé.

"I'm so sorry," she told them, when at last all this had been elicited by Bobby's patient questioning, "I know it wasn't quite nice, but then he really did promise me his photo, and I'm sure he only forgot, or else he would, and so I thought it wouldn't be Really Wrong to pretend. I used to put it on my table at the library sometimes, it was so Comforting, if you know what I mean, when I was feeling low or Mr. Broast was more cross than usual. Of course, I never let him see it, but I do remember it was on the table once when Mr. Virtue was there, asking if he might see over the library, only Mr. Broast wouldn't let him, and he was looking at it—Mr. Virtue, I mean—so I told him who it was— at least, I mean to say, I told him who I said it was."

This story finally got down in more or less coherent form and Miss Perkins's signature to it obtained, the Major and Bobby departed. Once outside, the Major said:

"Well, I don't see that her story helps much, but it does clear up one point—how the little fool got hold of the photograph and why Virtue's description corresponded with it."

"Yes, sir," Bobby agreed, though in a troubled and worried voice, for there were points in the story as she had told it that did not seem to him quite consistent, and yet he did not see what bearing it could have upon the main problem of Nat Kayne's murder.

Major Harley did not seem fully satisfied either, or else he noticed the hesitation in Bobby's voice.

"Well, if she's lying, what's she lying for?" he demanded irritably. "Doesn't seem to link up anywhere that I can see."

"No, sir," answered Bobby. "Only I can't help thinking there's a lot more to this case than we've any idea of yet—a lot going on behind the scenes, cross currents, old hidden enmities and motives, things like that. I can't help getting the idea that it's all centred on the library somehow, though I can't imagine how."

The Major grunted and muttered and growled uneasily and inaudibly. Finally he said aloud:

"Can't see it—nothing more innocent than a library surely, lots of old books dating from the year one, most of them."

"Yes, sir," agreed Bobby. "I know a library doesn't seem quite a likely centre for crime—murder. Only—" He turned and stared at the building they had just left, and his eyes were dark and heavy with thought. "I can't help feeling, too," he said, "that the Nat Kayne murder is only on the fringe. There are so many little points that seem as if they ought to give a lead somehow if we could only find it, and yet none of them seem to point towards Nat Kayne. For one thing, if Virtue had seen that photo before, why did he seem so surprised when we showed it him—rather more than surprised, indeed."

"Put on," growled the Major. "They're all of them keeping things back, like that Adams fellow. I'll get the truth out of him, though, somehow, or I'll charge him as an accessory before the event."

"I think that would be a good plan," agreed Bobby. "There's another thing. I've been thinking over Mr. Killick's report, and there's one point seems interesting."

"I know," said the Major, interrupting with a smile, "I've been doing a bit of thinking myself—can't leave it all to you young yard men. You mean that it shows Kayne's decision to walk over to the Lodge, through the wood, was taken quite unexpectedly, so that the murder couldn't have been premeditated. I think the answer is simple. The murder was premeditated, but not the occasion. That presented itself quite unexpectedly, and was at once seized on. I think everything suggests the murder had been contemplated and prepared for, and then an opportunity came along and was taken. That's all."

This was not quite what Bobby himself had meant, but he decided that though the possibility suggested to him by the Killick report differed from that put forward by the Major, yet perhaps he had better not attempt to explain further, especially while it and its implication all remained so vague, so unformed in his mind.

CHAPTER XVII
REVOLVER FOUND

All this questioning, of the old librarian and of his typist, had taken so long that there was little time left for anything further to be done that day. Major Harley, indeed, had plenty to occupy him in the shape of ordinary routine work, and in reading various reports to hand concerning other aspects of the investigation. Then, too, Superintendent Killick had to be seen and consulted, the withdrawal of so many men from ordinary work involving a complete re-casting of duties.

The chief constable, therefore, had plenty to occupy his time, but Bobby was left with no more definite instructions than to stand by, think things over, and report again first thing in the morning. So he went back to the Wynford Arms to get some tea and have a rest, and also partly to assure himself that young Virtue and Mr. Adams were still there, though indeed he knew precautions were in force to prevent either of them taking an unnoticed departure.

That, however, neither of them had shown any sign of wishing to attempt, and when Bobby reached the inn they were both there, sitting together over tea cups and cigarettes and engaged in what seemed earnest and confidential conversation. They stopped talking as soon as Bobby appeared, and seemed to expect him to join them, but that he did not do, contenting himself with a nod and word of greeting as he passed.

Natural and to be expected, no doubt, that they should have much to talk over, even though hitherto they had been complete strangers, since both were concerned in some measure in what had happened, and both were under some degree of suspicion—Virtue on account of the doubtful and unsupported tale he had told, Adams because of his calm admission that he had given a false description of himself in an attempt to secure admission to the library, and of his refusal to offer any explanation.

Bobby seated himself in a corner and ordered tea and scones. He saw Virtue and Adams whispering together and looking at him. He took no notice. Then Mr. Adams got up and came towards him.

"May I venture to inquire," he said in his precise, formal way, "if there is any likelihood of the situation becoming sufficiently clarified to allow of my taking my departure in the near future?"

"None at all," said Bobby cheerfully.

Mr. Adams sighed.

"I should be loath," he said, "to question your right to inflict upon any citizen this kind of prohibition of his movements, but I must consider my position. Mr. Virtue informs me he is willing to stay around, as he expresses it, until the case cracks, which I understand means until a satisfactory solution is arrived at. But for me the inconvenience is considerable."

"Then why not," Bobby asked him, "tell us the truth? If I were running the inquiry," he added, though not quite truthfully, "you would have been before the magistrates already, on a charge of being an accessory before the fact."

"That would be most unpleasant," observed Mr. Adams sedately, with no sign of undue alarm; "a situation so repugnant indeed I can hardly conceive. But I am unable to—er—speak the truth as you express it, with, if I may say so, a certain crudity, a certain lack of courtesy even, some might hold. I am between—er—the devil and the deep sea, if I may employ a well known locution."

He paused, shook his head, sighed deeply. Bobby said.

"Meaning the police by the first term?"

"On that point," said Mr. Adams, with mild but firm decision, "I must request you to be so good as to draw your own conclusions, which I shall beg leave neither to confirm nor to dispute."

"What about the deep sea?" asked Bobby.

Mr. Adams turned pale. He seemed far more affected, far more frightened, than he had been by Bobby's hint of a possible arrest and charge. But he made no reply, and went back to join Virtue, to whom he began to talk in low whispers, with occasional glances in Bobby's direction. They might have been complete strangers before, Bobby thought, but they certainly seemed on confidential and intimate terms now. He wondered if there could be any truth in the theory that had seemed to put itself forward once or twice, to the effect that these two were accomplices in some elaborate plan to secure burglarious possession of some of the Kayne library treasures. A rare book differs in this from other artistic and antiquarian treasures that while, say, a Holbein miniature is unique, there is no reason why another copy or two of perhaps the first edition of Bunyan's *Pilgrim's Progress* should not be found any day in any attic. Impossible often to prove, if some such work were stolen and then offered for sale, that it was identical with the stolen book, and not merely another copy recently discovered by a bit of good luck. Bobby was still turning over this possibility in his mind when there appeared one of the waitresses with a telegram that had just arrived for Mr. Adams. Bobby saw him read it and look more worried still, and then show it to his companion before putting it in his pocket. That decided Bobby. If Virtue could see it, so could he. He got up and went across to them.

"Have you any objection to showing me the telegram you have just had?" he asked.

Mr. Adam perpended.

"I conceive," he said finally, "you have no authority entitling you to inspect private communications. I fear, therefore, I must oppose a direct negative to your suggestion."

"In that case," said Bobby bluntly, "I must ask you to come to the police station with me."

"You can do a bit of third degree over on this side, too," murmured Virtue.

Mr. Adams still hesitated.

"Well?" said Bobby sharply. He added "Telegrams aren't so very private, and I saw you show this one to Mr. Virtue."

"Under compulsion then, I submit," said Mr. Adams, "more especially as I think the message will convey no meaning whatsoever to you."

He produced it. Bobby took it and read:

"For God's sake, don't say a word."

There was no signature. It had been handed in at Charing Cross Post office, where they probably handle hundreds of telegrams every day. Not much chance of tracing the sender. Bobby said:

"Who is it from?"

"I propose," said Mr. Adams sedately, "to give you no further information whatsoever."

"Do you object to my keeping the telegram?" Bobby asked.

"I should most certainly object," answered Mr. Adams, "if I thought there was any likelihood that my objection would be respected. As I do not, I refrain from expressing it."

Bobby, therefore, put the telegram in his pocket and went back to finish his tea, feeling completely baffled; for what to make of Mr. Adams's enigmatic personality, he had no idea. The incident of the telegram seemed to him, however, sufficiently important to be reported at once. So he took it to the police station, where, as a natural result, he told himself ruefully, he was at once caught up again in the routine of the investigation and dispatched to verify some entirely unimportant and irrelevant facts.

A hopelessly blind trail, it turned out, but it had to be followed up, and it kept Bobby busy both the rest of that evening and the whole of the next day. Some ingenious neighbour of Len Hill, the young man who had discovered Nat Kayne's body, had unearthed, invented, misinterpreted, and otherwise distorted a few simple facts to make it appear that Len Hill himself must be the murderer. Not till evening, after a trying and exhausting day, was Bobby able to report that the story had no foundation other than the neighbour's busy imagination. All that, however, was quite normal, since in every serious investigation the blind trail along which the police are directed by would-be assistants, is common enough. So Major Harley, to whom Bobby made his report, thanked him, agreed that that at least was cleared up, and told Bobby he could go off duty for the rest of the evening.

"And," he added, "just at the moment, sergeant, I don't quite see where we are going on from in the morning."

Bobby didn't either, so having a little time to spare before it was time to think of supper or bed, he took the road to Wynford Lodge, in the hope of catching a glimpse of Olive.

As, after her own tea, which she had been obliged to take in solitude, since Miss Kayne spent most of her time now shut up in her own room, Olive had set out towards the village in the hope of catching a glimpse of Bobby, their common hope was presently fulfilled when they encountered each other near the Lodge gate.

They strolled on together, both of them glad to forget as far as they could, recent events in more personal matters, when they met Mrs. Shepheard, the wife of the vicar of the parish, and a lady of whom it was said that having been vicar's wife for thirty years she knew far more of all the inhabitants of the village, than any of them knew about themselves.

She and Olive had met several times. She stopped now, evidently determined on an introduction to Bobby, and he at once sank to zero in her esteem when she learned that he had never been to the new police college at Hendon.

"I thought that's what it was for, to have gentlemen in the police," she said, "and very upsetting, too, though I'm sure everything is, nowadays, and not in the least what it was when I was a girl. But I suppose, Mr. Owen, you'll be a chief constable soon, like our dear Major Harley, because, of course, he's a gentleman, too."

Bobby admitted that he saw no immediate chance of obtaining that advancement, but Mrs. Shepheard, having now satisfactorily classed him with Major Harley and not with Constable Mills, went on to talk about Miss Kayne.

"It's all so very trying for her," she said, "all this and the responsibility and everything—such a pity she never married."

"I suppose that was her father's fault, wasn't it?" Bobby remarked.

"Oh no, he wanted her to marry, he often said so, only how could she when she never saw a man who wasn't as old as Mr. Kayne himself, and his head just as full as his of books and first editions and all that kind of thing."

"But wasn't she engaged at one time?" Bobby asked. "Didn't her father think it unsuitable and make her break it off?"

"Good gracious no, certainly not," declared Mrs Shepheard with vigour. "That's nonsense. Who ever told you such rubbish? The poor girl was never engaged to anyone, never saw anyone to be engaged to, never the least hint of such a thing."

Bobby asked one or two more questions, but Mrs. Shepheard was quite clear and emphatic.

"You've just been hearing silly gossip without even the tiniest foundation," she repeated. "Though it is true Mr. Kayne did change a little towards the end, though not quite in that way. He did tell me once that he was afraid when he was gone his daughter might make a bad choice, and that he wished she had had more opportunity to make friends of her own age. Of course, he was quite right, it wasn't intentional, but the poor child was sacrificed to that library of his."

With that she took her leave, and when she had gone Bobby and Olive turned back towards the Lodge, both of them looking a little puzzled. Bobby said:

"She seems quite certain about it, and yes Miss Kayne told you herself she was engaged and her father made her break it off."

"Perhaps Mrs. Shepheard never heard about it," Olive remarked, but doubtfully, so plainly evident was it that Mrs. Shepheard was precisely the sort of person who would have heard all about it, down to the smallest detail and even more.

"Anyhow, Miss Kayne ought to know best," Bobby remarked. "I suppose she wasn't only trying to be funny when she told you about those letters she said she had buried?"

"I am sure she wasn't," Olive declared. "She was awfully upset and nervous; I can't describe it, it might have been the most awful thing she was telling me about. I think she thought it was."

They went back through the Lodge grounds and out towards Wynton wood, where a sporadic, though by now hopeless, search for the missing pistol was still in progress. Behind the Lodge the ground rose slightly, and their way led them through a clump of trees growing just before the old boxwood hedge that here marked the boundary of the Lodge gardens. A fine view over the surrounding country was to be had here, and there was a seat in position from which it could be enjoyed. They went behind this seat and onwards through the trees, passing, as Bobby noticed, a fine bed of forget-me-nots, a bed some six feet long and two or three wide and that seemed to be carefully looked after. Bobby said:

"They look nice."

Olive did not answer, but hurried on. Bobby said, thinking of Miss Kayne's story and Mrs. Shepheard's unconscious denial of it:

"This thing seems full of contradictions of one sort or another, but none of them seem to have anything to do with Nat Kayne's death—or with each other for that matter."

He began to tell Olive of Mr. Broast's discovery that his pistol was missing. Olive agreed that she, and no doubt a great many others, knew that he possessed such a weapon.

"But you can't think," she protested, "that Mr. Broast would want to shoot poor Mr. Kayne? why should he?"

"Well, someone did," Bobby pointed out, "and Mr. Broast's pistol is missing. That doesn't prove it was used. If it was used, that doesn't prove Mr. Broast did the using. Only it's got to be found somehow. If it were, one or two little discrepancies are worrying. You don't know what's behind them—like Miss Kayne saying she had been engaged and Mrs. Shepheard being sure she never had the chance.

"I don't see why Miss Kayne should have told me all that story if it wasn't true," said Olive, looking both thoughtful and uneasy.

"Major Harley would say it was more sex starvation, probably," remarked Bobby. "Then there's Sir William Winders saying he never left the house after he heard what had happened till we got there. He said he was expecting us and didn't want to miss us. And his butler says he started out for the village, went as far as the entrance to the wood, and then turned back by the pond and home."

"By the pond?" repeated Olive. "It's rather a long way round."

"It's not very big, is it?" Bobby asked. "Didn't you say it wasn't deep?"

"Oh, no, only a foot or two, a little more perhaps. I used to play there sometimes when I was a tiny."

"Let's go round by it, shall we?" Bobby said. "I'd like to have a look."

They walked on, and before long reached its somewhat muddy banks. They stood still, Bobby thoughtful and Olive wondering what was in his mind.

"If you are suspecting poor Sir William now," Olive said, "I don't think you need. I think he is rather horrid, I always hated him when I was a child, but I don't think he would ever murder anyone. Too flabby."

"There are times when a murder happens easily," Bobby said.

They went closer to the pond. Bobby walked along by the banks, his eyes intent and searching. He found footsteps presently where someone had been standing, close to the water's edge. The earth was damp and the footprints were quite plain. They had evidently not been made by a labourer, but by someone wearing well cut, well made shoes; by someone, too, who had been standing there a few minutes, since the imprints were deep and well-defined. They pointed directly to the water, as though the person making them had walked straight up to it and then stood still.

"What are you doing?" Olive asked.

Bobby was taking off his shoes and socks. He rolled up his trousers above his knees. He took off his coat and rolled up his shirt sleeves. Olive watched him, but asked no further questions. Bobby waded into the water. It hardly came up to his knees. In the middle of the pond it was a little deeper, but not much. Several times he stubbed his toes against stones. Once or twice he trod on old tins, though without hurting himself, for he proceeded very carefully. When his feet touched anything hard he felt for it and brought it to the surface. Once in this way he brought up some old wire and once an ancient and battered kettle. He flung them aside. In the centre of the pond he paddled to and fro, searching with his feet, with a stick he had picked up, getting himself thoroughly wet. Presently he found what he was looking for. He paddled back to the bank again. He was carrying a revolver in his hand and the water dripped from it and from the muzzle, splashing in a shower of drops on the surface of the pond. Olive said:

"You'll get cold, getting so wet." Then she said: "What's that?"

"I think it's the murder gun," he answered. "I think Winders must have thrown it in to hide it."

"Bobby," Olive whispered, "Bobby, does that mean—he did it?"

CHAPTER XVIII
MURDER AGAIN

Bobby had at least learnt that it is never wise to jump to conclusions. Doubts, suspicions, questions, all had to be welcomed and considered, but a conclusion must be examined and tested and weighed in every possible manner before acceptance could even be thought of. It was not, for instance, even certain yet that this was the pistol missing from the library, nor, if it were, that that was the one from which the fatal shots had been fired. Quite possible that Sir William, knowing that he had a pistol in his possession and remembering that he had no licence for it, had chosen this method of getting rid of the thing.

The discovery had to be reported at once, however, and of equal importance was it to make sure that the footsteps were preserved till they could be properly examined and measured. Leaving Olive, therefore, on guard he hurried back to the village, handed in the pistol, told his story, and was soon back with Superintendent Killick and some of his expert assistants. While they were doing what was necessary in the way of securing measurements, photographs, plaster casts, and so on, Bobby took Olive back to the Lodge, left her there, and then went on to the village to write out a full report. He was hurrying along at his best speed, when he heard his name called. Peering through the darkness, for by now it was night, he saw young Virtue stepping out of the shadow of a hedge where he had apparently been waiting.

"You've found the pistol Kayne was shot with, haven't you?" Virtue asked.

"How do you know?" Bobby demanded sharply.

'All over the village," Virtue retorted. "Someone saw them handling it at the police station. Look here, I was waiting to see if I could spot you. There's something I want to say, I know you think I'm holding out on you."

"Well, you are, aren't you?" Bobby asked. "Very silly, too. It's got to come out."

"If it did, it wouldn't help you, not about who killed Kayne. If I knew" —Bobby thought he emphasized slightly this last word—"anything at all, I would tell you at once."

"Even if you had done it yourself?" asked Bobby.

"Well, now, that's just crazy," declared Virtue, though looking distinctly uncomfortable. "Why on earth should I do a thing like that to a man I didn't know the first little thing about?"

"Is that quite accurate?" Bobby asked. "Did you never write to him, for instance?"

"Oh, you've got on to that, too, have you?" Virtue asked. "Well, if you've seen the letter, you ought to know there's nothing in it. I wrote to him as a library trustee. I asked if he knew anything about my cousin."

"Did he answer?"

"Yes. He didn't say much. But I got the idea he was a bit excited, as if he thought there might be something worth getting after. He said he might write again. I thought I would wait developments. I didn't reckon on these developments. I was hoping he might help me find out what happened to James A. So why should I shoot him? unless you think it was all a bit of fun of mine?"

"You told us a very peculiar story, and I don't mind saying that for my own part, I don't believe a word of it," Bobby retorted. "Only if it is accepted, well, then it gives you an alibi. Perhaps that's what it was told for?"

"Well, it wasn't," Virtue grumbled. "Trying hard to pin it on me, aren't you?"

"If I am, you've only yourself to thank," Bobby answered steadily. "Telling lies, suppressing the truth, it's equally suspicious."

"Oh, I know I'm in a jam," Virtue admitted, "but I don't mean to make it worse by shooting off a lot of guesses that might bring a whole heap of trouble. I promised not to, for one thing. There's a little old business way back home that needs looking after if she's not to go to glory. That's all. Means nothing to you, but a whole heap to some of us."

"It means something to us," Bobby said, "to find out who killed Kayne. We don't like killings in this country."

"No one does," retorted Virtue. "You're being hostile. It's no good our taking cracks at each other. Get us no-where. Listen, will you? That typist girl, Miss Perkins, has been trying to pump me. Did you put her up to it?"

"What did she want to know?" Bobby asked in his turn without answering the question, for though he felt quite certain Miss Perkins had not been 'put up' to anything by the police, he saw no reason for saying so to Virtue.

"Blessed if I could make it out," Virtue answered. "Something about that photo you dug up. Wanted to know a lot about it, about me, about a whole heap of things. She's a sticker when she gets going. I nearly had to throw her out to get quit of her."

"What did you tell her?"

"Not a thing, why should I? A dumb little idiot like her," Virtue answered. "I thought I would mention it. If you set her on, you can pull her off again. If you didn't, you had better ask her what was back of all those questions she piled in with. Or I will myself. I shouldn't wonder if she doesn't know something, seen something, heard something. She gave me the idea she was dropping hints she wanted me to pick up. If it's about me, I want you to make her come out in the open, that's all."

It did not seem altogether unnatural to Bobby that the little typist was in a mood for asking questions, especially for asking questions about that photograph which seemed in some way so oddly connected with recent happenings. It occurred to him that Virtue might be trying to throw suspicion on the girl. Presumably Virtue would not know she was the only one whose alibi seemed to be supported by independent testimony—that of Mrs. Somerville, her landlady.

Bobby went on to the police station to write his report. Killick got back while he was there, but Major Harley had an appointment at Mayfield he was obliged to keep, and he had not yet returned. However the discovery of the pistol had been reported to him over the 'phone and the further fact that it had been immediately identified as the one entered in the Firearms Register, as owned by, and in the possession of, Mr. Broast. The pistol itself had already been sent off by special messenger to a firearms expert for him to decide whether it could be proved that the bullets taken from the body had been discharged from this pistol. It had previously been examined for finger-prints, but without anything being found except vague traces too faint and uncertain to be of any value.

It seemed also that one eager reporter, and already there were many in the village, all eager, had heard of the discovery of the pistol. Killick was very annoyed. So was Bobby for that matter, though more resigned, for he had more experience of the newspaper fraternity. But there was nothing to be done, though Killick said a few brief poignant words on the general subject of newspaper enterprise.

From the police station Bobby went on to Mrs. Somerville's to find Miss Perkins, as he thought it might be as well to ask her a few questions. She giggled a good deal, seemed enormously impressed by Virtue's good looks— indeed when she looked ecstatic and compared him to Mr. Ronald Colman, whom he did not in fact in the least resemble, Bobby began to remember Major Harley's sex starvation theories. She admitted, too, with her usual apparently incurable discursiveness that she had been asking Virtue questions, because, as she put it, she felt he 'must Know Something.'

"It all seems so Strange," she told Bobby earnestly, "I mean to say, telling us he saw someone dead on the library floor when it was dark, and the shutters fastened, and him saying, too, it was like my photograph I found. Because how could it be, unless it was him, and it couldn't be, could it? So I thought if I asked him perhaps he would explain it, but he didn't, he was almost Rude."

She sniffed at the memory, and Bobby advised her not to ask any more questions, either of Mr. Virtue or of anyone else. She promised not to, and said she would go to bed instead, and indeed she looked so pale and worn and excited that bed was evidently the best place for her.

"It's all been so very trying," she said. "And Mr. Broast ready to jump down your throat if you so much as open your mouth, especially about his pistol being lost, and he asked me if I had taken it, and I said I wouldn't touch one of the things, not if you paid me, because I shouldn't know if I was letting it off, and such a small thing like that could easily get lost. I told him most likely it was there all the time, in one of the drawers, under something, and he—he Swore at me. He did. I know every one's upset and only Natural they should be, and I am, too, but I've quite decided. To-morrow I shall tell him," said Miss Perkins with a great appearance of firmness, "he must either apologize or accept a month's notice. I will Not be sworn at. He told me—" She lowered her voice to a whisper: —"He said right out I was to get to the Devil out of that. And I will not be sworn at," Miss Perkins repeated with even greater firmness than before.

Bobby agreed gravely that such language was indefensible. He had noticed that Miss Perkins spoke of the missing pistol as being 'such a little thing'. But a Colt three-two revolver is not so very small, and Bobby thought the point worth taking up. He thought so still more when as a result of his questioning it became plain that what Miss Perkins declared she had seen in a drawer of Mr. Broast's writing table was almost certainly a two-two automatic, which can no doubt be described as small.

Satisfied on the point, Bobby did not press it. He thought it might turn out highly important, though he did not quite see how, and at any rate he did not wish to let Miss Perkins guess the significance he was inclined to attach to the information she had let slip. The less she thought it mattered in any way, the less likely she would be to talk about it, and Bobby's impression at the moment was that no means existed of preventing her from talking, if she knew of anything to talk about. As well attempt to bridle the tides or check the stars in their courses, he thought, as keep Miss Perkins's tongue from wagging once it knew there was something to wag for.

So he merely repeated his former advice to her to go to bed, confirmed with a yawn his own overwhelming desire to seek a similar refuge, and departed. Looking back as he was going, he saw the light go up and her figure at the window as she drew the blinds. He hoped she would sleep well, as he felt he most certainly would himself. However, he had still to report this further odd and perhaps significant information of the small two-two automatic Miss Perkins appeared to have seen in Mr. Broast's possession. He did so, and Killick thought the information interesting, but decided that it would be time enough to question Mr. Broast in the morning. They all, observed Killick feelingly, needed a rest.

Bobby felt he did, anyhow, and as soon as he had some supper, departed for bed and a sound slumber.

He was up in good time next morning and made the sort of breakfast it is wise to make when the time and the place of the next meal are highly problematic. Then he went on to the police station and almost as soon as he got there, Major Harley arrived. Two reports had reached him that morning, both significant. One was from the firearms expert to the effect that the bullets found in the murdered man's body had undoubtedly been fired from the revolver sent to him. A full report would follow presently, but the fact could be taken as clearly established. The other report had been received from the New York police by transatlantic 'phone and explained that there was no hope or prospect of tracing the photograph of which the particulars had been given them. All the records of the photographer in question had been destroyed in a fire, after which he had retired from business and was now believed to be dead.

"And that's that," said Major Harley, "so far as the photo's concerned. The pistol business looks bad, and I don't understand the complication of the two-two automatic Broast is supposed to have had. He'll have to be questioned about it, but it doesn't seem important. The three-two revolver looks conclusive. I think it justifies us in thinking of making an arrest. It's undoubtedly the weapon that was used. It belonged to Broast. Winders had access to where it was kept. It is found in a pond there is evidence Winders visited. There are footprints believed to be his. If they agree with his shoes when we test them—well, we shall have to hear anything he has to say. Winders may have some explanation to offer, but it looks bad, Owen, very bad."

"Yes, sir," agreed Bobby, who was of the same opinion.

Their preparations completed, a little party, consisting of Major Harley, Superintendent Killick, Bobby, and one or two others set out for the pond where a sad and weary constable sat and thought the hours would never pass.

The footprints were duly shown to the Major, examined, considered, talked over. The plaster casts were examined, too, and pronounced successful. There was a long argument as to whether it would be safe to dig up a portion of the bank containing them to be transported to police headquarters and kept as evidence, but finally it was agreed that the ground was too soft for that to be practicable, and they were all on the point of making a move when Wilson, Sir William's butler, appeared, looking very pale and excited.

"You're not thinking he's in there, are you?" he asked. "My heart went into my mouth when I saw you."

"What do you mean? what are you talking about?" Major Harley demanded sharply.

"It's Sir William, sir," explained the man. "We can't find him, he's not in the house, his bed's not been slept in, we can't make it out."

The little party of police looked at each other. The significance seemed plain. Major Harley beckoned to Bobby. Killick joined them. The Major said:—

"Bolted? Is that it, do you think?"

"Shouldn't wonder," said Killick.

Bobby did not say anything, but he thought much the same.

Major Harley asked Wilson a few questions. The man had little to tell. He had locked up as usual. At that time his master had been sitting in the study, reading. The study was the room where he generally sat at night. Wilson was certain he had bolted the side door. It was provided with a spring lock, a mortice, so it was not really necessary to draw the bolts to make it secure. In the morning he had found it unbolted. That was not in itself very unusual or alarming. Sir William often took a stroll last thing at night, sometimes going to see Mr. Broast, and then would generally return after the rest of the household had gone to bed. When that happened he always came back by the side or garden door, and occasionally forgot to draw the bolts. After all, the mortice lock was safe enough in the ordinary way. Wilson therefore had not been unduly alarmed. Elsewhere downstairs everything seemed as usual, nothing disturbed, and it was only later on that he grew alarmed when he took early morning tea to his master and found the room empty and the bed apparently not slept in.

He went at once to inform Miss Winders, Sir William's daughter. A search had been started. No trace of the missing man had so far been found. But when Wilson saw, he said, the little group of police near the pond, it had given him a real turn.

The Major asked Killick to organize as complete a search as practicable of the immediate vicinity, and told Bobby to come up with him to the house.

"Must hear what they have to say, may find something," he said, "though his running for it like this is as good as a confession. Only what did he do it for? The murder, I mean. Can't understand that. And how did he know Nat Kayne was coming through the woods?"

"Well, sir, as you said yourself," Bobby remarked, "the occasion may have been offered by chance and seized upon."

"What about Broast's pistol?" the Major asked. "Winders hadn't that with him just by chance."

"Do you see over there, sir?" Bobby asked.

A man was running towards them. As he came nearer they recognized Adams, looking a good deal less prim and precise than usual. He was calling to them and waving. What he said seemed incoherent, incomprehensible. But something about him, about his attitude, his waving arms, the tones of his voice uttering these words they could not plainly hear, all suggested urgency, urgency and terror. The Major began to run. Bobby followed. Behind them puffed Wilson who had come with them and who was not much used to running. Adams's cries became clearer.

"Over there," he was shouting, "by the hedge, the ditch, over there."

He turned round and began to run in the direction in which he had been pointing. The Major caught him up. He tried to speak but could not. Less breathless, Bobby said:

"What is it? Sir William...?"

"Dead," Adams answered, still running. "Dead," he said, his voice rising in a shrill scream as with sudden panic. "Dead," he whispered, but in a whisper that carried almost as far as the scream. "Murdered," he said and stood, as though all at once he dared go no further.

Bobby raced on. The Major was close behind. They had been crossing a field laid down in pasture. They came in sight of something that lay still and humped, half in, half out of the ditch that ran at the foot of the hedge about the field. Nearer, they saw it was Sir William Winders, supine, his calm face upturned to the calm sky, as still himself as was that still, clear morning, quiet and peaceful as though he slept.

Bobby stood, looking keenly around. The Major bent over the dead man.

"Shot through the body half a dozen times or so," he said. "Riddled." He stood up. "Where is Adams?" he asked.

CHAPTER XIX

FORGET-ME-NOTS

For a moment they both thought that somehow he had managed to disappear, though that seemed difficult in an open field. Then they caught sight of him on the further side of the hedge, hurrying away. The Major shouted. Adams took no notice. The Major said to Bobby:—

"What's he up to? Fetch him back, will you?"

Bobby forced his way through the hedge and began to run. Adams, hearing him coming, look back. Bobby shouted to him to stop. Adams obeyed. Bobby caught him up and said:—

"Please go back at once. Major Harley wishes to question you."

Mr. Adams hesitated.

"Is that really necessary now? I confess to experiencing much discomfort at the spectacle presented. I am not accustomed nowadays—not to such sights. I find them unpleasantly reminiscent, most unpleasantly."

Bobby did not answer, but the gesture he made was eloquent. So probably was the long, searching look of doubt and suspicion he gave Adams. He was wondering what was the true cause of the agitation Adams was certainly experiencing. Was it only because this violent death in this quiet English scene reminded him of those scenes of horror in the past in France that dwell like a nightmare in the minds of some of our neighbours, controlled only by an effort of the will, ready to push themselves forward again in the silent watches of the night or when some chord of memory is touched? Or was there some other, some stronger, more immediate reason? He remembered that Adams had gone out a little before Nat Kayne's murder, and that there was no independent proof of the time of his return. Now he was first on the scene of this fresh murder.

Adams began to walk towards where the dead body lay. Bobby followed. They pushed through the gap in the hedge where Adams had passed previously and went on. Major Harley looked up as they approached. He said angrily to Adams:—

"What was that for, hey? what's it mean?"

"As I have already explained," Adams answered, "I found myself unpleasantly affected. I became aware of a sensation in the pit of my stomach—to express myself vulgarly, I was in some apprehension that vomiting was about to occur.

Nor do I feel altogether certain," he added, "that the danger is entirely of the past."

He then proceeded to demonstrate that this last surmise was entirely correct.

"Get over there and sit down on the bank," the Major growled, "and don't try to run off again or I'll put you in handcuffs. I'll hear what you have to say later on. Owen, cut off back to the house. There's a 'phone there. Tell them to get a doctor and send help. Hurry up and get back here as soon as you can.

Bobby set off at a run. From the further end of the field he glanced back. Mr. Adams was sitting on the ground, his head supported on his hands. Major Harley was examining the body and the ground near. Several of the cartridge cases ejected from the pistol used were lying close by, and he was picking them up and marking the spots where they had lain, in between pausing to give angry and doubtful glances at the seated, huddled figure of Adams.

Bobby was aware of a very uneasy feeling as he reflected that he was leaving the chief constable alone with one who might be a murderer, who might still have on him the weapon so recently used, who might feel that anything was better than waiting for arrest or even for further questioning.

Adams had not been searched. In the general flurry and excitement the advisability of that had been overlooked. Bobby wondered whether he ought not to return and warn Major Harley. But he had received direct orders to proceed at once to the house, orders are always orders, the Major was presumably able to look after himself and certainly would not welcome any suggestions to the contrary. Bobby ran on therefore, quickening his speed though, and as soon as possible, hurried back to the field, running again.

To his relief his fears had been unnecessary. The Major was still busy with his careful examination, Adams was still sitting on the ground at a little distance, though he looked slightly better now. Very soon, as help began to arrive, the field became a scene of hustling activity. All the general routine of such cases was gone through, photographs taken, measurements made and noted, the ground near examined inch by inch, the actual spot where the body had lain roped off and a constable put in charge to keep away intruders. Spectators began to assemble. Journalists on the spot as a result of the previous murder and all agog with excitement at what they were already describing as 'Amazing Development, Sensational Sequel,' hovered around. The doctor, making a preliminary examination of the body where it lay, thought death had occurred between eleven and twelve the previous night, and was not too sanguine that further examination would enable him to be much more precise. Death, he said, must have been nearly instantaneous. A small calibre pistol had been emptied into the body at close range. Seven shots in all had been fired. Probably an automatic had been used and the trigger pulled till the magazine was empty. The doctor thought that possibly, but only possibly, the post-mortem examination might enable him to deduce something from the nature of the wounds. It was at any rate certain the shots had been fired with the pistol almost or quite pressed against the body.

The empty cartridge cases Major Harley had found, seven of them, came from a two-two automatic, a small weapon with small stopping qualities but deadly enough at close quarters. And this fact, once established, made both the Major and Bobby remember Miss Perkins's incidental remark that the pistol belonging to Mr. Broast was a 'tiny thing'. It looked therefore, if Miss Perkins were correct, as if a weapon of the kind used had been in the possession of the librarian, in addition to the one for which he had a licence. Bobby remembered, too, that occasion when he had seen in the librarian's hand something small and bright and hard that might have been a small automatic but afterwards appeared to have been only an electric torch.

The careful examination made of the vicinity revealed nothing else of interest. Traces were found of Mr. Adams's presence, but that was only to be expected since he had been the first on the scene. A half smoked cigarette found in the hedge, for instance, he agreed at once was his. He had been smoking it when he first saw the body, and he supposed he must have thrown it away, though he did not remember doing so.

From the field Major Harley went on to the house where the only fact of importance that emerged was that Virtue had called the previous evening and had apparently had some dispute with Sir William, since their voices had been heard raised as if they were quarrelling, and since Wilson, the butler, when he took in whisky and soda, noticed that they both looked flushed and angry. Mr. Virtue had left almost immediately, and Wilson remembered that when he cleared away the tray, the glasses had not been used, so that apparently the visitor had either refused a drink or had not been offered one.

Killick thought this very important. The Major agreed that it would have to be looked into. Bobby reflected that the quarrel had taken place about eight and the murder apparently between eleven and midnight—three or four hours later. The Major said:

"Only for what? What had Virtue to do with Winders? There's no motive."

"Motive no concern of ours, sir," said Killick firmly. "It's facts we want."

Bobby said:

"A jury always wants a motive." He added: "I get the feeling there's someone watching all the time, always just one move ahead of us, someone working out a plan we've no idea of yet."

Killick said:

"We always seem to trace the pistol back to Mr. Broast."

The Major went over to the 'phone and rang up Wynton Lodge. It was Olive who answered. Evidently no news of this fresh tragedy had yet reached there. Olive explained that Mr. Broast had left by the early train for London, and had not said when he would be back. It was a piece of news that made Major Harley, Killick, Bobby, exchange doubtful glances.

"Looks bad, very bad," Killick said. "Time after the murder to go back to the Lodge, collect what he wanted, and catch the early train. What about warning the Yard and trying to pick him up in town?"

"Hardly enough to go on," decided the Major. "He may come back of his own accord. If he is really running for it, well, that'll make things a bit clearer."

Further enquiries over the 'phone revealed that he had taken nothing with him, not even a handbag, and had said he would be back early in the afternoon or at any rate in time for dinner. A suggestion that he might be found at his club at lunch time, or that perhaps he had some favourite restaurant he usually went to, brought the information that he belonged to no club and when he went to London generally lunched at any tea shop he happened to be near when he remembered he was hungry—a glass of milk, roll, butter and cheese, total cost 7*d*., was his accustomed lunch, and, he used to say, the best value in nourishment obtainable for the money anywhere in the world.

Major Harley shook his head, hung up the 'phone, and decided that there was nothing to do but wait and see if Mr. Broast returned as he had promised.

The statements made by the other inmates of the house revealed nothing of importance. Sir William had been sitting in his study, reading, when the rest of the household retired about half past ten. He had not seemed in any way perturbed by his quarrel, if quarrel it had been, with Virtue, nor had he referred to it again. He had not said anything about taking a stroll before bed, but it was not at all unusual for him to do so. He had not been heard to go out, but there was no reason why anyone should, in fact, have heard him. The garden door was only a yard or two away from the door to the study, and Sir William was always quiet in his movements. Someone discovered an odd looking impression in a flower bed beneath the study window, and further investigation showed two morsels of earth on the window sill. It was consistent with the suggestion that Sir William's attention had been attracted by earth thrown against the window, and that he had then been induced on some pretext, when he had answered the signal, to proceed to the spot where he met his death.

The impression on the soft earth of the flower bed was too nebulous for any conclusion to be drawn, though Bobby spent a long time staring at it with all the slow concentration of his nature. Someone had once said rudely that it took him as long to bring an idea to fruition as it took for a blossom to take shape as fruit ripe for the plucking, and there was some truth in this, though there was also truth in the retort that generally his ideas, when ripe, were, like the ripe fruit, worth the plucking, and ready for digestion. Now, however, for all his slow and careful pondering as he turned one thing after another over and over in his mind, he could draw no clear direction from this odd, shapeless imprint on the flower bed.

"If only it could tell," he thought.

Careful search revealed nothing like it anywhere else, and in fact recent dry weather, broken only for some time past by faint and ineffectual drizzle on one or two occasions, made it little likely that the ground would have retained many visible tracks or markings.

All this had taken so much time that it was not till late afternoon that Mr. Adams could be interviewed again, though indeed Major Harley had been in no hurry to question him further. He had made a statement in writing, and it contained nothing of much importance. In it he admitted he had been out late the previous evening. He had gone for a walk after supper, but was sure he had been back by about half past ten or possibly a little later. He agreed, however, that he had spoken to no one on his return, and so far as he was aware no one had seen him come back. He had gone straight to his room and to bed, and so could produce no independent testimony to confirm his statement.

"A most unsatisfactory story," commented the Major severely.

Mr. Adams said that no one regretted it more than he did.

"You still refuse to give your real name and address or explain your business here?"

"I am constrained, I am under the compulsion," Mr. Adams replied slowly, "of an unfortunate coincidence of circumstances. It has been well said that self-preservation is nature's first law, and I do not wish to involve myself and others in risks that might produce the most serious consequences as a result of events in which we are not intimately concerned."

Major Harley looked at him for a long time in silence.

"Self-preservation? risks?" he repeated. "That's saying a good deal. You mustn't be surprised if we draw certain conclusions."

Mr. Adams looked worried and made no answer. The Major continued:—

"Where did you go when you went out last night? Did you meet anyone you can tell us about? Had you any special object?"

Mr. Adams described his route. He appeared to have made a fairly long circuit. It was late, dark, he had met no one he recognized or who could recognize him. Passing through another village some distance away, he had posted letters there. The postmarks would prove that at least. The Major retorted that it wouldn't prove he had posted them in person, and what was important was to have evidence of his whereabouts between eleven and twelve. Also, why had he gone to this other village to post his letters when there was a letter box within a few yards of the inn?

"I had no wish," explained Mr. Adams, "for the address of the person with whom I was communicating to be known at present, and from what I have perceived of the methods in this investigation I am not prepared to affirm any strong belief that strict propriety is always observed. I considered it wiser, therefore, to post my letters unperceived in a locality where a possibly surreptitious glimpse of the envelope would be harder to obtain."

Major Harley went red. Bobby, who was acting again as shorthand writer, rubbed his nose reflectively with the end of his pencil and told himself, not for the first time, that Mr. Adams was hard to place. Mr. Adams remained tranquil, apparently quite unaware of any effect his remarks had produced. The Major swallowed twice and, when his self-control was again firmly established, he said:

"Well, now then, about this morning—you were out early? Posting another letter on the quiet for fear it should be seen by the police?"

"On this occasion, I was actuated by no such motive," answered Mr. Adams sedately. "My mind has been much occupied by recent events, and I had decided to seek an interview with the unfortunate gentleman whose demise we must deplore and whose murderer I am no less desirous than yourself to see brought to a severe and condign judgement."

"Oh, you are, are you?" growled the Major blinking a little. He was beginning to have an air of knowing that he was waging a hopeless fight.

"Rather early for a call, wasn't it?" he asked.

"In the very remarkable circumstances prevailing," Mr. Adams explained, "I was inclined to think that the usual conventions of society might not unreasonably be set aside. I was well aware the interview might lead to disagreements of a marked character."

The Major stared. Killick gave a little gasp. Bobby leaned so heavily on the point of his pencil that it broke off. Mr. Adams again seemed serenely unaware of the effect produced. He appeared to be making these admissions without in any way realizing their significance. Once more he declined to be more explicit.

"Sir William," he explained, "having met with so tragic and melancholy an end, I am precluded, at any rate for the present, from entering into details."

"Very well," said the Major. "I remind you again that what you say may be used in evidence, if necessary. I ask you another question. How did you happen to find the body? The spot where it was is quite out of the way for anyone going from the village to Highfields?"

"I was not," observed Mr. Adams thoughtfully, "contemplating with any pleasure the interview I had felt it necessary to seek with Sir William, a violent and hasty-tempered person. I have a marked constitutional objection to scenes of violence, much heightened by the extremely unpleasant, indeed loathsome and even disgusting experiences I was force to endure in France, for reasons I never clearly apprehended. I even wondered whether to go through with my intention. It was in order to obtain time for further consideration that instead of proceeding direct to my destination I turned aside into the field in which I discovered the body of our unfortunate friend."

The Major fired off another series of questions. He learned nothing more. Finally he gave it up. He said:

"Mr. Adams, you will be called as a witness at the inquest. I advise you to consider your position very seriously. I advise you to secure legal assistance. At present it seems as though it may be suggested that you were the first to find the body because you alone knew where to look for it."

"It is an aspect of this unfortunate affair I have not overlooked," confessed Mr. Adams. "It has indeed been present very clearly to my mind. The suspicion is unjust, though not, I admit, in all respects unreasonable. You may be sure I shall continue to give it my most careful consideration, as also your valued suggestion that I should secure legal advice."

That concluded the interview, and when Adams had gone the Major wiped a forehead damp with perspiration and said "Ouf". Then he turned to Killick and Bobby and said:—

"Well, what do you make of all that?"

"Sweat it out of him in time," said Killick. "Give him a gruelling. What he wants is to be on oath with a good smart man having a go at him."

The Major agreed that that was probably the best way of dealing with Adams, and then sent for Virtue, who was in waiting.

Virtue agreed at once that he visited Sir William the previous evening, that high words had passed between them. But he insisted that the dispute had not been important.

"It was like this," Virtue said. "I told him you fellows weren't satisfied with what I saw in the library, and as he was a trustee I asked him to back me up about having a search made. I told him you said there were no grounds for insisting on one so would he agree. He seemed to resent the idea. Lost his temper about it. That's all."

Afterwards he returned to the inn and went presently to his room and to bed as usual. But as Major Harley remarked wearily there was no evidence he stayed there. From most bedrooms in most houses it would be easy for any one who wished to do so to leave and to return unseen.

With Virtue's dismissal after an interview almost as unsatisfactory as that with Mr. Adams, teatime arrived, and Bobby decided to go to the Wynton Arms, being not without hope that there he might find Olive, of whom he had not so far had a glimpse all day. As he was going out, a gloomy Constable Mills, returned limpingly to duty and much harassed by all these happenings, said to him:—

"As if we hadn't got enough on hand as it is, here's Mrs. Somerville complaining that two of her hand towels were stolen last night. Seems to think we ought to stop everything and go chasing after her towels. I told her we had two murders on our hands—two hand towels indeed," grumbled Constable Mills.

Bobby said vaguely that it was too bad, and hurried along to the inn, where he found for once his luck was in and Olive waiting for him, very quiet and silent, though, under the weight of this new tragedy.

"Miss Kayne wants you to go and see her as soon as you can," she told Bobby.

"What for?" he asked. "How is she now?"

"I can't make her out," Olive answered slowly. "When I told her about this new awful thing happening to Sir William, she said something about that was two, but two wasn't all. She wouldn't say what she meant only if you were as clever as I said you were, then you ought to know. After that, I couldn't get another word from her. She sits there, doing nothing, just as if she were waiting…"

"Waiting? what for?" Bobby asked quickly.

"I don't know. It's only what I feel. The way she sits— and, well, listens. I don't know if she knows something, but I'm sure there's something she expects. She was out last night herself quite late."

"Alone?"

"I think it was to meet Mr. Broast. He had been in town all day, he got back very late."

"Yes, I know," Bobby said moodily, remembering the theory that had been put forward that Broast had been to town to prepare for flight or concealment, had returned to commit the murder, and now this morning had put his escape plans into execution.

"I heard someone talking under my window," Olive went on, "and I got out of bed to see who it was, and I could see Miss Kayne and Mr. Broast standing talking near the house. He must have come back by the last train and she was waiting for him, I suppose."

"What time was that?"

"About twelve it must have been. I asked her this morning why she had been out so late. She wouldn't say, but she told me to tell you."

"To tell me?" repeated Bobby frowningly. He found himself wondering if that had been meant as defiance, as a challenge. "She gets about by herself all right," he remarked.

"Oh, yes, when she wants to," agreed Olive, "though sometimes she pretends she can't."

One of the maids attached to the inn tea-rooms came up. She was carrying a small box.

"It came this afternoon," she told Bobby. "It was in your room waiting so I brought it down."

Bobby thanked her and took the package. It had been posted in Mayfield and he noticed that it was addressed in block capitals. When he opened it he found within a number of freshly-picked forget-me-nots.

"Who are they from?" asked Olive.

Bobby made no answer but sat staring at them with a gloomy and a thoughtful air.

CHAPTER XX
MISS PERKINS WONDERS

"You've made a conquest," Olive said presently, but though she spoke in jest, her voice was heavy, her eyes, too, were dark and oppressed with thought.

To both of them those small and lovely flowers, shining up from the cardboard box they had come in, brought in some way they did not understand a message of foreboding, as of some dark crisis approaching, as of evil happenings still to come to pass. Bobby put the lid back in place with a quick, nervous gesture. It was almost as though he hoped in that way to shut up something he had fear of, to prevent thus its escape into the world. It was not like him. Olive, watching, looked on uneasily. The picture in both their minds was that of Miss Kayne, seated and silent, waiting for something that somehow she had long expected, perhaps because she herself had given to it that first impetus from which these happenings had ensued, in her eyes black hatred of that great library which more than once had been described as a source of pride even to the nation itself. Bobby said:

"What's she got against the library? It's hers, it's magnificent, it's one of the finest things going? What's wrong with it?"

Olive did not answer. Her fingers were plucking nervously at the folds of her skirt. Bobby said:

"There's a bed of forget-me-nots in the Lodge garden, behind the seat where the view is, under the trees there."

"Forget-me-nots are everywhere," Olive said.

Bobby had the impression that she did not wish to think that these came from the Lodge garden. After a long pause, when she saw how carefully Bobby was examining the address label, she added:

"It's the Mayfield postmark, isn't it?"

"Yes, posted last night," Bobby agreed. "Not much chance to find out who did the posting. We can try, of course, and we shall have to find out if anyone from here went to Mayfield yesterday. That might possibly give us a lead."

"No one from the Lodge," Olive said quickly. "I can tell you that. Miss Kayne hasn't been anywhere for ages—oh, except Mr. Broast, and he was in town. He went again to-day."

"Are you sure? about yesterday, I mean. He went off early this morning, didn't he? But about yesterday? Is it certain he was in town?"

"Well, he rang up twice. I had to put him through to Miss Perkins. She was there all day anyhow, and so were the maids, and so was I and Miss Kayne—Briggs, too."

"Do you know where he was speaking from?"

"He said he was at that big book shop at the corner of Mayfair Square. I forget the name. They have an important antiquarian book department."

"It'll be easy to check that," Bobby said. "He's a well known man in the book trade. They'll be sure to remember if he was there. Did he ring up from there both times?"

"I don't think he said where he was the second time. He said he had been delayed and wouldn't be back till the last train, and Miss Perkins needn't wait. She had gone home by then, so that didn't matter."

"Do you know if he has any special reason just now for going up to town, both yesterday and to-day?"

"I think it's some book, autographed copy or something, that they wanted his opinion on because they think it may be forged. Of course, he is almost the greatest expert in the world about that."

"Yes, I see," said Bobby, "I suppose so. He had come back by that last train then when you saw him and Miss Kayne together?"

"I don't know, I thought so. You could find that out, couldn't you?"

"Oh, yes, easily," Bobby agreed. "He's well known, someone at the station is pretty sure to remember. The last train's due about half past eleven, isn't it? If he walked home, and he hadn't the car, and there's no 'bus at that time, it would take him nearly an hour—three quarters, anyhow, even if he hurried."

"Oh, yes, quite that," Olive agreed.

"Seems to let him out, as far as this last business is concerned," Bobby mused. "Not quite perhaps. It'll have to be gone into. He might have had a car parked, a bicycle perhaps, not very probable on the face of it. Have to be gone into, though. Miss Kayne must have been waiting up for him. Did she say she meant to?"

"No. She always goes to bed early. Last night it was earlier than usual—before nine, I think, I'm not sure exactly. I went early, too. I think everyone was feeling tired out. The maids, too. It's all been so awful. Everyone's glad to get to bed and think one day is done and perhaps to-morrow will be better."

"Miss Kayne must have come down again? Most likely she hadn't actually been to bed, then?"

"I don't know. She didn't go straight to her room. When I went up about nine she was sitting in Mr. Broast's room. The door was open and I spoke to her. She wasn't doing anything. She was just sitting there, brooding."

"Yes," Bobby said, and seemed to see the old, fat, monstrous woman sitting there like some ancient goddess meditating thoughts of doom. "Did she answer when you spoke?"

"She said something about wondering how Mr. Broast had got on, and it was very worrying and difficult because he had to say whether something or another was genuine or not. I don't know why it was specially worrying this time. He is always being asked for his opinion. I suppose it's why she waited up."

"Did she stop in Mr. Broast's room?"

"No. She asked me to help her out of the chair, and I did and she went to her own room."

"You didn't hear her go down stairs again?"

"No. I don't suppose anyone would. She can get about very quietly when she wants to."

Bobby reflected again that an alibi seemed indicated for Mr. Broast; if, that is, his movements were confirmed on inquiry. But apparently none for Miss Kayne herself. Nothing to show where she had been or how she had occupied herself between the hour when she had retired, ostensibly to bed, and the hour when Olive had seen her talking to Broast in the garden at midnight, long after the hour when a man had died, shot through and through seven time over.

Again a vision came to him, no longer of a woman waiting and passive, but darkly active, slipping, huge, gross, and agile, silently through the night, on her way to keep a rendezvous where one at the meeting place would be death.

He remembered those huge, shapeless marks, footprints perhaps, made in the flower bed near the study window at Highfields. He remembered he had seen Miss Kayne wearing huge, shapeless shoes, almost like carpet slippers, on her swollen feet. Clearly, too, he remembered how she said that once she had committed, a murder never suspected even, never discovered. Had that boast been true? Was it to be made good once yet again? Or had it been, not boast of a past achievement but rather vaunting anticipation?

He felt the problem was for the present at least altogether beyond him. But one thing he made quite clear to Olive, in the plainest possible language. Olive must go back to London at once. There was danger in this quiet, peaceful village. Peril, and who could tell where it would strike next? After all, Olive was in business, wasn't she? A business woman? She had a hat shop, and very clearly that shop required the attention of its owner. One could not, Bobby pointed out earnestly, expect assistants or a manager to take the same interest as the proprietor. She must go and see about it at once. Immediately. The business might be going to rack and ruin. Probably was. Bobby made all that perfectly clear.

Unfortunately Olive made it equally clear she was going to do nothing of the kind.

"Miss Kayne was father's friend and she is mine, too," Olive said. "She was awfully good to me when I was a tiny. I'm not going to leave her in the midst of all this trouble. Of course," she added meekly, but not altogether as if she meant it, "when we are married I shall have to do exactly what you tell me—like all the other wives. Obey. But not till then, so don't expect it."

Nor from that position was she to be moved, and when he talked once more of danger, she said nothing, but put out her hand to his with a quick and sudden look that made him realize one reason why she would not go was that she, too, thought that there was danger was past and over, she did not mean to be very far away.

He tried to argue a little, but soon realized he might as well save his breath. She listened patiently but with a patience as impenetrable as the patience of eternity. He gave it up presently and said:

"Miss Kayne didn't tell you why she had come downstairs again, did she? Was it just to meet Mr. Broast? That wasn't usual, was it?"

"No. She's been so strange lately. She said a day or two ago:—'I knew her again the moment I saw her.' She wouldn't say who. She said over again she knew her at once, but I couldn't make out who she meant. I suppose you can't wonder at her being strange when things like this are happening. She was worrying about the forged book or whatever it is, and Mr. Broast having to go to town to examine it. I can't think why. She said he might buy it for the library. I shouldn't have expected her to care if every book they have turned out forged. I don't see what there's to worry about over the chance of his buying something else says is a fake. Anyhow, I told her Mr. Broast would be sure to know."

"What did she say?"

"She said yes, Broast would know. She said that twice over, and then she gave me a funny sort of look and she went away. If he does make a mistake and buy a fake for once, what's it matter?"

"Perhaps she might think other things in the library were fakes, too?"

"Good gracious, Bobby," said Olive, beginning to laugh, "why Mr. Broast—well, I should just like to hear anyone tell him he wouldn't know a fake a mile off. Murder would happen then all right. At least, unless he just lay down and died from the shock." She added more seriously: "Bobby, you may be quite sure. Mr. Broast would no more mistake a fake for the genuine article than you would mistake a football for a cricket bat."

"I see," Bobby said slowly, though a vague, a faint suspicion was beginning to stir, as it were, in his mind.

"It was a very early copy of youthful poems by Tennyson that friends of his printed privately," Olive explained. "Very rare, only copy known, all that sort of thing. Mr. Broast bought it for the library after he had examined it very carefully, he said, so that shows you what he thought. He paid £100 for it, he told Miss Kayne."

"Stiff price," Bobby remarked, though absently, for his thoughts were still busy. He said, half to himself:—"She would know where the two-two automatic was kept if he had it."

"What do you mean?" Olive asked quickly.

Bobby did not answer, but the troubled look on his features grew more marked. Olive had become very pale. After a pause she almost whispered:

"Bobby, you can't mean... you can't... not Miss Kayne, that's too awful."

He took her hand in both his and held it, speaking very gently:

"Dearest love," he said, "I've to follow the truth where it leads, no matter where it leads. If you are going to marry a policeman, you mustn't forget that. But," he added more lightly, "don't jump to conclusions; that's about the first thing we are taught, never to jump to conclusions." After another pause, he said: "I can't get it straight. Don't you worry, Olive. Nothing certain yet by a long way. Look here, don't you think you really ought to clear out of this? It's not the sort of thing to be mixed up in if you can help it?"

"I am staying with Miss Kayne," Olive answered. "She's my friend and that's all that matters."

She was looking straight at him, with something of anger and defiance in her expression, that changed suddenly as a flush spread over her pale cheeks and she looked away, for she had seen the admiration, the love, and the approval in his eyes.

It was time by now, and more than time, for Bobby to return to the little police station that had become such a centre of hustling activity, that existed now in a state of perpetual siege, with eager-eyed reporters swarming about it, like flappers round a film star. First he saw Olive on her way back to the Lodge, and then he went on to the police station, where he found Killick in some excitement over a fresh bit of information that had just arrived. Someone had come forward to identify Virtue as having been one of those in the library some weeks previously, when had been broken the glass of the case containing one of the library's most cherished treasures—the *Glastonbury Psalter*.

"What's more," said Killick excitedly, "he don't attempt to deny it—we've had him in and he owned up he was there. Gives a pretty clear lead, don't it? That was a try-on that didn't come off, and the whole thing adds up to attempted theft of some of the old stuff there that's worth thousands of pounds—to them as thinks so. The Major's very bucked."

"Has Virtue been held?" Bobby asked.

"No," admitted the superintendent with slightly diminished enthusiasm. "He wouldn't own up to anything except that he was in the library that day. He refused to say anything more, said he understood it was our job to prove it was him broke the glass, and he could swear he wasn't anywhere near at the moment, and there was a girl ran round by where he was standing could swear to his being on the other side of the library when they all heard the smash. Then he said he was a business man in good standing and he wasn't a thief. Perhaps he isn't, but you know how crazy these collectors are, everyone knows that. Anyhow, we can't hold him on it, except for malicious damage if we had proof. He meant to pinch the Psalms thing all right, if he got the chance, but you can't send a man up on intention. It's a clear lead, though."

"Any report in from America?" Bobby asked.

"Well, yes, there is," answered Killick, his enthusiasm dropping another point or two. "Cable from the Grand Rapids police, a bit snotty, too. Don't half like one of their prominent citizens being run in here. Family's communicating with the American Ambassador. Broad hint to us to watch our step. Well-known and respected Michigan citizen and all that sort of thing—they seem to have money to blow in on cables over there. Confirms, too, that one of the Virtue family disappeared on a European trip, and a sort of hint that if we had got busy about that at the time, it would have been a whole lot smarter of us. All very well, but prominent American citizen and all, he was there when a pass was made at that what-d'ye-call it thing, and that's a pointer we can't drop. Some of these collectors will give any amount of money for mouldy old stuff you and me would chuck on the dust heap."

"Yes, that's so," agreed Bobby with more fervour than he felt, for he could not imagine anyone in the world blind to the loveliness of that old manuscript with its lettering, its illustration, its exquisite border of birds and foliage in which the spring itself seemed eternally to laugh. He added:—"Things do seem to be falling a bit into place. I got a glimmer of light at tea just now on what perhaps may lie behind it all."

He went on to tell Killick what he had gathered from Olive's conversation. Killick told him to put it in a report. He pointed out, however, that they had known before that Mr. Broast had returned from London by the last train the night before and had left again for town by the first train this morning. His errand there, Killick remarked, was, of course, of no interest to them, no importance at all. All that mattered was the fact that he had gone, and the times of his arrival and departure, which seemed well established by independent evidence. A man arriving at Mayfield from town at 11.35 p.m. had a fairly sound alibi for a murder committed in such circumstances at such a distance. It seemed clear, for instance, that the attention of the murdered man had been attracted in the first place by earth thrown against the study window by some secret visitor, and it seemed clear again that that must have happened sometime well before half past eleven, since afterwards, Sir William had had to leave the house and proceed as far as the spot where the murder took place. Of course, there was no proof that the thrower of the earth against the study window and the murderer were the same person, but it was difficult to suppose anything else. As for Miss Kayne, when her name was mentioned, Killick laughed a little.

"No, no," he said, "I can't see a fat old lady like her cutting capers of this sort." He smiled again. Evidently before his eyes there was no such vision as that which had so impressed itself on Bobby's imagination. He went on: "Besides, why should she? It's all her property, isn't it? Kayne and Winders were only trustees."

To that there was no answer; and as for the receipt of the box of forget-me-nots, Killick's only comment was a broad grin and a warning to Bobby to mind what he was about with the village flappers.

There being nothing else to attend to at the moment Bobby went out again to make a little private investigation of his own, for he was anxious to assure himself that Mrs. Somerville was a trustworthy person, that, for example, she really had had two small hand towels stolen, and had not merely mislaid them, and that, too, her statement of the hour at which she had returned home on the night of the murder of Nat Kayne was really accurate. Unimportant points, perhaps, but such minor matters have a way of concealing major significance.

However, the verification of the second of these two minor points had to be postponed, for Mrs. Payne, the neighbour with whom Mrs. Somerville had been on the evening of Nat Kayne's murder, was away, visiting a married daughter expecting an addition to her family. But Bobby was able to establish two other details; first, that Mrs. Payne had no wireless, probably the only person in the village without that adjunct to the amenities—and the noises—of modern life, and, secondly, that Mrs. Somerville was the kind of housewife who turned out every room from top to bottom at frequent intervals, tracking down with grim determination every grain of dust within the four walls of her home.

Both facts he thought interesting, and tucked them away in his mind for future consideration, and then, as he was walking back to the police station, he came face to face with Miss Perkins, returning home apparently after a small shopping expedition, as she carried a paper bag or two in her hands.

"Oh, that's luck," he said, "I was rather hoping to meet you."

She looked a little startled, even afraid, he thought, and her pale eyes from behind their heavy glasses flashed at him a sudden, intent, and questioning look.

"Oh, yes; oh, I'm so sorry," she said, pulling open her handbag, which was provided with one of the popular zip fasteners.

"Major Harley was asking for you," Bobby went on.

"Yes," she said, fumbling in her bag.

"About the pistol you told us you saw, the small one," Bobby explained. "You remember? You described it as small and flat, it was in a drawer of Mr. Broast's writing table."

"Yes," she agreed, "yes." She produced from her bag the handkerchief she had apparently been fumbling for, and put it to her eyes. "I'm so sorry," she said, "but it's all so Dreadful, isn't it?"

A few more questions Bobby put her she answered clearly and simply, describing the little two-two automatic quite plainly, though she would insist on calling it a revolver. Bobby, who had an exact mind, tried to explain the difference between the two types of weapons, but this she seemed incapable of taking in, in spite of the clear description she gave of the pistol she said she had seen. Another remark of hers made Bobby realize that she still believed Mr. Broast had returned the previous night by the six o'clock train, as he originally intended, and not by the last train, as was in fact the case. Indeed she looked as if she thought Bobby must be mistaken in what he said.

"Oh, I'm so sorry," she protested with her usual inane giggle, "but I'm sure that's what he said, and he's always so Particular, and there was a light in his room, too, last night, about nine."

"Are you sure of that?" Bobby asked.

"Oh, yes, indeed, at least, I mean to say, I think I am."

"Do you mean you saw Mr. Broast himself?"

"Oh, no, just that there was a light in his room, like there always is, when he's there, because he always gets his letters ready, so I can type them first thing in the morning, and I wondered if he had brought the Trial Tennyson back with him he had been to see, because it's so Interesting, isn't it?"

"Yes," agreed Bobby absently, for he was wondering if this new piece of information broke the Broast alibi.

In these days of cars and motor-cycles, great distances can be covered with great ease. If the modern man cannot yet be in two different places at the same time, he can at any rate be in two different places in extraordinarily swift succession. Anyhow, Mr. Broast's movements in town would now have to be checked with even greater care, and then Bobby remembered, too, that Olive had remarked on the early hour at which Miss Kayne had retired the previous evening—about nine, Olive said. She had said, too, that Miss Kayne had gone into the librarian's room for a moment or two, or, possibly, Miss Perkins had mistaken the window. That, however, Miss Perkins would not admit for a moment.

"Oh, no," she said, "I'm quite sure, ever so sure."

It occurred to Bobby to wonder why she had returned to the Lodge after her work was over, and he was about to put that question to her, though indeed he knew that when there was a pressure of work she sometimes came back late to try to finish it, when quite calmly she dropped a bombshell that drove everything else out of his head.

"Oh, I'm so sorry," she said, "but I do wonder if you've ever thought, and of course, it isn't Slander, because why shouldn't they? or Libel, or anything like that, is it? but I do wonder if perhaps Miss Kayne and Mr. Broast aren't married?"

CHAPTER XXI
THE TRIAL TENNYSON

Bobby merely gaped, too astonished at this suggestion even to say a word. Such an idea had never entered his mind. He had only thought of Miss Kayne as an enormous, fat old woman, of Mr. Broast as a withered, dried up old stick of a scholar. True, Olive had told him that Miss Kayne talked of some far off, distant romance in her life, but even that had failed to bring before him a picture of her as a young girl with such dreams as young girls have. Much less had he ever conceived the dried up old scholar as having also once been young, or ever thought that in his veins, too, as in Miss Kayne's, had at one time run the hot and careless blood of youth, that indeed for both of them there had been a time when ginger was still hot in the mouth. No one is born fat and old, no one comes into the world a dried up old scholar with a heart pumping ink, not blood. In this youth of theirs the two of them had been thrown into close companionship. Miss Kayne had apparently in her girlhood seen scarcely anyone else, except her father's friends of his own age. Was it perhaps love letters from Mr. Broast, concealed in the first place from her father's eyes, of which she had confided the secret hiding place to Olive? Perhaps Mr. Broast had written for her verses of which he was now ashamed, thinking they would damage his reputation as a serious scholar, while Miss Kayne cherished tender memories of them and a belief in their beauty she thought the world should be allowed a chance to admire as well. That might explain the secrecy shown. She dared not publish them now in face of Mr. Broast's objections, but hoped that in coming years a posthumous fame might be won for him—for her, too, perhaps as the Beatrice to his Dante.

Fantastic in a way, perhaps, and yet conceivable enough in the light of this suggestion Miss Perkins had just dropped.

Bobby remembered, too, those odd clauses in the will governing the disposition of the library, clauses that did now seem to suggest old Mr. Kayne had had some grounds for fearing the unsuitable marriage so carefully provided against. If Mr. Broast were, in fact, the person most specially aimed at by those clauses, then it seemed to Bobby that an entirely new set of circumstances came into consideration.

It was perhaps the extreme surprise Bobby's expression showed that now produced from Miss Perkins a faint giggle that reminded him of her presence.

"What gave you that idea?" he asked.

"Oh, I'm so sorry, it's only just what I thought," she answered, with yet another of those nerve-trying giggles of hers. "I suppose I oughtn't to have said anything, ought I? Of course, I don't Know, because how could I? and I don't think now they're very fond of each other either, but then that's so Usual, isn't it? I mean, when you're married, and I'm sure she's afraid of him, I mean to say, anyone can see that, can't they? and why is she? if he's only the librarian and she could send him away whenever she wanted, only not if he's her Husband, could she? at least, not very well."

"I suppose not," agreed Bobby, trying to adjust his ideas to this new suggestion. "Noticed anything else?" he asked.

"Oh no," she answered, "I'm so sorry, only I mean to say I simply couldn't Help, because of course I don't Listen. I wouldn't Think of such a thing, only it wasn't my fault Mr. Broast was almost Shouting at Miss Kayne. Bullying her, and I thought: Why, the horrid way he talks to her you would think they were married, and then it came over me just like a flash of lightning that's what it was."

Bobby asked a few more questions, but obtained no more information. The little typists had no actual facts to go on, apparently, but the more Bobby thought it over the more he felt that quite possibly she had hit upon the truth. There is Biblical authority, he reminded himself, for the belief that things hidden from the wise are sometimes revealed to the foolish. Clever people are apt to confuse their minds by the multitude of their ideas, while the simple folk see only the one that is sometimes, though not always, the truth.

Yet, even if Miss Kayne and Mr. Broast were man and wife, bound by a secret marriage, how did that affect the sole question before the police, the identity of the murderer?

Could it be that Knowledge of the secret marriage had somehow only now reached the two trustees, and that they had been murdered to prevent their taking action on it? But there was nothing they could have done except by acquiring a greater power of interference, to insist on a stricter supervision, a more careful control, and that would have been largely, if not entirely, offset, by the superior position and authority Broast would gain as acknowledged husband of the owner. The Courts, if appealed to, would almost certainly take the view that Mr. Broast was a quite suitable person: in view of his high standing as a scholar, a very suitable person indeed. Highly improbable they would exercise the powers they might have thought it proper to use if Miss Kayne—Mrs. Broast was she, really?—had married some heedless young spendthrift or indeed anyone unsuitable for a position of trust in connection with what was almost a national possession.

No motive for a double murder, Bobby told himself, in any knowledge of any such marriage having reached the trustees.

He thanked Miss Perkins for her suggestion, remarked doubtfully that he did not see how the marriage was any-one else's business, dropped a hint he hoped would be effective against repeating the story, received Miss Perkins's fervent declaration that she would never even Think of such a thing, only it was Different when it was the police, wasn't it? and then, leaving her, made his way back to the police station. Killick had gone, but Major Harley was still there, brooding over some of the other reports that had come in that day, and when Bobby asked to see him and repeated Miss Perkins's story, he looked half puzzled, half amused.

"It may be true," he agreed, "but I don't see what we can do. It doesn't seem to affect the investigation. There's no suggestion of this being a crime of passion or jealousy." He paused to smile as he thought of such words in connection with that gross, ponderous old woman—like a good many other people he always thought of her as old, though in fact she was nearly a decade younger than he was. He went on:— "We could ask them, of course, if they are married, but if they told us to mind our own business, I don't know what we could say. We may have to put it to them, but I would like to think it over first. Surprising, of course. Had any more gifts of flowers, by the way, from any more lady admirers?"

"No, sir," answered Bobby soberly.

It was too late now for any more work to be done that day, and Bobby went back for supper to the Wynford Arms, accompanied on the way by an escort of journalists, who were very friendly and jolly and asked him no questions at all, and invited him to have a drink, and now and again made some outrageous suggestion or another in the hope that Bobby would contradict it, and so be led into a general discussion from which the intelligent journalistic mind might at least garner a hint or two to be dished up next morning as "Exclusive to—" whatever national newspaper it happened to be.

But Bobby had been there before, and much as he liked the company of newspaper men, with all the information they possess they are so careful not to print in their papers, he had adopted the simple plan of listening to all they had to say with no other comment than: "Well, now, you do surprise me." So presently the newspaper men gave him up as a bad job, told him the latest scandalous story about a Cabinet Minister, made him a fresh offer of a drink to show there was no ill feeling, and then allowed him to depart to eat his supper in peace.

But before he was half way through his meal Mr. Adams came into the room, established himself at another table, gave the girl in waiting his order, and then came across to Bobby. In his careful, precise tones he said:

"I have just made a communication to Major Harley. I conceive that even in circumstances no doubt trying, a greater courtesy on his part would be by no means out of place. I refer to a manner and to language it would be no exaggeration to describe as menacing."

"Better look out then," said Bobby unfeelingly. "Menaces from a chief constable probably mean something. What did you tell him? Your correct name and address? your real business here? I suppose you've not forgotten the inquest is to-morrow and that you will be examined on oath?"

"The fact," admitted Mr. Adams, "is clear in my mind."

"You'll be asked a lot of questions," Bobby reminded him.

"I shall be prepared to answer them," said Mr. Adams slowly, "and I have indeed received instructions to do so. But only as regards facts within my own knowledge, such as the one I imparted to-night to Major Harley, though I fear he lacks the training and cultivation necessary for the full appreciation of its meaning and significance."

"Any objection to telling me?" Bobby asked, "though I expect you think I lack the necessary cultivation, too."

Mr. Adams put the tips of his fingers together and perpended. Bobby devoted himself to apple pie and cream, the agreeable stage at which he had now arrived.

"I confess," pronounced Mr. Adams finally, "I am not highly impressed by such signs of intelligence as I have so far had an opportunity to observe in you. No doubt," he added, evidently trying to be fair, "it is higher, and even considerably higher, than that of the average officer of police."

"Oh, indeed," said Bobby crossly, "well, perhaps you'll find the police have some intelligence before we've done with you."

"It would surprise me," said Mr. Adams gravely. He added: "The information I gave Major Harley to-night was to the effect that Mr. Broast purchased yesterday in town, for the sum of one hundred pounds, paid on the spot, an early trial Tennyson."

"Oh," said Bobby, obliged to admit that his intelligence had certainly failed to see anything significant in this fact he was already aware of. "Well, why shouldn't he, if he wanted the thing? I must say I don't see—"

Mr. Adams raised a hand.

"I have not finished," he said. "Allow me to conclude. Mr. Broast is, beyond cavil, one of the two or three greatest bibliographical experts now alive. Others," said Mr. Adams primly, "may be his equal, none is his superior. The Trial Tennyson in question is undoubtedly a forgery."

With that he rose, bowed, and returned to his own table, and Bobby thoughtfully consumed the last spoonful of apple pie and confessed to himself that that intelligence of his was unable to attach much importance to this piece of information.

From what he knew of experts, it was only necessary for one of them to declare that X was X for another to start up with indignant proof that X was in fact Z. Anyhow, what had the disputes of experts to do with thus business of murder?

Experts talk murderously enough, but fortunately they don't act like that.

He was not permitted, however, to indulge long in speculation, for one of the waitresses now brought him a note to say that Major Harley was still at the police station and before he returned home would be glad to see Sergeant Owen.

Attended, therefore, by two or three vigilant journalists who had watched the receipt of the note and hoped that something was going to happen at last, Bobby went back to the police station. It was Mrs. Mills's parlour Major Harley was using for his office, and to him Bobby repeated what Mr. Adams had been saying.

"That's what I wanted to see you about." The Major explained. "I can't see any significance in it. Why should Broast buy a faked article, and, if he did, well, why shouldn't he? I'm rather looking forward to seeing Adams in the witness-box presently."

"Yes, sir," agreed Bobby, "only Adams strikes me as a very downy old bird. I'm a bit inclined to back him against the smartest cross-examiner at the bar."

The Major looked as if he agreed, little as he wished to.

"We'll get the truth out of him somehow," he said with an air of great confidence. "Out of Virtue, too. I'm curious to see if he'll repeat that yarn of his on oath. I've dropped him a hint what the penalty is for perjury over here, and he didn't half like it. I suppose this story of the forged Trial Tennyson must be followed up. The story of Miss Kayne's marriage, too. If it's true, why was it kept secret? I've been looking through the will, we had a copy here, and there's nothing to prevent her marrying anyone she likes. The only thing is that the trustees get greater powers of action if they suspect mal-administration. That's all it comes to."

"Well, sir," Bobby said, "do you think that links up with Adams's story about the faked Tennyson? Suppose Mr. Broast couldn't face an investigation that might show up other fakes? Suppose the whole library is full of fakes?

Could that be why he refused to let Mr. Adams examine the
Mandeville pages? Perhaps they aren't Caxton's work at all,
just fakes?"

Major Harley shook his head.

"I've had that very much in mind," he said, "but it won't
do. The Kayne library is a kind of Mecca for bibliographers
from all over the world. The Mandeville leaves have been
publicly exhibited in Paris. I know that because I had to
provide an escort for the first part of their journey. All the
experts in the world had a chance to see them. And there's
never been an expert yet since the world began who
wouldn't give the eyes out of his head for a chance to prove
a brother expert wrong. Besides, the provenance of the
things is well known, the whole story of their discovery. No,
I think we must take it the Mandeville leaves are genuine.
After all, there's no doubt Broast is the expert in his own
line."

"Yes, sir," agreed Bobby, "only does that quite fit with
this new story of his having bought a fake? And if the
Mandeville leaves are genuine, why did he refuse to let
Adams photograph them?"

"No, I know it doesn't fit," sighed the Major. "I've been
telling myself that for the last hour. But then nothing fits.
Everything contradicts everything else. But all the same I'm
not satisfied about Broast. He'll have to be asked some more
questions. I don't call his alibi for the Winders murder fully
watertight. And he had none at all for the Nat Kayne
murder. He says he came back last night by the eleven
thirty-five and there's no doubt he was seen coming off the
platform somewhere before the train got in and then to
mingle with the passengers alighting and walk off with
them. No one would be likely to notice. There's no proof
that's what he did, but also there's no proof he was ever
actually on that train. He can't or won't say where he was
between the time he left the book shop in Piccadilly about
six till the time he says he caught the late train for Mayfield.

He says he met a friend to whom he gave the Trial Tennyson. He says he bought it for him. He won't give the friend's name because he is a dealer who hopes to sell for a much bigger price, and if it got about he had bought for a hundred he couldn't ask so much more. I told him all information given us was confidential, He was—well, rude. He told me no policeman was intelligent enough to understand how necessary it was to regard that kind of information as confidential. He had the impudence," said Major Harley darkly, "to ask me if I knew what a trial Tennyson was. I told him that was not relevant. Then he was good enough to say he didn't mistrust our good faith, only our intelligence. I pressed him again to say where he was all that evening. All I could get out of him was that he met his friend and they had a walk together, and after his friend left him he had a walk by himself. He says, too, he had something to eat at a tea shop, but he doesn't know whereabouts, or what firm it was, or anything. He says they are all much the same, and of course that's true enough."

"Yes, sir," agreed Bobby. "Then there's nothing to show where he actually was last night between about six and eleven thirty?"

"No," agreed the Major. "I was talking to Killick. Killick suggests he could easily have come from town secretly, a car perhaps, and been at Highfields about ten thirty, attracted Winders's attention in the way the earth on the study window sill suggests, made an appointment with him, returned on a bicycle maybe, to Mayfield, shown himself to the station staff, given up the return half of his ticket in the usual way, all as I suggested myself just now, got back to Highfields in time to keep the appointment with Winders and commit the murder, and then back to Wynton Lodge with what he would think looked like a complete alibi. The motive may be irregularities in the library Kayne had discovered and Winders begun to suspect. The pistol used to murder Kayne we know belonged to Broast, and Broast could have thrown it into the pond where you found it. Winders suspected as much, and that's why he went to have a look and why his footsteps were there. There's Miss Perkins's evidence that a pistol of the calibre used to murder Winders was in Broast's possession. You can't think she knows enough, has sense enough, to invent that story, and then, too, you remember you saw something Broast was holding, once when we had been questioning him, that you thought looked like a small automatic, though afterwards he let you see an electric torch in his hand. It all counts. Many a man has been hanged on weaker evidence. What do you say, Owen?"

"Well, sir," Bobby answered slowly, "it still seems to me there are a lot of things that don't fit. That yarn of Virtue's, for example, and then for another thing, where do I come in? I feel that's important. And then there are those forget-me-nots someone sent me? What was that for?"

CHAPTER XXII
ASSEMBLING FACTS

Major Harley looked faintly puzzled.

"Where you come in?" he repeated. "Why? And what about forget-me-nots? Killick did say something about flowers some girl or other… they were laughing about it."

"Yes, sir," agreed Bobby. "Mr. Killick pretended to think it was someone trying to start a flirtation." Bobby paused and spoke slowly. "It didn't strike me that way. Not now, not with all this happening. Besides, everyone here knows Miss Farrar and I are engaged."

"It wasn't Miss Farrar herself, I suppose?"

"No, sir. I asked."

"You mean you think something was behind it; you think the forget-me-nots meant something?"

"Yes, sir. At first, I thought it was to remind us of something—forget-me-not. Only I couldn't think of anything we had forgotten."

"We'll have to try to find who did send them," remarked the Major. "Not too easy. You've kept the box or whatever they came in?"

"Yes, it was a small cardboard box. It could have been posted in a pillar box. The address was in block letters. I'll bring it across, if I may, for further examination."

"Doesn't sound much to go on," agreed the Major gloomily. "What did you mean about where you come in? I don't follow that."

"Well, sir," Bobby said slowly, "everyone in the village knows I am at Scotland Yard. They all seemed interested, seemed to look on a C.I.D. man as a sort of minor edition of a film star, instead of just what he is, an ordinary chap doing his job in the best way he can. There's Miss Kayne, for instance, and her telling me about the perfect murder she said she had committed. I can't get rid of the feeling that it was because a C.I.D. man happened to turn up here, that all this started. Putting a match to it."

Major Harley looked more puzzled than ever.

"I don't follow that," he said again. "Surely knowing the police are about is more likely to stop things than to start them."

"Yes, sir, I know," agreed Bobby, looking almost equally puzzled. "Only can it be mere coincidence, that as soon as I come here, these things happen?"

Major Harley got up from his seat and went to stand by the mantelpiece. He looked very worried. He picked up a mug with a lurid view of Margate on it and the announcement that it was a present from that town. He examined it intently and then shook his head gravely, as if in final disapproval after careful thought, and put it back in its place. He said:

"Owen, you mentioned Miss Kayne and that absurd statement of hers. You don't want us to take it seriously, do you? Surely you haven't got her in your mind?"

"Yes, sir," said Bobby.

"Preposterous, ridiculous, impossible," said the Major slowly and distinctly. He came back to the table and seated himself again. "So have I," he said heavily. "It's incredible, but so have I."

"Only," Bobby added, "I'm not thinking of her more than of two or three others."

"She can hardly get out of her chair without help," the Major said. "Certainly, her manner's been very strange lately. But is she physically capable? I mean, could she get about?"

"I've tried to go into that," Bobby said. "I think she could if she wanted to."

"Well, even if we were able to prove it, no one would ever believe us," observed the Major gloomily. "That fat old woman! Do you think she sent the forget-me-nots?"

"There are forget-me-nots in the Lodge gardens," Bobby said, "by the trees, where the seats have been put for the view. But then there are forget-me-nots in pretty nearly every garden. Also it would be very difficult for Miss Kayne to send anything like that without someone knowing. I suppose it's possible."

"Well, why should she?" asked the Major. "The murders I mean? Two of them? What for? Of course, we haven't to prove motive in a murder case. Still—"

"Yes, sir," agreed Bobby.

"You don't suggest she's mad?"

"No sir, I can't see any suggestion of insanity anywhere. It all seems to me to hang together only I can't see how. It's the governing idea that we can't get hold of, it seems to me."

"There's always what she said to you," mused the Major, "about the perfect murder, I mean. What did she say that for, and what's its significance? If any. Anyhow, why should it make her commit two more murders, young Kayne and

Winders, too? Could they have found out something? Could they have known or suspected anything about this perfect murder she talks about? For that matter, who could she have murdered and what for?"

"There's one thing, sir," Bobby pointed out, "there does seem to be a record in this case of someone who disappeared and has never been heard of since."

"You mean, Virtue's story about his cousin, the one who vanished on a European trip. But he was traced to Paris, wasn't he? He vanished there, not here. Besides, there seems no record that he and Miss Kayne ever met each other, except perhaps casually. So far as appears, he had none but business relations here. He bought books from the library and consulted them sometimes. But that's all, as far as we know, and it would be almost impossible to find out anything different after all this time."

"Yes, sir," agreed Bobby. "Very difficult indeed. At the time one could have tried to find out more; if there was really satisfactory proof he was going about with some unknown girl and if it was really he who was traced to Paris. A false trail might have been laid, but it would be pretty hard to prove that now."

"Well, then," said the Major, "there you are, and where are you?"

"Yes, sir," said Bobby, quite agreeing with this somewhat involved remark. "Could we try to start from the beginning? I mean, go over what we do know for certain?"

"Precious little we do know for certain," grumbled the Major. "Well, go ahead."

"I thought," explained Bobby, "if we got clear in our minds what we do actually know, some kind of pattern might begin to show. The first thing we do know is that a relative of Mr. Virtue's disappeared on a European trip, and we also know he had some connection with the Kayne library and visited this village. It appears he was traced to Paris, but there's no confirmation. We don't know it's true."

"You mean—" began the Major and paused.

"I'm trying to keep to the facts we can be certain of," Bobby repeated. "If a murder were committed in one place and the body hidden there, it might be a good plan to lay a false track somewhere else."

"But his luggage? hotel registers? all that?"

"His murderers might have secured possession of his luggage. A signature in an hotel register could be forged. In busy hotels guests are not always clearly remembered. I can't agree that it is proved as actual fact that the missing man disappeared in Paris. It may be so. It may not. All we can be sure of is that he did disappear and there's no explanation known. Also we know as fact that Miss Kayne has talked about a perfect murder in the past. Those are two facts. There may be no connection."

"Yes," said the Major. "Yes." Then he paused and said: "Yes" once more. Bobby continued:

"Another fact we know and the next in the time order, is that Bertram Virtue visited the Kayne library on the occasion of the breaking of the glass case holding the *Glastonbury Psalter*. Afterwards he turned up again when for some reason Mr. Broast refused him admittance. Thereon Virtue told a story, almost certainly false, of having seen a dead man on the library floor. When challenged about that, he demanded that the library should be searched. He has pressed that point since. We know also that Miss Perkins has in her possession a photograph answering to the description Virtue gave of the dead body he said he saw. I think we may say also that Virtue had no knowledge of that, his surprise when he knew was certainly genuine."

"Yes, I think that, too," agreed the Major. "What you are getting at is that Virtue thinks his lost cousin was murdered, believes that the body is concealed somewhere in the library, only he daren't say so, but he thinks if he could fix up a search for a supposed other dead body, then some trace might be found of his lost cousin?"

"Yes, sir," Bobby said slowly. "that's what was in my mind. It seems to me a fair deduction."

"How did the Perkins girl get hold of the photograph, if it is that of the missing Mr. Virtue? do you think she's in with Bertram Virtue?"

"I thought of that, it's possible but not very likely. It may be she found it in the way she says. I don't know. It seems to have been in her possession ever since she got here. Possibly before. Of course, that will have to be gone into."

"Only," the Major pointed out, "all this, though it's interesting and important, doesn't help us much to know who is guilty of these two recent murders?"

"No, sir. At present we are just assembling facts, or trying to. Another fact we know is that Mr. Adams is here under a false name on an errand he won't explain, and that the attempt he made to examine and photograph the Mandeville pages made Mr. Broast extremely angry. Yet we also know—your evidence, sir—that the Mandeville pages are genuine, so why shouldn't any interested person examine them? We know also—my evidence—that Mr. Broast was again extremely angry when I happened to notice that Dryden's autograph was not in a copy of Milton's*Paradise Lost* where he had told us it was."

"Surely that's trivial," interposed the Major. "Temper at being found out in a mistake?"

"It's stuck in my mind, sir," Bobby said apologetically. "I thought it odd at the time, and then it is a fact, and we've so few facts to give us any kind of lead. It's just a fact, like the forget-me-not incident, and like the other fact that everything seems to have begun as soon as it was known a C.I.D. man was on the spot."

"You've something else on your mind," the Major said. "Go on."

"Well, sir, that's about all we know in the way of fact, but I do think we can deduce a few other things we can be reasonably sure of. If I'm right in thinking it's in any way significant that all this started with my own arrival here, then I think it means some one knows something, is anxious it should come out, and yet dares not act openly—either dares not," Bobby corrected himself, "or has only suspicions, and thought if the police got interested they might dig up something. Both Bertram Virtue and Adams have more or less admitted they're afraid of the consequences if they talk too much."

"Brings them both into the picture," commented the Major.

"Another thing I'm inclined to think a reasonable deduction from what we know," Bobby continued, "is that there's something wrong with the Kayne library. It's difficult to see what. Mr. Broast's reputation seems to make it impossible to think, as I did at first, that the library is full of fakes and forgeries she daren't allow to be seen. He does allow them to be seen, only not by Adams and not by Virtue. That seems to me very difficult to understand. Why are those two barred? Do they know something? Bertram Virtue's no expert, anyhow. Yet it does seem to add up to something wrong, and what else can it be but forgeries Broast is afraid may be discovered?"

"Doesn't seem to hold water," pronounced the Major. "Not when practically every bibliographical swell in the world knows, for instance, the Mandeville pages and all about them. They're famous. If Broast had made a bloomer about them, even, it wouldn't matter much. They aren't his private property, and if he's wrong, he's wrong in conjunction with all the other experts."

"Yes, sir," agreed Bobby once more. "I wonder why—it's another fact—Adams was so keen on letting us know Mr. Broast bought yesterday as genuine what Adams describes as a certain fake?"

"Broast is as likely to be right as Adams," observed the Major. "A difference between two experts, and Broast backs his opinion to the tune of a £100. Nothing in that, surely?"

"No—o, sir," said Bobby, though doubtfully. "It is a bit odd that Mr. Broast seems to have disposed of it pretty effectively, and won't say how, so that apparently no independent opinion can be obtained. That may mean nothing or it may mean a lot, but at any rate another fact is that apparently now we can't say for certain who was right—Adams in saying it was a fake or Broast in backing his opinion to the tune of a £100."

"Is it relevant?"

"I don't know, sir. I can't see where it fits, but it's there. It may be a part of the puzzle or it may be something altogether outside. It's a fact, though, that there's conflicting evidence, and the point can't be decided because the exhibit has disappeared owing to action on the part of Mr. Broast."

"If it's not genuine, why should he pay a good fat sum for it?" demanded the Major.

Bobby ignored a question to which he did not know the answer. He went on:

"Another fairly obvious deduction is that the murderer must be someone connected with the Kayne library in some way. Miss Kayne herself, if she is Miss Kayne and not Mrs. Broast; Miss Farrar, who is studying at the lodge; Miss Perkins, who works in the library; Briggs, the butler; the two maids; Mr. Broast himself; Virtue and Adams, who want to get into the library and aren't allowed. I think the murderer must be one of them, though I also think the innocence of some is fairly certain."

"Yes, but which of them, and which is the one we want?" asked the Major, shaking his head sadly at what seemed an almost unsolvable problem. "Take Adams. He has no alibi. He was the first to discover Winders's body. He won't give us his proper name and address or explain what he's doing here. For all his prim appearance, we know from his war record he is capable of a good deal when he's put to it. There seems to be no motive unless, as Broast has hinted, there's been some plan on foot to rob the library. Pretty valuable stuff there. Is it possible young Kayne was behind some such plan? He may have wanted to draw back, hesitated, quarrelled in some way, and his accomplices felt he had to be silenced. Winders may have suspected something, and so he had to be silenced, too. How is that for a theory to work on?"

"Quite good, sir, but not complete," Bobby said, "not enough to take action on."

"No," agreed the Major. "No. Or perhaps Adams has been selling Broast faked stuff and was afraid of its coming out? Not very strong that. Well, what about Virtue?"

"It's clear he is very anxious for the library to be searched, and the suggestion seems to be that he thinks his cousin was murdered there and the body hidden, but he daren't say so without proof."

"I should think not," growled the Major. "Bodies are hidden in queer places sometimes, I admit, in cellars and so on. But in a library, a world-famous library?"

"Well sir, the library has a cellar," Bobby remarked. "It's where a fifteenth century printing press stands. Mr. Broast uses it still, I believe."

The Major shook his head, evidently unconvinced. Then he said:

"Look here, Owen, how's this for an idea? Virtue does believe his cousin was murdered here, perhaps for the sake of some specially valuable book or as a result of some quarrel. Wasn't there something about the *Dictes* of Caxton he had bought? Well, Virtue can't get proof, but he doesn't mean the murderers to get away with it. So he takes the law into his own hands, shoots the two he believes guilty, and invent that yarn about seeing a dead body on the library floor to give himself an alibi?"

"Well, sir, in that case, if it's like that," said Bobby hesitatingly, "wouldn't you have expected Broast to be a victim, not the two trustees?"

Major Harley played absently with his fingers on the surface of the table. He was silent for a time, but his look was troubled, and Bobby watched him with some surprise. Slowly, in a low voice he said:

"Well, perhaps he'll be next."

Bobby, unnerved, muttered:

"Oh, well, now then, I never thought of that."

It had not struck him until then that perhaps even yet the series was not finished. He had advised and wished Olive to leave, but not because he had really thought any further danger existed, merely because he wished her away from unpleasant and depressing events. But now Major Harley's words, still more his anxious look, called up worse apprehensions.

He said presently:

"Thinking of Mr. Broast as a possible victim, rather takes us away from suspecting him of the murders."

"It's nothing but guess work and speculation all round so far," declared Major Harley. "I'm afraid we've got no further. Look at the time, too. We shall have to make inquiries in Paris. They may be able to give us an idea whether Virtue did actually disappear there, whether that's a fact or whether it was a false trail laid to divert suspicion from what happened here. Not that the French police bother their heads too much about what happens to foreigners. They are a bit inclined to think that if tourists poke their noses into all the most disreputable holes in Paris they can find, then they've only got themselves to thank for what happens. Well, Owen, what's the next step?"

"Well, sir," said Bobby hesitantly, "about those forget-me-nots..."

"Well, what about them? Are they the next step?"

"Yes, sir, if you agree," Bobby answered.

CHAPTER XXIII
ACCUSATION

Late as it was when Bobby left the village police station, he did not go straight back to the inn and his bed but made his way first to the Lodge, where he wished to leave a note for Olive so that the developments just planned by himself and

Major Harley should not come as a surprise to her. For to Bobby's suggestions the Major had now given a somewhat reluctant consent.

"Private property," he had said gloomily. "Common trespass, that's what it is you want, Owen. Police have no more rights than anyone else, only they've got to be more careful. If they look over the wall ten to one it's called stealing a sheep."

"Yes, sir," agreed Bobby sympathetically, more than sympathetically indeed, "but still trespass isn't an offence in itself. The only remedy is an action for damages, and we shan't do any damage to speak of."

"We can be ordered off the grounds," said the Major in a depressed voice. "Nice fools we shall look."

However, in the end Bobby had received authority to make the few arrangements necessary, and now, after pushing the note he had written to Olive through the Lodge letter box, he was returning home to the village, the inn, and bed, when he saw standing by the side of the road a man and woman talking. Immediately the woman slipped away, as though the sound of his approaching footsteps had frightened her, and it seemed to him that on the still night air there was borne back to him a faint and distant giggle.

From the shadows in which they had been standing the man who had been her companion detached himself and came towards Bobby. Bobby saw it was Bertram Virtue. Virtue said to him:

"I was looking for you. There's something I want to say."

"Yes," said Bobby. "Well, what?"

"It's this," Virtue answered, speaking very slowly and deliberately. "I've told you a cousin of mine, James A. Virtue, disappeared on a trip to Europe and we never knew what happened to him. Well, now I believe he was murdered. I believe he was murdered right here, in this village. I believe he was murdered by Broast, the man in charge of the Kayne library. I believe I can prove it."

"Yes," said Bobby, non-committally, though inwardly so excited his bed and his need therefor passed quite from his thoughts. "Well, better come along to the police station and make a statement. You understand, of course, you are making a serious charge? You said you had proofs?"

"There's this," said Virtue. "James A. visited here. We've letters, the last he ever wrote, dated from here. He came specially to show Broast a *Dictes* printed by Caxton he had found. It's a valuable thing, worth real money, worth more than money if you've got the collector's bug. It was in what they call mint condition. James A. found it in a farm down Cape Cod way, Massachusetts. In James A.'s last letter, the one dated from this place, he said Broast was more than excited about it, called it the finest example of Caxton's work he had ever seen. James A. said Broast would give almost anything to get hold of it for his library. Of course, James A. wouldn't part, it meant just as much to him, more, because he was so mighty proud of having found it. Well, after that, nothing more has ever been heard of James, but the *Dictes* is in Broast's library. How did it get there?"

"Are you sure it's the same copy?" Bobby asked. "Can you prove it?"

"Yes. James A. told us. He pricked his initials on the last page."

"How do you mean? pricked them?"

"With a pin. Pricked his initials in outline—J.A.V. You can't see them unless you hold the page up to the light."

"Your statement is that these initials, outlined in pricks made by a pin, are on the last page of the copy of the *Dictes* now in the Kayne library?"

"Yes."

"You would be prepared to say that on oath?"

"Yes."

Bobby remembered the woman he had seen slipping away as he came up and that faint sound of a distant giggle borne back to him on the quiet night air. Miss Perkins, he felt certain. It looked as if Virtue had persuaded her to examine the *Dictes* in the Kayne library and ascertain that it did in fact show the private marks described. It seemed good evidence. Virtue went on:

"There's not only that. I can give a full description of the book, the names on the title page former owners wrote in. I've got a copy of the description James A. wrote out after he had found it. It meant a lot to him, the sort of thing that only happens once in a lifetime, and the only to one collector in a thousand. It meant as much to him as being asked to run for President would mean to some folk. James A. would never have parted while he was alive."

"Sounds like the same copy," Bobby agreed. "Mr. Broast will have to be asked to account for its possession. But I don't know that it amounts to proof of murder. It's pretty late now, Mr. Virtue, too late to do anything to-night. I think your best plan will be to draw up a full statement and let us have it first thing in the morning. It will be for the chief constable to decide what further steps to take."

"You mean Major Harley?"

"Yes."

"All right. I'll do that."

"Mr. Virtue," Bobby said gravely, "when I say a full statement, I mean it. I mean everything. I'm thinking of that story you told us about what you said you saw in the library the night of the first murder. I think that needs explaining."

"Oh, well," said Virtue, "that was just a yarn."

"You mean it was a lie?" Bobby asked.

"I suppose so; nothing like talking straight, is there?" Virtue said with a little nervous laugh. "Only a lie means when you want to deceive anyone, doesn't it? and I didn't reckon that yarn would deceive anyone for long, not even British police. I just knew that book was there and I had to get to see it someway."

"What about the broken glass of the *Glastonbury Psalter* case?"

"Yes, that was me, too," admitted Virtue. "I used to be quite good with a catapult when I was a kid. I took a shot with one and hit that glass case square. I reckoned, in the excitement, I would get a chance to grab the *Dictes* and have a look. It was a good plan, but it didn't work. All the folk made a rush for where the sound of the smash came from,, all except one old fellow who stayed leaned right up against the case with the *Dictes* in it. His nose was so deep in some other book he was looking at, I don't think he had heard a thing. My big idea had been to force open the case—I knew it was locked, but it didn't look so strong as all that—and grab the *Dictes*. But I couldn't do a thing with him leaning right up against that very case. I asked him if he hadn't heard a smash, and what he thought was happening, and he sort of looked at me and said it was a most interesting variant and the use of signatures was characteristic and decisive, and then he put his nose back in the book and my chance was gone before I could make up my mind to slug him and do what I wanted. Anyway, he was too old to slug, and I couldn't expect him to stand for it if I yanked him out of there and smashed open the case and grabbed the *Dictes*. Even the way he had his nose in that book, he would have been bound to notice something was happening."

"I expect so," agreed Bobby.

"So I went away," Virtue continued, "and tried to think up something else. Not so easy. Then I heard there was a swell Scotland Yard cop down here for the weekend. So I worked it out to frame something, so there would just have to be a search of the library, and I thought if the Scotland Yard folk were so mighty smart as they are let on to be, then they might spot it. I reckoned to be let in on the search. I reckoned if I was, I would get hold of that *Dictes* someway. Well, that didn't come off either. Oh, and I described James A. the way I did because I thought it would give Broast a jolt, if James A.'s body was hidden there and someone said they had seen it lying on the library floor."

"Mr. Virtue," said Bobby with more severity than he felt, for it was difficult not to experience some degree of sympathy for this ingenuous young man, "you seem to have behaved very foolishly and in a way to make us doubt your whole story. You should have brought your suspicions straight to us."

"A fat lot of good that would have been," retorted Virtue. "Thank you. I've had some, British cold water I mean. And it's sure a colder brand than any other ever known. I got an introduction to one of your swell lawyers. He went all up in the air. Said if I didn't watch my step, I should be in for an action of libel, heavy damages, too, said a libel action in this country—well, it was a libel action, said making suggestions of that sort against a scholar of Mr. Broast's standing was mighty serious, said on my own showing James A. had been traced to Paris and his baggage was found there, and so how could anything have happened to him here? I tried to say it wasn't so difficult to fake a trail, but he wouldn't have it. I tell you I crawled away after that talk feeling I was mighty lucky not to be going inside for the rest of my life and a million dollar fine as well. All the same I had my own ideas still, and I meant to find out what had happened to James A. and if that *Dictes* was his. It didn't work out the way I expected, and you may call me a fool from the last house in Foolsville, but then I wasn't reckoning on two fresh murders. What I say is, Broast put them through, too, and you can call that libel or slander or any darn thing you like."

"At any rate, I wouldn't say it to anyone else," remarked Bobby dryly. "It's not wise to throw around accusations like that."

"That's the way the London lawyer talked," Virtue said. "All the same, now I know the *Dictes* is the one belonging to James A., I want that library searched. I want it gone over from roof to cellar. I've been in that cellar. It's lined with packing cases. Parts of it have been concreted—to keep out rats. I asked about that. First they tried to poison them with putting down strychnine because the concrete wasn't any good. Maybe it wasn't for rats, maybe it was for—for something else."

"It will be for the chief constable to decide," Bobby repeated. "You may be sure you statement will receive full investigation. Let us have it as early as possible. You know the inquests on both Mr. Nat Kayne and Sir William Winders are to-morrow? They will only be formal, won't take more than a few minutes, but it all means a good deal of work and time taken up. So the earlier we get your statement the more chance there will be to consider it at once."

Virtue promised to have it ready first thing in the morning and in fact by nine o'clock it was in the hands of Major Harley, who read it with a frowning brow and then sent for Bobby to question him about some of the details.

"Broast will have to be questioned, that's clear," he said. "If this book can be identified, and apparently it can be—" He paused, frowned. "Do you think the identification satisfactory, Owen?" he asked. "There seems no proof on the face of it when these pricks were made."

"No, sir," agreed Bobby. "I thought of that, and if Virtue is in touch with Miss Perkins, he may have induced her to make them and he may have got the description he talks about from her."

The Major nodded.

"That'll have to be gone into," he said. "We'll see what Broast has to say first. Busy day ahead. One thing, the Perkins girl is such a little fool that even if Virtue has been getting at her, I don't suppose there'll be much trouble in inducing her to tell the truth. She'll soon be contradicting herself, and then we'll get it all. Virtue's a good-looking youngster, got a way with him, too. Sex appeal," said the Major suddenly; "the Perkins girl would most likely do anything for any good-looker in trousers. But she'll soon break down if she's questioned."

"Yes, sir," said Bobby mechanically, his thoughts elsewhere.

"Six hundred pounds," said Killick, "for a book. These collectors—make you ready to believe anything of them."

"Broast will have to be questioned, that's clear," Major Harley repeated, and later on, therefore, after the brief, formal inquest proceedings were over, Major Harley and Bobby presented themselves at the Lodge. Briggs admitted them, and learning their errand handed them over to Miss Perkins, who greeted them with her accustomed giggle.

"Oh, I'm so sorry," she said. "I'm afraid Mr. Broast's awfully busy—he's so good-tempered to-day, and he always is when he is Really Busy. If he isn't, you hardly dare go near him."

"I'm afraid we must ask you to interrupt him," the Major answered. "Police business can't wait, you know."

"Oh, is it about all these Dreadful things?" asked Miss Perkins. "They are so Awful, aren't they? I can hardly Sleep thinking about them, and perhaps there'll be someone else next, because you never know, do you? Not when it's once begun."

With that she retired into the library to announce their arrival, and soon returned to say Mr. Broast would be delighted to see them. He did, in fact, receive them very amiably, and with a touch of old-world courtesy that went well with his white hair, his thin, ascetic features, his tall though now stooping form. Bobby found himself thinking again that in his youth Mr. Broast must have been singularly handsome.

"I suppose," he said, greeting them, "it is too much to hope that you have discovered anything fresh about these most distressing events?"

"A statement has been made to us we are obliged to verify," the Major explained. "We have been given information that a valuable book now in this library, the *Dictes*, one of the first actually printed by Caxton, I am told, and of considerable pecuniary value, was formerly the property of a Mr. James A. Virtue. Mr. Virtue, an American citizen, was on a trip to this country, and it is established that he disappeared in a manner at present unexplained. What happened to him is unknown. If the book I spoke of can be identified with that known to have been in his possession when he disappeared, it may provide some clue to what happened."

Mr. Broast had listened with apparent surprise, and he waited a moment or two before answering.

"I remember corresponding with a Mr. Virtue, somewhere in Michigan he lived, I believe," he said, then: "I remember he visited the library here once or twice, you will probably find his name in the visitors book. I think, too, I had a letter asking if I could give his present address. That was some time ago, and naturally I had no idea where he was. I don't remember him personally. There are so many visitors here—curiosity-mongers, tourists, cranks who think any incunabula must be worth hundreds of pounds. No, I can't say I remember him very clearly, and I don't know why you think our *Dictes*—a very fine copy—ever belonged to him. May I ask why you think that?"

"Our information," said Major Harley, "is that when Mr. Virtue first got the book, he put his initials in it."

Mr. Broast stared unbelievingly. He rose to his feet, his stoop gone, his eyes alight with indignation.

"His initials. In a mint *Dictes*? His initials? Like a schoolboy scribbling in his first reading book? I don't believe it." He flung out his hand. "Impossible," he said, "no man could be guilty of such a crime."

CHAPTER XXIV
DISCOVERY

Major Harley blinked and made no reply. He was a trifle disconcerted by the vehemence with which Mr. Broast spoke. Bobby, watching him closely, did not speak either. Upright, indignant, with flushed cheeks and angry eyes, the librarian stood, quite still, one hand outstretched. He said again:

"Incredible, utterly incredible. But I will look. If what you tell me is the fact—" He paused. He spoke slowly and deliberately. He said: "I shall use my utmost endeavour to let it be known as widely as possible. The world shall know. Scribble your initials in a mint Caxton, a *Dictes*. Inconceivable. Besides, I should certainly have noticed such an outrage."

"Well, not scribbled exactly," Major Harley said. "Our information is that the initials were pricked out with a pin on the last page. I understand they can only be seen if the book is held up to the light."

"Extraordinary," said Mr. Broast. "At any rate, that does show a glimmer of decent feeling. Bad enough, though."

He moved away and opened with a key a book-case at a little distance. From one of the shelves he took down the famous *Dictes*. Handling it as a mother might her first-born, he brought it back with him. He opened it and held it up to the light. The pin pricks showed clearly. Mr. Broast put the book down, and, still standing, spoke gravely to his two visitors.

"Imagine it," he said, one hand caressing the volume with light, loving fingers. "Handled by Caxton himself. Drawn from the press nearly five hundred years ago, among the first of all printed books to be produced in England, the first spark, as it were, that lighted the great blaze of our knowledge of to-day, the first thrust forward into the full daylight from out of the blackness of the medieval ignorance, the first child of the wisdom of man. There it is for our reverence and our wonder, and it falls into the hands of a man who can think of nothing but to stick in it his own beastly, trivial initials. We must be thankful he did no worse thing, but to think that such people exist! It's—it's bewildering," said Mr. Broast, deeply moved. "It's beyond words."

"Yes, most distressing," said the Major briskly, "but our present job is to trace the book. It may help us to find out what became of Mr. Virtue?"

"Does it matter," asked Mr. Broast, "what became of such a man?"

He moved away to close the doors of the book-case he had left open. The Major leaned across to Bobby and said in a whisper:

"Well, you know, he's really upset. You can't think a man like that could be guilty of deliberate murder, can you?"

Bobby made no answer, for he knew well what may issue from the obscure and tangled mind of man. Mr. Broast came back to the desk. He said:

"Of course, if I can assist you in any way, if you really conceive it your duty—"

"Our job," said the Major. "What we are paid for. Perhaps you wouldn't mind letting us know how the book came into your possession."

"From Dessein Frères, a Grenoble firm, very well known people," explained Mr. Broast. "They wrote to me about it. They knew I had a copy if the *Four Sons of Aymon* in a unique fourteenth century MS. they were anxious to secure for an important client of theirs. They suggested a part exchange. In the end I had to give them both that and a fine early Rabelais—a hard bargain, but the *Dictes*, a mint *Dictes*, such an opportunity might never occur again. You agree I was justified?"

"I am sure I shouldn't dream of questioning your judgment," said the Major politely. "Did Messrs. Dessein explain how they got the *Dictes*?"

"I think they said they purchased it from the widow of an American who had died in a Marseilles hospital. I forget the exact circumstances. They were not my affair. Dessein Frères was a well known firm, responsible people. When old Monsieur Dessein died the business was sold, but I've no doubt the records were still kept. You can see the correspondence that passed between us at the time if you like. I keep the files in the cellar. If you wish, I can get them for you. We try to be business-like, you know," he added smilingly, "and I flatter myself I can find any letter, written since I took control, within five minutes."

The Major said that was very commendable indeed, and most business-like, and then they all descended to the cellar, where the old fifteenth century printing press stood. From one of the packing case, after a certain amount of rummaging, Mr. Broast produced the required file. They took it upstairs, and there the Major and Bobby went through it carefully while Mr. Broast continued tranquilly with his task of examining and collating a batch of catalogues that had arrived by the morning post.

The story told by the letters seemed quite plain and straightforward. A woman had visited Messrs. Dessein's establishment in Grenoble and had offered them the *Dictes* for sale. Evidently she had only a vague idea of its value, for the sum she asked was quite modest. She explained that she was the widow of an American who had just died in a Marseilles hospital. On inquiry, the hospital confirmed this. The American had been taken ill at an hotel in a small village between Toulon and Marseilles. On his illness developing seriously he had been removed to hospital, and there had died. At the hotel he had registered himself and his companion as Mr. and Mrs. James A. Vivian, Chicago, U.S.A., and on his death his possessions had been handed over to Mrs. Vivian, who was presumably entitled to them. As the lady's claim to ownership of the book seemed clear—and possibly because it was highly valuable and offered at a very low price—Messrs. Dussein purchased. Mr. Vivian, before losing consciousness, asked that his possessions should be handed over to Mrs. Vivian, and signed a receipt for them. She had used the money left in his baggage at the hotel to pay the bill. He had, too, spoken of a book she would know what to do with, and he had always referred to her as 'ma femme'. After his death and the funeral, Mrs. Vivian announced her intention of returning to Chicago to communicate with his family and to settle up his affairs. With that she had gone on her way, and it was only accidentally that reference was made in the letters to the fact that the money found in Mr. Vivian's baggage amounted to a fairly substantial sum, so that there was a good deal left even after payment of all expenses.

"Are you satisfied?" Mr. Broast asked smilingly, when at last the reading and the consideration of the letters had been completed.

He made no objection to Major Harley taking the file of correspondence away with him, though he refused absolutely, and even with heat, to allow the *Dictes* to pass out of his possession.

"Library property," he said firmly; "I am responsible for its safe keeping. If you want to remove it, you will have to get an order from the Courts, and I tell you frankly I should fight it to the last. If I let it out of my charge," he added with some bitterness, "it might come back with more scribbling in it. I don't propose to risk that."

He seemed, too, quite unperturbed by a suggestion that the statements made in the correspondence would require to be investigated.

"I confess I never thought that necessary," he said. "Dessein knew what he was about. The man was certainly dead—there was a statement from the proper officials to prove that. He had described the woman as his wife, he has asked for his property to be handed over to her and it was actually in her possession. Everything quite in order. I had no reason to investigate, as you say. If you see any cause to do so, I suppose you know your duty."

Bobby had been talking in a low tone to the Major. The Major nodded assent. Bobby said:

"There are just one or two questions, Mr. Broast, we should like to ask if you wouldn't mind answering them.

When this book was first offered you, did you recognize it as the one Mr. Virtue had shown Sir William Winders and yourself?"

"When it was offered me," Mr. Broast answered slowly, "it was by letter. I bought on the strength of Monsieur Dessein's description. I was aware I could trust it. When the book reached me I saw his account of it as an unusually fine copy was fully justified. I had no reason to suppose it was identical with the one Mr. Virtue had shown us. Why should I? Mr. Virtue's copy indeed I had no opportunity to examine with any care. I do not remember that such a possibility ever occurred to me."

"When the other day you were shown the photograph found in Miss Perkins's possession and said to resemble the body Mr. Virtue claimed to have seen through the library window, you did not recognize it?"

Mr. Broast shrugged his shoulders.

"I am afraid I didn't take Mr. Virtue's story very seriously," he said. "A silly schoolboy hoax, I thought, for some reason of his own—his idea of a joke, perhaps. As regards the photograph, no, at the time, no. But later on it did strike me as having some sort of resemblance to someone I had once seen. I couldn't think who or when. I thought very likely it was only fancy. But I am not very good at remembering faces. They are all so much alike, they are all so entirely without interest."

"The fact that the initials were the same in both cases, James A. Vivian and James A. Virtue, did not suggest anything?"

"No. Why should it? For that matter I don't suppose I noticed it. I had no special interest in, or knowledge of, Mr. Virtue. I suppose you mean they were the same man? Very likely. That's your affair apparently. It's certainly not mine. So far as I can see the woman who sold to Dessein had a clear claim. I warn you I shall resist to the utmost any attempt to dispute ownership. I can't think any such attempt would succeed for a moment, but if I had to I should certainly take the case to the House of Lords."

"We've nothing to do with that," interposes the Major. "Disputed ownership is not a police matter. Our duty is to try to establish what became of Mr. Virtue. Of course, if it can be proved he died abroad, in France, our responsibility ceases."

The Major then proceeded to express his gratitude to Mr. Broast for having so kindly answered the questions put to him, and for having been so willing to give up so much of his time which, it was fully realized, was extremely valuable; and Mr. Broast made it perfectly plain that he considered it had all been a deplorable and most unnecessary waste of that time. He also made it quite clear once more that he would fight to the death against any attempt to claim the *Dictes*, and then he accompanied them to the little sanctum where Miss Perkins presided and asked her to type out a form of receipt, specifying the details of the letters taken. This done and the receipt duly signed, the Major and Bobby departed. Outside, the Major said:

"Sounds all right, eh? Quite a good, consistent story. Have to be checked, of course, but these letters seem genuine. I suppose there's no doubt Vivian and Virtue are the same?"

"I think so," agreed Bobby; "I think that's clear. Probably Virtue picked up a girl somewhere and went off with her to the Riviera. Previously he sent most of his luggage to the Paris hotel where it was found. He meant it to wait there for his return. Only he didn't return. He went to the Riviera under an assumed name and he passed off his companion as his wife. That's common enough. Makes things easier even in tolerant France. Probably they don't believe it, but they don't care. Using another name is convenient. Avoids complications, both present and future. One thing to be entered in an hotel register in your own name, quite another thing if the entry is Mr. Jones or Mr. Someone Else.

Unfortunately, if death happens, it makes complications, too. No reason, though, to suppose it was anything but a natural death. It took place in hospital, nothing in the least suspicious. He caught a chill perhaps or something like that. But the woman with him sees her opportunity. If she owns up she's only a chance companion, she has no standing. As his wife, she has naturally a right to his possessions, which indeed apparently she had got into her own hands before death actually took place. There was ready money, as well as clothing, and an old book she most likely guessed was worth something, though I don't suppose she had any idea how much. Anyhow, she sold it, and probably she could argue it had been a present to her by him before death, and so was her own property. His papers, letter of credit, passport perhaps, all that would be no use to her, and she probably destroyed the lot. She didn't want a lot of questions asked, and quite possibly she didn't know his real identity. She had lost her lover, but she hadn't done so badly. Of course, that's on the assumption that inquiry confirms the letters and that the death actually occurred as stated. There is just the possibility that the whole story was faked by Broast, with Dessein's assistance, in order to account for the possession of the *Dictes*, if that were challenged, and that the MS. and the Rabelais given Dessein were payment for his help. And now apparently Dessein is dead."

"Very difficult, very difficult indeed when there's such a time interval," the Major said. "And all this James A. Virtue business no help to finding out who murdered Kayne and poor Winders. You want to go on with our arrangements for the morning?"

"Yes, sir," said Bobby, "and another thing, I should like permission to send a telegram to Fromavon."

"Fromavon?" the Major repeated, not at first understanding this reference to the great West country port that is now rivalling both Bristol and Cardiff. "Oh, because

Miss Perkins comes from there?" he said then. "Because of that photograph?"

"Yes, sir. It seems certain Bertram Virtue had been in touch with her. He must have got his information about the *Dictes* from her. I thought it might be useful to trace her from Fromavon to London and see if anything else turns up. You see, sir, she had a copy of a photo of this James Virtue, and I don't much believe the story she told to account for its possession. I thought it might be as well to try to check up."

"Yes, it might be as well," agreed the Major, and Bobby duly sent the telegram, but on his own responsibility enlarged its scope a little.

"She bothers me," he told himself frowningly; "she's always turning up. She may know a good deal more than she's told yet."

There was nothing more to be done that day, but next morning, very early, almost as soon as it was light indeed, there assembled by the bed of forget-me-nots, under the trees near the seats giving so wide a view over the surrounding country, a little group of men. The Major was there, and Bobby, and with them two uniformed policemen and two others of the police in plain clothes. Superintendent Killick looked on doubtfully from a distance, and with much satisfaction and complacence they perceived that for once no single journalist had got wind of their intention.

The two constables in plain clothes began their work. They had brought spades, picks, so on, with them. First they removed as carefully as they could the top layer of soil with the growing forget-me-nots. It was hoped these might be replaced undamaged. Then they started to dig, using the utmost care, thrusting in their spades with slow deliberation, examining each morsel of earth as they turned it up. For some minutes the work proceeded in silence. A light rain began to fall and stopped again. Each spadeful of earth was carefully laid aside. The ground seemed hard and well packed. Plainly it had not recently been disturbed. Two rabbits came out from among the trees and stopped to watch. Killick threw a clod of earth at them to make them go away. They scampered off, their little white tails upheld. The hole was about three feet deep now. One of the diggers looked up and said:

"There's something here. My spade touched something."

Bobby handed him a trowel.

"Go carefully," he said.

The second man ceased work. Cautiously his companion loosened the soil where he had thrust in his spade. He scraped away the earth. Gradually he freed from the soil a round white object. Lifting it in both his hands, he laid it on the ground where Major Harley stood, and Bobby, and Superintendent Killick, all watching.

"Human skull, sir," said the man who had found it.

They all looked at it in silence, that poor relic of humanity round which now the fresh sweet air of the morning blew, on which the first rays of the sun fell for a moment and then vanished again as though they dared not stay.

The rain began again, but very slightly. Major Harley said:—

"What about that long story Broast told us?"

No one answered him. The digging continued. Gradually a complete human skeleton was exposed. One of the diggers said:—

"There's been lime used—a lot of lime."

Killick said:—

"Broast will have to find another yarn now."

Then he said:—

"It's a long time ago. How are we going to prove identity? how are we going to prove anything?"

"Yes, there's that," agreed the Major. He was looking with close attention at the bones, now nearly free from earth. He said to Bobby:—"Do you notice anything?"

"Yes, sir," Bobby said. "It's a woman."

"Yes," said the Major. "Yes."

"It's been a woman all right, sir," agreed one of the diggers.

"Well, now," said Killick, "what the hell's that mean?"

"Hell, I think," said Bobby softly, "is the right word."

They were all silent and still, bewildered, so engrossed in their own thoughts they did not hear a quiet, approaching step. Now there passed through them Miss Perkins, walking slowly, walking almost as one might walk in sleep. None of them might have been there for all the awareness of them she seemed to show. Killick put out a hand to stop her, but drew it back again. A uniformed constable stepped aside as if compelled to let her pass. There was about her something aloof and even daunting, so that they watched and were silent. It was almost as though she moved in another world to which they had no access. She stopped by the spot where the small skull lay. She knelt down. She put out a hand towards it and touched it with the tips of her fingers.

"It's been a long time, very long," she said in a voice that did not seem her own. "How long to wait, but now at last it's done."

Once more she put out her hand and touched the skull, very softly, very gently. It was a grave, a solemn gesture that she made, one, as it seemed, of promise and of greeting. She got to her feet, and as she did so she seemed to assume once more the personality they all knew best, as though it were a garment she put on and off at her ease.

"Oh, I'm so sorry," she said, "but I mustn't be late because of my work that's waiting still."

CHAPTER XXV
A MEMO

In an odd silence they stood and watched her go, and even after they had turned again to the task awaiting them, one or other would pause and give a glance over the shoulder at that small figure as it moved steadily on its way, back to its daily task of typing and copying and filing.

"Bit of a shock for a girl like her," one of the diggers said presently, the first to break the silence.

His companion answered:

"Notice how she touched it like? She'll have dreams to-night?"

"Look at that! Someone else coming," Killick said crossly. "Beats me, the way things get about."

It was footsteps he had heard, and he had caught a glimpse of a form coming near through the trees. A moment later there emerged from them the figure of Mr. Broast, peering shortsightedly through his gold-rimmed spectacles, his hands behind him.

"Well, well, well," he said, "now then, what's all this?"

No one answered. He came a little nearer. He took off his glasses and looked thoughtfully at the skull still lying by the side of the freshly dug earth.

"Remarkable," he said. "A grave apparently? A woman buried in secret? But after so many years, what can be done? Identification, I imagine, will be difficult."

"How did you know it was a woman, Mr. Broast?" Major Harley asked.

"How did I know?" repeated Mr. Broast mildly. He put his glasses on again and came a little nearer still, so that the skull lay almost between his feet. "Well, well," he said, "it's what we all come to in the end."

"How did you know it was a woman, Mr. Broast?" Major Harley asked again.

"How did I know?" Mr. Broast said as he had said before. "Why, really, did I say I was? You know, if there were still eyes in those round, vacant holes, they might be watching us. But then there aren't, are there?"

"No," agreed the Major, and for the third time asked: "How did you know it was a woman?"

"I hardly think I did know," Mr. Broast answered now. "Was it not perhaps a natural assumption? This skull, for instance—obviously small, the jaw, the bones, fine and slender. I suppose it might be a boy. I had not thought of that. You think it is a boy?"

"No, a woman," Major Harley answered. "Can you give us any help? suggest any way to identify her? or explain why a body should be buried here?"

"My dear sir," said Mr. Broast gently, "I have not the least idea. None. You should know more than I, since I presume you had some reason for digging here? Hardly chance, I imagine." He paused as if expecting a reply. None came. He went on: "Identity? That will be difficult, I imagine. The teeth perhaps, I have heard that dentists—" Without finishing his sentence, he stooped and looked more closely at the sad relic lying there, almost between his feet. "No," he said, "no trace of dental work, small teeth, fine, regular, well-shaped. They must," he said, almost as if he were speaking to himself, "they must have been charming when she smiled. I remember—"

"Yes," said Major Harley. "You remember—?"

"I was going to say," Mr. Broast answered slowly, "that I remembered a girl I knew—oh, many years ago. She had the loveliest teeth. When she smiled, it went to your head like wine. Of course," he added apologetically, "I was younger then."

Killick said in an aside that was audible:—

"Cold-blooded old devil."

Mr. Broast heard and turned and bestowed on him a charming smile.

"I'm so sorry," he said, "but after all—well, I am old, and one day your skull and mine will be a subject for contemplation, too. It is the universal law of death."

"Of life," Bobby said from behind.

Mr. Broast swung around to look at him.

"Ah, our young policeman," he murmured. "Now, I wonder what he means? Just said for the sake of saying, or do policemen sometimes turn philosophers? Anyhow, both begin with a 'p'. An interesting thought, and no doubt policemen and philosophers both deal with mystery—

insoluble mystery, I fear, very often. The unknowable, in fact, as forgotten Herbert Spencer would have said. But very fortunate for me, I imagine, it is a woman, or you would be trying to prove the missing Mr. Virtue had been found at last. Yes, I think it very fortunate, or I should be anticipating endless questioning on a suspicion that the missing Virtue had been knocked on the head—probably with his own *Dictes*—and buried here one still, quiet, moonlight night."

"Why still, why moonlight?" Bobby asked.

"Oh, merely to be picturesque. Can't you imagine it? Someone, myself perhaps, frantically digging, perspiring, the sweat running down on each spadeful turned up. One does not perspire so easily when one is old. Every sound an agony in the silent night. The moon watching, fortunately quite indifferent, and under that tree, lying very still, a bit of bare, stripped machinery that had run down, regrettably, perhaps, but also unavoidably."

"You might have been there," Major Harley said.

"Oh, a scene easy to reconstruct," Mr. Broast retorted.

"Can you tell us anything about any woman you remember disappearing suddenly from the neighbourhood?" Major Harley asked.

"My dear sir, surely you, as head of a police force, chief constable I believe, surely you know very well that girls disappear with considerable frequency. It is indeed, among girls, a not uncommon procedure. I know it happens at times to the maids employed at the Lodge. I can recollect two or three cases. One, some years ago, an unusually prepossessing girl. I forget her name. Her mother was frantic. A lad of the village had been seen in her company. He admitted a quarrel. I believe he was closely questioned by members of your admirable and persevering force. Afterwards it became known that she was doing very well in town—in the neighbourhood of Piccadilly and of Leicester Square. Very well indeed. Another girl—her name was Gladys, I remember that, it seemed somehow so appropriate—disappeared, too, a year or two later, but that was simpler, for a certain number of silver spoons disappeared simultaneously. Putting two and two together in their inimitable way. Your colleagues of the times drew certain conclusions. But in this case I understand, there's nothing in the way of silver spoons?"

"Nothing," said Major Harley briefly. "You can't help us then?"

"My dear sir," protested Mr. Broast, "you expect too much. What help can you suppose I should be in a position to offer? Indeed, I greatly fear you will find identification exceedingly difficult."

"We shall do our best," said the Major heavily.

"I am sure you will," Mr. Broast agreed. "Do you know—all this reminds me most oddly of the grave digging scene in *Hamlet*. You remember? 'Alas, poor Yorick,' and so on." He looked down again at the skull where it lay so close by his feet. "Alas, poor—But your name wasn't Yorick," he said.

None of them spoke. They were listening, watching, with a kind of fascination. Mr. Broast looked round slowly.

"I mustn't interrupt you any longer," he said. "You have your work to do and I have mine."

With a gesture of farewell he turned and walked away, back towards the Lodge, and again the little party stood and watched him go, and again, even after they had turned once more to their task, one or other would pause and give a glance over the shoulder at that tall, receding form.

"What I say," declared Killick suddenly, "is he knows all about it."

"What proof is there?" Major Harley asked. "After all this time, what chance is there even of establishing identity?"

One of the men digging paused suddenly. He was very pale, and there were beads of sweat making channels down his cheeks through the dust and grime that had settled on them. He said slowly:—

"I never thought to hear a man stand up and tell how he had done a thing like that—and us police and all."

"Murder all right, and he done it," his companion said; "and he knows we know, and he don't give that—" The speaker snapped finger and thumb together. "For why? because he knows he'll never hang."

"There are worse deaths than hanging," Bobby said, and wondered, when the others looked at him, why he had said that, for the words had come spontaneously, as if his tongue had repeated something whispered in his ear.

"We'll never even know who she was, poor soul," Killick said.

Major Harley turned to Bobby.

"What do you think, Owen?" he asked.

"I think, sir, if we both wrote down a name, it would be the same," Bobby answered.

"You'll write the same name, Killick, when you've had time to look through the papers more carefully," the Major explained to the puzzled looking superintendent. "At least, I expect you will but we'll see. Only I don't know what action we can take."

They went on with their work. The poor remaining relics were collected. The turned-up earth was examined almost grain by grain to see if anything further could be found, but without success. Not even a shred or remnant of clothing, no button or clasp or buckle, no article of jewellery, none of those more durable objects that most of us carry in our pockets or that are a part of our clothes.

"He said 'stripped'," one of the searchers remarked. "You noticed that? 'Stripped', he said. Means she was put in there stark naked so as to make sure nothing shouldn't ever be found. How did he know that if it wasn't him did it?"

"Never be proved," said another, "and so he'll never swing, and if there's worse waiting for him, same as the London bloke said just now, well, I hope it won't be long."

"Well, anyhow," Killick said, "the poor soul will have Christian burial now."

This fresh discovery involved a good deal of extra work. The coroner had to be notified, since an inquest would be necessary. Various other formalities of routine had to be gone through. Journalists, for the news was beginning to get about now, had to be dealt with. It was late before Bobby could slip away to get lunch—his breakfast had been no more than the hurried outline of a meal—and at the inn he found as he had hoped might be the case, Olive waiting for him.

"I suppose you've heard," he said.

"It's so terrible," she said, "to think all this time—and often and often I've gone there to sit. Bobby, who can she have been?"

"You heard it was a woman?" he asked. "We were trying not to let that out yet."

"Miss Perkins told me," Olive explained. "I met her in the drive as she was coming to work, and she told me a woman had been buried there, and you had found the skeleton."

"Oh, yes," Bobby said. "She came up while we were digging. I am wondering how she happened to be there?"

"She told me she couldn't sleep. I don't wonder either. She said she got up to have a walk because of having been awake all night, and she thought a walk would do her good, and then she saw you there and went to see what was happening. Mr. Broast was there, too, she said."

"Yes, he was," agreed Bobby moodily.

"Miss Perkins said he laughed. He said you would never be able to do anything because it was all so long ago. Then he laughed. Miss Perkins said he needn't be too sure. She was very excited and upset, almost as much by his laughing as by what you found. She said it was dreadful to hear him laughing, and I expect it was."

"He shouldn't have laughed," Bobby said. "He shouldn't have let her see him laughing."

"I think it was horrid of him," Olive said, "only I think every one is so upset, we are none of us quite normal. What's going to happen now?"

"I don't know," said Bobby. "Major Harley's very worried. He doesn't know what action to take. Not much he can do. Does Miss Kayne know?"

"Yes. We told her as soon as she came downstairs. She didn't say anything except one thing, I don't know what it means. She said:— 'I knew her at once.' She said that before. Does she mean she knows who it is was buried there? She went to ask Mr. Broast about it. It's the first time I've known her visit the library for ever so long. She looked awful. Bobby, how long is it since—since it was done?"

"Since the body was hidden?" Bobby asked. "I haven't much idea. Major Harley will try to get expert opinion. Good long time anyhow—some years. I wonder if Miss Kayne has any idea?"

"She won't say anything," Olive said. "She just sits there and you can almost see her waiting, but you don't know what for. It's almost like the way you think people condemned to death sit and wait. Bobby, I don't think I can stand it much longer."

"I don't think you ought to," Bobby said. "I don't think you ought to have stood it as long as you have."

"I shall tell her I can't, it's not right," Olive said passionately. "I shall tell her she must come away to London with me. Bobby, what is Major Harley going to do?"

Bobby shook his head.

"I've no idea," he said. "There's to be a conference."

"Do you think—do they think this was murder, too?"

"There's nothing to suggest murder, except, of course, the secrecy of the burial," Bobby answered. "That suggests murder, but it's not proof. There does not seem to be any injury showing to prove violence. Major Harley was talking of having the soil analysed to see if any trace of poison could be found. Doesn't sound very hopeful to me. There'll be all sorts of experts turned loose, I expect. I don't see what they can prove, I don't see how identity is going to be proved, either. You may know things you can't prove. It looks as if the body had been stripped"—he hesitated before he used the word—"stripped of everything that would be likely to resist decay and afford any clue. All we have to go on is that it was a woman of a certain height, and most likely the doctors will be able to make a good guess at her age and weight, and perhaps give some idea of her appearance—I believe they claim they can reconstruct a face from the line of the skull, though only to a very limited degree. There'll be a lot of inquiries made, but they'll have to be made in the dark. Of course, there's always the chance of someone knowing something and coming forward."

"Will Miss Kayne have to be questioned? I don't think she's in a fit state."

"Well, I believe Major Harley intends to see her this afternoon. I heard him say something to Killick."

"Not to you?"

"No. My job this afternoon is to draw up a memo. I've put a theory to Major Harley he wants me to get down on paper in full details. He knows what it is, of course, but he wants it for the conference, and then I think he means to take the advice of the Public Prosecutor's office. I think, myself, we ought to act at once. I'm afraid of—well, of something else happening. I don't feel as if we were at the end yet. We ought to take precautionary action. I know it's difficult."

"Doesn't Major Harley want to do that?"

"It would be his responsibility. It's one thing for a sergeant to advise, privately, another for a chief constable to act publicly. In this country the police have jolly well got to watch their step. English people keep a sharp eye on their police—quite right, too. A policeman can easily turn into a bully, he has a little brief authority and it's up to the public to see he plays no fantastic tricks to make the angels weep. Killick is strongly against taking any action—yet. Against precipitate action, he says, before it's ripe."

"What does he mean—ripe?"

"Cunning old beggar. No flies on Killick. His idea is for us to lie low and wait for a mistake. It's a good plan very often. If you do nothing, then they think you must be doing something, and they get nervous, and then they do something themselves, and that's where you get them. Only—sometimes what happens isn't what you expected."

"You've got something in your mind, Bobby? The theory you are putting in your memo?"

"Yes," he admitted. "I've got to have a chat with Mrs. Payne first though—you know, Mrs. Somerville's friend. She's been away visiting a daughter, but I did make sure that she was about the only person in the village who isn't on the wireless."

"Is that important?" Olive asked, and Bobby nodded, though without explaining why, and after they had talked a little Olive returned to the Lodge firm in her resolve to insist on Miss Kayne's leaving at once for London, while Bobby devoted himself to the composition of his memorandum.

It was long and elaborate, a mass indeed of small details. But now it began to seem to him that in this accumulation of detail the pattern of a logical development and plan was becoming manifest.

It was possible now, for instance, to be sure that of those points so carefully lettered from A to K that he and Major Harley had from the start thought worth careful consideration, only those they had called H and K seemed wholly irrelevant. In the others, the whole series of recent events had been implicit, if only it had been possible then to appreciate their full and true significance.

Of course, besides these, there were other incidents and details that now appeared invested with a meaning hidden at the time.

Very important, for instance, seemed that glimpse of Miss Perkins at her bedroom window he and Mills had had as they drove by on the night of the Kayne murder. Important, too, in the same connection was the fact he had just mentioned to Olive that in a village of wireless devotees Mrs. Somerville had that same night been visiting the only one of the inhabitants not provided with a wireless set.

In his memorandum, too, he drew special attention to three things said and done by Miss Kayne: first, her cry mentioned by Olive that there was an unspecified person she had recognized again at once. Bobby now felt fairly certain who that person must be, and why Miss Kayne had been so sure of her recognition. Secondly, there was her half contemptuous, half challenging declaration to Bobby himself that Virtue's story was both a lie and the truth. Bobby felt he could now understand how that might be. Thirdly, too, there was her futile, and on the face of it meaningless, accusation of theft against Miss Perkins, the accusation that Mr. Broast had simply laughed away. Bobby was inclined to think that he could guess both why the accusation had been made and why it had been withdrawn.

Another point to which he felt that it was necessary to attach great significance was the abrupt manner in which Miss Perkins had announced her belief in a marriage existing between Mr. Broast and Miss Kayne. She must have suspected it long enough, and Bobby thought he perceived now why she had chosen that particular moment to tell him of it.

Miss Kayne's story of her former lover's buried letters and poems had naturally always been in the forefront of his mind, and though now he was inclined to think it untrue, yet he felt also it might well contain the cause and origin of these so many deaths that had come, as a stranger, into this quiet countryside.

Finally, there was the incident of the damage done to the portrait Olive's father had painted of Miss Kayne as a young girl as well as the more recent incident of the forget-me-nots some unknown person had sent him.

All these things it seemed to him now took their place in a coherent scheme, a closely-woven pattern of cause and effect: a series in terms of, because that was, therefore this must be.

When at last he finished, feeling that now his theory was complete and that even the Public Prosecutor's department, adepts though they are at the job, would have some difficulty in picking holes in it, he went back to the police station, where he found Killick. He handed in his memo, and with some hesitation, for it is a delicate matter to suggest a course of action to superior officers, he said:

"You know, sir, if I may say so, and if Major Harley agrees, I do think it would be better to act at once without bothering about the Public Prosecutor's office or anything else. I feel a bit uneasy after that scene this morning."

"Yes, I know," agreed Killick, not usually a nervous man, but now evidently on edge. "I'll get in touch with Major Harley at once. I'll back you up now, and I don't suppose he'll object. It's taking a big responsibility, but then so is waiting any longer."

The telephone bell rang. They heard the constable on duty answer it. He was one of those who had helped in the digging that morning. A moment later he came running.

"The Lodge, sir—that was Miss Perkins. She says as Mr. Broast has done himself in and will we go along at once? Poison, she says, and she saw him take it."

"Suicide," said Killick dispassionately. "Well, that's that, and some ways it's best."

"Plain enough it was, after how he carried on this morning," said the constable. "Defiant, I call it. Defiant, a sort of 'Yes, that's me, and what are you going to do about it?' Well, now he's gone and been and saved us a lot of trouble."

"No hurry now," observed Bobby. "We can take our time, now."

"Only," said Killick thoughtfully. "I wonder why? when he made it so plain this morning he felt as safe as houses."

"It gets them in the end," said the constable; "it does that, I've seen it before. In the end it gets them."

CHAPTER XXVI
TEACUPS

At the lodge Major Harley, Killick, Bobby, were received by
Olive, who had been obliged to take charge of a thoroughly
disorganized household, with two maids in recurring
hysterics, Miss Kayne shut up in her bedroom and refusing
to answer knocks at her door, the butler, Briggs, in a state of
dithering helplessness.

He had called up apparently every doctor he could think
of, and two were already on the scene. Mr. Broast's body
had been carried into the dining-room and laid on a couch
there. Death had already taken place before the arrival of
either doctor, and the characteristic symptoms of poisoning
by strychnine were too plainly marked for any doubt to exist
concerning the cause of death.

On the table lay, too, a neatly-typed statement, signed
'Eliza Perkins,' giving a very brief, yet clear and detailed
account of what had happened.

Two cups of tea had been brought to the library by one of
the maids at four o'clock, as was part of the established
routine of the household. Tea was always served at four and
Miss Kayne always poured out two cups, which were taken,
with a plate of biscuits, to the library, one cup for Mr. Broast
and one for Miss Perkins. Miss Perkins kept one cup for
herself and one or two of the biscuits, and took the other
cup and the remaining biscuits to Mr. Broast.

On this occasion all had passed as usual. But the
statement went on to say that Miss Perkins had seen Mr.
Broast shake a few grains of a white powder into the cup as
soon as she put it down by his side. She had not, the
statement said, attached any importance to the incident at
the time. She had merely supposed that he was taking some
kind of medicine or tonic. He had made a rather odd
remark. It was: "Well, they've dug something up, but I know
the answer to that." She had not known what he meant. She
had not asked because it was never wise to ask Mr. Broast

what anything meant. He expected you to know. Sometimes, of course, you had to, and then you nearly got your head bitten off. On this occasion she had not thought it necessary to ask the meaning of a remark apparently not specially addressed to her. She had gone away to get on with her work, of which there was plenty waiting. At five o'clock, having occasion to speak to Mr. Broast to get his instructions, she had gone into the library again and had found him lying on the floor in convulsions. She had at once given the alarm.

The statement was precise, very nicely typed, quite clear, and phrased in curiously formal language. When he had read it, Major Harley said discontentedly:

"Might be a letter to a bookseller, ordering new stuff. Owen, ask if we can see Miss Kayne."

Bobby went to find her. Meanwhile the little party adjourned to the breakfast-room and the dead man's body was removed to his own apartment. Miss Kayne was still not visible, and when Bobby got Olive to go to her room, Olive returned looking a little worried.

"She's not there," she said. "Briggs says he saw her a few minutes ago going down the library corridor. Bobby, why is she going to the library? Briggs says she looked so strange he asked if he could do anything, and she said, no, but there was something she must do, because now it was enough. What did she mean?"

"What did she mean by the 'something' she had to do?" Bobby countered.

"I don't know," Olive answered. "I think it's the library, I mean something about the library. I think she hates it more and more every day, I think she thinks it has been the cause of everything."

"Better see what Major Harley thinks, I suppose," Bobby said.

He went back to the breakfast-room where the police party had now established itself. Major Harley was reading a telegram that had just arrived. It was the reply to the one

Bobby had sent off to the Fromavon authorities and the Major handed it across to Bobby to read.

"Much what you expected," he said, and then returned to question the maid for whom he had sent and who now came into the room. She was still hovering on the border of hysterics, but finally, by tactful treatment, was induced to explain that she always collected the used tea cups from the library at half-past four, but on this occasion when she went for them she was given only Miss Perkins's cup, Miss Perkins explaining that Mr. Broast had not yet drunk his tea. That had surprised her a little, but she hadn't thought much of it.

"It was unusual?" Major Harley asked.

The maid could not remember that it had ever happened before. Not that she had given it a second thought at the time. But it was notorious that Mr. Broast liked his tea scalding hot. He always drank it at once, and grumbled if for any reason it had gone cold. It was the same at breakfast. He always drank it the moment it was poured out, and if it wasn't hot—'fair boiling' was the maid's expression—he would ask for it to be thrown away and fresh poured out at the desired temperature. Olive, questioned, agreed that this peculiarity was well known.

"He didn't much mind whether it was strong or weak, but he made a fuss if it wasn't hot enough," she said.

"On this occasion," Major Harley asked the maid, "there was nothing said about wanting fresh tea because the other had gone cold?"

"Oh, no, sir," the maid answered. "Miss Perkins only said he wasn't finished yet."

"Were those her actual words, what she actually said?" the Major asked, a little slowly, and he and Bobby exchanged uncomfortable glances.

"Yes, sir, that's what she said," the girl answered. "So I took her cup and went away."

"That would be about half past four?"

"Yes, sir."

"Miss Perkins had drunk her tea, I suppose."

"Oh, yes."

"I don't quite see," observed the Major thoughtfully. "how she knew Mr. Broast hadn't finished his tea, when she says in her statement that after taking him his cup, she didn't go into the library again till five."

"Miss Perkins was in the library when I came to clear," the maid told him. "She wasn't in her own room, so I knocked at the library door—Mr. Broast didn't like you going in and interrupting—and she came out and said that about he wasn't finished yet."

"Ah, yes," the Major said heavily, and the hand with which he held the paper before him shook a little.

He asked one or two more questions about the supply of strychnine which apparently the whole household knew was kept in the library basement for use as a rat poison. So far as the maid knew, it had not been employed for some considerable time, two or three years perhaps, as the rats had been either exterminated, or, with their uncanny instinct, thought it better to seek less dangerous haunts. She agreed everyone knew the poison was there and where it was kept, in a tin box secured by a padlock. An ordinary tin box and an ordinary padlock so far as she knew, but plainly marked 'Poison' in big white letters, so no one could make a mistake. She remembered having seen the box once, though her duties seldom took her into the library, and she was completely and absolutely certain that not a single grain of strychnine had ever been brought out of the library into the dwelling quarters of the house, for any reason or on any pretext whatever.

The girl was dismissed and Major Harley referred again to the telegram that had just arrived.

"We had better see what Miss Perkins has to say," he remarked, and then, looking a little worried: "Owen," he said, "Briggs states he saw Miss Kayne going to the library?"

"Yes, sir. I think she's there now," Bobby answered.

"Better go along ourselves then," the Major said. "What's she doing there?"

No one answered this inquiry, and the three of them, Harley, Killick, Bobby, went together down the corridor leading to the door that separated the library annexe from the house proper, and that admitted into the small ante-room where Miss Perkins sat day in and day out behind the big writing table, busy with her typewriter.

She was there now, very much occupied evidently, for as they drew near they could hear the swift, impersonal rattle of the machine as the lettering levers rose and fell, as the carriage was banged to its starting point. When they entered she looked up, executing a final fanfare on the machine.

"The work must go on," she said.

"Some door," Killick remarked to Bobby, struck by its size and weight.

"Fireproof," Bobby explained, "The one to the library proper is stronger still."

"Is Miss Kayne here?" the Major asked. "Have you seen her?"

"She came in a few minutes ago. She went through to the library," Miss Perkins answered. "Oh, I'm so sorry, but I do Wonder who will sign the letters now. I asked Miss Kayne when she came in and she said 'No one', but no one can't Sign letters, can they? Only you see this is an important one, because it's about something someone thought mightn't be genuine, and it's worth a Lot of money, only not if it isn't, is it?"

"Can you smell something," Bobby asked Killick.

"Burning garden stuff probably," Killick remarked, sniffing at the air.

Bobby said to Miss Perkins:

"You mean a forgery? something in the library?"

"Oh, No," answered Miss Perkins with her accustomed giggle, "I'm quite sure there's no forgeries in Our catalogue. I'm sure poor, Dear Mr. Broast made quite certain of that. There might be in other catalogues, of course, and poor Mr.

Broast used to Laugh quite a lot when he saw entries he was ever so sure were only forgeries. But he won't laugh any more now, will he?"

"Nothing to laugh at in all this," said Major Harley with some distaste.

"Oh, no, there isn't, is there?" agreed Miss Perkins meekly.

"Perhaps they've been forgeries on your shelves though," observed Bobby, "that have found their way, not into your catalogues but into other people's."

"Oh," said Miss Perkins, looking at him suddenly. She drew nearer her handbag that lay by her on the table. "Oh, yes," she said, and into her manner as she uttered those words there had come a sudden and a startling change.

Major Harley noticed it and made up his mind suddenly.

"I won't bother Miss Kayne yet," he said. "Miss Perkins, there are some questions it is necessary to ask you. I am not satisfied with some of the replies you have given, and with certain other matters. I am not satisfied that your real name is Eliza Perkins. I have received a telegram from the police authorities at Fromavon. The suggestion is that your real name is Agnes Elizabeth Moult, that you are the daughter of John Moult, of Fromavon, and of Agnes Mayne Moult, née Windham, of whom nothing is known since she left her husband, taking her child, Agnes Elizabeth, then about five years of age, with her, in the company of a junior assistant of the Fromavon College library, named Basil Royston Oast."

"You think that's me?" said Miss Perkins. "Suppose it is, can't you change your name if you want to?"

"Certainly," agreed the Major. "A change of name is, however, sometimes matter for suspicion."

"Suspicion?" repeated Miss Perkins. She was evidently a little nervous now. She was fiddling with her handbag, drawing the zip fastener to and fro. Her manner was still quite different from that she ordinarily showed. "Suspicion? what about?"

"Of complicity in or knowledge of recent events," answered the Major. "You understand I am questioning you in connection with these murders; that anything you say will be used in evidence, if necessary; and that, if you prefer, and it would probably be wise, you need answer no questions till you have received legal assistance?"

Miss Perkins shook her head gently.

"Yes, but I don't think I do understand at all," she said. "Do you mean you suspect me of shooting poor Mr. Nat Kayne? Why should I? He was always ever so nice. I was dreadfully sorry when I heard. Besides Mrs. Somerville can tell you I was talking to her. We were both in her kitchen at ten o'clock when it happened."

"I am not satisfied on that point," Major Harley said. "Sergeant Owen has been making inquiries. Mrs. Payne thinks it was much later when Mrs. Somerville left that night. Mrs. Payne has no wireless, Mrs. Somerville seems to judge times entirely by the wireless programme, and to set her clock by it. It is easy to alter the hands of a clock and if that were done that night, Mrs. Somerville may be entirely mistaken about the time."

"Oh, you are Clever," said Miss Perkins, dropping back into the manner that was familiar to them. She even produced her characteristic giggle. "So is Sergeant Owen, awfully Clever. But then everyone says so, don't they? Oh, you don't really think it was me shot poor Sir William too, do you?"

"We notice there is no alibi for you," Major Harley said. "We notice two hand towels were missed that night by Mrs. Somerville and that an imprint in a flower bed near the window of Sir William's window was made apparently by a foot round which something, it might be a towel, had been wrapped. A search will be made for the weapon used, a small two-two automatic."

"Oh, yes," said Miss Perkins, and took her handkerchief from her handbag and wiped her eyes and her lips. "Oh, yes," she said again. "I suppose if you find it, you will be Quite Sure. Oh, and then there's poor Mr. Broast, too. It's quite a List, isn't it?"

"Several people, including yourself," Major Harley answered slowly, "had access to the strychnine kept in the basement here. Our information is that you were in the library when the maid came at half past four to take away the empty tea cups. In your statement you say you did not enter the library after taking Mr. Broast his tea until five o'clock. I must ask you to accompany us to the police station. You will be wise to obtain legal assistance before saying anything further. Will you please let me have your handbag?"

"Oh, no, I Couldn't," she answered at once. "I've got Everything in it."

"I must insist," the Major said.

"Oh, I see," she exclaimed, pulling the zip fastener to and fro. "You think if I had strychnine in it, tiny traces of it may be there still?"

"That is a question for the experts," Major Harley said. "Examination will be necessary."

"What I'm wearing, too?" she asked. "Perhaps you think some of it may have stuck to my clothes or my gloves?"

"You were wearing gloves?" the Major asked. "Yes, I think your clothing will have to be examined, too. May I have your handbag, please?"

"Oh, dear," Miss Perkins said, "what a lot of things you have thought of—so Clever of you. I daresay now the tiniest little grain of strychnine... So Clever. I expect it's Mr. Owen really. Miss Farrar said he was, and so I thought perhaps he might be. Oh, there's another murder, too, you haven't said a word about—the murder of whoever it was you found buried up there by the trees, and nothing left of her but only bones—bones, a skull, and nothing more."

"We think perhaps it was your mother buried there," the Major said gently.

"Oh, well," she said. "Now, then. Well?"

"However that may be," Major Harley said, "these other murders must be accounted for. One murder is no excuse for others."

She drew back the zip fastener of her handbag again and replaced her handkerchief. She appeared to be fumbling for something. There came into Bobby's mind an oddly clear memory of how once before, when he was questioning her, she had fidgeted with the zip fastening of her handbag. Her look, her manner, had been the same—oddly the same. It crossed his mind that possibly it was the same thing she was feeling for, both now and then. The heavy writing table was between them or he would have tried to take the bag from her. She said:

"I do think it's so Silly. I mean, blaming it all on poor little me. Don't you think so? I mean, I do think it's Silly. Don't you? I mean, have I got to go with you?"

"It will be my duty to detain you," the Major answered. "You will be charged with the murder of Nathaniel Kayne, with the murder of Sir William Winders, in both cases by shooting, with the murder of Basil Royston Oast, commonly known as Basil Broast, by the administration of poison."

"Oh, I'm so sorry," said Miss Perkins, and finding at last what she fumbled for in her handbag she drew out a small point twenty-two automatic and levelled it at them and began to fire.

CHAPTER XXVII
FIRE ENDS ALL

It was so sudden, so unexpected, that for the fraction of a second they remained all three perfectly still, motionless targets. Bobby felt a blow over his heart. He found afterwards a bullet embedded in his notebook. Killick instinctively flung up his hand to guard himself. A bullet that otherwise would have passed harmlessly by, struck his wrist watch and was deflected upwards. Major Harley felt one bullet stir his hair, like the touch of a caressing hand. Yet another passed between his coat and arm, and a fifth cut the string by which the 'No Smoking' placard was suspended, so that it hung awry.

Then it was all over before they had well realized it had begun. Between them and Miss Perkins was the heavy writing table at which she worked. She was still firing at them from her deadly little automatic as she stepped back to the inner door, the one admitting to the library proper. She opened it and passed through, slamming and locking it behind her.

The three men stood and looked at each other, a trifle dazed by the storming death through which they had just passed, though unharmed. Killick was swearing to himself in a soft monotone as he nursed his damaged wrist and examined his broken watch. Major Harley, with an air of almost ludicrous surprise, said:

"Well, now then."

For the moment none of them remembered that Miss Kayne had last been seen making her way hither, and that now presumably she, too, was within the library, behind that locked door. Killick suddenly ran to the door and shook it with some vague idea of forcing it open. The air was full of the acrid smell of powder. There was another smell, too, but fainter, and one they were for the moment too confused and excited to pay much attention to. Killick, still shaking the door, said:

"It's locked, she's locked it."

"Solid bit of work," said the Major. "Fireproof. Strong. What's next?"

"I think there should be a spare key somewhere, sir," Bobby said.

"See if you can find it, look sharp," the Major said. He added, still with his air of surprise: "Well, now, you know, I never expected that." Bobby was already out in the corridor. The Major called after him: "Send someone round to watch the windows in case she tries to get away there."

"Yes, sir," said Bobby, and ran on.

"Has she any more ammunition?" Killick said. "It was a seven shooter—even if she hasn't another clip, she'll have a shot or two left."

"What about Miss Kayne, where is she?" Major Harley asked, suddenly remembering. Then he said: "Yes, one or two shots left, I think—nasty things at close quarters, those two-twos. Lucky she missed us. I hope Owen gets that key quick."

Bobby had, in fact, secured it at once from the glass case in the hall where it and others hung. As he took it down he heard his name called, and saw behind him Mr. Adams who had walked in by the open and unattended front door, since Briggs was in no state to carry out his accustomed duties.

"Is it true Broast has killed himself?" Adams asked quickly. "If it is, I must see the Mandeville leaves at once."

"Why? do you think they are fakes?" Bobby asked.

"No," answered Adams, "not these, not the ones here, the ones he sold. He kept the genuine and then forged copies he sold. He was doing that all the time. Half the things he sold, autographed copies and all, were forged, and he used the money he made like that to buy genuine. He filled other libraries with forgeries that he might have genuine himself for his own. Old Kayne started it and Broast carried on."

"If you had told us that before—" Bobby said angrily.

"How could I when I wasn't sure?" Adams retorted. "I wasn't going to risk ruining myself and my firm and my clients, too. I kept to my instructions."

"Sergeant, sergeant," roared the Major's voice.

"Yes, sir," answered Bobby, recalled to a sense of the urgency of the position.

He went back at a run, the key in his hand. Adams followed. Major Harley was standing in the doorway of the ante-room with his hand outstretched. Bobby gave him the key. The Major ran across to the inner door and fitted the key to the lock. Adams said:

"What's burning? there's something burning."

"It's powder, young lady doing pistol practice," grumbled Killick, looking ruefully at his wrist.

"There's something burning, too," Bobby said.

Major Harley threw open the door of the library. A trail of smoke issued, and within they saw a great column rising to the roof, shot through by the dull glow of flame.

"Good God, it's on fire," shouted the Major. "Get help— quick. Where are the women?"

Killick rushed away to give the alarm. Adams stood still. The Major, Bobby following him, ran forward. Smoke eddied round them. They could feel the heat of the flames. Under the impact of the fresh current of air from the open doors, the central column of smoke changed to a pillar of fire, licking even the roof, then died down again into black, swirling, suffocating smoke. An armful of books, a shower of books, came flying through the air, thrown from above. The whole air became full of books, descending in a kind of heavy hail, as though the heavens rained books. They looked up. On the iron gallery above they saw a heavy, gross, running, maniacal figure: Miss Kayne, running at speed along that narrow iron gallery, and as she ran plucking books from the shelves at her side and hurling them down to feed the growing, leaping flames that burned beneath, flames that already leaped to reach the roof, that curled round and about the projecting wooden bookcases, that showed, too, for one clear instant, the glowing colours of the *Glastonbury Psalter* before wrapping it in a fiercer light.

Instinctively Bobby made a movement to save that lovely relic of an age when men might still make beauty without thinking of its market value, but Major Harley stopped him.

"You go this way, I'll go that, we must catch her," he said, and even as he spoke a heavy volume, a product of the Kelmscott Press, the *Chaucer*, perhaps the most splendid book ever printed in England, came crashing down and struck him on one shoulder and sent him spinning and sprawling. Another volume, less heavy though, Bobby warded off with his hands, or it would have caught him on the head. Another and another followed, and they saw Miss Kayne looking down at them from above, ringed round with smoke and fire.

She vanished. The Major scrambled to his feet.

"Catch her, stop her," he repeated, "I'll go this way, you go that"; and an enormous iron-clasped 'Breeches' Bible fell heavily between them, missing them by inches.

Then began the strangest, weirdest chase. Up the iron, spiral stairs, along the iron galleries, raced Bobby, ran Major Harley. Before them, agile and swift, for all her enormous bulk; light on her feet, it seemed, as any girl, raced Miss Kayne, still plucking as she fled books from the shelves to hurl down to feed the increasing flames beneath. She ran, she leaped as though her frantic spirit took no heed of the gross burden of her flesh. At one moment when Bobby was close behind she somehow swung down by an iron support from the upper gallery to the lower, and when next he saw her through the swirling smoke, through the flames so richly fed that now by their own force they were licking up the serried ranks of books below, shelf after shelf, book after book, bursting into flames, opening their leaves in fire as rosebuds into beauty, she had climbed back into a third yet higher gallery that ran across the lower end of the library hall.

For one passing instant he had this glimpse of her. Then she was running again, the wreathing smoke concealing her, the only evidence of her presence fresh showers of books that came flying down as she swept whole shelves clean and tossed the contents to the floor.

Smoke-grimed, choking, half blinded, Bobby still pursued, the Major still ran and climbed from gallery to gallery and back once more. In the doorway below Mr. Adams watched despairingly. He was hugging in his arms the great Kelmscott *Chaucer* he had run forward to pick up after it had felled the Major, and then had retreated again to the doorway. Above Miss Kayne still darted here and there, obese and quick as a darting bird, and only once did they hear her speak when she cried with a great voice:

"Burning, burning, burning, it'll do no more harm."

Now they saw her once more upon the uppermost of the three end galleries, whither she had fled again with that incredible speed, that strange intensity of speed which seemed to make nothing of her gross and heavy body, of her encumbering flesh now so subdued to the wild energy of will and spirit that possessed her. The Major shouted to Bobby:

"She's got a devil in her, she's mad, possessed, where's the other one?"

Bobby pointed. There on the floor, in the midst of a circle of flame, on a space as yet itself comparatively free from fire, lay a small, still body, hardly bigger, it seemed, than the great volume, a fifteenth century incunabula, a psalter, that lay close by. A flame shot out as they looked, and showed them a stain of red upon the floor, yet another on one corner of that vast, ponderous tome.

"Knocked out," the Major said. "Get her out, Owen, if you can. You attend to that and I'll go after this lunatic woman again."

Bobby hesitated, for indeed he saw that to reach that uppermost gallery where they had last seen Miss Kayne, had now become a task of extreme peril. But the Major snapped:

"An order."

He ran as he spoke towards the nearest spiral stair. Bobby followed and ran down the same stair to the library floor, and through the heat and flame and smoke fought his way to where he had seen that prostrate body lying. He managed to reach it. Crouching on the floor, dragging it behind him, choked, suffocating, his clothing actually smouldering in one or two spots, he reached at last the doorway; and Adams helped him to drag himself and his charge into the comparatively clearer air of the ante-room.

Killick, who had been busy at the 'phone getting through to the Mayfield fire brigade and giving instructions for help to be sent from the village, came running back now. He said:

"Where's the Major?" Bending over Miss Perkins's body, he said: "She's gone—she's dead."

"In there," Bobby panted. "Miss Kayne—he's trying to get her out." To Adams, still hugging the great *Chaucer*, he said: "Don't stand there, do something, get help, water, anything."

"Quite useless," answered Adams, hugging his*Chaucer* closer still. He went again to the open doorway and peered within. "It burns," he said. "The treasures of three centuries, all burning, all."

Bobby, still carrying the body of Miss Perkins, staggered out into the corridor. Though there was no one to hear him, he said:

"Yes, she's dead."

Olive appeared at the end of the corridor, running. She was carrying two small fire extinguishers she had remembered were in the garage and had run out to find. She said:

"Briggs has run for help. He panicked really. The maids are in the garden. Where is Miss Kayne? Oh, Bobby—"

She did not complete the sentence, but with a gesture of pity she bent above the body Bobby had just laid down.

"She did what she meant to do," Bobby said. "She paid her mother's account—paid in full," he said, and from within they heard a loud, triumphant cry:

"It burns, it burns, all burns."

"That's Miss Kayne," Bobby said, and Olive caught his arm.

They heard Killick shouting.

"Major Harley—Harley—where are you?"

Bobby ran back. The two little fire extinguishers were so patently useless against the furnace that once had been a library that Olive left them lying where she had put them down and followed him. He and Killick had both disappeared into what had now become, for it grew with giant strides, a sea of smoke and fire and leaping flame. Olive would have followed, but Adams held her back, loosening even his hold upon his precious Chaucer to be able to do so.

"None will ever see the like again," he said sadly, "of what is burning there—the best of the harvest of nearly five hundred years, and now they burn."

"Who cares for a pack of old books?" retorted Olive, trying to push by him. "Let me go."

From the mirk and the flame emerged Killick and Bobby, staggering, reeling, gasping, suffocating, their hair singed, their clothes smouldering, bearing between them the unconscious form of Major Harley. In the clearer air of the corridor into which they had all reeled together he revived sufficiently to gasp:

"The Kayne woman—got her?"

He half raised himself but stayed there, crouching, fainting, supported against the wall, The other two reeled, staggered, struggled back towards the open library door. A flame licked out to welcome them as it were, wrapped itself round the big writing table in the anteroom, and the chair before it. The chair began to burn. Olive cried:

"You can't—even if she's there. Is she there?"

By some freak of the fire, some new eddy of air, the centre of the library suddenly cleared. At the further end, still on the highest of the three galleries there, they saw her plainly. She stood with the smoke curling in dark wreaths about her body, with fire and flame on either hand, with arms uplifted holding on high more books. She flung them down, as it were a conquered enemy she tossed at her feet. She lifted arms again with a gesture of triumph, of victory, of farewell. So for a moment they saw her. Then the iron of the gallery seemed to buckle as by the heat of the fire. It gave way. They saw her fall. The curtain of flame and smoke rolled back. They could see no more. Only an ocean of smoke, of flame, that filled the whole of the interior of what once had been the world known Kayne library.

"She is beyond our help," Major Harley said from behind. "Close the doors. We can do no more."

CHAPTER XXVIII
CONCLUSION

Bobby opened his eyes and looked vaguely around. He seemed to remember something about a fire. He could not imagine where he was. A small, bare room he did not recognize. But he could not feel that it mattered much, and he was tired, tired to the point of an utter indifference to all around. So he shut his eyes and went to sleep again, and when he opened them once more, he saw Olive sitting by his side.

"Hullo!" he said.

"Hullo!" said Olive.

"What's up?" asked Bobby.

"How do you feel?" asked Olive.

Bobby considered.

"Empty," he said wistfully.

Olive went away and returned, not, as he had hoped, with a large tray heaped up and up with pile upon pile of edible matter, but with a doctor and a nurse. Bobby discovered that various parts of him were swathed in bandages. These the doctor and the nurse proceeded to undo and then to replace. Bobby found that this process caused him a considerable degree of discomfort. He emphasized this fact by saying "Ow-w" at intervals, sometimes loudly, sometimes more loudly. The doctor seemed uninterested. The nurse remarked once or twice that he must be brave. Bobby asked "Why?" and said "Ow-w-w" again and with greater emphasis. The nurse said that the bigger and stronger the man, the worse patient he made. She had often noticed it. The doctor said Bobby could now have something to eat. Bobby at once forgave him all, but was still determined to say "Ow," whenever the nurse and opportunity combined. Olive appeared with that large tray, piled high with eatables, whereof Bobby had dreamed before. When he had dealt with it and asked for more and been refused, he said:

"What's this place, anyway?"

"Mayfield Cottage Hospital," Olive explained.

"Oh," said Bobby. "Well, what am I here for?" Olive did not regard this question as worthy of an answer, and he suggested cigarettes. They were supplied. He said: "What happened? I don't seem to remember much after someone said to shut the doors—to keep the fire back, I suppose. Did it?"

Olive shook her head.

"There's nothing left of the library except the walls and a pile of charred paper poor Mr. Adams sits and looks at, nearly crying," she told him. "Not much more of the house either. The fire was checked by the fireproof doors, but it got through the roof and then the house caught, too. They saved some of the furniture, but that's about all. Now you must go to sleep."

He obeyed, and the next day was allowed up. One or two official interviews had to be gone through, and a long statement made, but presently a time came when he and Olive were left alone. A statement had been required from her, too. She said thoughtfully:

"You know, Bobby, even now I can hardly believe that giggling, insignificant, silly-seeming, little Miss Perkins was behind it all. You couldn't imagine there was such determination, such a fury of will and purpose hidden in her."

"If we had thought about it," Bobby said, "we might have known it was there. A girl who teaches herself shorthand and typing in secret after working all day as a slavey in a cheap lodging-house—that takes some doing."

"Was that what made you suspect her first?"

"No," Bobby answered. "Hadn't enough imagination, I suppose. What really bothered me was trying to think why it all seemed to start as soon as I got here. In that book of his you lent me the other day, Somerset Maugham says when he was young he coined the epigram: 'Follow your inclinations, but remember the policeman round the corner.' Well, most people do that all right—remember the policeman, I mean. But this time it seemed they were remembering him by way of wanting him to be there.

"That worried me a lot. It might all be just coincidence, but I never like to take coincidence for an explanation. Too easy by half. But if it was all happening because this time there was a policeman round the corner, then it seemed logical to suppose there could only be one reason. Someone wanted something found out. Only that seemed difficult. People responsible for the sort of thing that interests the policeman round the corner, don't generally want it found out.

"I tried to worry out some sort of explanation. One was that the policeman was meant to find it out wrong. Or else there was something behind, something hidden he was expected to dig up, and his being on the spot had hurried up events meant to point somewhere else.

"Those two words 'dig up' I used in my mind in a slangy sort of way—kind of metaphor—began to associate themselves somehow with that yarn Miss Kayne told you about the letters and so on she had buried in the garden. I wondered a little if 'dig up' was to be taken literally, and if Miss Kayne really wanted them dug up. But then why shouldn't she go and do it? Nothing to stop her, apparently. Unless there was someone else who didn't want them dug up. Then I remembered you showed me that portrait of her your father did, and the odd slit in the throat it showed. Odd place for a picture to get damaged, and it did just cross my mind as a possible explanation that someone had been threatening her, and had shown her on that portrait what might happen to her if she wasn't careful.

"Only who was likely to threaten violence to prevent a few old letters being brought to light? Unless it was something more than letters that was hidden there. But I didn't see what that something else could be, and I just kept it in the back of my mind as a rather vague idea hardly worth remembering.

"What I really thought was that there must be something wrong with the library, and that some rival or enemy of some sort wanted whatever it was exposed. I thought up all kinds of theories. That Broast had been selling valuable stuff on the quiet and replacing with forgeries. That Miss Kayne suspected. That Miss Kayne was helping. I remember Broast refused to let Adams examine the Mandeville leaves, and there was the way Broast went all up in the air that time I couldn't find Dryden's autograph in the *Paradise Lost* I looked at.

"Only none of that fitted. If Broast or Miss Kayne or both or either were selling on the quiet, what were they doing with the money? All they got seemed to go back into the library when, on that theory, they were robbing it. And all the evidence I could get seemed to show that all the library treasures were absolutely genuine.

"It didn't make sense.

"I couldn't see either where the murder of Nat Kayne came in. At that time I hardly gave Miss Perkins a thought. She didn't even seem in the picture, except for a rather odd confusion about whether, when Sir William Winders 'phoned, he said he was walking through the woods or driving over in his car. But it was Miss Kayne who had taken the message, and besides it was Nat Kayne who had been murdered, not Winders, so what had any confusion over his 'phone message got to do with another man's death?

"But we had to consider there was evidence of quarrelling. Nat Kayne was trying to get the library sold, and apparently Miss Kayne, the other trustee, and the librarian all resented his efforts. We had to consider that one or all of them might be responsible for his death, which certainly seemed to suit them. Broast, for instance, would have lost his job. Winders might have reasons, too. At that time I was still worried by the idea that there was something wrong with the library itself, with its contents, rather. Something wrong that perhaps only murder could cover up.

"Almost as worrying was the complication of the wild yarn young Virtue told. It seemed incredible, but we had to consider that it might be true. Anyhow, it was plain that he really wanted to get the library premises searched. When he told us about his missing cousin, it was fairly plain he suspected his cousin had been murdered, and the body concealed there. He didn't dare make such an accusation outright, especially after a warning he had had from some K.C. in town about the risks of letting himself in for a libel action, but he hoped his story would result in a search being made. Especially he wanted to make sure if the *Dictes* he knew was in the library, was the one his cousin had owned. It seemed to him that would be conclusive evidence. As a matter of fact Broast was able to explain both how it had come into his possession and what had really happened to Virtue's lost cousin. Broast had kept quiet because he was afraid of the *Dictes* being claimed, though I think he could have proved a clear title. His story about all that has been confirmed.

"An even more puzzling complication was the discovery that Miss Perkins had in her possession a photo of the missing cousin. She gave first a fairly obvious false account of how she had got hold of it, and then substituted a slightly more probable yarn about having met the original of the photo in London. That could neither be proved nor disproved. Only if the second version was true, we were up against coincidence again, and I never like coincidences, even though they do happen and you have to allow for them. The photo brought her back into the picture, though, and I began to notice how often she seemed to pop up, as it were. It made me wonder, though only vaguely at first.

"Anyhow, it seemed a fact that both she and Virtue were genuinely puzzled, so it didn't look as if there was any connection between them."

"Have you any idea how she really got hold of it?" Olive asked when Bobby paused to suggest that as he had talked so much, now a drink would be acceptable.

She got it from him and he went on, answering her question:

"I'll come to that later. It's only a guess in a way, but a fairly safe one. We had to leave all that, though, when the discovery of the pistol used in the murder seemed to point to Winders as guilty. It was clear he had been in the neighbourhood about the time of the murder, we knew there had been quarrelling, it began to look as if the confusion over the 'phone message had been deliberate—the clumsy beginning of an attempt to prove an alibi.

"But then he was murdered, too.

"It was then I began to think that the murder of Nat Kayne might have been a blunder and that Winders was the intended victim. For one thing, we knew Kayne's intention to return to the Lodge had been sudden and unexpected. No one could have known he would be coming along that path through the wood, and yet it seemed probable that the murderer had been lying in wait there. So perhaps it was Winders who had been expected, and that suggested either Miss Kayne or Broast as guilty, since they were the two who knew about the 'phone message. I remembered, too, that it had passed through the hands of Miss Perkins—quite naturally, but there she was again.

"I don't know whether there would have been proof enough to satisfy a jury, though I think we should have got it in time, but anyhow there's no doubt that she was waiting that night by the path through the woods with Broast's pistol she had taken from the drawer where it was generally kept. When she saw Kayne coming, she took him for

Winders. They were of much the same height and build, it was dark, and it was Winders she was expecting. She left the revolver lying there. That was where I was to come in. I was to exercise my detective abilities by tracing the revolver, and therefore the guilt, to Broast. Very likely she had some more evidence cooked up all ready to make his guilt clear. But she had shot the wrong man, and Winders, coming back that way, found the revolver, wondered how it had got there, picked it up and put it in his pocket. Next morning, when he heard what had happened, he got into a panic, remembered his quarrel with Kayne, knew he had been near when it all happened, didn't like the idea of acknowledging the pistol was in his possession, and could think of nothing better to do than to throw it into the pond where we found it.

"That made it look bad for him, and he might have been arrested if he hadn't been murdered himself. Adams found the body, and so came under suspicion, suspicion strengthened by his previous refusal to explain who he really was or his errand here. Broast's alibi was not too good. There remained Miss Kayne and young Virtue to consider. And there was the incident of Mrs. Somerville's missing hand towels. Outside Winders's study we found a mark that looked as if made by a foot wrapped in something to prevent leaving a clear print.

"I think perhaps that was the first time I began to consider Miss Perkins seriously. Only what could be her motive? I began to think about her history. You had told me something and Mrs Somerville told me some more. Apparently her mother had left her father for another man and had been divorced. Then her father had committed suicide and her mother, deserted by the blackguard with whom she had run away, vanished entirely. A tragic sort of story altogether, and the child was left without a friend, for the father's family would have nothing to do with her. They were people of considerable wealth and some social position, and the child, instead of being brought up with all the social advantages she might have expected from her birth, became a friendless little waifs, a maid-of-all-work in the cheap lodging-house where her mother had left her, and where the landlady saw a chance to get an unpaid servant.

"Probably most girls in her place would have accepted it. She did not. She showed an intensity of will not many would have been capable of in fitting herself for a better position, and it began to seem to me as if Miss Perkins, with her gigglings and her footling way of talking, was hiding her true self.

"If so, why, and was there some purpose she had it in mind to carry out?

"I wondered. The father had committed suicide, but what had become of the mother? No one seemed to know. She had disappeared, But Miss Perkins had a photo of the missing James A. Virtue. I wondered if he could be the man with whom the mother had run away. Apparently he had a pretty loose reputation where women were concerned. However, dates and places didn't seem to fit, so I had to give that notion up. There was nothing to suggest James Virtue had ever been to Fromavon, nor did it seem quite likely that Miss Perkins would show people, as her own fiancé, the portrait of her mother's seducer. But we knew Virtue had visited this neighbourhood, we knew Miss Perkins had somehow got hold of a photograph of his, and it struck me the photograph might have reached her through her mother. The mother could have got it from Virtue if he had ever tried to start a flirtation with her. In that case she could have sent it on to the Fromavon lodging with other of her possessions. That was only guesswork, of course, but the possession by Miss Perkins of the photo was a fact that had to be accounted for, and if the guesses were right, it suggested that this woman, whose present whereabouts no one seemed to know anything about, had been at one time in this neighbourhood.

"That seemed pretty important.

"Only why was she here? Had she followed the man she had run away with and who had deserted her? and had Miss Perkins been showing the photo round in the hope of getting some more information?

"Whether she did get any information or not, I don't know.

"But she seemed to be coming more and more into the picture.

"More than ever I felt the silly, footling airs she put on were hardly consistent with the character of a girl who had spunk enough to teach herself shorthand and typing—and make herself expert at them—so as to get a better job. You have to have plenty of will and energy, more than most, if you've any left over after working all day as a little slavey in a cheap boarding-house. Intelligence, too.

"Seemed Inconsistent, somehow, and I don't like inconsistencies any more than I like coincidences.

"I noticed other things too.

"I noticed that she brought out her extremely unexpected and rather staggering suggestion of a secret marriage between Broast and Miss Kayne just exactly at the moment when I was wondering what she was doing near the Lodge to notice a light in Mr. Broast's room at nine at night. There was no reason, that I could see, unless she wanted to make sure Broast had in fact returned from town. If so, why did she want to be sure of that? was it so as be sure he would have no alibi for the Winders murder? At the moment, of course, I hadn't got all that thought out. I was only wondering why she was near the Lodge at that hour, after she had finished her day's work and gone home, and when she brought it out about a marriage between Broast and Miss Kayne I was so surprised and the idea seemed so full of possibilities, I forgot everything else.

"But afterwards it came back to me, and I began to wonder if she had said it when she did just to stop me from asking why she had gone back to the Lodge."

"But why did she want to kill poor Sir William?" Olive asked.

"She evidently thought he was partly responsible. I think myself it's more than likely he must have known something. He was too close with Broast not to have some idea of what was going on. I feel it is certain he had some knowledge. Very likely, if he had chosen to act, he could have prevented it all. What further information Miss Perkins got I don't know, or whether she got any at all, but it seems certain she came to believe her mother had been murdered and her body buried here in secret. She even came to suspect the actual spot, and that is why she sent me the forget-me-nots as a hint. I suppose she couldn't try to do the digging herself, so she put us on to it. Things were anything but clear in my mind, but I did guess what was meant, though it puzzled me at first. I began to remember what she had said about the possible marriage between Broast and Miss Kayne. So I thought, suppose the marriage, so advantageous to a man like Broast with his tastes and capacities, wasn't valid, because of a previous marriage with another woman after that other woman had left her husband for him and been divorced?

"It began to link up.

"There was a possible theory, I thought. Miss Perkins's mother might have gone to Miss Kayne and told her things, and Miss Kayne thereon had taxed Broast with the story? I had seen something of Broast's temper. It was at least conceivable that the result of that was murder. Perhaps that is what Miss Kayne meant when she told me about having committed the perfect murder. Perhaps, though, when you think of Broast's fits of fury, murder wasn't intended. It may have been the result of a quarrel, manslaughter rather than murder.

"Anyhow, he couldn't face exposure, and the poor woman's body was buried secretly where it lay hidden till—till we started digging.

"Whether Winders knew, as Miss Perkins, to give her the name she went by here, evidently believed, or did not know, Miss Kayne must have known. It was that knowledge she was brooding on, that that made her seem so strange. I think she had lost any love she ever had for Broast, but he still dominated her. She was still afraid of him, I think, and dared not tell, even if she had wanted to. I think that injury to her portrait suggests that much. I can't believe that was the result of any accident. I think it hung there as a perpetual reminder. Do you remember telling me Miss Kayne said something about knowing 'her' again. 'I knew her again at once', was what she said. I remembered that afterwards because it seemed to fit in with the idea that Miss Kayne had seen someone of whom Miss Perkins reminded her, and who could that be but her mother?"

"Bobby," Olive cried out, "do you mean Miss Kayne knew all the time?"

"I don't know about all the time—I think she did know finally," Bobby answered. "I think recognition came to her, and an understanding of what was the girl's errand here. I think that is what made her seem so strange, why she sat apart so much, why she tried to get rid of the girl by that rather futile accusation of theft she started to make. She told me once, too, in a challenging sort of way that Virtue had told the truth, had told a lie, when he said there had been a dead body on the library floor. She meant it was the truth because once a dead body had lain there—that of Miss Perkins's mother—and yet it was a lie because he had not seen it."

"It seems almost the most dreadful thing of all," Olive said slowly, "to think of Miss Kayne sitting waiting, knowing what was going to happen, waiting and brooding, and waiting like some poor soul in the condemned cell."

"Miss Perkins was waiting and watching, too," Bobby went on. "That must be how she came on the scene of our digging. I shan't forget soon the way she stood there, looking, with the skull between her feet that she knew was her own mother's. Or how she bent down and touched it with her fingers. But it must have been a shock to Broast. He carried it off, though. It might have meant nothing to him as he watched while what was left of his victim was being brought to the light of day again after so many years. Yet he knew we knew, he must have, and we knew he knew, too, and still he as good as told us there was nothing we could do. That was his mistake, though. We could do nothing, but Miss Perkins heard his boast, and it seems it was that finally decided her.

"She tried to get him thought guilty of the Kayne murder and she failed. She tried again to put the guilt of the Winders murder on him and that failed, too, for he had a fairly strong alibi thanks to his having stayed in town later than he had said he would; so that he could destroy one of his own forgeries he had been obliged to buy up to stop awkward inquiries.

"Because all those forgeries by which the great Kayne library had been built up were beginning to come back. Adams had been commissioned to investigate by the American collector who bought the forged Mandeville pages. Inquiries were being made by the Virtue family. They were really aimed at finding out what had happened to James Virtue, but were misunderstood by a collector already a trifle uneasy. So he got Adams, who is really manager to a big Scottish firm dealing in rare books, to take it up, but on the strict condition that Adams wasn't to let anyone know what was suspected. Adams thinks the American collector had some idea of himself passing the forged pages on before the forgery was generally known. In any case, though, they would have had to be pretty sure of their ground before making an accusation of that sort against a man of Broast's standing. That is what Adams wanted the photograph for. He thought if he could get a good snap of the genuine pages and enlarge it, then comparison with the forgeries would give the proof wanted.

He thinks Broast printed the fake pages on that old printing press in the cellar, possibly on blank leaves taken from other contemporary books. Most likely Broast produced his other forgeries in the same way on the same old fifteenth century press. There's no doubt, too, that he forged a number of the autographs and inscriptions in the presentation and association books he sold. That's what upset him so much when I spotted there was no signature of Dryden's in the *Paradise Lost* he showed us. He was afraid if he sold it, duly autographed, I might turn up with my story.

"If Miss Perkins had realized all that, and how every day he was getting deeper and deeper into troubles of all sorts so there was bound to be a smash pretty soon, she might have waited. I suppose, like a lot of other people, she couldn't believe how things in the end work themselves out. You can't dodge consequences. So she had to take a hand. Give Providence a leg up. What upset her in the end was Broast's boasting that the skeleton we had found could never be identified. If he had held his tongue, perhaps she would have held her hand. But his boasting and swaggering about being safe were too much for her. She had already provided herself with strychnine, and she put some in his tea that afternoon—and then waited in the library to watch him die. I expect she told him. She was worked up to it. She came straight from his side, when the maid came for the tea cups, and she said Mr. Broast had not finished yet. Quite true. He hadn't finished. But it wasn't long. A death worse than hanging. I don't know what made me give him that warning, but it turned out true enough."

"Why do you think she went into the library after she had tried to shoot you?" Olive asked.

"I've been wondering whether she did try," Bobby said slowly. "I have an idea she wanted chiefly to keep us off so that she could get the library door open and slip inside. I don't know what was in her mind. She may have had some thought of escaping by the windows. She may have meant to round off what she had done by trying to shoot Miss Kayne. She may have intended to shoot herself. Probably it was just an instinct to gain time. As it turned out one of the books Miss Kayne was throwing down must have struck her on the head and stunned her, and the fire did the rest. Death was actually due to suffocation—suffocation and shock."

Olive said slowly:

"I can't help feeling sorry for her. I can imagine how she brooded on the wrong done her father, her mother, herself, till it seemed intolerable the man responsible for it all should escape punishment. It's almost as if there were something in her that might perhaps have been great—great in other ways, not only a great criminal."

THE END

AFTERWORD

E.R. Punshon's detective novel *Comes a Stranger* carries an epigraph from the seventeenth-century poet Francis Quarles: "Death has no advantage, but when it comes a stranger." A 1657 edition of *Enchiridion*, the original source of this epigraph, currently is available from a Swedish rare book dealer for over 2100 US dollars. How appropriate this is readers of *Comes a Stranger* will surely comprehend, since in the novel Punshon's sleuth, Detective Sergeant Bobby Owen, finds that the ambiguous origins of certain rare books in the fictional Kayne library figure centrally in the maze of mystery he enters. The Kayne library's highly-respected librarian, revealed in the course of the novel as a charlatan forger and fraudster (not to mention a murderer), is based, as far as forgery and fraud are concerned, on a real individual, Thomas James Wise, an eminent and influential English bibliographer and book collector whose astonishing literary misdeeds were exposed a few years before his death in May 1937. With Wise's passing, England's restrictive libel laws became far less of a pressing concern to Punshon and his publisher, Victor Gollancz, and *Comes a Stranger* duly appeared sixteen months later, though not without a protective note by the author, in which he assured readers that although "[t]his story was suggested by, and is indeed founded upon, certain recent occurrences, on which, however, for good reason, little emphasis was laid in the public press...[t]here is, there never has been, any library, public or private, in any way resembling the Kayne library. The owner, the trustees, the librarian, are all equally creatures of the imagination, and have no relation to any person, living or dead." This statement is something less than the truth, at least as concerns the librarian of the Kayne library, a certain Mr. Broast, who in the course of the novel is revealed as the malefactor behind a shocking series of crimes, including, as in the case of Thomas J. Wise, literary forgery and fraud.

In real life, Thomas J. Wise entered the decade of the 1930s as one of Britain's most respected bibliographers, a former President of the Bibliographical Society, an honorary Masters of the Arts at Oxford University and an Honorary Fellow of Worcester College, Oxford. A longtime avid collector of first editions, Wise owned an enviable private library of rare books, dubbed the Ashley Library, after the street where Wise had lived when he first started his collection. Wise funded the Ashley Library through the sale of duplicate copies and his services as a purchasing agent for wealthy book collectors in the UK and US. Ironically, given his later exposure as a forger, Wise had won for himself among bibliophiles in both countries an authoritative reputation as an exposer of forgeries. "Easy as it appears to be to fabricate reprints of rare books," Wise once prophetically commented, "it is in actual practice absolutely impossible to do so in such a manner that detection cannot follow the event." (For a recent convenient summary of the career of Thomas J. Wise and the investigation of the Wise forgeries, see David Thomas, *Beggars, Cheats and Forgers: A History of Frauds through the Ages*.)

Wise's edifice of probity, already viewed with skepticism by some discerning individuals, began its total collapse in 1934, upon the publication of *An Enquiry into the Nature of Certain Nineteenth Century Pamphlets*, an outstanding instance of literary detective work by John Carter and Graham Pollard, two of the twentieth century's most renowned bibliographers and booksellers. In their *Enquiry* Carter and Pollard definitively established that great numbers of rare privately printed, pre-first edition nineteenth-century pamphlets, depending solely on Wise's word for authentication, were fakes. For example, a pamphlet pre-first of Elizabeth Barrett Browning's *Sonnets of the Portuguese*, dated 1847, was shown to have been printed not on paper made from rags, but rather on chemically-treated wood pulp, which did not become available until 1874. The spurious works authenticated by Wise included, in addition to the famous 1847 Browning *Sonnets*, alleged pre-firsts by such nineteenth-century literary luminaries as William Wordsworth; Alfred, Lord Tennyson; Charles Dickens; William Makepeace Thackeray; Robert Browning; Algernon Charles Swinburne; George Eliot; and William Morris. Strict English libel laws restrained Carter and Pollard from accusing Wise outright of being behind the forgeries (in *Comes a Stranger* Punshon has an American character explain that the reason he refrained from publicly accusing Mr. Broast of fraud was fear of English libel laws), but their implication was sufficiently clear: "In the whole history of book collecting there has been no such wholesale and successful perpetration of fraud as that which we owe to this anonymous forger. It has been converted into an equally unparalleled blow to the bibliography and literary criticism of the Victorian period by the shocking negligence of Mr. Wise."

With the publication of Carter and Pollard's *Enquiry* what had been mere whispers about Wise became the subject of polite yet pointed discourse in literary periodicals in both the UK and US. In a review of Carter and Pollard's *Enquiry* in the *New York Times Book Review*, Philip Brooks suggestively observed that the "activities described point to the work of one forger," a person of uncanny skill and resource. A.J.A. Symons, himself a noted bibliophile and the author of the classic biography *The Quest for Corvo* (and also the elder brother of E.R. Punshon's future Detection Club colleague, the crime writer Julian Symons; see below) quickly joined the affray with a 1934 article supporting Carter and Pollard and demanding that Wise explain himself, which was published in *The Book Collector's Quarterly*; and later that year he privately printed (25 copies only, under the signature "A.J.A.S.") a three stanza poem mocking the discredited bibliographer, entitled "Is It Wise?" Faced with exposure, Wise pled that illness prevented him from responding to the allegations, though his cause was ineffectually taken up by a few loyal supporters, including the prominent American bookseller Gabriel Wells, who published his own pamphlet in defense of Wise's integrity.

At his death three years later, Wise's reputation for integrity was in tatters, yet his Ashley Library, an undeniably fabulous repository of rare books, was purchased by the British Museum for nearly four million pounds in modern value. (With rich irony it later was discovered that Wise had stolen leaves from rare books in the British Museum to replace missing leaves in copies he owned.) In 1939, a year after Punshon published *Comes a Stranger*, bibliographer Wilfred Partington published the picaresque *Forging Ahead: The True Story of the Upward Progress of Thomas J. Wise*, which frankly acknowledged the fraudulent actions committed by his famous subject, revealing, according to a notice in the *New York Times Book Review*, a learned charlatan in all his fascinating complexity: "a paradoxical blend of ambition, effrontery, treachery and enthusiasm, a man perfectly adapted to shady operations, a pirate and a braggart, and yet underneath a substantial Englishman and a deliberate scholar if not a true one." E.R. Punshon seems to me to have captured as well many of the facets of Wise's roguish character in his brash and boastful Mr. Broast.

In the 1940s, evidence continued to mount concerning the offenses of Mr. Wise. University of Texas librarian Fannie E. Ratchford published a book on the matter, in which she argued persuasively that the long-deceased bibliographer and antiquarian bookseller Harry Buxton Forman had collaborated with Wise in the production of the forgeries. (Like Mr. Broast in *Comes a Stranger*, who, we learn early in the novel, keeps a printing press in the cellar of the Kayne library, Forman was knowledgeable about printing and typography.) Additionally, Wilfred Partington, as well as Carter and Pollard, returned in print to the subject during the course of the decade. (Partington's book, *Thomas J. Wise in the Original Cloth: The Life and Record of the Forger of the Nineteenth-Century Pamphlets*, included an appendix authored by George Bernard Shaw.) Finally, there appeared two detective novels that were inspired, like *Comes a Stranger*, by the Wise affair: American Lee Thayer's *Murder Stalks the Circle* (1947) and Englishman Julian Symons's *Bland Beginning* (1949). When Julian Symons, the younger brother of A.J.A. Symons, was proposed for membership in the Detection Club, it was on the basis of *Bland Beginning*, his third detective novel, that he was accepted. E.R. Punshon wrote Dorothy L. Sayers that he disliked Symons's first detective novel, *The Immaterial Murder Case*, but that he considered *Bland Beginning* "certainly an intelligent and clever book." (As seems often to have been the case, Sayers was of the same opinion as Punshon; see my discussion of Symons's acceptance into the Detection Club in my *CADS* pamphlet essay "Was Corinne's Murder Clued? The Detection Club and Fair Play, 1930-1953.") In his surviving correspondence with Sayers Punshon did not mention that the novel, like his own *Comes a Stranger*, had heavily drawn upon the Wise forgeries scandal, but I assume that this fact was, as far as Punshon was concerned, a strong point in the book's favor.

Curtis Evans